The Hades Project

**A novel
by
Justin Gustainis**

TO MARK —

HARPY NGHTMARES!

Justin Gustainis

10/31/03

Brighid's Fire Books
a subsidiary of Wahmpreneur Publishing, Inc.
P.O. Box 41
Sidney, New York 13838

The Hades Project

Library of Congress Control Number: 2003102225

ISBN 0-9713278-6-6

Cover art (c) 2003 by Misty Paiement.

Acknowledgements

In writing this novel, I was fortunate to receive encouragement, criticism, and useful information from a number of people.

Several friends read the manuscript at various stages and gave me helpful feedback, so my sincere thanks to Carrie Brady, Gwen Brown, Hope Corbin, Deb DeSilva, Melody and Barry Dimick, Carla List, Jess Litwin, Dan O'Rourke, Karen VanDerlyn, Pat Yoos, and especially to Craig Sample, whose mastery of language helped make this a better book.

Michael Kanaly and C.J. Henderson, both successful authors in their own right, were kind enough to read the manuscript and offer both support and valuable suggestions for improvement.

Jim Andrews transliterated an English phrase into Russian for me, thus helping to make the demon Asmodeus multilingual. Janette Kenner Muir provided key information about the geography of Fairfax, Virginia. Troy Collin shared his knowledge of shotguns and shotgunning. Richard Lacki, M.D., was kind enough to answer some medical questions. However, any errors of fact or interpretation involving these areas, or any others, are my responsibility alone.

My wife, Pat Grogan, provided unflagging support, encouragement and love to keep me going. She believed in me when no one else did, including me.

Terry Bear helped, too.

To
Patty Ann,
who makes it all worth doing.

"Hope I live to tell
the secret I have learned.
'Til then, it will burn
inside of me. . . ."

–Madonna

A Caution to the Reader

The spells, rituals, and magical paraphernalia described in this novel are an amalgam of diligent research and a healthy dose of the author's imagination. In other words, I made some of it up. This is fiction – I get to do that.

This book is not intended to be a *grimoire* for the conjuring of demons, and should not be employed for that purpose. If you are unwise enough to ignore this advice, don't blame me if nothing happens.

More important, don't blame me if something *does*.

J.G.

Prologue

Quang Tri Province, Republic of Vietnam
May 24, 1971

The village of Do Lac lay stoically underneath the merciless afternoon sun. It was a small place – fifteen bamboo hootches and a corral containing three tired-looking water buffalo.

From a distance, Do Lac appeared to be deserted, apart from the broken-down livestock. There were no children running around yelling; no village elders gossiped or dozed in the shade outside the huts.

From certain places in the jungle, it was possible to get a clear view of the village's fields and rice paddies. Such observation, aided by a good pair of field glasses, would show the paddies to be unattended, the fields deserted.

A reasonable man might have concluded that Do Lac was uninhabited, just another abandoned village in a land ravaged by war. The men watching from the jungle, who were not reasonable, thought they knew better.

Then the screaming started, and they were certain.

The anguished sounds came from one of the hootches – the biggest one, which was probably used for communal purposes. The screams, unmistakably those of a man in mortal agony, went on for a long time.

The six watching men were lying prone just inside the jungle's edge, about 180 yards from the closest hut. One of them, the big American with close-cropped blond hair, took the field glasses from his eyes and blew out his breath in a soft whistle. "Well, he's in there," he said quietly.

"Not much doubt, is there?" the other American said. He was smaller than the blond, with dark hair and eyes and slightly swarthy skin. Even the Vietnamese on the team, to whom most round-eyes looked as alike as grains of rice in a bowl, had no trouble telling the two Yankees apart. Size and pigmentation aside, they were distinguishable in another way the four Vietnamese knew well – the big, blond American was dangerous; the smaller, darker one was lethal.

Neither one had yet reached his twenty-first birthday.

The dark-haired American glanced at the Rolex diving watch on his wrist. "Full dark in about four hours," he said. "We go in then, before moonrise."

The blond looked dubiously at him, then back at the village. "Sounds like he's pretty busy in there, man. Havin' too much fun to worry about watching his back. Shit, we go in now, we can be on top of him before he even knows we're there."

The other American just shook his head.

"Come on, Mike," the blond said. "Let's get in, get it on, and get it over with. I'm tired of trackin' this motherfucker."

"You tired of living, too?" The smaller man's voice was patient. "We never did figure whether he operates alone or as part of a team, right? Hell, this might even be his home base. Could be a couple dozen of Victor Charlie's finest in those hootches, Chops. We'd never know it until they lit us up like a Christmas tree." He shook his head again. "Fuck that shit. We wait until dark."

He made a summoning gesture to one of the Vietnamese. Like everyone on the team, the man who crawled over was wearing tiger stripe jungle fatigues, patched and faded and sweat-stained. Coming up to the American named Mike, he whispered, "What happens?"

"We're going in after dark, about four hours from now. You and the other guys grab some sleep, if you can. Me and Chops will handle security."

The Vietnamese, whose name was Tran Van Dinh, looked at the one called Mike thoughtfully. "Wait for darkness is safer, yes?"

The American nodded.

"So we wait," Tran said, "even if some poor bastard getting his guts torn out, inch at a time, yes?"

"Yeah, that's right. Orders are to take this fucker alive, if possible. We got a better chance to get close in the dark. So we wait."

"Good. Many 'Mericans sentimental assholes. Get people killed that way."

"Not me," Mike said grimly.

"Me, either. Wake me in four hour."

———◆———

The dark came down swiftly, as it does in the jungle, covering the land like a black velvet cloak. Even with the night to hide them, the six men had been leery about the open ground that separated the village from the bush. The cleared land could be mined, or booby-trapped in some other way. Or they might be halfway across when someone in the village decided to send up a flare, leaving the team exposed, discovered, and in very bad trouble.

Fadeout they called it, at the Royal Jungle Tracking School the Brits ran in Malaysia. "Fadeout's what happens when the blokes you're after get after *you* instead, on account of you fucked up." The instructor, an SAS Sergeant Major named Callan, had looked sourly around at the group of students before going on. "And just you remember this, mates: *fadeout* is generally followed by *rigor mortis*."

So, using the jungle for cover during the last half-hour of daylight, they made a cautious semicircle around the village. When darkness fell, they came in through the rice paddies, on their bellies. Their bodies were almost submerged, but they were careful to keep their weapons dry. Vietnamese farmers use the dung from their water buffalo as fertilizer. The odor is both distinctive and unpleasant, but the six men were prepared to put up with an awful lot of buffalo shit if it were the price of staying alive.

They came out of the paddies quiet as ghosts, one at a time, and slipped into the village. Silently and efficiently, they checked every hut in Do Lac before approaching the larger communal building. In almost every dwelling they found the mutilated bodies of villagers – men, women, and children. They did not linger over the corpses, but even cursory examination showed that the mutilations had been carried out while the victims were still alive. The six men had some experience in these matters, and they recognized death by torture when they saw it.

After all of the hooches had been cleared, the team

prepared to move on the larger building, from which the screams had only recently ceased. Using hand signals, the American named Mike quickly deployed the four Vietnamese as security at different points around the building. Then he and the tall, blond American took turns moving in on the entrance, one man providing cover as the other scurried closer to the objective. Finally, they were near enough for the final rush.

As usual, the smaller American had taken upon himself the dangerous task of breaching the door. Crouching behind the village well, the blond brought his Swedish "K" submachine gun to his shoulder and drew a bead on the door of the hut. *"Fuckin' Mike. Gotta be the first one through the door, every goddamn time. Bet if he was six foot four he could give this shit a rest once in a while."*

Seeing that his partner was ready to provide covering fire, the American named Mike took a firm grip on the shotgun he was carrying. He sprinted the last twenty yards to the hut, sent the door crashing open with one powerful kick, and dived through the entrance.

Outside, the one called Chops waited, the sound of his pulse pounding in his ears. The seconds ticked by in aching, empty silence. Finally, after more than three minutes, he decided that something was seriously wrong. He was just getting to his feet when the screaming started inside the hut, the voice different from the one heard earlier.

Then, a moment later, the roar and flash of a shotgun blast split the night wide open.

The big blond man was running now, flat out, sprinting toward the door of the hut, all the while sick at heart with the knowledge that whatever had gone bad in there, he was already too late to do anything about it.

Justin Gustainis

Chapter 1

Michael Pacilio leaned forward in his chair and placed the videocassette on McGraw's desk. Sitting back, he said, "We can play it whenever you're ready."

McGraw glanced at the cassette then quickly looked away, the way some people do when driving past a bad accident. "Just what do these assholes think they were trying to accomplish, anyway?"

Pacilio looked at him and said softly "*Did*, not *do*, I think. Since they're all dead now, the past tense seems appropriate."

McGraw bowed his head briefly. "All right, past tense, then, and all due respect to the departed. But, what were they up to in that lab?"

"I really can't say. I've read the project file, just as you have, but I haven't got the scientific background to make much sense out of it. The only phrase of any importance that I recognized was *space-time continuum*, and I think that's because I heard it once in an old *Star Trek* episode. You're going to need someone with a physics background if you want anything like a useful answer."

"That's in the works even as we speak," McGraw told him. "I've got a couple of Ph.D.s with security clearances on loan from Georgetown. They're downstairs going over the file now. I told them I wanted a preliminary assessment before close of business today. Naturally, they have no idea of any connection between the file and . . . what happened in Fairfax overnight."

Pacilio nodded wearily. There were lines of strain and fatigue in his face that McGraw had never seen there before. Pacilio was a smallish man, no more than 5'8", with a slightly swarthy complexion. Although pushing fifty, he still moved with the economy and unconscious grace of a matador – and, in Spanish, *matador* means nothing more than *killer*.

There was no bravado about Pacilio, no machismo. Sit next to this well-dressed, carefully groomed man on an airplane and you would have no idea you were coming across anything special – unless you took a good look at the brown eyes, which, McGraw thought, contained all the warmth of a couple of pennies left out in a November rain.

He tried not to use Pacilio much. Most of what crossed McGraw's desk involved run-of-the-mill investigations of scientific fraud, and sending someone like Pacilio after a government-funded cancer researcher suspected of fudging his data was akin to using a leopard for chasing down runaway lab rats – it offended McGraw's sense of proportion. But when he had been awakened by the telephone at 5:19 that morning with the first report of what had been found at the lab in Fairfax, McGraw had realized very quickly who he needed. He had called Pacilio at 5:33.

And now it was just past two in the afternoon and here was Pacilio sitting across from McGraw's desk and there, in the middle of the desk, was the videotape Pacilio had been instructed to make.

McGraw had asked for an oral report first, and Pacilio had provided one that lasted three or four minutes. While listening to the soft, precise voice, McGraw had experienced an odd physical sensation.

He was a big man, McGraw was, and about thirty-five pounds of it was fat. As a result, summer was hard on him. The excess weight meant that he was usually warm, even in air-conditioned environments. And here it was June, in Washington, even more humid than usual, with the cranky government air conditioning working erratically at best *and McGraw was cold.* Pacilio had been speaking for less than thirty seconds when McGraw had begun to feel as if ice crystals were forming in his bloodstream.

McGraw wondered if he would ever feel warm again.

He looked back to the videocassette that lay on his desk like a patient cobra. Something printed on the tape's cardboard sleeve caught his eye. "Did you buy the blank tape yourself? It's not department issue."

Pacilio shrugged. "I brought it from home. It had a couple of episodes of 'Nigella Bites' on it, but I've already watched them. I'll get reimbursed out of petty cash. Or, if you're feeling stingy this month, consider it my contribution toward the budget deficit."

"You always buy this 'EXP Hi-Grade' stuff?"

"Yeah, I guess so."

"Why?"

"Better picture fidelity. It's got more – what do they call it? – iron oxide coating than the cheaper tapes."

McGraw shook his head, pleased to be one up on Pacilio. "Not true," he said. "Saw an article in my dentist's waiting room a couple of weeks ago. In that place, the walls are so thin, you read anything just to keep from listening to the sound of the drill going in the next room. Anyway, this was in one of those consumer magazines. It said that they had run tests on the kind of picture you get from the various grades of videotape, and they found that the differences between the lowest grade and the highest grade of brand-name tapes were negligible and couldn't be seen by the naked eye. Can you believe it? Article said that these more expensive 'high grade' tapes were just a marketing gimmick to make more money for the manufacturers."

Pacilio nodded a couple of times and looked down at the carpet. "You're stalling, aren't you?"

McGraw was silent for several seconds. "Yeah, you're right. I guess I am."

"If you don't want to look at it, it's no skin off my tender parts. I can write you up a detailed summary, if that's what you'd prefer."

"No, it's good of you to offer, but we both know that won't wash. I've got a report to put together, and I've got a feeling it's going to prompt a lot of questions from upstairs that I'll have to answer later. If you could stand to make the fucking thing, I guess I can stand to watch it."

Pacilio shrugged. "Up to you."

"Go ahead and cue it up, will you?" McGraw's tone of voice was not very different from the one you hear in the gas chamber just after the warden asks *"Do you have anything to say before sentence is carried out"*?

Against the far wall was a credenza containing a VCR and a 26-inch monitor. Pacilio inserted the tape cassette and picked up the remote control. He looked at McGraw as if giving him one last chance to back out. "Okay?"

"Sure. Play it again, Sam."

"My name's not Sam, Bogart never said that, and this is the first time it's ever been played."

McGraw's smile was thin to the point of emaciation. "Then I hope you remembered to take the damn lens cap off," he said. "Go ahead, you literal-minded bastard."

Pacilio pointed the remote control at the TV and pushed a button. The set came to life with one of those syndicated freak shows that have proliferated across the TV landscape the way algae takes over a pond. Six people, four men and two women, were seated in armchairs lined up across a bare stage. One of the men, an Indiana farmer with more tattoos than teeth, was trying to explain to the show's pudgy young hostess, amid jeers and catcalls from the studio audience, that incest wasn't *necessarily* bad in all cases; you had to look at the *circumstances*; you had to consider a person's *needs*. Pacilio pushed another button. The farmer disappeared and the tape started to roll.

On screen was a shot of a low red-brick building as seen from across the street. Pacilio said, "I'll give you a running commentary, all right? There's nothing on the soundtrack. Nobody in there was making any noise by the time I arrived."

"All right, fine." McGraw's eyes never left the screen. After a moment he said, "It looks more like a school than a lab under government contract."

Pacilio nodded. "Used to be a high school gym. Our Lady of Perpetual Motion, or something." A thoroughly lapsed Catholic, Pacilio was irreverent as a reflex. "The diocese closed the place down a few years ago, due to low enrollment. They tore out the bleachers, put in a bunch of interior walls over the basketball court, and rented it out to Uncle Sam."

The camera's eye had moved close to the front double door of the building, which was mostly glass reinforced by what looked like crosshatched chicken wire, when McGraw suddenly said "Wait. Run it back a little, will you, and then let it go forward again."

As the camera approached the door again, McGraw said "Stop. Go back just a hair and freeze frame. Okay, see that puddle on the concrete just to the right of the door? What is that? We haven't had rain all week."

Pacilio was looking at the floor again. "It's vomit," he said quietly. "A small pool of human vomit."

McGraw sat up straighter. "Did one of the victims get outside? Could it have come from one of the killers? Has it been sent to a lab for analysis?"

Pacilio sounded both irritated and embarrassed as he said, "No, no one got outside, as far as I can tell, and no, the puke has not been sent to a lab."

"Why the hell not? It might be–"

"Because it's mine."

"*Yours*"?

"I took a walk through the place without the camcorder the first time. I wanted to know what I was dealing with. There might have been some kind of chemical or biological hazard – how would I know? What you gave me over the phone was pretty sketchy. You said we had dead people, but nothing about how they died. If it was murder, maybe the perp was still on the premises. In any event, I wanted to be able to move fast if I had to, so I left the camera in my car."

"And what happened?" McGraw's tone was not unkind.

"It was murder, all right, and that's putting it mildly, but whoever did it was long gone. Once I figured *that* out, I went back out to the car to get the camcorder. On the way, I had my little accident just outside the front door. I could have made it to a restroom inside, probably, but I didn't want to contaminate the crime scene by tossing my cookies all over it."

McGraw tried to get his mind around the idea that Pacilio had encountered something in that lab that had made him vomit in revulsion. People like Pacilio weren't supposed to do things like that.

McGraw thought he had a pretty good idea about the sort of man Pacilio was; he'd known him for four years, and had access to his Personnel File, as well.

Even more important, McGraw had a son-in-law who had served in Vietnam.

———◆———

Labor Day weekend, four years earlier:

McGraw, wearing a well-stained apron that says "Kiss the Cook" across the front, is gingerly placing raw hamburgers in rows across his hot barbecue grill. Without looking up, he says to the tall, fiftyish man leaning against the nearby deck railing, "You were with Naval Intelligence, weren't you, Jack, during the Late Unpleasantness in Southeast Asia?"

Jack Braithwaite, who is married to McGraw's eldest daughter, swallows a mouthful of potato chips and smiles slightly. "Yeah, it seemed like pretty good duty at the time they offered it, especially if you wanted to avoid getting shot at. But if I'd known up front about all the bullshit involved, I might've taken my chances in combat."

"While you were over there, did you ever run across a guy named Mike Pacilio?"

Braithwaite's eyes narrow, and the smile vanishes from his face. After a moment he asks, "Did he serve with the SEALs?"

"So I understand, yeah."

"No, I never met him." The tone of voice does not encourage further discussion.

"You say you've never met him, but yet you knew right away that he was in the SEALs?"

The younger man sighs a little. Then he shrugs and says, "He'd be mentioned sometimes in reports that would pass through our office." Braithwaite looks at his father-in-law. "What do you care about this guy, Mac?"

"The Department hired him last week, and he's been assigned to my office as a field investigator, starting Tuesday. I like to know about the people who work for me, so I had his Personnel File sent over."

McGraw fusses with the grill a little more. "Fella's had a varied career in government service, I'll say that much. Several years with DEA, back when it was the Bureau of Narcotics and Dangerous Drugs. Then the U.S. Marshals for a while, followed by ATF for three or four years. Most recently, he's been with that State Department outfit, the Diplomatic Security Corps."

"So, what's the deal with him? He keeps fucking up and getting canned?"

"Nope, he's never been fired, far as I can tell. He keeps transferring out. And, you know what? Every one of his supervisors write him great evals, really outstanding – even while they're approving the guy's request for transfer."

Braithwaite shrugs. "If you've seen his file, what more do you need?"

"Nothing, I guess. But I got kind of curious when I saw that his service record had been expunged."

Braithwaite nods, as if he finds this unsurprising.

"I mean, there are a few bits and pieces that somebody missed," McGraw says. "A copy of an

Honorable Discharge from the Navy, a couple of references to 'Overseas service, Republic of Vietnam,' and one passing mention of 'Navy special warfare units.' And that's about it."

There is silence between the two men that lasts long enough for McGraw to apply generous amounts of salt and pepper to the burgers he has grilling. Finally, Braithwaite says, "I'm not supposed to talk about that stuff, Mac. A lot of it is still classified, even after all this time."

"What *stuff* might that be, Jack?"

"Special Ops stuff. Like a lot of the SEAL missions." Three or four seconds go by before Braithwaite adds, "And like Phoenix."

McGraw blinks a couple of times. "I see," he says quietly. His war was Korea, not Vietnam – but even McGraw has heard of the Phoenix program.

McGraw says nothing more about it, but during the meal that follows, he finds Braithwaite's eyes on him whenever he happens to look in his son-in-law's direction.

Later, McGraw is enjoying a post-dinner beer and watching his grandchildren tear-assing around the back yard when Braithwaite, carrying his own can of beer, wanders over. They stand side by side, watching the kids in a companionable silence.

Suddenly, Braithwaite says, "Your newest employee did two tours in-country, Mac. He volunteered for the second one, but that's not unusual among Spec Op types. They don't go through the hell of all that training just so they can sit around a Pentagon office, counting paper clips. They tend to be what you might call highly motivated."

"Or maybe they're just crazy," McGraw says dryly.

Braithwaite doesn't smile. "Could be that they are. To carry out the kinds of missions those guys do, maybe being crazy helps." He takes a swallow of Coors. "Anyway, Pacilio's first tour was typical SEAL stuff: raids, ambushes, recon patrols – the usual snake-eater shit. Then some spook from The Company talked him into Phoenix. He did his second tour with them, operating mostly out of I Corps."

"Was the Phoenix program really as sinister as the news reports made out, Jack? They made it sound like a military version of Murder, Incorporated."

"You don't believe those pinkos in the liberal media, do you?" Braithwaite's voice gives the words a light coat of irony. "Assassination was part of it, that's true. But it wasn't the whole ball game, not by any means. See, the basic idea was to fuck up the Viet Cong organization in the South. Sometimes, Intelligence would identify somebody who was a big wheel in the VC cadre, and a team would be sent in after him. Or her."

"What was considered a 'team?'"

"Generally two American Spec Op types, and three or four Viets. Pacilio was partnered with a Green Beret, name of . . . some Polack guy . . . Chopko, that's right, Carl Chopko. Him and Pacilio and four Vietnamese Rangers. Best team in I Corps, or so I heard."

"And these bad-asses would do what, exactly?"

"Whatever they were told to do. Sometimes, the mission was to locate the identified VC and take him out. That's where all that "Murder, Incorporated" crap comes from. But, other times, the orders would be to snatch some guy, bring him back, then turn him over for interrogation by our democratic and freedom-loving allies, the South Vietnamese National Police."

Braithwaite pauses, staring at his beer can as if the contents had suddenly turned bitter. "Tell you this much, Mac," he says bleakly, "no VC suspect who ended up in one of those little rooms underneath the Saigon Jail was ever heard from again, and the luckiest of those poor bastards were the ones who broke early."

McGraw nods acknowledgement in the silence that follows. Thinking that his son-in-law's tale is done, McGraw is about to thank him when Braithwaite suddenly says, "It was early in '71, I think, when the word came down from MACV about the new 'psywar offensive.' The people in Phoenix were assigned to play a major role in it."

McGraw's brow furrows. "Psychological warfare? Spreading leaflets around – 'Surrender now, you will receive good treatment'– that kind of thing? Why would they waste special ops guys on a pissant job like that?"

Braithwaite shakes his head. "There's all kinds of psychological warfare, Mac. What they had in mind for the Phoenix teams . . . well, when the other side did it, we usually called it terrorism."

McGraw's voice is carefully neutral as he says, "I see. Or, rather, I don't see."

"Look – most Vietnamese are Buddhists, right? Even the VC, who were supposed to be good, atheistic Communists, still followed the old ways, most of them. You don't wipe out something like 3,000 years of tradition with a couple of decades of Marxist-Leninism, you know?"

"Sure," McGraw says. "Makes sense."

"So, Buddhism teaches that when somebody dies, you have to bury the body intact, with all of its . . . parts. Otherwise, the dead guy's soul can't find peace and it's doomed to wander the earth forever."

"The light begins to dawn," McGraw says. "So these Phoenix teams –"

"– Would sometimes be sent after a particular guy, with instructions to go in at night, find him, hit him, and then leave the body near his village where it was sure to be discovered the next morning. And when the guy *was* found, he'd be missing some important organ – usually the liver, for reasons I can't remember."

"And this stuff was supposed to help us win the war, somehow?"

Braithwaite shrugs. "It was supposed to send a message to the locals: *Be careful how much help you give to the Viet Cong, or we might come for you some dark night. And if we do, we bring not only death, but damnation.*"

McGraw shakes his head in wonder. "Damnation. Jesus."

A few moments go by before Braithwaite says, "One more thing, Mac: you and me, we never had this conversation."

"What conversation?"

———◆———

And so McGraw was well aware that he was sitting across from a man who was capable of breaking somebody's neck with his bare hands and then cutting the liver out of the corpse. Pacilio, who had done these things, and worse, and yet managed somehow to retain his sanity, had seen something in that building that had caused him to vomit in disgust. *Mother of God,* McGraw thought, *I knew it was going to be bad, but if it made Pacilio throw up then it is so far beyond bad that I haven't got the words for it. I just know that I don't want to see it.*

But he knew he had to see it.

And so, after a deep breath and a silent thanks to whatever gods there are that he had been too busy to have lunch, he did.

Justin Gustainis

Chapter 2

"We're through the front door now, and here's the foyer. Nothing interesting here, so I just gave it a quick pan. This is the interior door, the one that needs an electronic security card to unlock it. There's going to be a brief jump here–right, there it is–where I turned the camcorder off, got the door open, and turned it back on again."

"I should have thought to provide you with a key; careless of me not to. How did you get in?"

"I have a selection of master security cards. Each one opens about 700 different combinations."

"Jesus Christ. I thought that was the whole point of electronic locks – to keep some guy with a skeleton key from getting into hotel rooms and places like that."

"There's no such thing as a skeleton key, but basically you're right. Still, the maids have to clean the rooms, right? So there have to be master keys. I've gotten to know a few guys who work hotel security."

"So have some hotel thieves, no doubt."

"Always use the hotel safe. Okay, we're going down the main hallway here. Offices along both sides, as you can see. I checked them out during my first walk through, and they're all empty. I think everybody who was on shift last night was in the main room when it happened."

"*It* being what, exactly?"

"You'll see, just be patient. Look, the hallway forms a T-junction here. Left is to the main lab, right leads to the lavatories and some vending machines. We'll get to the big room soon enough. I turned right because there's something I wanted you to see in the men's john. It's the first thing of consequence we're going to look at, although I don't figure it was Event Alpha. More like Event Omega. This guy probably tried to run, although there's no way out from this corridor. Maybe he panicked. Anyway, it looks like he tried to hide in the can. As you'll see, it didn't turn out to be such a great idea."

"Stop the tape for a second. How do you figure this was the last thing to happen? None of the autopsy reports are in yet, so we haven't established time of death for any of them."

"Because this is the only body I found outside the main lab area. It's not likely that what happened here in the men's john happened quietly. Somebody would have heard the screams and come running, but nobody did because there was nobody left to hear."

"*In Fairfax, nobody can hear you scream.*"

"Excuse me?"

"I was just thinking of the ad for a scary movie I saw once."

"Yeah, well, trouble with this movie is, it's *real*. In fact, there's probably a certain number of people who would pay some serious bucks for a copy. It's a collector's classic, you know? The next best thing to an honest-to-God snuff film."

"Some people are fucking nuts."

"True enough. It looks like at least one of them was loose in Fairfax last night. Start the tape again?"

"Yeah, go on."

"Okay, we're going into the john now. Got this dividing wall on the left so that nobody passing by in the hall when the door's open can look in and see some guy waggling his weenie around. Now we're past the dividing wall and turning left and . . . here we are."

"Yes.... Yes, I see. Where's the rest of him?"

"The torso's in one of the stalls. We'll get to that in a minute."

"I can hardly wait."

"Are you all right, Mac?"

"Anybody who could be 'all right' looking at this stuff belongs in a rubber room. Just keep going."

"Okay. A couple of things you need to notice here."

"You mean the eyes? I can see they're gone."

"No, that's not what I meant. I zoomed in on the mouth here, because I knew from my first trip through that there was something there. Do you see it?"

"There's something in the mouth, but I can't tell what it is. Is his tongue swollen? Is that it?"

"No, it's not his tongue. It's his penis."

"I see."

"The second thing to notice is the position of the head in the sink. See how it's turned so it's looking at the entrance, so that, as soon as you come around the corner of that dividing wall, you're making eye contact with it."

"True, but so what?"

"So, this was planned carefully. The first person in there is supposed to see this thing in the sink, right? It's looking right at you. So you shit yourself, or scream, or whatever. But sooner or later, your peripheral vision is going to pick up on something to your left, and you're going to turn that way, just as I'm doing with the camera, and then you see the big mirror and what's been written on it."

"*How about a nice blow job*? Jesus fucking Christ. What is it written in, blood?"

"I think so. I tried to smell it to get a better idea, but the stench of blood in there is so overpowering that I couldn't be sure. Still, blood's probably what it is. It's consistent with the scenario, you know what I mean?"

"Yes, I do, unfortunately. I see you're moving off to the right here. The stall with the torso?"

"Right. I warn you, our friend's sense of humor hasn't exhausted itself. Okay, opening the door now . . . and here's the next installment of your nightmares."

"I'm surprised the body is still sitting up like that on the can. I would have thought, with all the muscles gone slack in death, that it would fall over quickly."

"I wondered about that, too. But the body's jammed in there pretty good. The perp is one strong son of a bitch. I won't be surprised if the autopsy report shows fractured hip bones on this poor guy. Look, the light isn't too good in this area, they've got some burned-out bulbs in the ceiling, so this part of the tape isn't as clear as the earlier stuff. But ... you can see what he did, right?"

"You mean jamming the roll of toilet paper onto the stump of the neck, like a toy head on a doll? Yes, that's clear enough, unfortunately. Are those the eyes stuck on in front?"

"Yeah. He cut two holes in the side of the roll just big enough so that the eyes would stay in position, more or less in the same place they would be if the toilet paper was really a head. This is a careful boy, takes a lot of trouble with his work. He wasn't in a hurry, either, which also supports my belief that the restroom was his last stop."

"Why did you tilt the camera up, here?"

"Oh, that's right, you can't see it in the lousy light. It's another little note, this time on the wall above the toilet."

"Okay, I can just about see something now, but I can't read it."

"It says, *'What a shithead.'*"

"Does it, now?"

"I took a closer look at it my first time through. I'd say it was actually written *in* shit. And once they get what's left of this poor guy off of that toilet, I expect we'll be able to tell where the stuff came from."

"Yes, I agree. It would be consistent . . . what did you call it?"

"Consistent with the scenario."

"Right. Since the camera lens seems to be on the move again, I assume we're off to see other horrors. Is it fair to say that they're also 'consistent with the scenario'?"

"Yeah, I'm afraid so. Do you follow boxing, Mac?"

"A little. I catch a heavyweight bout on HBO once in a while. Why?"

"Where we're going next might be considered the main event. Do you know what that makes the stuff we just saw?"

"What?"

"The warm up."

Justin Gustainis

Chapter 3

"So we've got ten corpses in all," McGraw said to his boss, "which is kind of interesting, considering that a normal night shift in that lab was three people – we were able to establish that from their records and log books."

It was 7:15 p.m.. In the four hours since watching the videotape, McGraw had read the autopsy protocols, hand-delivered from Walter Reed Army Hospital by a Warrant Officer with a "Top Secret" security clearance and a 9mm Beretta holstered on his hip.

He had also spent forty-five minutes with the two physicists from Georgetown University, who tried to explain to him the nature of the scientific research that had been carried out, at government expense, in the laboratory located in a former high school gymnasium in Fairfax, Virginia.

The two scientists' conclusions were tentative, since they were not at all certain they had understood everything contained in the project file. But on two points they were in firm agreement: first, neither one of them would have recommended that a dime of taxpayers' money be allocated to the project, and, second, the fact that 4.3 million dollars had actually been awarded was simply incomprehensible. McGraw had listened to the two of them, asked a few questions, and politely thanked them for their valuable service. He reminded both men that the project file, ludicrous though they might consider its contents to be, was still classified information. He then called his boss, requesting an urgent meeting.

McGraw's boss was Hiroshi Kimura, a thin, balding Japanese in his late fifties. He was the only person in the history of the Cal Tech physics department to earn a perfect 4.0 average through all three degree programs: Bachelor's, Master's and Ph.D.

"Ten people," Kimura said, shaking his head. "So sad. Such pain for their families." He looked at McGraw closely for a moment. "You don't look so good yourself, Mac. Have you eaten?"

"Not since breakfast. I haven't had either the time or the inclination."

"Cafeteria's still open. Would you like me to have something sent up? A sandwich, maybe? Some soup?"

"Thanks, Kim, but no. The stuff I've been dealing with today isn't good for the appetite. I've put away the better part of a bottle of Mylanta as it is."

"Then all I can do to help is to share your burden. Why don't we sit over at the table? That way you won't have to balance all that stuff on your lap."

Kimura rose from behind his desk as McGraw, weighed down with file folders and notepads, struggled out of his chair in front of the desk. They walked over to the conference table that was usually employed for staff meetings. Kimura gestured McGraw to a chair and settled into the one directly opposite. He folded his hands in front of him and said, "So, what terrible thing do you have to tell me, Mac? What happened to all these people?"

McGraw hesitated for a few seconds before answering. "There are two answers to that question.

The first answer, the medical one, is clear, if unpleasant. The second answer is elusive and maybe even more unpleasant." He glanced up from his notes for a moment and met Kimura's gaze. There was something in McGraw's expression that reminded Kimura of the faces of child prostitutes he had once seen on the streets of Bangkok – a sense of too much knowledge, gained at far too high a price.

"Anyway," McGraw said, "as far as the medical aspect goes, the pathologists are calling it 'massive trauma' in each case."

"They make it sound like a car crash. Are we talking about an explosion here? Something like that?"

"I wish we were. No, they didn't all die at the same time. Maybe I'd better describe for you how each one was found." McGraw picked up a legal pad and began to flip through the pages. "Here it is. This is culled from the autopsy protocols, the report of our man on the scene, and my viewing of the videotape made by him at the scene."

"And who was that?"

"Mike Pacilio."

Kimura looked as if he had just tasted something bitter. "Him."

"I thought he was the best one for the job. I still think–"

"No, I'm sorry," Kimura said, waving a hand back and forth. "I was unfair. Mr. Pacilio has caused us some difficulties in the past as a result of his . . . single-mindedness. But he is a good man, in his way. I think you were right to send him. Please go on."

"All right. These are the deceased, along with relevant pathological information." McGraw cleared his throat, although his voice had not sounded husky beforehand.

"Steven Muller, 42. Cause of death: shock and massive blood loss, both of which stemmed from his being disemboweled, apparently with a box-cutting knife found at the scene. Also, his right leg was broken.

"Richard Clayborn, 48. He was the project director, by the way. Cause of death: massive internal injuries, probably as a result of being repeatedly struck with a metal folding chair that was found nearby. His pelvis was also broken, and this injury preceded the others by at least an hour.

Charles Merritt, 37. Cause of death: shock, combined with widespread tissue damage. He'd been burned over 80 percent of his body, probably with a Bunsen burner that was found near the corpse, which was nude, by the way. His left kneecap was shattered, as well.

Rosemary Pavlico, 43. Like Muller, she was eviscerated. Unlike him, she was apparently raped—vaginally, anally, and orally. Both her ankles were broken.

Reynaldo Sanchez, also 43. Cause of death: multiple skull fractures. Also, he was castrated, although this seems to have been post-mortem.

Thomas VanderMark, 48. Cause of death: shock and blood loss as a result of being partially flayed—that is, skinned alive. The body, nude, was found tied over the top of one of the lab tables.

Joseph Kearney, 45. Cause of death: shock, blood loss, and strangulation. He was disemboweled and then strangled with his own intestine. He was also raped, anally.

Philip Weinberg, 53. Cause of death: heart failure. His right thighbone was broken, ante-mortem, and he, also, was castrated, although that was almost certainly post-mortem. Lucky bastard must have had a heart attack while waiting his turn, although I realize that 'lucky,' in this context, is an extremely relative thing.

Rita Wozniki, 34. Cause of death: massive internal injuries. She was apparently beaten or kicked to death after first being comprehensively raped. Both her eyes were gouged out, apparently ante-mortem. The penises of Sanchez and Weinberg were inserted into the empty eye sockets. Written on her forehead, apparently with lipstick, were the words "Brow Job." These nine were all found in the main laboratory.

Then, in the men's lavatory, we have Hobart Longtin, age 38. Cause of death probably strangulation, although that's uncertain because he was decapitated, instrument unknown. Unlike the others, with the exception of Weinberg, he appears to have died fairly quickly."

McGraw went on to describe how Longtin's head and torso had been found, as well as the messages written on the lavatory mirror and the toilet stall. Then his macabre narrative was finally done.

Kimura sat silently for some time. He was looking off into space, his eyes slightly unfocused. McGraw suspected that the other man was contemplating some of the mental images created in response to McGraw's words. McGraw felt a twinge of sympathy, but then thought, *"No matter how bad it is, my friend, I bet it doesn't hold a candle to a certain videotape I've got locked in my file cabinet downstairs."*

Kimura brought himself back to reality with an effort, and his voice was barely above a whisper when he said, "Who could do this? And *why*? What sort of mind could justify such barbarity?"

"Well, I have a theory, sort of," McGraw said. "I have a few facts to hang it on, but a lot of it is pure supposition."

"Any theory that can make some sense of this butchery would be very welcome, suppositions and all," Kimura replied. "But, please – begin with the facts, if you would."

McGraw flipped to another page of his legal pad. "Well, here's an interesting fact for you. In virtually each corpse, the wounds seem to have occurred at different times."

The wrinkles over Kimura's eyebrows deepened. After a few seconds he said, "I don't follow you."

"The pathologists are saying that each of the deceased, except for Weinberg and Longtin, has two kinds of ante-mortem injuries – one occurring earlier, the others later," McGraw explained. "Further, in each case the first injury was relatively minor – that's relative to the massive trauma occurring later, of course. Muller's broken leg, for example, probably occurred an hour or more before the other things that were done to him."

"I'm sure that's significant. It must be. But I can't quite see why –"

"Disabling injuries, Kim. Broken leg, broken ankle, fractured pelvis. Disabling, but a long way from fatal."

"But *why?*"

"He didn't want them to get away, or get to a phone. He didn't want to be interrupted, is my guess."

The two men sat there for several moments, looking at each other. Finally, Kimura broke the silence. "You said *he.*" Are you thinking this is the work of one man? Ten people dead, and without a single gunshot wound among them? One man alone? Is such a thing possible?"

"Within the context of the evidence, yeah, it's possible. Mind you, I'm not talking about your average guy here. This isn't some crack addict who wandered in off the street looking for something to steal."

"I imagine not. But why do you say it was just one?"

"Those disabling injuries themselves suggest it. Look, let's say you've got a group with you – or a gang, if you prefer. They can help you subdue everybody, keep them under control, tie them up like Christmas turkeys until you're ready to do your number on them. Right"?

"Yes, I suppose." Kimura's voice showed his distaste.

"But one man alone has got problems," McGraw said, "especially given what he had in mind. If one of the victims gets away, or gets to a phone long enough to dial 911, it's all over. So you've got to secure the environment. And even if he had a gun – and I'm assuming he did – it's still pretty hard to tie up one person while keeping an eye on nine others."

Kimura nodded slowly several times. "So he crippled them first."

"I think he must have. It's the only way those initial injuries make sense. Of course, this whole fucking thing is insane, so maybe the motivation for the injuries is as twisted as everything else that happened. There is something else that supports the single assailant theory, though."

"Yes? What is that?"

"There was a lot of semen around. It was found in, what – " McGraw consulted his notes. " – three of the bodies, although, in the case of the women in all three orifices. The FBI lab is still doing tests on it – the DNA results won't be ready for a couple of days – but they've been able to get a blood type. It's O-negative, all of it. I'd be willing to bet that it all came from the same guy."

There was silence in the room. McGraw assumed

that Kimura, who was prudish about sexual matters, was trying to formulate a question, and he made a small bet with himself about what the nature of that question would be.

McGraw won his wager when Kimura blushed and said, "Mac, this can't be right. We're talking about how many separate, uh, ejaculations, here?"

"Looks like seven."

"Seven times, over how long a period?"

"Near as we can figure, four hours. Five, tops."

Kimura spread his hands. "Can't happen, right? Can't be just one man."

McGraw shrugged. "It's a stretch, but it's possible. There are probably some teenage boys who could manage it. But you're forgetting the most important thing about sex, Kim."

"And what do you consider that to be?"

"It's mostly mental. If the proper mental stimulation is present, the body will often follow along. And whoever did these things enjoyed it Kim. That's plain as day." Anger was growing in McGraw's voice now. "Some day, I have no doubt, a team of shrinks will write a journal article on this mess and describe this guy's kink in the proper jargon: 'pathological rage complicated by deep-seated megalomania and the inability to restrain sadistic psycho-sexual impulses,' or some such bullshit. There's probably even a DSM-IV category for it. But what it comes down to is this: *the bastard did it for fun.*"

———◆———

As McGraw and Kimura were speaking of these horrors, something that had once been Peter Barbour was driving north through Pennsylvania along Route 95.

It maintained a steady speed of 64 miles per hour – fast enough to make reasonable progress but slow enough to avoid the attention of the State Police.

The blue 1999 Toyota Camry, on which Peter Barbour owed sixteen payments that would never be made, had both an AM/FM radio and a cassette player as standard equipment, but both were silent now. The driver had no need of music; it had a fresh soundtrack of screams and sobs and pleas for mercy running through its memory that it found sweeter than any song known to this world.

The driver sat behind the wheel calmly, even serenely. The hands, which had once belonged to Peter Barbour, held the wheel lightly and did not fidget. Those hands had been washed thoroughly, and were clean of anything that might have drawn a second glance. The fingernails were another matter, however. They were a little long and overdue for the trim that Peter Barbour had been meaning to give them. Underneath several of the nails were small quantities of a brown substance. The driver was not concerned. No one would be getting a close enough look at the hands to discern what the substance was. Besides, most people associate blood with the color red, forgetting that the stuff turns brown when it dries.

The face, like the hands, was placid – except for the eyes. It amused the driver to keep a little of Peter Barbour's consciousness present to observe and appreciate the interesting new things that his body was up to. From time to time, that tiny sliver of humanity showed itself in what used to be Peter Barbour's baby-blue orbs, and for those occasional few seconds the eyes held an expression that would not have looked out of place on the face of a Jew in Auschwitz.

Justin Gustainis

Chapter 4

Kimura asked a few minutes' indulgence of McGraw in order to call home. He had already advised his wife that he would be late for dinner; now he wanted to tell her not to wait up for him.

As Kimura walked over to his desk, McGraw said "Tell Louise I said 'Hi'" and got up from the conference table. To restore full circulation and also to give Kimura privacy, he walked over to the windows. The setting sun had made the western sky a gently glowing tapestry of red, blue and purple.

After a few moments, McGraw tore his attention away from the view and reached into his suit coat pocket for his cellular phone. He switched on and checked his voice mail. The first two messages concerned mundane matters but the third was from Pacilio: "I'm back from that errand you sent me on. I'll be in my office when you want me."

McGraw punched in Pacilio's number. The two men spoke for about three minutes, with Pacilio doing most of the talking. Then McGraw said, "I'm in Kimura's office. I think you'd better come on up. Okay, good."

McGraw put the cellular away and turned back to the table, where Kimura had resumed his seat. As he returned to his own chair and sat down, McGraw said, "We may have something. Remember how I told you that the normal night shift in that lab was three people?"

Kimura nodded. "Yes. I wondered what the entire project staff was doing there at that hour."

"Ten corpses, right? All identified as members of the project staff. The personnel records were in a file cabinet, undisturbed. Which is how we found out that the number of people under contract to that project was *eleven*."

Kimura thought about that. "So, it would seem we have an odd man out," he said.

"We sure do," McGraw agreed. "Which is why Pacilio is on his way up. I asked him to join us."

Kimura shrugged. "If you think it's important, I won't object. But why?"

"Because I sent him to burgle the odd man out's apartment."

Kimura was quiet for several seconds, gazing at McGraw with an intent expression. When he spoke, his voice was calm and measured and very careful, the way you speak to a small child who has just picked up a loaded gun. "Mac, listen to me. I know we're dealing with a serious matter here. But we have to keep some sense of proportion. We already have a bad situation. We have to watch out that we don't make it worse, you see? Breaking into people's homes, that kind of thing, it can bring down a lot of trouble on you, me, the whole department. This isn't the Nixon administration, Mac. If Watergate had any lesson for us, it's that the government of the United States of America should not act like the damn Mafia."

"I know, Kim, I know. But there's a difference between bugging the Democratic National Committee and entering the apartment of a material witness, maybe even a suspect, in a mass murder. Besides, Pacilio was discreet. He always is."

"I hope so," Kimura said grimly. "For everyone's sake. But, you know Mac, I think I remember that 'discreet' was used to describe another fellow one time."

"Oh? Who was that?"

"Gordon Liddy."

Before McGraw could respond, there were three soft taps on the door. Kimura rose, let Pacilio in, and directed him to a seat at the table.

After Pacilio was settled, Kimura sat down again and said to him, "So, Mr. Pacilio, I understand you are returning from what our friends in Langley would call a 'black bag job.'"

Pacilio glanced sideways at McGraw, who said, "Mr. Kimura is a little unhappy about your illicit entry into the apartment of this guy, uh –"

"Barbour. Peter Barbour," Pacilio told him, then turned to Kimura. "I can see how you may have some concern about this, sir, but it's uncalled for. Believe me."

"I very much want to believe you, Mr. Pacilio." Kimura was always formal with people who were more than one level away from him in the chain of command, either above or below.

"You *should* believe me. This was a very minor deal, legally speaking."

Kimura permitted himself another small smile. "A 'third-rate burglary,' perhaps?"

McGraw said to Pacilio, "We were trading Watergate references just before you arrived."

Pacilio made a face. "When I said this was a minor

deal, I meant there's no chance of it turning around to bite us later. Barbour has an apartment in Alexandria. I went over there and knocked on his door. No answer."

"And what if he had answered the door"? Kimura asked.

Pacilio shrugged. "Then I show him my ID and ask to come in. I've got a perfect right to talk to him, considering that everybody on his research team but him got killed last night. But, like I said, there was no response. The lock on the apartment door is a joke. I had it open in less than ten seconds. Nobody saw me. And if he comes home while I'm there, which he didn't, or if I find something that ought to be passed on to the police, I can say that the door was unlocked, or maybe the latch hadn't caught when he left. So no matter what happens, I'm covered. And that means Mac here is covered. And that means that you're covered, too, Mr. Kimura. So what do you say we all stop worrying about how I got in there and focus on what I turned up, instead?"

Kimura's eyes flickered at that last remark, but he merely nodded twice and said, "A sound idea. And what *did* you find?"

"Nothing much, at first. I was about ready to give it up and leave when I remembered the answering machine. The red light was blinking, so I played the tape. There was a message from his mother, one from the Toyota dealer, about a part on order that came in, something from his dentist about a check-up – and this."

Pacilio pulled from an inside pocket a microcassette recorder and placed it on the conference table. Kimura looked at it and said, "You didn't remove the tape from his answering machine, did you?"

"No, I left it there, and the police are welcome to it, if they ever get that far. I just replayed the message and recorded it directly onto this. The fidelity is a little off, but it's understandable. Listen."

Pacilio pushed a button. After a few seconds, the machine emitted a "beep," followed by a woman's voice: *"Peter, it's Rita. We're all meeting at the lab at 10:30 tonight. If all goes well, the door opens at midnight, the witching hour. Pretty apropos, don't you think?"* There was a giggle, then: *"Are you as excited as I am? See you tonight. Bye."*

Pacilio switched off the recorder. For a few moments, the three men were silent. Then Kimura said, "So they were all told to be at laboratory at 10:30. But what is this about a door opening at midnight? Can't be the door of the lab – hard to be in the lab at 10:30 if the door to the place doesn't open until ninety minutes later."

McGraw nodded. "I doubt that anything would be served by having the ten of them milling around in front of the building for an hour and a half, as if waiting to buy tickets to see Led Zeppelin, or something."

"Led Zeppelin broke up fifteen years ago," said Pacilio, ever the literalist, "but I agree that there must be another door that this lady is talking about. Are we assuming that 'Rita' is Rita Wosnicki, one of the victims?"

"Must be," McGraw said. "The message puts her at the scene."

Kimura nodded. "All right, say that's the case. Then what is this 'door' the woman refers to, and does it have anything to do with this massacre? And what is this about 'the witching hour'? What does *that* mean?"

"Those are all important questions," Pacilio said, "but before we get into them, can I make a suggestion?"

"Of course," Kimura replied.

"You need a pickup order on Barbour, the sooner the better. Maybe he's involved in the massacre, maybe not. Even if he isn't, I'd sure like to hear his explanation for why he didn't meet the rest of them at the lab last night."

McGraw nodded agreement, then asked "Is he on the run, do you think?"

"Probably not," Pacilio said. "There were two empty suitcases at the back of the bedroom closet. The closet itself had very few empty hangers, so there aren't a lot of clothes missing. His checkbook is still in the apartment, and so is his savings account passbook. He hasn't written a check since he paid his electric bill last week, and the most recent withdrawal from the savings account was last December. If he *is* running, I'd say he's only got the clothes on his back and whatever money was already in his wallet."

"Plus credit cards, maybe," McGraw said. "They can take you a long way, providing you're not nudging the edge of your credit limit."

"So he *could* be on the run," Kimura said.

"Yeah, I guess he could," Pacilio said. "But if he is, he didn't plan it in advance. And let's not forget this: wherever he is, he's not necessarily our killer just because he took off. Could be he arrived at work late last night, got a good look at that slaughterhouse the lab had been turned into, and suddenly decided that Nova Scotia must be lovely this time of year."

"We won't know for sure until he's picked up," Kimura said, "so I'd better get that in motion. Mac, I assume you've been in contact with the Bureau?"

McGraw nodded. "The guy you want is Pennypacker, Special Agent Charles Pennypacker, out of the Washington field office. He's heading their investigation."

Kimura excused himself and went over to his telephone.

McGraw looked at Pacilio and said softly, "What do you think, Mike? Is Barbour our guy? Whoever did all that awful shit in Fairfax has got to be a major-league nutcase, and that kind of thing usually leaves signs. Did you find anything at his place that would make this Barbour appear psycho?"

Pacilio thought briefly, then shook his head. "Nothing that points that way. No signs of obsessive fixations or compulsive behavior. No drugs, legal or otherwise. No journals or scrapbooks. No diary that I could find, and I gave the place a pretty good toss. No magazine photos or news clippings tacked to the wall. No unusual or prolific religious icons. No copies of *Mein Kampf* or *The Search for Aliens among Us* or whatever the nuts are reading these days. Several recent issues of *The Washington Post* but no supermarket tabloids. In short, not a damn thing."

McGraw made an exaggerated shrug. "Well, if not him, then who? And how? And, for Chrissakes, why?"

Pacilio just shook his head.

Kimura, his phone call completed, returned to the conference table and sat down. "I was thinking about that answering machine tape," he said. "There are several things there that bother me. Could we listen to it again, please?"

"Of course," Pacilio said. He rewound the tape, then replayed the message from the woman who identified herself as Rita. When it was over, Kimura said, "She refers to midnight as 'the witching hour.' What does that mean?"

"I think I know," McGraw said pensively. "I read an article some years ago about the European witch trials, most of them seemed to take place in Germany. The prevailing wisdom – if you want to call it that – was that midnight was the peak hour for the dark powers that the witches served. That's why, supposedly, the Witches' Sabbath began at midnight. And Black Masses, too, I believe."

Kimura looked at McGraw curiously and said, "You read some damn funny stuff, Mac."

"You're probably right," McGraw admitted. "But does it lead us anywhere?"

Pacilio said, "This 'door,' whatever it is, was supposed to open at midnight, according to Rita. She says that's 'apropos' for some reason. Then she says she's 'excited' about it."

Kimura looked at McGraw, then at Pacilio. "What was going on in that lab"? he asked, softly. "What on earth were they trying to *do*?"

"Here's a better question," Pacilio said. "What *did* they do?"

———◆———

The blue Toyota Camry formerly owned by Peter Barbour pulled into the deserted highway rest area just south of Wilkes-Barre, Pennsylvania at a few minutes after midnight. Barbour's bladder was uncomfortably full, and the driver did not want to push the human's body beyond the limits of what it could stand. Barbour's mind, of course, was another matter.

It shut off the Toyota's engine, got out of the car, and went into the men's restroom, where it relieved the bladder problem and checked Peter Barbour's appearance in the scratched and dingy mirror. Everything was satisfactory, although it found itself surprised by the feeling of hunger emanating from Peter Barbour's stomach. Physical hunger was a new sensation, although it was thoroughly familiar with many other kinds of appetites.

It went back to the car and was about to start the engine when headlights appeared in the rearview mirror. Another car was pulling into the parking lot, a white Lexus with New York plates. The new arrival pulled into a space five or six places away, and the thing that had once been Peter Barbour watched as a man and a woman emerged from the Lexus and began to walk toward the restrooms. The man appeared to be in his mid-forties, the woman at least ten years younger. Neither spared the Camry more than a passing glance, but its driver stared at them intently while contemplating a hunger that had nothing to do with Peter Barbour's empty belly. In a perfect imitation of a popular cartoon character, it said, softly, "*Oooh, if I dood it, I gonna get a whippin.*" Then, after a brief pause, it smiled a terrible smile and continued, "*I dood it!*"

It got out of the Toyota and began to walk toward the restroom building.

Justin Gustainis

Chapter 5

The man might have been crucified. Both arms were outstretched, the clenched fists were level with his shoulders. And he was naked, which lent a certain authenticity to the image. As the man himself could have told you, those subjected by the ancient Romans to crucifixion usually died naked as the day they were born; the countless images of Jesus on the cross wearing a discreet loincloth were the artists' gestures in the direction of propriety, not historical accuracy. Further, every muscle in the man's slim body was knotted, and the face was twisted into an expression that might have been taken for agony.

But then he came, in a series of groaning spasms that sent his hot spunk into the mouth of the young woman whose lips were engulfing his penis. He was riding not a cross, but a bed, and the harsh, grunting sounds he made were not those of mortal anguish but of sexual ecstasy.

The French refer to orgasm as *le petit mort*, the little death. The French may be on to something, even if they do regard Jerry Lewis as a genius.

As he caught his breath, the man gazed fondly at the young woman, whose name was Julie. He had known many women in his life – girlfriends, mistresses, prostitutes, and two wives. But Julie got to him like none of the others ever had. She was more than twenty years younger; that was part of the attraction, along with the thrill of forbidden fruit. And God, she was beautiful: hair shiny and black as a raven's wing, a tall, willowy body that she kept taut through daily aerobics – she was the answer to all his prayers. And she worshipped him, obviously, and would do anything for him, sexual or otherwise. For his last birthday he had asked her to put on an exhibition with another woman (an expensive call girl hired for the occasion), and she had agreed without hesitation or complaint, although he didn't think she was attracted to women sexually. For him, that had added even more spice to the proceedings.

She was kneeling between his splayed legs now, relaxed, her job well done. Then she glanced at her watch and said, "It's coming up on 2:30. Don't you have that session with the Board at 3:00?"

"Shit, is today Tuesday? Yes, of course it is." He lifted his legs over the side of the bed and sat on the edge for a moment. "God, I may never walk again," he groaned in mock agony. "But if I'm a cripple, it was worth it."

She smiled into his eyes, which were the same shade of blue-gray as her own, and tossed him his undershorts. "Better get a move on," she said. "Some of those tight-asses will develop heart palpitations if you start the meeting late."

Five minutes later, he slipped on the jacket of his custom-made gray suit, then checked his appearance in her floor-length mirror. "Not bad, for an old fart," he said to his reflection.

She knew he was fishing, and gave him what he needed. "Not too old to be a marvelous fuck, either" she said. "Now you better get going. The heathens are lurking everywhere, and they'll rule the world unless you're out there to smite them hip and thigh."

The Reverend Tom Pascoe, who *Time* magazine had recently called "the most powerful television evangelist in America," gave his lapels a final tug, then kissed the girl on the lips. "See you at dinner tonight?" he asked, walking to the door.

"Of course," she replied, the smile on her lips somehow failing to reach her eyes. "Bye."

She waited for the click of the closing bedroom door before calling him by the name she knew he hated to hear. "Bye, Daddy," she said softly.

———◆———

The meeting had been plodding on for almost two hours, and Reverend Pascoe was having difficulty maintaining his concentration. He found high finance boring. He was at heart a preacher, not a CEO. Pascoe enjoyed his great wealth immensely, but he did not have the soul of an accountant.

However, these board meetings were necessary if he were to hold his empire together. Each segment of it— the cable TV network, the university, the radio stations, the political action committee, and all the rest – had competent people in charge, but they relied on him to set broad policy. In turn, Pascoe relied on these meetings to remind them who was really in charge of things.

Pascoe looked down the length of the conference table at Miles Miller, who had been speaking for the last five minutes and showed no signs of winding down. Miller was head of Believers United, the political arm of Pascoe's widespread organization. Pascoe had founded

Believers United in an effort to bring Christian values (as he and his fundamentalist followers defined the term) into American politics. A *New York Times* editorial had used another word – "theocracy" – to describe what it thought Believers United was trying to achieve, but Pascoe and Miller were used to such carping from the hell-bound liberals of the establishment media.

Pascoe was pleased with his decision to entrust Believers United to Miles Miller, who was dedicated enough to give his all to the organization, and loyal enough never to contemplate any course not pre-charted by Pascoe. Although in his mid-thirties, Miller looked like a sophomore at some freshwater college that was caught in a Fifties time warp.

Miller's blond good looks, youthful appearance, and slavish devotion had once prompted Julie to describe him privately to Pascoe as "the Hitler Youth poster child." Pascoe had laughed so hard that tears ran down his face. After recovering his composure, he had made Julie promise never to repeat her observation to anyone. "I shudder to think what those bastards from People for the American Way could do with that," he'd said, "especially considering the source."

The Hitler Youth poster child was not happy today. "Donations are down 16% from last quarter, even though most local chapters have stepped up their fundraising activities," Miller reported glumly. "Even worse, membership is also down. Only two new local chapters were opened last quarter, and the existing chapters are reporting a decline in membership for the third straight quarter. Overall, membership is down 9.3% from this time last year."

Pascoe tapped his pen on the table a couple of times and said, "This is worrisome, Miles. We've been showing steady growth for over five years, and now this . . . reversal. Do you have any notion of what's behind it?"

"Nothing certain," Miller said, "but our chapter president in Minneapolis had an idea he was telling me about last week."

Typical Miles. Somebody else has an idea and Miles gives him the credit instead of taking it for himself. I love this boy, but he is such a putz. Pascoe smiled in his warm, fatherly way and asked "And what was his explanation?"

Miller glanced for a moment at a pad in front of him. "He calls it the Law of Increasingly Hostile Environment. It's supposed to be a marketing theory, but Sid thought it might apply in this case. Basically, it says the more you expand, the harder any additional expansion will be."

"I would have thought just the opposite." This came from George Poundstone, head of Pascoe's university, a place where drinking, gambling, blasphemy, and the playing of rock music were all cause for expulsion. "The bigger you get, the more powerful you are, and the harder you are to resist. You can just overwhelm the opposition."

"I'm not so sure," said Larry Constantine, who ran Pascoe's cable television network. Pascoe never ceased amazement that anyone as politically and socially conservative as Constantine could wear such garishly loud sport coats. Today's number was roughly the same color as a tangerine; it made the pudgy Greek look to Pascoe like the world's biggest Florida orange. Constantine continued, "That might be true in an army, or some other situation where size equals physical force. But what we're doing is basically persuasion. Size may not be such a factor there."

"Of course not, Larry," Pascoe said. "Everybody knows that size doesn't matter. It's what you *do* with the organization that really counts."

Pascoe's witticism caused the others to erupt with laughter – except for Miles Miller, who smiled weakly as if he didn't get the joke. When the laughter subsided, Miller said, "As I understand what Sid was saying, we've already reached the people who were most receptive to our message. They were, in a sense, the easy ones. Those remaining are the hard ones. People who belong to some country-club religion, like the Episcopalians. Or cultists, like the Catholics. Or those who are simply not godly."

"Or those whose minds have been poisoned against us by the liberal-atheist media," Poundstone rumbled in his double-bass voice.

"Them, too, of course," Miller said. "All of which makes for a hard sell, as I think they say in advertising."

"A 'hard sell'?" The words, on a rising tide of righteous indignation, came from Calvin de Groot, director of Pascoe's divinity school. "Take care, young man," he said sternly to Miller, a flush infusing his gaunt face. "You are speaking of the word of God – not some brand of dishwasher detergent!" His first name, combined with his thin, gangly body and old-fashioned suits, caused some of de Groot's colleagues to call him "Coolidge" behind his back.

"Gentlemen, gentlemen," Pascoe interrupted. He was irritated to have to break up yet another fistfight in the choirboys' locker room, as he thought of these quarrels; but none of this showed on his face, which was full of pastorly concern as he said, "I'm sure Miles meant no irreverence; we all know the depth of his love for the Lord Jesus. Although, Calvin, you were certainly right to remind us of what we're about, here. With all the trappings of the modern world with which we have to surround ourselves, it's so easy, isn't it, to focus on the secular and forget the real nature of our mission – the bringing of the Lord's word to those who need it so desperately."

"You know what we need to do, don't you?" This was Poundstone again. "We need to dance with the guy what brung us, as they say down home." Poundstone had grown up in the cosmopolitan college town of Chapel Hill, North Carolina, but he liked to pretend to rustic origins in a kind of reverse snobbery. He went on, "We need to remember that our message has always had two sides to it: what we stood for, and what we were *against*. I hope it's not un-Christian of me to say it, but you can motivate people a lot better and quicker with hate than you can with love."

Pascoe looked at him and said blandly, "We're not in the hate business, George. We represent a God of love." But Pascoe found that he was fully alert for the first time in two hours, and that had to mean something.

"A God of love, sure," Poundstone replied. "But he is also known as Jehovah, and Jehovah was known to deal severely with those who pissed him off, wasn't he? Your pardon, Calvin."

"So you're saying what, exactly?" Pascoe asked with a touch of impatience.

"I'm saying that we ought to be more aggressive in invoking the wrath of the Lord on His – and our – enemies. We need to make clear who those enemies are, and why they are God's enemies, and thus the enemies of God's people."

"No shortage of enemies of the Lord," de Groot said with a snort. "None at all. Sodomites, of both sexes, clamoring for their 'rights' to flaunt their perversions. Pornographers, preying on our children. And, worst of all, the baby killers, and those who dare to defend their butchery." He glared around the room, as if expecting to find pro-choice activists lurking in the corners.

"That brings us back to the question, doesn't it?" Constantine said. "What enemy, of the many that are out there, will unite the people of God?"

"All the enemies of God are ultimately tools of Satan," Miles Miller offered. "But the Evil One tends to operate behind the scenes, which makes it hard to point him out to others."

"Pity, in a way," Poundstone said. "The Devil himself – now *there's* an enemy everybody can agree on."

"Oh, I'm not so sure," Constantine replied. There was a smirk on his face that meant an attempt at humor was about to be made. "A fella was explaining to me just last week how Satanism might just be the perfect religion."

Pascoe decided to feed Constantine his line and get it over with. "Why's that, Larry"?

The smirk was a full-fledged grin, now. "Because if you screw up, you go to Heaven."

On that note of hilarity, the meeting ended.

Chapter 6

When the telephone rang at 6:38 A.M., Pacilio was sitting in the living room of his condo, wearing an old terrycloth bathrobe and trying to wake up. For help, he had a mug of Jamaican Blue Mountain coffee and "The Adventures of Rocky and Bullwinkle" on TV.

Pacilio sometimes felt a little decadent drinking the pricy beverage, which went for forty dollars a pound in gourmet coffee shops. But it was so rich and full-bodied, in both taste and aroma, that he couldn't help himself. Compared to Jamaican Blue Mountain, he'd found, the stuff they sell in those two-pound cans at the supermarket tastes like boiled goat vomit.

Pacilio smiled as Bullwinkle tried, yet again, to pull a rabbit out of a top hat. "Nothin' up my sleeve," the moose assured Rocky the flying squirrel, then reached into the depths of the cavernous chapeau − only to produce a very pissed-off looking rhinoceros. "Wrong hat," Pacilio remarked solemnly. A moment later, Bullwinkle arrived at the same conclusion.

Pacilio's cable package included both CNN and Headline News, as well as the two C-Span channels, Fox News, and MS-NBC. A confirmed news junkie, Pacilio watched them all when he could, but not first thing in the morning. The real world was more than he could usually cope with at 6:30 a.m., but "Rocky and Bullwinkle" was just about perfect.

Especially after a night like last night.

There was a recurring nightmare that plagued Pacilio during times of stress, and yesterday had been more stressful than anything he had experienced in years. No surprise, then, that his dreams had found him back in the jungle.

He was creeping through thick growth, alone, scared shitless, searching for Carl Chopko, his Green Beret partner on the Phoenix team. Pacilio and Chopko had saved each other's lives more times than either could remember, and in the dream Pacilio was near panic because he had heard the reports. The stories that Chopko and the rest of the team had been ambushed by the Viet Cong. The rumors that Chopko had been taken alive.

All of the men, American and Vietnamese, who did the ruthless work of the Phoenix Program were aware of the dangers, and the biggest risk of all was capture. After what they had done to the VC, night after night, village after village, the Phoenix operatives knew better than to expect anything like mercy.

Pacilio moved through the bush slowly, carefully, the way he had been taught. Eventually, he began to notice a buzzing sound that slowly grew louder as he walked on. The sound was not mechanical, but it was not a typical jungle noise, either. Finally, the thick brush gave way to a small clearing, where Pacilio saw that the buzzing was coming from about a billion flies and other insects, and under that living, seething mass was something that had been wired to a tree, something that had once been a human being, and the billion bugs were eating and fornicating and laying eggs all over what was left after the Viet Cong had finished with Carl Chopko. And as Pacilio stood there gaping, there came the sound, distinct and unmistakable, of a weapon being clicked off safety and in that instant he suddenly knew they were behind him.

That was when Pacilio had started thrashing around and screaming, eventually waking himself up. The time was just after 3:00, but he was up for the rest of the night. Having the dream once was bad enough; there was no point in inviting reruns.

He answered the telephone on the second ring, after carefully putting his coffee mug on an end table and pressing the "mute" button on the TV's remote control.

"Hope I didn't wake you for the second day in a row," McGraw's voice said.

"No, I was up this time. Did you sleep as badly as I did?"

"Didn't even try. I was up writing reports and drafting memos and making lists of people to call today. I could probably have managed two or three hours sack time, but I had a pretty good idea of what was waiting for me as soon as I closed my eyes, so I decided to pass."

"Guess I know what you mean." To keep his mind from returning to the images of his nightmare, Pacilio glanced at the silent TV screen, where Boris Badinov was being screamed at by Fearless Leader.

McGraw said, "Since I didn't go to bed, I wasn't awakened twenty minutes ago when Special Agent Pennypacker called."

"He's the FBI guy working our massacre, right?"

"That's him. Apparently he *did* get some sleep last night. He tells me he was up at 5:30, though, and one of the first things he did was check his computer, which is plugged into the NCIC hotline."

"Why do I have the feeling that this means more bad news for somebody?" Pacilio said. "Is it Barbour? Did he turn up dead?"

"No, but a two other people did. A married couple, apparently killed in an unusual way. There seem to be elements involved that are – how did you put it? – consistent with the scenario we saw in Fairfax. At least Pennypacker thinks so, but I want a second opinion, so I'm sending you up there to take a look. See if you think it was the same sick fuck who was in that lab."

"Still sticking with your 'lone gunman' theory, are you?"

"Until I get some information that contradicts it, yeah, I am. And that's what we need, information – which is why I want you to get up there and see for yourself."

"'Up there' is where?"

"Northeastern Pennsylvania. A highway rest area off Route 81, just south of someplace called Wilkes-Barre. I don't know if it has an airport, but–"

"No, it doesn't," Pacilio said, and there was something odd about his voice. "You have to fly into the Wilkes-Barre/Scranton airport, which is actually in Avoca. Then it's about a seven-mile drive to Wilkes-Barre, and probably another two, three miles to this rest stop you're talking about."

"You know the area, then."

"I guess I ought to. It's where I grew up."

———◆———

Pacilio's plane touched down in Avoca at 1:15 that afternoon, eight minutes ahead of schedule. He hoped that the luck that had brought his flight the hastening tailwind would stay with him long enough to produce a break in the investigation. Pacilio was as baffled as McGraw, Kimura, and everybody else involved, but some kind of idea was starting to form in the back of his mind, like a thunderstorm brewing on a distant horizon. He couldn't get a good look at it yet, but it made him uneasy. He assumed his subconscious would move the thought, or memory, or whatever it was, into his forebrain when it was good and ready.

The perky blonde at the Avis counter was happy to rent him the car he had reserved. Since his luggage had not been mis-routed to Omaha and the rented Chevy Cavalier seemed clean and free of mechanical problems, he considered that his good fortune was holding.

It was a short drive to the Howard Johnson's restaurant on Route 309. To get there, he passed through the small township of Dupont, the only place he knew where the municipal Christmas lights remained up all year long. They were only illuminated from Thanksgiving to New Year's; the rest of the time they just hung there in mute testimony to the parsimony of the city fathers. Driving through Dupont for the first time in three years, Pacilio found himself smiling at the unlit multicolored bulbs swaying gently in the June breeze. Some things, it seemed, could still be counted on.

The hostess at Howard Johnson's asked him if he wanted smoking or nonsmoking. "I'm meeting someone," he told her. "The gentleman in the corner booth." She followed his gaze to the man in the State Police uniform and said "Of course, sir. Right this way."

Once Pacilio was seated, the hostess placed a menu in front of him and took his beverage order. As she hurried away, Pacilio extended his hand across the table and said, "Mike Pacilio, Lieutenant. Thanks for meeting me."

The other man took the offered hand, squeezed lightly, and said, "Mitch Keenan. Troop B Crime Lab."

Keenan looked to be about thirty-five, which Pacilio thought was a little young for his rank. That probably meant that Keenan was good at his job. Or maybe he had an uncle in the state legislature.

A waitress brought Pacilio's ginger ale and asked if they were ready to order. Pacilio looked at Keenan and asked, "Are you going to get something to eat?"

"This is probably my only chance for lunch," the other man said. "I'd like to grab a bite, if you're not in a big hurry."

"No, go ahead. I haven't eaten, either. Airplane food always gives me gas."

Pacilio sipped his soda and watched as Keenan ordered. The State Policeman's brown hair was short, as per regulation, and parted on the left. His blue eyes were set wide apart, and seemed to have some intelligence behind them. The nose showed evidence of having been broken at least once. Keenan's uniform tunic looked tailored, Pacilio thought. It fit the broad shoulders well, and was cut to accommodate well-developed deltoid muscles that suggested reqular acquaintance with heavy weights.

Pacilio ordered clam chowder. He had decided to eat lightly, given the sights he was likely to be viewing later. Watching the waitress walk away, he said to Keenan, "So, I understand you had yourself a double homicide last night."

Keenan nodded glumly. "In a rest area bathroom, just off 81 North. Weirdest fucking thing I've ever seen, and I thought I'd seen it all."

Pacilio thought, *You haven't seen it all until you've spent a few hours poking around in the Fairfax Fun House, buddy.* Aloud, he said, "Weird in what way?"

Keenan shrugged his big shoulders. "The crime itself, for starters. I mean, I've seen rape before – what cop hasn't? Even a rape-murder, a couple of times. But a double-rape, double-gender double-murder? This isn't L.A., it's the Wyoming Valley, for God's sake. That kind of stuff doesn't happen around here."

Pacilio resisted the temptation to say, *"It does now."* Instead, he spent a few moments forming his next question. "Was there anything about the crime scene that had the aspect of a ... tableau about it"?

A couple of small frown lines appeared just above Keenan's nose. "Afraid I don't follow you."

"I mean, did it look like the killer was leaving something for you to find? Something that had been laid out in a particular way so as to maximize the gross-out factor?"

Keenan stared across the table for several seconds, then said softly, "So you *do* know him."

"Maybe I do. I'll have a better idea once I've seen the photos and the crime scene. You did bring the pictures, didn't you?"

Keenan nodded. "Sure, they're in my cruiser. Not the kind of thing to wave around in here, unless you want some civilians to lose their appetites in a hurry."

"That's fine," Pacilio said. "I don't much want to look at that stuff when I'm eating, either. Speaking of which, I think lunch is on the way."

The waitress served Keenan his bacon cheeseburger and fries and placed a bowl of steaming clam chowder in front of Pacilio, along with some Saltines and a fresh ginger ale.

They ate in silence for a while. Then Keenan said, without looking up from his food, "So, who is he? Or is it *they*?"

"My boss thinks it's a *he*, and he could be right, although some of his reasoning seems tenuous. But as far as the identity of the killer goes, we don't know yet. One possibility is a guy named Peter Barbour, who lives in Northern Virginia. Or did, until very recently. He seems to've disappeared, the same night that everybody he worked with was murdered. Ten people in all."

Keegan looked up at the last part. "Ten dead? Christ Almighty. What is this guy – one of those disgruntled postal workers"?

"No. He's an engineer working on a government-funded research project. And these ten murders were all pretty . . . elaborate. Not the kind of thing you might expect from some GS-7 with a Smith and Wesson and a grievance."

Keenan ate a couple of french fries, then said pensively, "I don't know anything about those ten homicides you're talking about, of course, but I'm thinkin' that maybe you made the right move, coming up here."

Pacilio's mouth was full, so he used raised eyebrows and a tilt of his head to show, "Oh, really?"

Keenan nodded. "Yeah. That word you used – 'elaborate.' I didn't put it in my report, but maybe I should have. Because that's exactly what that crime scene was: fucking elaborate. Set up like a window display in a department store during Christmas season." Keenan thought for a moment. "Well, Christmas in Hell, maybe."

"I doubt they celebrate it there," Pacilio said. "But what you're talking about sounds promising, in a perverse sort of way." He had another spoonful of chowder. "Actually, my life would be greatly improved if

I never had to look at this bastard's handiwork again – except they're paying me to find him, if I can. Pretty good definition of mixed feelings, wouldn't you say?"

Keenan swallowed the last of his coffee and shrugged. "My brother told me one I like better. He says mixed feelings is watching your mother-in-law drive off a cliff – in your new Cadillac."

Pacilio gave the old joke more of a smile than it deserved, then said "Guess it's time we found out if my mixed feelings are justified. Can I follow you out there?"

Keenan picked up his trooper's hat from the seat next to him and nodded. "Sure, no problem."

"Then let's go." Pacilio stood up and put some money on the table for a tip. Picking up the check, he said, "Lunch is on me."

"I certainly hope so," Keenan replied.

———◆———

Pacilio stepped over the yellow Crime Scene tape and followed Keenan to the door marked "Men." There was a police seal on the door, and Keenan busied himself removing it. Pacilio let his gaze wander around the outside of the long, low building. It looked like every highway rest area he had ever seen, apart from the lack of traffic through the parking lot – the police barricades had seen to that.

A chubby gray squirrel, made semi-tame by travelers' handouts, approached Pacilio cautiously, a few bounds at a time. It stopped about eight feet away and rose up on its hind legs, begging. "Hey, little guy," Pacilio said softly. "Do you know Bullwinkle? Where's your goggles?" He checked his pockets, but found nothing that was edible, even by squirrel standards.

Keenan finally got the seal off the door and called over, "Okay, we're in." The squirrel, recognizing a stiff when it saw one, gave a disgusted snort and scampered away. Pacilio turned back to the men's room door and followed Keenan inside.

Just inside the door was a light switch. Keenan flicked it on, flooding the lavatory with harsh light from three ancient ceiling fixtures. The place contained two chipped sinks with a streaky, scratched mirror above them. To the left were three urinals, then two stalls, their green metal walls and doors pockmarked with rust. That was it – except for the chalk outlines on the floor.

Pacilio stared at the crudely drawn silhouettes, then shook his head a couple of times. "I can't figure it," he said.

"Can't blame you for that," Keenan said. "It's not the kind of thing you run into every day." He took a manila envelope from under his arm, pulled out a file folder, and handed it to Pacilio. "Here – try this."

Inside the folder, a metal brad held some papers in place, and there were a number of loose eight-by-ten black and white photos. Pacilio looked through the photos once, then again, more slowly. Next, he skimmed the reports. Then he went back through the photos, even more slowly. Finally, he closed the folder, looked back at the chalk outline for long seconds, then turned toward the mirror. There were words written there in what looked like lipstick.

Turning back to the chalk outline, Pacilio said, "So they were found with their clothes disarrayed, lying on their stomachs, facing each other."

Keenan took a couple of steps closer. "That's right,"

he said. "As you saw in the photographs, their arms were extended over their heads and the hands were tied together – his right to her left, his left to her right. The killer used the man's tie and a scarf from the woman, both silk. You know, good quality silk has a hell of a lot of tensile strength. There was a guy in England named Rusk, I think, used to strangle women using silk ties. They called him the Necktie Killer."

"But the tie wasn't used that way here."

"No. He used his hands. Or they did. The finger marks are clear, and the bruise patterns are strongly suggestive of manual strangulation."

Pacilio noticed that Keenan had taken on a formal, academic aspect since they had been in the lavatory. *Maybe that's how he keeps it at arm's length,* Pacilio thought. *He becomes Professor Keenan, lecturing at the State Police Academy about a case study in some old textbook someplace.* Aloud, he asked, "But the strangulation was later, right? After he sodomised them."

The trooper nodded. "Yes, in both cases the anal rape was almost certainly ante-mortem. Assuming he assaulted them while they were laid out like that, it means that each one was looking into the face of the other while it was taking place."

Pacilio took a couple of steps to the side and peered at the chalk outline from a different angle. "Well, looks like this setup challenges my boss's theory about a lone perpetrator," he told Keenan.

"How so?"

"It 'd be pretty difficult for one guy to do all this by himself, even if he was armed. That binding of the wrists together isn't going to control the victims all that well, especially when he starts raping them."

"Technically, what you mean is forcible sodomy, not rape." Clearly, the Professor was still in class.

Pacilio decided not to show his annoyance at Keenan's nitpicking. "Whatever. My point is, the way they were tied still allows a lot of mobility, and when it started to get nasty for them, the victims would have started squirming around, kicking, and so on. Hard to make this scenario work unless he had some help. Remember the Freeway Killers out in L.A.? Bianchi and what's-his-name? Those bastards worked as a team. A couple of real hunting buddies. Maybe that's what we've got here."

Keenan pursed his lips briefly. "It's an interesting theory," he said. "But I bet you wouldn't have advanced it if you had read the autopsy reports more carefully."

Pacilio looked at him. "Why? What's in there that says it was just one killer?"

In a patient voice, Keenan said, "Why don't you look at the report again?"

"*Better idea: why don't you just fucking tell me?*"

Pacilio's voice seemed to bounce off the dingy walls in the silence that followed. He and Keenan looked at each other for what seemed like a long time. Finally, Keenan said quietly, "I know how it is. It starts to get under your skin after a while, doesn't it, even when you're used to this kind of stuff. I know, believe me."

Pacilio took a deep breath and let it out. His eyes focused on the chalk outlines, he said, "I've been looking at a lot of corpses lately. People who weren't just killed, but tortured and mutilated and then laid out like trophy marlins that some rich fuck hooked from his cabin cruiser off the Florida Keys." He tapped the file folder he was holding. "People a lot like these."

He looked up at Keenan. "I'm a little out of practice dealing with this kind of thing." A pause, another deep breath. "But that's no excuse for talking like that to someone who's helping me out as a courtesy. I apologize."

"Forget it," Keenan told him. "Look, what I was getting at with –"

"No," Pacilio said. "You were right. Let me figure it out myself, if I can. Just give me a minute."

He read the autopsy protocols again, slowly. Then his eyes suddenly stopped moving. "Fractured pelvis?" He flipped ahead several pages, scanned downward, then stopped again. After a moment, he said to Keenan, "Is that what you were talking about? They each had a fractured pelvis?"

Keenan nodded. "I don't say it was one man, or two, or a whole platoon. And if it was just one, I don't know exactly how he worked it. But if he hit them hard enough to fracture the pelvis before the real fun started, that would serve as a –"

"*Disabling injury*," Pacilio said quietly. McGraw's voice seemed to be echoing in his head.

"Right. A disabling injury. Combine that with the tied hands, and these people weren't going anywhere without help, no matter what was being done to them -- or being done to somebody else."

"I think you've got a point there." Pacilio thought for a few moments. "But there's another aspect to this, as well. Have you ever broken a bone? Maybe not your pelvis, but an arm, leg, something?"

Keenan nodded. "Sure. Three or four times, if you go back to high school football. So?"

"Hurts like hell, doesn't it?"

Keenan nodded again.

"Okay, so imagine that you have a fracture of your pelvis, which is a fairly important anatomical structure. Imagine the agony. Then imagine laying on a concrete floor with your broken pelvis, face down, and having the weight of a man's body on top of you, pounding you over and over and over as he drives his dick into your unlubricated asshole. And then, after all of that torment, which was probably awful enough to make the Gestapo envious, imagine watching him do the same thing to the person you love more than anyone else in the world, as he or she is screaming right into your face. And then, finally, imagine watching him strangle the one you love to death, right in front of you, while you're powerless to do anything about it. Oh, and top it off with the knowledge that, as soon as he's finished with that little chore, he's going to come over and do the same thing to you."

Despite the professorial detachment that Keenan had put on like an overcoat, there was something in his face now, something that looked frightened.

"And so," Pacilio continued, "when you view it that way, you can see that the kindest thing the bastard did for these people was when he killed them."

Pacilio walked over to the restroom's mirror. Staring into it he said, "And then this creature that we're supposed to consider a human being gets up and goes through the woman's purse until he finds her lipstick. And he leaves us this little note."

Keenan couldn't tell whether Pacilio was looking at his own reflection or at the words on the mirror, which read, in neatly-printed letters three inches high, "IF YOU THINK SEX IS A REAL PAIN IN THE ASS, MAYBE YOU'RE DOING IT WRONG."

———◆———

Four hours later found Pacilio sitting on the edge of a hotel bed, phone to his ear. Newspapers (the two Wilkes-Barre papers, one from Scranton, and *The New York Times*) were scattered around the room. In the background, Dan Rather had just finished describing the mess the world was in today. Pacilio had the sound turned low.

McGraw was saying, "Any possibility this freak isn't our guy?"

"Possibility? Shit, anything's possible. But the probability seems high that it's him. The style is too distinctive to be a chance resemblance. Especially that business with the mirrors." He felt anger growing in him again, and took a deliberate deep breath to quell it. "You've done a good job keeping the Fairfax thing out of the media, so far."

"The details, anyway. We're trying to get it into the books as an explosion and fire, to explain all those closed coffins. If the reporters ever get hold of the juicy details, it's going to make the coverage of the O.J. trial look like a model of restraint and good taste."

"True, but I was thinking of something else."

"What's that?"

"A media blackout means no copycats."

McGraw thought about that for a moment. "Yeah, you're right. Guess we'd better try to keep the lid on as long as possible. How about the Pennsylvania people? Will they help us with that?"

"They'll try. It helps that the victims weren't locals. But you know that this is going to break open sooner or later."

"True. Frankly, I prefer later. Sometime in the next century would be good, although I'll settle for the day after this lunatic is in custody. Listen, are you flying back tonight?"

"No, I'm staying over. I've got a room at the Sheraton in Scranton." Pacilio read off the hotel's telephone number as well as his room number. "I can get a flight tomorrow morning that'll have me back before lunchtime."

"That'll be fine. I remember you saying that you were from those parts. Are you getting together with your family tonight?"

"No. I don't have much family left up here. But I do want to look up a guy I know. Did I mention that I went to college in this area, too?"

"No, I don't think you did," McGraw said. "What did you do, live at home while going to school?"

"That's right. After two tours in Vietnam, I was ready for a more stable environment – that, and my mom's cooking."

"So you're going to look up an old college buddy?"

"No, he's more of an old professor buddy. I think he may be able to help me with an idea I have about the case."

"I assume this is someone whose discretion you can rely on," McGraw said pointedly.

"You mean, am I sure he won't be calling *A Current Affair* two minutes after I finish talking to him?"

"Well, yeah. Something like that."

"I trust him. He won't blab if I ask him not to."

"Is he a criminologist? Someone I might have heard of, maybe?"

Pacilio sighed quietly. Sometimes McGraw could be as nosy as a Hollywood gossip columnist. "No, he's more of a half-ass theologian. We used to call him Dirty Eugene."

"Theologian? Are you suffering a spiritual crisis, or something"?

"I'm just playing a hunch, Mac. Look, it's a long story. I'll tell you about it tomorrow, if it amounts to anything."

"Fair enough," McGraw told him. "Me, I'll think I'll head home and go to bed."

"Maybe we can both get a decent night's sleep tonight," Pacilio said. "It would be a nice change."

"*To bed, to sleep. To sleep, perchance to dream.*"

"You were doing fine there, until you got to the 'dream' part."

"I hear you, podner." McGraw left his native Texas long ago, but its patois sometimes found its way into his speech when he was tired. "Listen, stop by the office when you get back into town tomorrow, all right?"

"I will," Pacilio told him, and hung up. He said quietly, "I just hope Dirty Eugene is sober, that's all."

Justin Gustainis

Chapter 7

The University of Scranton, despite its secular-sounding name, is a Catholic institution run by the Society of Jesus. Like most Jesuit colleges in the United States, Scranton is an urban campus, which means there isn't a great deal of green space, with one exception: the Jesuit Residence. The rambling old building, which houses the twenty or so priests who form part of the college's faculty and administration, is surrounded by grass, trees, and plantings, about half an acre of it.

The grounds behind the Residence are not well lit at night, so all Pacilio could see of his companion was the glow of the older man's cigarette, along with an occasional bounce of moonlight off the priest's mostly bald head as they walked.

"I was surprised by your last letter, Eugene," Pacilio said. "Surprised, I mean, that you were even back in the States, let alone back at the U."

The Reverend Eugene Grady, S.J., flicked ash from the tip of his Winston. "Lot of people in the Order make jokes about Scranton, Mikey. After being assigned to the Gregorian in Rome, or even Georgetown, they find Scranton kind of slow, you know? Some of them call it the boondocks." The priest snorted, which brought on a brief fit of coughing. "Boondocks my hairy ass. I just spent a little more than three years on top of a fucking mountain in Bolivia. You haven't seen boondocks until you've seen Bolivia – my part of it, anyway. After that place, this looks like Heaven to me, as the Bishop said when the actress dropped her drawers."

There had actually been two Jesuits named Eugene Grady at the University of Scranton when Pacilio was a student there. One taught Theology, the other, English Literature. To distinguish between them, someone came up with the names "Clean Eugene" and "Dirty Eugene." The designations stuck.

Clean Eugene was the literature guy – a tall, thin ascetic with a fine mind, an even temperament and no sense of humor whatsoever. He took everything seriously, including himself, and was a total, repressed tightass in his attitudes, language, and behavior. One of his lay colleagues, an English professor named Warner, once said, "Clean Eugene missed his calling. He should have been a nun."

Dirty Eugene taught Theology and Moral Philosophy. He was a small man, balding even back then, with a seamed face and sardonic green eyes. He claimed to know more dirty jokes than any other Jesuit in the Maryland Province, and his students believed him.

"Besides," Dirty Eugene was saying, "I've always had a soft spot in my heart – or is it my head? – for this place. It was my first assignment after I got out of the slam, you know."

"What did you serve – two years?"

"Just under. Twenty-two mother-frigging months at Danbury. God, the chow was lousy in that joint. Almost as bad as Bolivia, although Bolivia smells better – if not by much. Still, you can't say that I didn't ask for it."

"You and the Brannigan brothers. What was it you called yourselves?"

"*The Allentown Eight.* The Brannigans, me, a couple of nuns from one of the more liberal orders, a Christian Brother from Baltimore, and two seminarians. God, we thought we were big stuff, torching all those draft files."

"The clerks at the Allentown draft board probably thought so, too," Pacilio said.

"Yeah, they were pretty pissed. Can't blame them, really." They were passing a low brick wall used to set off some flowerbeds. "Let's sit for a little while," Grady said. "The old pins haven't been too reliable, lately."

They perched on the top of the wall, side by side, and the priest lit another smoke.

"But there's one thing that puzzles me, Mikey." Grady was the only person in the world who Pacilio would allow to call him "Mikey."

"What's that?"

"Just what the fuck do you want?"

There was a thoughtful pause before Pacilio asked, "I don't suppose the pleasure of your company, the sheer poetry of your discourse, or the way the moonlight glints on your scalp would be enough of a reason?"

The priest snorted, which got him coughing again. "Don't bullshit a bullshitter," he managed, finally. Then, in a more gentle tone, he said, "So come on, spill. What's bugging you?"

There was silence for perhaps ten seconds, then Pacilio cleared his throat and said, "Eugene, what do you know about demons?"

There was silence for ten or twelve seconds.

"Demons, Mikey?" Dirty Eugene's voice sounded the same, but his face had changed. Pacilio couldn't tell in the dark, but the laugh lines around the priest's eyes had disappeared, and the eyes themselves no longer sparkled with humor. Father Eugene Grady's countenance had lost all expression and become a mask. Of course, in many cultures, the *shaman* dons a mask before beginning the difficult and dangerous task of casting out evil spirits.

"What makes you think I know anything special about demons? The guy who played the priest in that movie still lives in Scranton, I think. Why don't you check with him?"

"Jason Miller's dead," Pacilio said. "It was in the alumni magazine. And stop yanking my fucking chain, because I know what you were doing during most of the Eighties."

"What, teaching bonehead seminarians at Woodstock? Nothing too exciting about that, unless you get off on cows."

"No, there isn't," Pacilio agreed. "But I'm talking about your special duties – the ones that took you away from the seminary, sometimes for weeks at a time."

"Mikey, someone's been feeding you a line of bullshit, and I don't –"

"Give it a rest, Eugene. I told you – *I know*."

"Know *what*, for Christ's sake?"

"That you were the Maryland Province's principal exorcist for almost ten years."

After a while, Dirty Eugene said matter-of-factly, "That's not supposed to be common knowledge, Mikey."

"It isn't," Pacilio said. "An old Navy buddy of mine got religion after the war and entered the Jesuits. But he still comes to the SEAL Team One reunions, and he gets talky when he's drunk."

Eugene went on as if he hadn't heard. "I mean, Mother Church is kind of embarrassed about all that exorcism stuff. None of the other churches, or, I should say, Christian churches, do it anymore, although you still see it in some of the African tribal rituals. Lots of Catholics, including quite a few clergy, think exorcism's both medieval and bad publicity, and I can't argue with 'em – it is. But it's something else, too."

"What's that?"

"A vital spiritual necessity. At least, it is on those rare occasions when you've got genuine demonic possession. When it's not Tourette Syndrome, not schizophrenia, not some kind of multiple personality disorder. I'm talking about the real article, direct from the gates of Hell."

Pacilio nodded. "That's what I want to know about. The real article."

Dirty Eugene Grady closed his eyes and massaged the bridge of his nose with a thumb and forefinger. Without opening his eyes, he said, "*Why*, Mikey? Why do you want me to give you nightmares that'll probably last for weeks?"

"I already have nightmares, Eugene," Pacilio said, and the priest marveled at the utter lack of self-pity in the younger man's voice.

"So why, then? Why the sudden interest in demons?"

"Because it's possible that I'm on the trail of one."

The old priest opened his eyes and turned to look at Pacilio in the semi-darkness. After a long moment of silence he said, simply, "Tell me."

———◆———

"In order for this to make any sense," Pacilio said, "I'm going to have to delve into ancient history a little bit."

"You mean the war."

"Yeah, the war. You have some idea of the kind of shit I was doing in those days, and you know about the team I led when I was with the Phoenix Program. Me, another American named Chopko, and four Viets."

The priest nodded. "Yes, I remember. You used to talk about them sometimes, especially after a few beers."

"Well, one time they sent us on a mission that I never told you about, no matter how much beer I'd had. In the briefing, we were told that there was some kind of VC hit squad roaming around I Corps butchering people. They'd killed a bunch of South Vietnamese, both military and civilian, and several Americans, including one Army Colonel assigned to I Corps Intelligence. His murder was the one that got people paying attention."

"Yes, I can imagine," Dirty Eugene muttered.

"And when I say 'butchered,' I mean it. These people were tortured before death and mutilated afterward. Intelligence had put together a file with photos of the victims, and some of those pictures would have given Jack the Ripper the dry heaves."

"Why the cruelty?" Eugene asked. "I mean, what was the point?"

Pacilio shrugged. "The working theory was that it was all part of some VC terror campaign – you know, psychological warfare. I thought it was bullshit."

"Why? Terrorism wasn't exactly unheard of in that war, was it?"

"No, it wasn't," Pacilio said. "In fact, you could say that I'd practiced some myself. And that's why I knew that terror wasn't the point of these killings: there was no propaganda."

"Ah! The light begins to dawn."

"'*The purpose of terror is to terrify*,'" Pacilio said, the way you do when you're quoting somebody. "Lenin came up with that, and he would know, the bloodthirsty old bastard. He understood that terror only works if the people you want to frighten know who's doing it, and why. The VC cadres weren't talking up the killings as a way of scaring the villagers into paying their rice tax, or whatever – we had sources in the villages, and they weren't reporting so much as a whisper about this stuff. Radio Hanoi didn't have anything to say about it, either. That bitch Hanoi Hannah would've loved to use something like that. You know," – Pacilio pitched his voice higher and took on a Vietnamese accent – " '*You are safe nowhere, GI. We go where we want, we kill whoever we please. You cannot stop us.*' But she never said a word about it."

"So the point of the murders wasn't terrorism, because no one was taking credit for them."

"Right. Unfortunately, some genius on Westmoreland's staff had already decided that the killings *were* being carried out for psywar purposes. So that was that, end of discussion – for everybody on down the line, including us poor spec op types, who were expected to go after the motherfuckers."

Dirty Eugene nodded. "Bureaucracy wins again, as usual."

"It always does," Pacilio said. "Thing is, this staff guy, whoever he was, apparently was very impressed by the little messages that were left at the scenes of the killings. He figured that was proof that the VC were behind it all."

"Messages?" The priest frowned. "You mean notes left on the bodies, or something?"

Pacilio snorted. "'There were notes, all right, but the guy writing them didn't use anything as ordinary as pencil and paper. Messages were found on walls, mirrors, the headboards of beds, sometimes right on the bodies themselves. A lot of the time, they were written in blood, although the killers would use anything that was handy: a magic marker, lipstick, whatever."

"So, what did these messages say?"

"Well, one time they went into some village and wiped out a whole family: mother, father, and two kids. Nobody else saw or heard a thing. The victims were found inside their hut, decapitated, the heads resting inside the family members' individual rice bowls. And on one wall was written, in perfect Vietnamese, "SOMETHING NEW FOR DINNER!"

"Jesus H. Christ," Dirty Eugene said softly.

"And that American Colonel from Intelligence, he was found in his quarters, lying on his bed – dead, mutilated, and so on. His eyes were gone, although whether he was dead or alive when they were cut out wasn't clear. On the wall over the bed was printed, in the Colonel's blood, "IN G-2, WE ALL HAVE EYES IN THE BACK OF OUR HEADS. And when they went to move the body, and somebody lifted its head off the pillow –"

"You don't mean . . . ,"

"I absolutely do," Pacilio said. "His eyeballs were stuck to the back of his head, somehow. I bet the guy who found him still dreams about it."

"Christ, I'll be lucky if *I'm* not dreamin' about it tonight, myself."

"Anyway, the Powers That Be latched onto these little displays as proof positive that this was all part of a psywar campaign by the Viet Cong. So, since my team had some experience in psywar, and a lot of experience finding people out in the boonies, we got orders to track the son of a bitch down. And, shades of old Frank Buck, they wanted us to bring him back alive."

"What on earth for?"

Pacilio's shrug was barely visible in the darkness. "Interrogation, I guess. Or maybe they wanted to use him in our own propaganda, as proof of enemy atrocities, or something. They never told us."

"Hold on a second," Dirty Eugene said. "I just realized that you've been referring to the killer as 'him,' but earlier you were using 'them.' So, which is it?"

Pacilio thought for a moment. "I guess I was just reflecting the thought process we went through at the time. At first, we figured it was a team. Hell, they told us it *had* to be. No way one man could do all that shit alone, they said. Later on, we started to wonder. And, later still, we found out for sure."

"Found out it was one man?"

"One . . . *something*."

Dirty Eugene nodded slowly. "I get the feeling that we have finally reached the heart of the matter."

"Maybe we have," Pacilio said. "Anyway, we were out in the field for almost three weeks before we cut this guy's trail, then we followed it for four days. We finally caught up with him in a little hole-in-the-wall village called Do Lac."

Pacilio explained what his team had seen and done in the village of Do Lac, and described his final rush into the hut where their quarry was believed to be.

"I did it just the way they had taught me, Eugene. Kicked the door open, dove in fast, rolled once, and came up on one knee with my weapon ready. Did I mention that I favored a shotgun in those days?"

"No, you didn't, but go on."

"There were four people in that hut, but only one of them was still alive. There was a coleman lantern burning, so I could see that much. Two of the corpses were Vietnamese children. The best you could say for them was that they weren't feeling any more agony from the things that had been done to them. The third corpse was an adult male, also Vietnamese, hanging by his hands from some rope that was tied to one of the bamboo roof timbers. I couldn't take the time to look at him closely, but it wasn't hard to see why had had been screaming so loud, and for so long. And the bastard who had done all this was sitting on the floor a few feet away, calmly eating a candy bar.

"And here's the real ass-kicker: he was an American. *And I knew him.*"

"Who was he – somebody military?"

"I guess you could say that. His name was Hank Bitner, and he was a Master Sergeant in the Green Berets."

"Mother of Mercy. And he had killed all those people?"

"Well, in a sense, yeah."

"What the fuck does 'in a sense' mean?"

"Just be patient," Pacilio said. "See, we'd assumed that Hank was either dead or a prisoner. He'd been reported MIA four months earlier – which was about the same time the murders started, although nobody made the connection. His A-team had gone out on a mission into the Rung Sat Zone, and none of them ever came back."

"What's 'MIA?'" Dirty Eugene asked.

"Missing in Action," Pacilio told him. "One way or the other, I never thought I'd be seeing old Hank again, and inside that fucking abattoir was about the last place I would have expected to run into him.

"So, there I am, shotgun ready, sweating like a pig from the heat and the adrenaline rush, and Hank just sits there chewing on this fucking Hershey Bar. He finishes off the last bite, then looks at me and says, 'I wondered when someone would come. It would appear my curiosity is now satisfied.' Now that quote, Eugene, is pretty much word-for-word, and that's important."

"Why does it matter how he said it?"

"Because Hank Bitner never talked like in his whole life. I ought to know – I spent enough time with him, both in the field and in a couple of dozen bars in Saigon and Da Nang. See, Hank came from some shithole in the West Virginia hills – you know, one of those places with 'Hollow' in the name, where your uncle is also likely to be your cousin, and everybody's biggest worry is that the 'revenuers' will bust up their still. Hank told me once that he'd quit high school halfway through tenth grade."

"A real redneck, in other words."

"Don't get me wrong: the guy was no dummy – I never saw anybody read aerial recon photos as well as Hank could, or repair a generator as fast – but he wasn't what you'd call real refined. He sure as shit didn't talk like Lawrence Olivier doing *Hamlet*."

"So what happened after you recognized him?"

"I say to him, 'I don't know what the fuck you think you've been doing, Hank, but they sent me to bring you back.' And he just stares at me with this blank expression, like he's thinking about something else.

Then he finally says, 'Yes, I know you. You're Pacilio, which means the one called Chopko must be close at hand. Are the others with you, too?'

"I just nod at this, because even though he's finally recognized me, this guy is still not talking like Hank Bitner. But I know that he damn well *is* Hank Bitner. So I kind of gesture at him with the shotgun barrel and say, 'On your knees, Hank, then put your hands behind your neck. Do it very slow and very careful.'

"And the son of a bitch looks at me and smiles and says, 'No, I don't believe I will.'

"So I say something like 'I wasn't giving you a choice, motherfucker! Now move it!' And he does – except the movement is to his belt where he's got a sheath holding his K-Bar combat knife. He pulls the knife, but he does it slowly, so I don't fire. But I'm ready, in case he has some idea of throwing it at me. What I'm *not* ready for is what he does next."

"I'm almost afraid to ask," Dirty Eugene said.

"He jams that knife into his own gut and starts disemboweling himself."

"Oh, sweet fucking Jesus."

"Now, I'm so freaked out by what I'm seeing that I just kneel there gaping for four or five seconds. And then, with blood spurting all over and his fucking intestines spilling onto the floor, something like, *changes* in Hank's face. All of a sudden, he looks horrified at what he's doing to himself, Kind of like a sleepwalker who just picked a real bad moment to wake up. And he looks at me, and in a voice that sounds a lot more like the Hank Bitner I know, he croaks out, "Mike, stop him! Please, man, make the fucker *stop*!" And meanwhile, that hand with the knife is still carving away at Hank's guts, it's like he can't control it. So I do the only thing I can think of to make it stop.

"I raise my shotgun, take aim, and splatter the contents of Hank Bitner's skull all over the back wall of that hut."

"Mikey, listen –"

"Used to be, you know, not a day would go by that I wouldn't think about Do Lac. Remembering what happened, trying to figure out what it all meant, thinking that I should have been able to save Hank's life. Then, gradually, over a period of years, I was able to let it go. Weeks would go by when I wouldn't think of it at all.

"But now it's back inside my head." Pacilio's voice was slightly unsteady. "And the reason why it's back is because they've sent me after some guy who's doing the exact same kind of shit that my old buddy Hank Bitner used to do, and I'm finally starting to think that maybe I know why."

Pacilio turned and looked at the priest, who was only a silhouette in the darkness. "And *that*, Eugene, is why I want you to tell me what you know about demons."

Justin Gustainis

Chapter 8

Pacilio followed Dirty Eugene Grady through the front door of the Jesuit Residence. "Come on, Mikey," the priest said. "We can talk in the smoking parlor."

They passed from the spacious foyer into a large room full of old but well-preserved furniture. Bookcases lined the walls, and heavy glass ashtrays sat atop every table.

"Pick a pew and sit down," Grady said. He gestured toward a small wet bar against the far wall. "Care to wet your whistle?"

"Something soft, if you have it," Pacilio told him, easing into an overstuffed armchair. "Club soda is fine, if it's cold or there's some ice."

"Well, let's see here." Dirty Eugene was peering into a small refrigerator that was built into the bar. "There's some club soda, but wait – didn't you used to be nutty for ginger ale?"

Pacilio nodded. "Still am, I guess. Have you got some?"

"Um-hmm. Looks like a couple of cans of Schweppes."

"Best ginger ale ever made – sure, I'll take some off your hands."

The priest produced a can from within the refrigerator and placed it on the bar. "You want a glass? Some ice?"

"No, the can's fine."

Dirty Eugene mixed himself a generous Jack Daniel's and water. He handed Pacilio the can of Schweppes and carefully lowered himself into the armchair directly across from the one Pacilio had chosen. Lighting another cigarette, he said, "Lot of priests still smoke, you know, despite the wise words from the Surgeon General. Quite a few of us drink, too, although not necessarily to excess. Compensation for celibacy, or so we like to tell ourselves. We all have our little vices."

Eugene took a pull at his drink, set it down and asked, "And what about you, Mikey? Is chasing after demons *your* latest vice? If so, there's more at stake than lung cancer or a bad liver. A *lot* more."

Pacilio shrugged. "I realize that I might be full of shit, Eugene. In fact, I hope I am." He tilted the can of ginger ale and took a couple of swallows. "But the savagery of these murders, and the amusement the bastard apparently gets out of displaying the remains . . . I don't know. It's been striking a chord, that's all. Some of it goes back to the war, and the rest comes from stuff you used to teach in class about the nature of evil."

The priest nodded grimly. "And that was just book knowledge I was passing on. Those days, I hadn't yet experienced the real thing." He shook his head a couple of times. "I didn't know the fucking half of it."

Dirty Eugene flicked his Winston in the general direction of an ashtray. "You know, it used to be widely believed that a person possessed by a demon was not dangerous, in a physical sense. The only damage, the books said, might be to the poor son of a bitch who was hosting the thing."

"When you say 'dangerous in a physical sense,' that implies some other sort of danger *is* present," Pacilio said. "Like what?"

"Spiritual, of course. It's been church doctrine for a long time that the reason God allows demonic possession is to test the faith of those around the possessed – the family, friends, and so on. What the *demon* wants is to destroy the faith of those people, or at least sow the seeds of doubt and despair. It's purely a spiritual battle, you see. Or so it was thought."

Pacilio's eyes narrowed slightly. "But you don't believe that now?"

"No," Dirty Eugene said. "Not anymore."

"When did you change your mind?"

"When I saw one of them kill."

Pacilio took another swig from his can of Schweppes and asked, "So someone under the – what would you call it, influence? – of demonic possession is capable of murder?"

Dirty Eugene Grady nodded grimly. "Capable of anything, really, because demons are capable of anything. Until the demon is driven out, the person afflicted has no real will of his own."

Pacilio thought for a moment, then asked, "Why do they do that?"

Dirty Eugene made an impatient gesture. "Don't confuse an old man, Mikey. Why does *who* do *what*?"

"Why do demons do what they do? You said that the Church's line on why it happens is that it's a test of faith for those who have to put up with the possessed person, or whatever the proper Vaticanese is for all that. Okay, say that's true. That explains why God, or whoever's in charge, *allows* it to happen. But what's in it for the demon? What is it getting out of the experience?"

The priest stared at him for several seconds. Finally, he sighed and said, "Everybody needs to believe in something, so I believe I'll have another drink. You want another can of that kiddie stuff?"

Pacilio shook his head and watched Dirty Eugene make his slow, unsteady way to the bar. Twisting the cap off the bottle of Jack Daniel's, the priest said, "Mikey, you need to get some things clear in your noggin if you're going to be messing around with a demon, although I pray to God, literally, that you're wrong about that." He poured himself a generous measure of bourbon. "Understand this for starters: you are not dealing with some human being who happens to have a hostile attitude, combined with a pitchfork fetish. We're talking about evil incarnate. If the baddest, meanest, most depraved motherfucker you ever heard of, maybe somebody like Charlie Manson, or that cannibal fella in Milwaukee –what was his name? Dahmer? – was to meet up with one of these things, he'd head for the horizon at full speed, screaming for his mother the whole way. Keep that in mind as a first principle, all right?"

Dirty Eugene returned to his chair as Pacilio said, "All right, they're terrifying. I accept that. What I don't get is *why* they are the way they are."

"That's a tall order, Mikey," the priest said. "The Church doesn't have an awful lot of information, and half of what it *does* have comes down to pure speculation by people who have never encountered one of the damned things, and you can imagine what *that's* worth. Kind of like a lifelong celibate moralizing about sex, although, come to think of it, Mother Church has no shortage of that sort of bullshit, either."

"So, what is there to go on?" Pacilio asked.

Dirty Eugene shrugged. "A few scriptural references, both Old and New Testaments, as well as the Apocrypha. The writings of a few saints who had run-ins with demons in their lifetimes. And the testimony of surviving exorcists, which amounts to more material than you might imagine. Did you know that the Vatican has been collecting written accounts of exorcisms since the Fifteenth Century? No, of course you didn't – that's the Church's equivalent of a state secret. They still do it today, though. If the exorcist is a diocesan priest – which is pretty rare anymore – the report goes to his Bishop and from there to Rome. If he's in a religious order, like the Jebs, the account goes to the Province director, from him to the head of the order, and then on to the Vatican. The complete collection of exorcism accounts is kept in a special room at the Gregorian University in Rome. And, believe me, you need some pretty heavy authorization to get inside that room."

"Have *you* been inside?"

Dirty Eugene nodded. "Yeah, I once spent three months immersed in that material. Back in 1979, that was. It's required reading, if you're going to serve as an exorcist. It was slow going for me, since the whole fucking file is written in Latin, a dead language that somebody really ought to give the last rites to and bury."

The priest pulled another Winston out of its pack. He held it between his fingers for a moment, looking at it sourly. "God, I hate these fucking things," he said softly, then lit up and took a deep drag. "I'll tell you what the Church knows, or thinks it knows, about demons, Mikey," he told Pacilio. "It won't take long, because it doesn't amount to a great deal."

"Anything at all will be more than I've got now," Pacilio said.

"Okay, we'll start with their nature. Demons are fallen angels. Created by God, as were all the angels, but some of them did something to piss Him off and were cast out of Heaven and consigned to the place known as Hell, Hades, Gehenna, call it what you will."

"Why so many different names?" Pacilio asked.

"'Hades' is the ancient Roman name for it, 'Gehenna' is the Hebrew." Grady shrugged. "Different cultures, different names, same nasty place."

"You said these angels 'did something.' I thought they rebelled against God, and that's why they were kicked out of Heaven," Pacilio said.

Dirty Eugene smiled thinly. "See? You know more than you thought – except you're wrong." He took another swallow of his bourbon and water. "Actually, you might be right, for all anybody knows. But what you're thinking of comes from Milton's *Paradise Lost* – not an approved Scriptural source on the subject of demons, although it's pretty good poetry, I'll grant you. A lot of what our culture thinks it knows about demons comes from Milton. *Better to reign in Hell than to serve in Heaven,* and all that. It's a good line, and as good an explanation as any. But we don't know for sure, okay?"

Pacilio shrugged. "You're the expert," he said, "but that's what Sister Mary Rose told me in fifth grade."

The priest snorted in disdain. "Okay, second thing," he continued. "Demons are pure spirits, which means they lack physical bodies. That's why we talk about demonic *possession* – one of them takes possession of someone's body for a period of time and uses that to do its work."

Pacilio leaned forward. "So, unless they take possession of a human bring, we'd never be able to see them?"

Dirty Eugene made a face. "Usually, but not necessarily. There are cases on record of direct apparition, both angelic and demonic. You remember some of the accounts of angelic visitations, don't you? They show up in the liturgy often enough."

"You mean like when the angel appeared to Mary and told her she was pregnant with God's son? Sure, I heard that one often enough growing up – but you're saying that demons can do that stuff, too?"

"They can. Not much in scripture about that side of things, apart from Satan's tempting of Jesus while He was in the desert fasting and praying. But sacred scripture isn't our only source for knowledge about demonic apparitions."

"What else is there?"

"There's the evidence of my own two eyes." The priest hesitated briefly. "I just hope your discretion is still up to snuff, Mikey. If the Powers That Be get wind of all the shit I'm telling you, I'm on my way back to Bolivia faster than you can say *'Ad majorem gloriam Dei.'* And if I have to eat one more fucking tortilla, I swear it'll be the death of me."

Pacilio started to speak, but Dirty Eugene made a brusque gesture. "No, spare me your reassurances. I'm just getting windy in my old age. If I didn't trust you, I wouldn't be talking about this stuff in the first place."

The priest leaned forward in his chair. "All right, then: did you know that it's actually possible to conjure up a demon, Mikey?"

Pacilio sat back, looking like he had been punched in the solar plexus. "Conjuring demons?" he said quietly.

"Are you telling me all of that black magic crap you see in bad movies is real?

"More or less. I've seen it done, myself, quite a few years ago."

"Jesus Christ," Pacilio said. "What did you do? Sneak into a Witches' Sabbath and sit in the back, hoping not to be noticed?"

Dirty Eugene shook his head. "The *Sabbat* isn't an occasion for conjuring demons – it's an entirely separate ritual. No, this was specifically a conjuring. It was pretty interesting. In the same way that going scuba diving would be – especially if, while you're down there with the fishies, you were to turn around and find a Great White shark staring at you from twenty feet away, licking his chops."

"How did you ever manage to get close enough to watch something like that?"

"I was invited to be there," Dirty Eugene replied, "by the person doing the conjuring."

"You were invited by a *witch*?"

"You're making an unwarranted assumption, Mikey. It's true that a black witch can conjure a demon, but it's not only a black witch who can do it."

"I hate it when you're didactic, Eugene," Pacilio said. "So, all right, who was doing the conjuring?"

"Another Jesuit. A friend of mine, actually."

Pacilio stared at the old man. He was starting to wonder if his mind was capable of accommodating all the revelations that Dirty Eugene seemed determined to dispense. "I don't get it," he said. "I figured you had to be one of the bad guys to do that kind of thing. You know, sell your soul to the devil, all that stuff."

"No, that's the kind of crap that was commonly held in the Middle Ages, and a lot of it has found its way into our popular culture. It's true that the 'bad guys' have been known to conjure demons, but sometimes the 'good guys' do it, too. It takes years of study, and an awful lot of guts, but it can be done."

"But why? Why would a *priest* do that?"

"To get information. Demons know a lot, both about the spirit world as well as the material one. And, there are ways of compelling them not only to speak, but to speak truthfully —or as truthful as one of those creatures ever gets. Sometimes there's no other way to find out what the 'good guys' need to know, so somebody like my pal, Father Joe Lorenzo, would be asked to make the attempt."

"'Asked?' I thought all you guys took a vow of obedience," Pacilio said.

"We do, but there's no Jesuit rector in the world who would *order* someone to conjure a demon. He would not want that responsibility on his soul."

"What responsibility? Is it supposed to be a sin, or something?"

Dirty Eugene picked up his empty glass and handed it to Pacilio. "Would you mind, Mikey? J.D. with just a drop or two of water."

Pacilio hesitated. "You're half in the bag already, Eugene," he said, not unkindly.

"I know, I know. And it's the whole bag I'm plannin' to get into before I'm done, or it's no sleep for me tonight." Then Father Eugene Grady used a word that Pacilio had rarely heard pass the old man's lips: "Please."

Pacilio immediately took the glass and stood up. He walked over to the bar and made a strong Jack Daniel's and water. Returning, he handed the glass to Dirty Eugene and sat down again.

The priest drained half his drink in two quick swallows. He then put it down and shook the last Winston out of the crumpled pack beside him. Firing up the cigarette, he took a deep drag and let it out. Finally, he said, "Well, Mikey, the reason no Jesuit, or any other kind of priest, even those pukes in the Dominicans, would order somebody to conjure a demon, is because there's always the danger of something going wrong."

"Meaning what?" Pacilio asked. "The demon gets loose?"

"Bite your tongue," Dirty Eugene said. "That's never happened, thanks be to God."

Until now, maybe, Pacilio thought. Aloud, he asked, "Then what? The demon kills the conjurer?"

"Sometimes," the priest agreed. "There are some cases of that happening. But there's another possibility, too, a kind of worst-case scenario."

"Which is what?"

"The demon returns to Hell, taking the conjurer with him *in the body.*"

Pacilio shook his head. "I don't get it."

Dirty Eugene sighed. "You've got no excuse for bein' thick, Mikey. I'm the one who's drinkin', for God's sake. Look, both Scripture and tradition give us some indication of the torments that Hell holds for the damned. Pretty bad, right?"

"Sure. Pitchforks, fire, all kinds of gross stuff. Not to mention what Dante came up with."

"Exactly. The demons of Hell inflict all sorts of profound torments on the souls of the damned. Now, what do you imagine they'd be able to do with a live human being? Huh? And, here's the kicker: after you finally expired from their ministrations, that would only be the beginning!"

Pacilio, understanding at last, could only shake his head.

"And that is why, Mikey," Dirty Eugene continued, his voice starting to break up now, "every day of my life, when I say Mass, I offer prayers that a compassionate God will have mercy on the poor damned soul of the Reverend Joe Lorenzo, S.J., who played with the fire one time too often."

⎯⎯⎯◆⎯⎯⎯

Pacilio stayed up with Father Eugene Grady until almost 4:00 a.m. Then he put the thoroughly drunk priest into bed and went back to his room at the Sheraton, where he requested a 7:30 wake-up call and went to sleep. It was not the most restful slumber he ever experienced.

But Pacilio's evening was quiet and mundane, compared to Carol Sefchek's.

At a little after 11:30 that night, Carol was drinking a vanilla Fribble in the Friendly's Restaurant just off Wolf Road in Albany, New York when her pager began its insistent beeping. She reached into her large handbag and turned the thing off. She had no need to look at the LED display; there was only one place the call could have come from.

Carol took one more sip from her Fribble, picked up her bag, and headed for the pay phone in the corner. A couple of male customers watched her progress with some interest. Carol was not dressed provocatively, but her trim body looked good in the beige blouse and long brown skirt, her long brown hair was clean and shining, and she moved with a grace that men often found appealing.

Carol put a quarter in the pay phone and tapped in a number. Anyone sitting near enough to overhear Carol's end of the conversation would have heard her say, "Hi, it's Natasha." After a pause, she asked, "Which Holiday Inn?" Then: "Oh, sure, I'm five minutes away. He sound all right?" Then: "OK, I'll take it. What's the room number?" She wrote something on a scrap of paper with a pen that she had ready, then said, "Okay, call you later," and hung up. She paid for the ice cream and went out to her car.

Carol wasn't a bad person. She was simply a logical product of a consumer society that preaches that happiness comes from the things you buy. And the financial institutions made getting credit cards so easy. So when Carol was bored, she shopped. When she was upset, she shopped. When she felt like celebrating, she shopped. After a while, her debts began to exceed the income she made as a secretary at the New York State Department of Transportation. Creditors started calling her at home, asking for payment on her overdue accounts. Those who called were polite, but, when Carol was still unable to pay, the people from the collection agencies were not so polite.

When the man from Albany Savings started talking about repossessing her car, Carol made a decision. It was the same reached every year by hundreds of nice, middle class girls who get in money trouble and are too proud to ask their families to bail them out. She answered a small, discreet ad placed in the *Times-Union* by an escort service and became a part-time prostitute.

Adopting the work name "Natasha" because she thought it sounded exotic and mysterious, she worked, on average, four nights a week – it was up to her. After five months of this carnal moonlighting, Carol Sefchek found that her debts were almost paid off. Most of the men she met were nice, and if she did have a couple of bad times, well, they were no worse then some of the back-seat experiences she'd endured in high school.

Carol drove her black Dodge Shadow out of the Friendly's lot and then took the next left onto Wolf Road. Except during the morning and evening rush, traffic moves rapidly along that street, and Carol was pulling into the Holiday Inn's parking lot a few minutes later. Spotting the right room number, she pulled into a nearby parking space. After checking her makeup and lipstick in the rearview mirror, she locked the car and double-checked to be sure the lights were turned off. Carol Sefchek was a careful girl.

The man who answered her knock seemed okay, which meant he didn't look like either a cop or a weirdo. Carol smiled at him and gave her head a toss to get the hair out of her face, a move she had seen Kathleen Turner do in *Body Heat*.

"Hi, are you Peter?"

The man nodded.

"I'm Natasha. I understand you'd like some . . . company."

Another nod.

"Can I come in?"

"Sure, please do." He stepped back to allow her into the room, then closed the door. After looking her up and down he asked, "Did you say your name's Natasha?"

She smiled into his eyes. "Yes, that's right. Do you like it?"

"Very much," he said, then: *"Ty znaesh' chto ty sevodnia vecherom umresh' s agonii?"*

Carol blinked, but the smile never left her face. "Golly, is that Russian? I'm sorry, I don't know any." After a second she said, "Hey, you must be pretty smart to know another language like that, huh?"

He shrugged, then gave a nervous little laugh. "I used to have a lot of time to study different things."

She nodded. "I know what you mean." She didn't, but being agreeable was part of the job. If she was pleasant and friendly and agreeable, they'd like her, and if they liked her she'd probably get a nice tip.

"So, Peter, did you fly into town?" An airline ticket would establish that he wasn't a cop.

"No, I drove."

"Really? Where from?"

"Down in Virginia."

"Wow, I bet that was a long trip, huh?"

"Yes it was, but I made a few interesting stops along the way."

"Okay, listen, do you mind if I take a quick peek at your driver's license?" A license from out of the area, and especially from out of state, also probably meant he wasn't the law.

"Sure, no problem." He rummaged through his wallet for a moment. "Here you go."

She looked at the Virginia license, compared the photo with the man in front of her, and was satisfied.

"That's a pretty last name," she said. "How do you pronounce it, 'Bar-bore'?"

"No, 'barber.' Just like the guy with the scissors and the razor."

"Excuse me?"

"For cutting hair, you know? Snip, snip."

"Oh, right, yeah. Listen, what do you say we get the boring old money part out of the way, so we can just relax and have fun?"

"Sure, no problem. It's two hundred, right?"

"Two hundred cash, two twenty-five if you use a credit card."

"I have the cash, that's fine."

Carol counted the twenties carefully, then put them in her purse. "Okay, great," she said. "Do you mind if I use your bathroom? I had some coffee half an hour ago, and it went right through me."

He gestured toward the bathroom door. "No, feel free."

She picked up her purse and headed in that direction. She didn't really have to pee, but it would give her a chance to check for toilet articles, which should be in there if he were actually staying in this room. More important, it would give her the opportunity to lubricate the walls of her vagina with K-Y jelly; this would allow her to have sex without discomfort, and also create the illusion that she was wet for him. That was often worth a tip all by itself, especially when combined with endearments like, "Oh baby you make me so HOT!" Men, she'd found, would believe almost anything that flattered their sexual vanity.

She paused at the bathroom door and turned back to him. "I'll just be a second," she said, her voice low and throaty, "and then you can tell me what you want to do. I hope it's something nice and nasty."

He was smiling at her like a kid in a candy store.

"Oh, it is," he said happily. "This is gonna be *great*."

Justin Gustainis

Chapter 9

Louise Dillon was tired. As she pushed her maid's cart down the walkway that ran along her assigned stretch of rooms at the Holiday Inn, she would have sworn that the damned thing had gained fifty pounds since yesterday. Louise was not a morning person at the best of times, although the three cups of Maxwell House that she habitually drank with breakfast usually helped. But she had been up a good part of the night with her youngest son, who had contracted the stomach flu that was going around among his playmates. The boy seemed better this morning, but Louise's butt was dragging, big time. She hoped that she'd have the chance later on to lie down on one of the motel beds and close her eyes for half an hour or so.

She had just finished room 125, and saw on the chart from Housekeeping that 126 and 127 had been empty the night before. She stopped in front of 128, noted the absence of the "Do Not Disturb" sign, and knocked twice, firmly. "Housekeeping," she called, loudly enough to be heard inside the room.

Getting no answer, Louise put her key in the lock and opened the door a few inches. It wasn't chained from inside, which suggested that the room was unoccupied. But Louise had learned to be careful about these things. People discovered in various stages of undress by a hotel maid sometimes got nasty about it (as if it were *her* fault they didn't chain their damn door), and those who were interrupted while having horizontal choir practice on the bed were guaranteed to be pissed off. Louise didn't need the grief, so she was always careful to announce her arrival in several stages.

Now she was at the last stage. "Housekeeping!" she called through the gap in the doorway. There was no answer. She moved her cart closer so as not to block the walkway, opened the door of 128 all the way, and went in.

Her routine was to start with the bathroom, and she had actually taken two steps toward it before her peripheral vision picked up what seemed to be an unclothed figure on the bed nearest the window. For one heartbeat she thought she had, despite all precautions, walked in on a couple in the throes of passion. She turned her head, an apology on her lips, and got her first good look at what had been left on the bed.

It took three tries before Louise Dillon was able to pull enough air into her lungs to scream.

———————◆———————

Pacilio was sitting in what passed for the USAirways departure lounge at the Wilkes-Barre/Scranton airport, trying to wake up by drinking a cup of what the airport restaurant insisted on referring to as "coffee." Although vile, it was better than nothing. If the caffeine didn't bring him to full consciousness, then the second-degree burns that the foul brew was inflicting on the inside of his mouth ought to do the trick.

Pacilio could function on little sleep, or none at all, if he had to. He had proven that a long time ago during Hell Week. The fifth week of the seventeen-week SEAL training course was officially designated Motivation Week, but no one who went through it ever called it by anything other than its vivid nickname. During the six days of almost nonstop physical exertion, noise, mud, and harassment, the trainees averaged fifteen minutes' sleep per day, usually in five-minute snatches. It was during this period that people began to drop out and wash out of the course in large numbers. That was one of the main purposes of Hell Week: to weed out those who were unwilling or unable to adopt the proper mental posture. The attitude that the SEALs were looking for was unknowingly articulated by Pacilio's bunkmate Carter Pelham during the fourth day of their ordeal. Cart had grunted it out between clenched teeth as he and Pacilio and the rest of their squad struggled to raise a Zodiac assault raft over their heads while one of their instructors was reclining in it. "Motherfuckers," Cart groaned in Pacilio's ear as they wrestled with the raft. "They can't make me quit. No way. They'll have to fuckin' kill me first." Pacilio would have replied, "Yeah, me too," but he had no breath to spare. Somehow, he and Carter Pelham and thirty-seven of their classmates made it through Hell Week. They had begun the week with sixty-one.

So Pacilio knew he could keep going on the three hours of restless sleep he had managed the night before, but sleep deprivation tended to make him grumpy, and his mood was not being improved by the awful coffee. Nor was it helped when he heard himself being paged from the USAirways check-in counter. The hot liquid in his gut seemed to turn to ice in the few seconds it took him to walk to the counter, identify himself, and be directed to the white courtesy telephone; he thought he knew who was calling, and why.

"I'm glad I caught you," McGraw's voice said in his ear. "I think you'd better change your travel plans."

"Why?" Pacilio asked tautly. "It's Barbour, isn't it?"

"Yes, it is. I just heard from Agent Pennypacker about twenty minutes ago."

"What did they find, him or –" Pacilio was mindful of the clerk standing within earshot. "–another one of his exhibits?"

McGraw picked up on it immediately. "Somebody listening?"

"Maybe," Pacilio replied. "Hard to tell."

"Okay, I'll do most of the talking. To answer your question, it's another victim, just one this time. Name of Carol Sefchek, looks like a working girl. Maid found her in a hotel room in Albany, New York."

"Are we sure it's our boy?"

"Dead solid certain," McGraw told him. "He booked the room in his own name. That means New York can issue an arrest warrant, and it's about time somebody did. Pennypacker says the feds are working up one, too."

"Good. That should help."

"In the meantime, you'd better get on up to Albany. Eastern has a flight leaving from your airport in just under forty minutes. If you have trouble getting a seat, call me and I'll see if I can threaten somebody at the airline."

"I can do that myself," Pacilio said, "but, look, Mac, I don't think I need to check out this Albany thing. I've learned some stuff that I think has a bearing on the investigation, and it'll take us a lot farther than me standing around another crime scene trying to pretend I'm Sherlock Holmes."

"Stuff? What stuff? What are you talking about?"

Pacilio grimaced into the phone. "I need to talk to you about it in person," he said. "Trust me on this, will you? Besides, anything we need to know about this latest one we can get from the Albany P.D. or Pennypacker's people in their Albany field office, right? They can fax the whole thing as soon as the reports are ready, pictures and all. I don't need to fly up there."

"I'm afraid you do, Mike."

"*Why*, for Christ's sake?"

"Because the victim is still alive."

———◆———

The Reverend Tom Pascoe was on the air and on a roll. He said to the blonde woman seated to his left, "You know, Marcie, it amazes me to contemplate the kind of utter filth that anyone can buy almost anywhere in this country for only a few dollars. Pictures of young women, spread-eagled for all the world to see." For just an instant, an image of Julie from earlier this afternoon appeared in his mind.

He continued, "There are videotapes for sale showing every possible human depravity: oral sex, anal sex, group sex, homosexuality, women with animals, innocent children being molested by depraved adults. There is nothing that is considered off-limits or taboo by these merchants of smut. The wickedness of ancient Babylon, of Sodom and Gomorrah, why, it's like a children's game of spin the bottle compared to the sinful licentiousness of our own age."

The blonde woman nodded her head solemnly. "I know," she said. "It is so awful."

Pascoe allowed scorn to mix with the disgust already present in his voice. "And, of course, if some of our morally spineless public officials should ever bestir themselves to actually prosecute these perverts-for-profit, these spoilers of our society, why it's practically a waste of time. The so-called American Civil Liberties Union is right there immediately with their lawyers and writs and injunctions, as if raping children and taking pictures of it is somehow protected by the Constitution." Pascoe was well aware that child pornography is illegal in every state, and under federal statutes as well, but he never let inconvenient facts interfere with a good, righteous rant.

He went on in this vein until the commercial break. Once a week, he hosted this live show on his television network, the Sacred Word Channel. The broadcast was brought by cable into an estimated 2.8 million homes. The show was live because it featured a call-in segment that was the principal reason for the program's existence. Each week, hundreds of people called the toll-free 800 number that would appear at the bottom of their TV screens, in the hope of conversing with the man they considered their spiritual leader. Only about a dozen carefully-screened callers (no crazies, no journalists, no intellectuals, no liberals) would actually get to talk to Pascoe, but that wasn't the point. As part of the screening process, each caller would be asked for his or her name, address, and telephone number, as well as a statement about what the caller thought was the biggest problem facing Bible-believing Christians today.

Later, this information would be entered into a computer. The answer to the "biggest problem facing Christians" question would determine whether the caller's data would end up in the file headed "pro-life," "pornography," "school prayer," "UFOs," or any of two dozen others. Thereafter, and for years to come, the caller could expect to receive fund-raising material from one or more divisions of Pascoe's organization. The accounting people had estimated that currently this program, called "The Prophecy Fulfilled," generated contributions in excess of six million dollars a year.

During the weekly diatribes leading up to the calls, Pascoe's nominal partner in conversation was his co-host, Marcie Madison, a former Miss Tennessee. "Co-host" was a misnomer, of course. The show was, and would remain, Pascoe's forum. Marcie's job was to nod adoringly at anything Pascoe said, feed him an occasional line, and look decorative.

After the commercials, Pascoe and Marcie began to take the first of the selected calls. A woman from Pomona, California wanted advice on reining in her rebellious daughter (Pascoe and Marcie advised prayer and a Christian counselor); a woman from Dayton, Ohio called to castigate baby-killing abortion doctors (Pascoe and Marcie agreed, although, mindful of the potential legal pitfalls, carefully refrained from appearing to support any violent action against abortionists); a man from Windsor, Ontario offered thanks to Pascoe for his prayers on a previous show – the man's back was feeling much better now, praise Jesus and the Reverend Tom Pascoe! Each of these calls was the kind of thing that Pascoe and Marcie had handled dozens of times before.

The fourth call was not.

Marcie glanced off-camera at the monitor that displayed information about the next caller and said, "Reverend Tom, we have a call from Florence in Alexandria, Virginia."

Pascoe gave the camera his practiced, fatherly smile. "Hello, Florence," he said. "Thank you for joining us in the love of Jesus this morning."

"Oh, thank you, Reverend Pascoe. This is such a thrill for me, to actually speak with you. I watch your show every week, right after my wrestling program, and I always feel closer to the Lord when I turn it off."

"Well, Florence," Pascoe replied, "I think it's only fitting that you tune us in after you watch wrestling, since I like to think that what we're doing here is wrestling with Satan on the Lord's behalf."

The woman from Alexandria laughed with delight. "I never thought of it that way, Reverend, but I think you must be right, yes indeed." Her voice grew suddenly serious. "That's actually what I'm calling about, in a way. There's a very evil thing that's happened, and I wanted to ask for your prayers."

"It would be an honor to pray with you, Florence." Pascoe replied. "No matter what has happened to you, it can by made better by the love of Jesus Christ."

"Well, it didn't exactly happen to me, but I'm just so upset about it. You see, my cousin Hugh is on the police over to Fairfax, which is a bit west of here?" She paused as if waiting for a reply.

"Yes, I see," Pascoe said. This was going on too long. If the old woman didn't get to the point soon, he would make an unobtrusive signal to the floor manager, and Florence would be "accidentally disconnected."

"Well, he tells me," Florence went on, "that a whole bunch of people were murdered over there a few days ago. Not just murdered, but horribly, horribly butchered. Ten people!"

"Oh, my God, how awful," Marcie exclaimed. "Was it one of those drug deals?"

"No, I don't think so," Florence said. "Hugh said it was in some sort of laboratory. He heard later it was owned by the U.S. government, can you imagine?"

Pascoe was suddenly interested, although he would have been hard pressed to explain why. But he had learned to trust his instincts, and they were telling him that there was something important in the old woman's story.

"That is a terrible thing," he said. "Truly awful. Does the government know who's responsible for this atrocity?"

"Well, they must have some idea, Reverend," Florence answered, "because they're covering it all up!"

Pascoe's eyes narrowed. "Are they really?" He was starting to wonder if the woman was a nutcase, after all.

"They must be! Reverend Pascoe, there hasn't been one word about this in the paper, or on the TV, neither! Ten people murdered, and some of them, I don't rightly know how many, were tortured first, and there was even" – Florence seemed momentarily at a loss for words – "sexual violation. And not one word in the paper."

"Florence, let us pray together," Pascoe said soothingly. "Let us all pray for the souls of those poor people, and let us also pray that our godless government will take steps to acknowledge its responsibility and punish this wickedness."

After extemporizing the prayer, Pascoe somberly announced another commercial break. As soon as the floor manager declared that they were clear, Marcie turned to Pascoe and said, "That poor woman. Was she delusional, do you think?"

Pascoe had already decided that, if it turned out that the phone room had let another nut call through, then the manager of the phone room was going to be applying for unemployment benefits sometime in the near future.

"I don't know," he said to Marcie. "There's no way to tell."

The first of those statements was true, although, Pascoe hoped, only temporarily so. The second was a lie. When you had the resources at your command that Tom Pascoe did, there were always ways of finding out what you wanted to know.

———◆———

Albany Medical Center is a modern, sprawling complex located well away from the city center. It took Pacilio several minutes to locate the wing he was interested in. But once he found the correct corridor, the rest was easy, since only one of the rooms had an FBI agent standing in front of the door.

To save time and trouble, Pacilio had his ID folder already in his hand. It might invite misunderstandings if he were to reach under his suit coat before the agent at the door knew who he was. Some of these Feebies, especially the younger ones, liked to impress you with the speed of their reflexes, and Pacilio was in no mood to be manhandled by any junior G-man. A couple of years earlier, he'd lost his temper after being shoved around by some macho nitwit from the Drug Enforcement Administration. The letter of reprimand was still in Pacilio's personnel file, even though the DEA man had long since regained full use of his limbs.

But this Fed seemed to be of a different school. He examined Pacilio's identification then handed it back, politely. "Thank you, Mr. Pacilio," he said, and extended a hand. "Tim Hanrahan, FBI."

Hanrahan looked to be about thirty. He was taller than Pacilio, but not by much. His sandy-colored hair was a cap of tight curls against his head, and the dusting of freckles across his nose made the FBI man look very Irish and very young. Hanrahan's brown eyes were several shades lighter than Pacilio's, and they looked intelligent. Pacilio hoped they were.

The FBI agent put one hand flat against the door of room 920. "Shall we go on in?"

Pacilio nodded and followed him into the hospital room.

It was a double room, but only one bed was occupied. As Pacilio approached it, he saw that Carol Sefchek appeared to be either asleep or unconscious. She looked to be in her mid-twenties and was pretty without being in any way memorable. Her long hair was spread out across the starched institutional pillowcase.

Glancing around the room, Pacilio noted the absence of a respirator, cardiac monitor, or any of the other high-tech gizmos with which hospitals usually surround seriously injured patients. He also saw that the young woman's face and head were unmarked. "I don't know what she looks like under the sheet," he said softly, "but she's in a lot better condition than I would have thought. Hell, I was expecting to find her in Intensive Care, not a regular hospital room."

"I'm not sure what you had in mind," Hanrahan replied in a normal voice, "but she's had a pretty rough time, by most standards." After a moment he added, "There's no need to whisper, by the way. They've got her on Thorazine – 50 ccs every four hours. Shoot off a howitzer in here and you might make her twitch, but I doubt it."

"Thorazine?" Pacilio went to the foot of the bed and picked up the clipboard that was hanging there. "Since when do they use Thorazine as a first-choice painkiller?" He began to flip through Carol Sefchek's medical chart.

"They don't, far as I know," Hanrahan told him,

"but this lady's got troubles that go beyond her physical injuries."

Pacilio looked up from the clipboard. "What are you saying? That she's psycho?"

The FBI man shrugged. "They've been treating her as if she is," he said. "Here's the way it went down, as I understand it: the kid's in shock when they bring her into the ER downstairs, but they pull her out of that okay. They put some blood into her, and some stitches, and get her stabilized. Medically, she's looking pretty good, all things considered. Then she starts to come around. A nurse is right there, ready to do the usual number: tell her where she is, reassure her that she's going to live, give her some Darvon, or maybe something stronger, for the pain, all that good stuff. Never gets the chance."

Hanrahan pulled a spiral-bound notebook from his inside breast pocket and began to page through it. "I don't know if you want a bunch of medical jargon," he continued, "so let's just say that Carol here pitched a real nutty."

"You mean she had hysterics? That's not too surprising, is it?" Pacilio looked back at the clipboard. "Says here he broke every finger on her left hand, thumb included. And either before or after that, they're not sure which, he sliced off her nipples." Pacilio replaced the medical chart where he had found it. "Compared to several people who've met up with this guy recently, she was pretty lucky – although I'll be the first one to admit that in this instance 'lucky' is a relative term. Still, I don't think it's hard to see why she might have become hysterical in the ER."

Hanrahan shook his head. "I'd agree with you," he said, "but apparently this went way beyond hysterics.

The attending physician described it to me as a 'full-blown psychotic episode.' One of the nurses said it was like the girl didn't know where she was, even though the people working on her kept assuring her she was safe. They tell me she kept screaming 'It's in the mirror!' over and over again, even though there was no mirror anywhere in the emergency room." He closed his notebook. "That was when they decided to hit her with the Thorazine."

Pacilio stared at the unconscious young woman for a long moment. "Her chart says she's due for the next dose in about 45 minutes," he said. "I think I want to talk to the attending physician before that happens. What's his name? His signature's on the chart, but I can't read it. Fucking doctors all seem to write in Sanskrit."

Hanrahan had a slight smile on his lean face. "*Her* name is Rojas, first name Muriel, I think."

Pacilio nodded. "Think Dr. Rojas is still in the building?"

"I don't know, but somebody at the nurse's station probably will. I'll go check."

"I'll go with you," Pacilio told him. "I want to be sure that nobody sticks another needle in this kid's arm until I've had a word with that doctor."

<hr/>

"I don't like this," Dr. Muriel Rojas snapped. "It is unnecessary, it is medically questionable, and I will not be a party to it."

Pacilio looked at the woman standing next to Carol Sefchek's bed and tried to stifle his impatience. He could probably go over Dr. Rojas' head, but it would take time, and he would have to do it through the Albany FBI office, who might or might not cooperate. He could go over *their* heads, but that would take even more time. So he needed Dr. Rojas, and offering to fracture her lumbar spine for her, as he was tempted to do, would probably not help to move matters along.

He was fairly sure that threats would be useless, anyway. Murial Rojas barely topped 4'11", but size is no indication of ferocity – ask any Australian who's ever run into a Tasmanian devil while trekking through the Outback. The woman had steely gray eyes that were an odd contrast with her slightly olive complexion. Her long black hair had its share of gray in it, too, but Pacilio suspected that she had caused a lot more gray hair in others than she would ever develop herself.

Dr. Rojas took her left hand out of the pocket of her white lab coat, glanced at her watch and said "If there's nothing else, Mr. Pacilio, I'll have to ask you to leave the room. My patient is due for her medication, and she is not authorized visitors at this stage of her recuperation."

Pacilio said, "Doctor, this is extremely important. Nobody wants to hurt your patient, least of all me. But I *have* to talk to her. There's a good chance that lives depend on it."

Dr. Rojas looked at him with one eyebrow raised. "I believe I've heard that expression, 'Lives depend on it,' before. In my experience, it's a police code phrase that means 'My next promotion depends on it.'"

Pacilio's mouth compressed into a thin line. "Do you have the use of a fax machine here in the hospital, Doctor?"

Frowning slightly, she replied, "There's one that I share with several other doctors, yes."

"That's fine. If you'll give me the number, I want to have some material faxed to you."

Dr. Rojas tilted her head a little to one side. "What kind of material?" she asked. "And what do you expect to accomplish with it?"

"What I hope to accomplish should be obvious," Pacilio said. "I want to delay this woman's next dose of Thorazine so I can talk to her when she comes to. The material that I'm going to have faxed to you consists of ten autopsy reports, along with some crime scene photographs. The ten deaths were all homicides, what the newspapers like to call 'torture-murders.' Oh, and I've got two more reports, with very similar contents, out in my car. I can hand those to you personally, if you'll tell me where you're going to be in fifteen minutes. I should be able to find my way out to the parking garage and back by then."

"Do you believe you can gross me out with some gory police photos, Mr. Pacilio?" The scorn in her voice was unmistakable. "If so, think again. I've worked in emergency medicine for a long time, and I know all too well the horrendous things that human beings are capable of doing to each other. I've probably seen more messy corpses than you have."

Pacilio looked at her in a very direct way, but his voice was mild when he said, "No disrespect intended, Doctor, but I bet you haven't."

Muriel Rojas had encountered enough bullshit so that she had no trouble recognizing simple truth when it was, literally, staring her in the face. After a moment, she said, "Perhaps not." She took in a deep breath and exhaled loudly. "But let's not get sidetracked here. One of the basic principles I learned very early in this job is that you can't do anything for the dead, so it's best to focus your energies on the living. That's what I'm trying to do."

Pacilio nodded. "That's my concern, too. But maybe we've got different concepts of what that means." He gestured toward the unconscious Carol Sefchek. "When you talk about taking care of the living, you're referring to your patient, here. That's only natural. But I'm hunting a monster, Doctor – the man who brutalized this young woman, and who did a hell of a lot worse to twelve other people over the last three days. That's why I wanted you to see those files. Not because I think you're soft." He smiled with one side of his mouth. "I'd say you're about as soft as anthracite coal. But I wanted you to know what this guy has been doing, because unless we catch him soon, he's going to do it again to some other people. *Those* are the people I'm worried about, Doctor – his next victims. You might say that I'm trying to practice some preventive medicine."

Dr. Rojas folded her arms across her chest, turned away from Pacilio, and took a couple of slow paces away. Then she turned back to him. "Twelve murders, you say."

"Twelve that we know about, anyway."

"Then why wasn't Ms. Sefchek here number thirteen?"

"That," Pacilio said, "is one of the things I'd like to ask her."

———◆———

The blackness was a warm, comfortable blanket wrapped around Carol Sefchek's mind. As long as the blackness was there, she was safe. On the other side of the blackness might be pain, and terror, and something unutterably evil, but she was safe here within her drug-woven cocoon, and she slept in peace.

But slowly, gradually, the blackness began to lighten. Carol Sefchek's sleep became uneasy. Within her blanket, she began to grow anxious. If the blackness went away, she would have to become Carol again. She would have to see things again, she would have to feel again, feel the pain, feel the fear, see his face, hear his soft voice cooing foul obscenities, see the one in the mirror, in the Mirror, In The Mirror, IN THE MIRROR, **IN THE MIRROR!**

Dr. Rojas had Carol's good hand clasped in both of hers. In a calm, soothing voice she was saying, "It's all right Carol, it's okay, I'm here, it's safe, it's all right, it's all right." It was the kind of voice a mother uses with a child having night terrors. Gradually, Carol Sefchek responded to it.

The hyperventilating began to subside, and Carol's eyes focused on the woman seated on the bed beside her. The woman's face seemed familiar. Then Carol noticed the white lab coat and the name tag pinned to the breast pocket. "Dr. Rojas?" Carol pronounced it with a hard "j" sound, but then something from high school Spanish class clicked in and she said, "No, wait, it's 'Ro-has,' right?"

Murial Rojas smiled gently. It was an expression seen frequently by her patients but rarely by her colleagues. "Yes, that's right, Carol. I'm your doctor. I've been taking care of you."

"I'm in the hospital?"

"Yes, this is the Albany Medical Center. You were brought in this morning, around eight o'clock. You're going to be fine. I fixed you up, and did a hell of a good job, if I say so myself."

Carol Sefchek's eyes widened. "What did I . . . oh, my

God, that guy, that fucking *freak* . . . ." She started hyperventilating again, her lungs like a bellows in overdrive. "And then the mirror, he was in the mirror, oh God his eyes, I couldn't look, oh Jesus, oh mama save me please, he's in the mirror, *the fucking mirror!*"

Dr. Rojas had a capped hypo of Thorazine in one of the pockets of her lab coat. She was thinking about using it just as Pacilio came over to the bed. He had been sitting quietly in the corner, as per Dr. Rojas' instructions. "Let me see if I can get her calmed down," Dr. Rojas had said, "then we'll find out if she'll talk to you."

But Pacilio could tell that Dr. Rojas' concern for her patient was going to lead her to administer another dose of the Thorazine, putting Carol Sefchek out of his reach for God knew how long. He had one card left to play. Win or lose, this was the time to play it.

Pacilio knelt on the floor next to the bed, so that his face was on the same level with Carol Sefchek. "Carol, my name is Michael," he said softly. "Michael, just like the archangel. You've heard of him, haven't you? Michael the archangel?"

Carol was still half in a Thorazine haze, and Pacilio was counting on that to help him. "Michael?" she said. Some of the panic was gone from her voice. "Archangel?"

"That's right, Carol, just like Michael the Archangel. You know who he is, don't you?"

"Yeah, I guess so." Pacilio could spot a fellow ex-Catholic a mile away. Besides, "Sefchek" was probably Slovak in origin, and Czechoslovakia, or whatever they were calling it these days, is a very Catholic country. Even if he was wrong, Pacilio knew that the popular culture was full of angel mythology these days – TV shows, magazine articles, even "I believe in angels" bumper stickers.

"Michael was the one who defeated Satan, you remember? Defeated him and kicked him out of Heaven. Michael the archangel can defeat any evil thing, Carol. He's God's right-hand guy. You know that, don't you?"

The young woman in the bed nodded. "Uh-huh. I remember from school. Long time ago. But you're not him, are you?"

"No Carol, I'm just a man. But I was named after St. Michael. He's my patron saint, you know? I have to figure he keeps a special eye on me, right?"

"Yeah, I guess. Maybe."

"Besides, St. Michael and me, we're kind of in the same business. We both chase after bad guys."

"Are you a cop? I don't like cops."

"I'm an investigator with the federal government, Carol. Nothing to do with the state of New York, and I don't care how you make your money, okay?"

"Yeah, okay."

"The thing you want to keep in mind is, I don't want to upset you. Your doctor here, Dr. Rojas, she's got a big needle in her pocket and she told me she'd stick it in my butt if I got you all upset, and you've got to believe me, Carol, I really *hate* needles."

"Yeah, me too."

"So you have to promise to stay cool, so I don't get stuck, you know what I mean?"

Dr. Rojas put on her most serious face and said, "He's right, Carol. All you have to do is say the word, and I'll jab him with my needle and kick him right out of here."

Carol Sefchek shrugged and said, "Sure, okay. Whatever."

Pacilio figured the groundwork was as solid as it was going to get; time to venture out onto it and see if it would hold.

"Like I said, Carol, I chase after bad guys. And right now, I'm chasing after the guy who hurt you last night."

As soon as he said those last words, he saw the pupils of the young woman's eyes contract. The rapid breathing started again, but Dr. Rojas was ready. She held Carol's right hand tightly and spoke soothingly. "It's all right, Carol. It's okay. Take some deep slow breaths. Deep and slow. Come on, please, just for me. That's it. Nice slow breathing. That's my girl. Nice and slow."

"All right," Carol Sefchek said several moments later. "I'm okay, it's all right."

"Carol," Pacilio went on, "I need you to tell me what happened last night. I know it's hard. And I won't lie to you: I want to know because it's my job to hunt this guy down. But I think it might help you, too. You've got all that bad stuff inside your head, but if you tell me about it, some of it will pass on to me. It's like taking the lid off a saucepan before it boils over, you know? Come on Carol, what d'you say? Let some of the pressure out. Dr. Rojas is going to stay right here. She won't let anything bad happen to you." He paused for a beat, then said softly, "And neither will I."

As the Thorazine wore off, Carol Sefchek told her story.

"I've got this part-time job," she began. "I mean, I have a regular job, too. I'm a secretary at DOT, full time, forty hours a week. But secretaries don't get paid squat until you've been there twenty years. I like to shop and stuff, so I ran up a lot of debts. Then people start calling me at home, calling me at work – which my boss absolutely just *loves,* the asshole – you know, they're like, "When can you make a payment, your credit rating will suffer, we'll repossess your stereo, blah, blah. So I started moonlighting, you know, going out on dates, and stuff."

Carol Sefchek stopped for a moment and looked from Pacilio's face to Dr. Rojas', and back. After a long moment, she sighed and said, "Okay, I guess I'm dealing with grown-ups here. Sometimes I forget what that's like. All right, we all know I'm a whore. I fuck for money. And the money's real good, which is the reason why I do it. Okay?"

Pacilio nodded and said, "Money's a good reason. I didn't figure you were in it for the exercise."

Perfectly deadpan, Dr. Rojas said, "No, the exercise benefit would be negligible. Nothing aerobic, to be sure. Possibly some slight muscle toning might result, although certain muscles would benefit rather more than others."

Carol Sefchek stared at Dr. Rojas, her eyes widening. Then she started to giggle. The giggle turned into full-throated laughter. Pacilio wondered if this was going to end up as more hysterics, but it never went beyond healthy, healing laughter. Looking at Dr. Rojas, then at Pacilio, Carol said, "Well, damn, aren't you two the comedy team! Been working together long?"

Dr. Rojas smiled slightly. "No," she said. "Not long."

Pacilio was looking up at Murial Rojas as she said that. He thought that her smile seemed genuine and that it also made Dr. Rojas look quite attractive. *She ought to smile more. But then, it would probably undermine*

the hard-bitten bitch image she's worked so hard to develop.
With a minor effort, he dragged his attention back to
Carol Sefchek.

"All right," Carol said resignedly, "you guys wanna
know what happened, I'll tell you. But you oughta know
up front, some of it is real weird shit. Just remember,
you asked. I don't want to hear any crap later about
shipping me over to the nut ward just because you don't
believe what you hear, okay?"

"Don't worry yourself over that, Carol," Pacilio said.
"There's been nothing *but* weird shit ever since I started
looking for this guy. I don't think you're going to
surprise me too much."

Carol Sefchek snorted. "Wait and see," she said.
"Okay, here's how it went down last night. I'd had a
couple of dates already, and I'm at Friendly's, having
some ice cream and chilling out. I get a message on my
pager, so I call the service I work for. I'm not going into
which one it is, or any of that stuff, okay?"

Both of her listeners nodded. "We're not the vice
squad, Carol," Pacilio said. "Go on."

"All right, so I call in. They tell me they've got a date
for me if I want it. The Holiday Inn on Wolf Road, room
such-and-such, guy sounds all right."

"What do they mean when they tell you that he
sounds all right?" Pacilio asked.

"That means he doesn't sound crazy, or drunk, or
whacked out on something. And it means they called
him back, and the number he gave checked out. Okay?"

Pacilio nodded.

"I was close by anyway, so I said I'd take it. I drive
over there, find the room, and knock. Guy answers the
door. He looks okay. I mean, he looks *fine*." Carol closed

her eyes tightly for a moment, then opened them. "Shows you what I fucking know."

Pacilio asked, "Can you describe him?"

"Kinda tall – six feet or maybe a little over. Slim, but not like somebody who works out a lot or anything, his muscle tone wasn't that great. Brown hair, dark brown, I mean. Looks like he gets it cut every other week at a three-chair barbershop, you know what I mean? Clean shaven. Kinda pale skin, like he doesn't get outside much. Blue eyes, pale blue, I guess you'd say."

Pacilio nodded. "So, you're inside the room now, right? What happened then?"

"Well, I don't think I said before that I use 'Natasha' as a work name. A girl I went to high school with was called Natasha – I used to think it was the *coolest* name. Course, with a lot of the older guys, after I introduce myself I get these 'Rocky and Bullwinkle' jokes, you know?"

In a passable imitation of Boris Badinov, Pacilio growled, "*Queek Natasha, moose and squirrel are getting away wit' Mooseberry Bush. We must come up with fiendish plan to stop dem.*"

In his normal voice, he asked Carol Sefchek, "That kind of thing, you mean?"

Before the young woman in the bed could respond, a voice to Pacilio's right said, in an almost perfect rendition of Natasha Fatale's low, sexy murmur, "*Boris, dahling, the way you did that was simply wonderful. Fearless Leader would be so proud.*"

Both Pacilio and Carol Sefchek stared at Dr. Muriel Rojas with amazement. After a moment, Carol asked, "You two guys spend a lot of time rehearsing this stuff?"

"Less than you might think," Pacilio said thoughtfully, his gaze still on Dr. Rojas, who combined a Latinate shrug with a wry smile. "Secret vice," she said. "It's on every morning."

Pacilio nodded. "Yeah, I know." He looked at Dr. Rojas a moment longer, then turned back to Carol Sefchek. "So, okay, you call yourself 'Natasha' when you're working."

"Kind of a strange thing happened when I introduced myself: he rattled off something in Russian. I mean, *Rocky and Bullwinkle* I'm used to, but not *Doctor fucking Zhivago.*"

Frowning, Pacilio asked, "Do you remember what it was he said?"

"Hell, no, I don't speak Russian. I'm Polish. My grandma speaks some of the old country lingo, but I never picked up any of it from her. I only know for sure it was Russian 'cause I asked him." She stopped, as if a thought had just struck her. "This Barbour isn't some kind of spy, is he? Like on TV?"

Pacilio made a noncommittal gesture. "The Cold War is over, they tell me, but, still, you never know."

That was a lie, but a benevolent one. He was beginning to think he knew where the thing calling itself "Peter Barbour" was from, and it wasn't anywhere near Moscow. But he didn't think that Carol Sefchek's peace of mind would benefit from that knowledge. Instead, he asked her, "So what happened after he spoke Russian to you?"

She shrugged. "He paid me – you *always* get the money up front, you know – then I went into the bathroom for a couple of minutes. I remember thinking that he was acting like a kid on Christmas Eve. Eager, you know? This guy was practically rubbing his hands together, he was so happy.

"So, okay, I come out of the bathroom, and damn if he isn't ready and rarin' to go – sitting naked on the side of the bed with a hard-on you could pound nails with. Some clients are like that. I mean, it's an hourly rate, and after sixty minutes I'm dressed and out of there, unless he pays to extend for another hour. So a lot of them, especially if they've had some experience with working girls, they want their money's worth. Fine with me, I'm not there to play checkers. But I was a little surprised with this Barbour. I had him pegged as the other kind."

Pacilio asked, "What kind is that?"

"One of the shy ones. Wants a little conversation first, so we can 'get to know each other better,' you know? Like we have a real *relationship*, right? But not this guy, uh-uh.

"So I take a look at him and his hard-on, and I say something like, 'Well, you're all ready to go, aren't you?'

"And gives me, 'You bet I am.'

"Then I ask him, 'Do you want to undress me?' Some of them like that."

"But he says, 'No, you can do it quicker.'

"So, okay, I can take a hint as good as the next girl, and I start getting undressed without a lot of fooling around. I get my blouse and skirt off, then I turn toward him, arch my back a little, put my hands on my hips and let him have a good look. They all like to look, that's what guys do, so I try to give them a little show at the start. It's good for tips.

"I'm wearing a black push-up bra with a matching garter belt. The garter belt is holding up my nylons – no pantyhose. No panties, either. I've got on black pumps with three-inch heels. My legs are kind of heavy, but in the heels they look pretty hot, if I say so myself.

"So I let him take all this in, and then I say, 'You want me to leave anything on?'

"I mean, a lot of them like to feel the nylon on your legs while they fuck you. And, besides, that outfit is what most of the girls in porno films wear, so I'm like a fantasy come true for a lot of these guys. They can only jerk off to Nina Hartley, or whoever, but they can really fuck me. And you know what else? I think the garter belt reminds the older ones of mommy, and all those nasty thoughts and dreams they had about her as boys.

"Only he's not having any fetishes today. He shakes his head and says, 'No, take it all off.'

"Okay, the customer's always right – up to a point, anyway. So I get naked, and I stroll over to the bed and stand in front of him. I've practically got my bush in his face, and I say, 'Like what you see?'

"And he says, 'Very much, but what's that you've got in your hand?'

"So I show him. 'Just a condom,' I say. 'For when we're ready.'

"And he *laughs*, like I just told him the funniest joke he's heard in months. I mean, he really cracks up. Then he calms down and says to me, 'Of course. You want to be protected.' I'm smiling, like I get what the joke is, but I'm really thinking, 'What the fuck?' So I say, 'It's for your protection and mine, honey. These days, you just can't be too careful.'

"And he cracks up *again*, and I'm starting to wonder if I'm in trouble, here. Little did I fucking know, right? But he stops laughing pretty soon, and he says 'No, you're quite right. It's always wise to be careful.'

"And I'm still not sure, so I say, 'We're not going to have a problem about this, are we?'

"And he smiles up at me and says, 'No, no problem at all. I'll wear your condom.' So, I'm thinking, okay, maybe he's a little wacked, but he's not gonna try and go bareback on me. No way I was gonna let *that* happen. I mean, I *know* people with AIDS.

"Then he says, 'But tell me – is this condom the only one you have with you?'

"Now I'm wondering where *this* is going, but I say, 'No, I've got some more in my purse.'

"And he gives me this smile, But it wasn't a nasty, 'I'm gonna hurt you, bitch,' smile. It was almost *sweet*, you know? And he asks, 'How many do you have?'

"And I say, 'I dunno, about a dozen.'

"And he nods, and says, 'Better get 'em.'

Carol Sefchek paused and looked over to the bedside table, on which stood a large plastic flask and some paper cups. "Is there water in that thing?"

Pacilio, who was closer, looked inside. "Yep, full of ice water," he reported. "Want some?"

The young woman nodded. Pacilio looked over to Dr. Rojas. "Okay?"

Dr. Rojas nodded. "Sure. Be sure to use one of those straws, and bend it, so she doesn't choke."

After sipping some water, Carol Sefchek continued.

"Turned out I had nine more Trojans in my purse. With the one I had took out, that's a total of ten."

She looked from Pacilio to Dr. Rojas and back again. "Well, kids, I'm here to tell you that we used every damn one of them."

Pacilio was not as surprised as he might have been, given what he knew about "Peter Barbour," but Dr. Rojas' eyes widened. "Ten times?" she asked in amazement. "Ten *separate* ejaculations?"

Carol Sefchek nodded.

"Within one hour?"

"No, I'm sorry," Carol said. "I forgot to mention that he had me extend. So, it's ten times within two hours."

"Oh, well, that's very different," Pacilio murmured.

"Still. . . ." Muriel Rojas said, shaking her head. "It's quite an unusual, um, accomplishment."

"Fucking incredible, is what it was," Carol Sefchek said. "I mean, he didn't just fuck me. He put on a damn *clinic*. He had me doing stuff I'd never even done for *fun*, let alone with clients. And, as long as we're being honest with each other, and all. . . . Well, you're going to find this a little hard to believe – shit, I know *I* do."

She took in a long breath and let it out. "The thing is, well, I came six times."

After a moment's silence, Dr. Rojas cleared her throat and said, "Well, surely that's not really unusual, given the extraordinary circumstances."

"Of *course* it's unusual," Carol Sefchek said impatiently. "I don't come with clients. It's unprofessional. Well, all right, once or twice with regulars, guys I got to know pretty well so that by now it's almost a social thing. But this guy was a complete stranger, and potentially wacko, besides. No way I was going to get personal with him."

"Except you did," Pacilio said quietly.

"Yeah, I sure did," Carol said. "Six times. It was like I got caught up in it all somehow, like we were both nothing but fucking machines. Once we started getting it on, it was like he changed. It was as if he knew, I mean really *knew*, everything there was to know about sex, and he just wanted me there to work out on. He was like someone possessed, you know?"

Pacilio just nodded, careful to keep his face expressionless.

Carol was silent for several moments. Then she said, "You know, if it had ended there, if after the two hours I just got dressed and went home to count my money and soak in a hot tub for the soreness, it would have been one hell of an evening. Something to remember for a long time, even if I couldn't tell anybody about it. But, instead, it had to get *weird*." There were tears running down Carol Sefchek's cheeks now. "After the last time, I was starting to say, 'Well the two hours are up, don't think it hasn't been interesting,' and all that. I was lying on my stomach, trying to find the strength to get up and get dressed, when I feel his hand on the back of my neck with the fingers pressing in, hard. Must have been some kind of sleeper hold, because the next thing I know I'm on my back in the bed, with my hands and feet tied to the bed posts. I think he used strips of sheet, or something. And there's a gag around my mouth, and it's so tight I can't hardly make a sound. And he's standing there, and he tells me the *real* fun is going to start now.

"And, just for a second, I think maybe he's a bondage freak who wants to give himself the thrill of fucking me while I'm helpless, and I figure, hell, that's not so bad, I can take *that*. But then he shows me his *tools* – the knife, and the scissors, and the other stuff, and I know that he's not going to let me go, not ever."

She was crying hard now, and the words came out, a few at a time, between sobs.

"I mean the motherfucker hurt me, and he cut me, and god fucking damn it, that's not even the part that scared me the most. He said he was going to kill me slow, and I believed him, and I was so scared, I didn't think I could ever be so

scared and still keep breathing, but then that thing with the mirror happened, that face in the mirror, and I was even more scared than before, more scared than I ever thought it was possible to be, and I still don't really know what happened, or why, or why the hell it all had to happen to me."

Chapter 10

Pacilio and Dr. Muriel Rojas were in the hallway outside Carol Sefchek's hospital room. They stood about ten feet apart, their backs leaning against the wall. Each was absorbed in solitary thought.

Then Dr. Rojas turned, looked at Pacilio and said, "I think we ought to talk."

Pacilio nodded. "Fine with me."

"I would normally suggest my office, but perhaps the hospital cafeteria would do. It's not usually crowded at this hour, and we can probably get a table to ourselves. I want to get something to eat while I have the chance. Low blood sugar impairs my efficiency. And some people," she added with a tiny smile, "even claim it makes me bitchy."

Without changing expression, Pacilio said, "Then by all means let's make it the cafeteria. Otherwise, they'll have to get the children and small animals off the streets."

Then he grinned at her.

He was gratified when she returned the grin. "The last time I missed lunch, I do believe the governor was forced to declare a state of emergency," she said. "But I think there may have been a flood that day, as well."

Muriel Rojas gestured to her left. "The elevator's this way." As they walked down the corridor, she said,

"The cafeteria has the advantage of being close, which may well be its only advantage. But, to my knowledge, nobody has actually contracted a fatal illness from eating there."

Pacilio shrugged. "I suppose I've taken bigger risks, although maybe not recently." He gestured with his head in the direction of Carol Sefchek's room. "Is she going to be okay?"

"The answer to that," Dr. Rojas said, "depends on what you mean by 'okay.' Speaking of which, excuse me for a moment."

They were approaching the nurses' station. Dr. Rojas went over and spoke to a very thin middle-aged black woman in starched nurse's whites who was sitting behind a computer keyboard. "Corinne, let me have the chart on Sefchek in 843, please."

"You bet," the nurse replied. She stopped typing and pulled a clipboard from one of the narrow cubicles to her right. "Here you go, Doctor."

Dr. Rojas took the clipboard and put it on the counter. She read the contents of the top page then took a silver Cross pen from her breast pocket and wrote busily for twenty or thirty seconds. Then she checked what she had written – twice.

Handing back the medical chart, Dr. Rojas said to the nurse, "I'm taking her off the Thorazine immediately and prescribing 80 mg. Valium every six hours until further notice. I want the first dosage administered stat, please, and make note of the administering instruction: oral only. No needles. Okay?"

The nurse nodded and said, "I'll get someone down there right away, Doctor." And she did, too – because she was herself a dedicated medical professional, and also because she did not wish to share the fate of the last nurse who had failed to carry out one of Dr. Rojas' instructions promptly and precisely.

Dr. Rojas rejoined Pacilio and they continued toward the bank of elevators. "You were asking about Ms. Sefchek's prognosis," she said. "Some of it is really pretty good. The broken fingers were all simple fractures, no bone matter puncturing the skin. The pain as they were broken must have been excruciating, but we've got each digit immobilized in plaster now. She's young; the bones will heal. There may be some residual stiffness in damp weather, and she'll be a good candidate for arthritis in that hand as she gets older. But full function should be restored with time and some physical therapy."

"And what about the other injuries," he asked, "the ones to her, uh. . . ."

"The proper medical term is 'nipples,' Mr. Pacilio."

"Yes, them. And, listen, why don't you call me 'Mike,' all right?"

One of the elevators gave a "ping" to announce its arrival. A moment later, the doors slid open to reveal an empty car. As they got on, she said, "All right, Mike. And you may call me 'Dr. Rojas.'"

Unsure whether he was being kidded, Pacilio said in a neutral manner, "Sure, whatever."

She laughed briefly. "No, please, I'm not quite *that* stuffy. Call me Muriel, at least until you manage to annoy me again."

"That seems fair," Pacilio said. He pulled back his left sleeve to reveal an old Rolex diving watch. He stared at the watch's face far longer than was necessary.

"Something wrong?"

"No," Pacilio said. "I just wanted to make note of the exact time. I'll check it again when I do something annoying and have to start calling you 'Dr. Rojas' again. Maybe I can reach a personal best."

She looked up at him, her expression unreadable. "Personal best for you or for me?"

"Either one. At this stage, I'll take any victory I can get."

She nodded slowly and said, "Yes, I have no doubt you will."

The elevator arrived at the ground floor, and Muriel Rojas exited to the right. "This way to the chamber of horrors."

As they approached the door to the hospital cafeteria, she said, "What they serve here isn't all that bad, really. I think most people who have to eat institutional food make fun of it, deservedly or not. It's kind of a fringe benefit we reserve for ourselves."

"I think you're probably right," Pacilio said. "Everybody always bitches about the food. I know we did when I was in the Navy. Of course, back then the chow really *was* lousy."

Pacilio noted that the cafeteria was quite large, with seating for several hundred people. Many of the tables were empty.

They picked up trays and got in line. Since it was past the lunch hour, their progress through the serving area was rapid. Dr. Rojas selected a dish of baked ziti with cheese and tomato sauce. Pacilio picked up a ham and cheese sandwich, and from a rack nearby added a small bag of potato chips. Further on, Dr. Rojas poured herself a large coffee with lots of milk, while Pacilio looked in vain for ginger ale and settled for Diet Pepsi.

Dr. Rojas insisted on buying Pacilio's lunch. "I invited you, after all," she said. "Besides, I'm a rich doctor, remember?"

"All right," Pacilio conceded, "but it's my treat next time." He waited for her to ask him why he thought there might be a next time, but she said nothing.

They found an empty table in a corner with nobody else nearby. Dr. Rojas started on her baked ziti as she watched Pacilio tear open his one-ounce bag of Ruffles. "I don't mean to be a health Nazi," she said, "but I'm probably obligated by the Hippocratic oath to point out that those things are absolutely awful for you."

"I know," he said. "Although I think the Reagan administration once classified them as a vegetable, didn't they?"

She nodded. "Yes, but I believe that classification only applied if the chips were being consumed by minority children."

They ate in silence for a while. Then Pacilio said, "You were starting to tell me upstairs about Carol and her missing nipples. Is she going to be disfigured for life, or can something be done to fix that?"

Muriel swallowed a mouthful of pasta, then said, "Quite a lot can be done, actually. The severed tissue was completely necrotic by the time the EMTs got to her, so there was no question of reattaching it. However, reconstructive surgery can go a long way in repairing that kind of injury."

"You sound very certain about that. You're not a plastic surgeon yourself, are you?"

"No, as I told you earlier, emergency medicine is my specialty. There are some physicians who just put in a little ER time to pick up extra money, but I'm there *all* the time, it's what I do. The reason I can speak with some authority on the eventual restoration of Ms. Sefchek's nipples is because I've consulted reconstruction specialists in the past about that very kind of trauma."

"You're kidding me. Really?"

Dr. Rojas nodded. "It's not common, of course, but I have seen it in the ER more than once. It's a nasty sort of injury, but repairable."

She put her fork down and looked Pacilio in the eyes. "Of much more concern to me at this point is Ms. Sefchek's mental health."

"Well, if you tell her what you just told me – that she can expect pretty much a full recovery from her injuries – that should go quite a ways toward making her feel better, don't you think?"

Dr. Rojas made an impatient gesture. "I *will* tell her, and, yes, it should cheer her up a bit. But that's not what I'm talking about, and you know it."

He shrugged irritably. "If there's something you want to ask me, then ask. I'll either answer you or not. If it's 'not', then I'll start calling you 'Dr. Rojas' again without waiting to be told."

"All right, start with this: should I be writing instructions to have Ms. Sefchek transferred to what she so charmingly called 'the nut ward' of this hospital?"

"That sounds like a medical issue," Pacilio said. "And even if you're not a shrink, you're still a lot more qualified to address it than I am."

Dr. Rojas leaned forward across the table that separated them. "Look, I realize this is difficult for you to discuss with me. What we heard in Ms. Sefchek's room, combined with your official status, and the presence of the FBI, tells me that something extremely unusual is going on. But I am not asking about this because I'm nosy. I want to do the best thing for that young woman in Room 843, and to accomplish that I need to know whether she is delusional or whether she was describing something that, unlikely as it seems, actually took place."

Muriel Rojas leaned back and took a sip of coffee. "I understand that you don't want to read about this business, whatever it is, in tomorrow's *Times Union*. If you want my word that I will be discrete, I will give it to you. And if you want to know what my word is worth, I can provide you with the names of several people in this hospital who will tell you."

Then she sat quietly, her hands folded on the table in front of her, and waited.

Finally, Pacilio said to her, "I guess this all comes down to the wise advice of Lyndon Baines Johnson, who once said about a political rival, 'I'd rather have him inside the tent pissing out, than outside the tent pissing in.'"

"By which elegant analogy you mean that it is safer for you to take me into your confidence, since in doing so you make me a sort of co-conspirator."

"Yeah, that pretty much says it. I'd like you on my side, if possible."

"And what exactly *is* your side, Mike?"

"That's a little hard to explain at this point, but I'm pretty sure it's the side of the angels."

"And the other side consists of – what? Peter Barbour, sexual athlete and serial killer?"

"The other side? Barbour is part of it, that's for sure. But maybe not the whole thing. Hard to know all the players without a scorecard, and I haven't found the scorecard yet." He held up a hand to stifle her objection. "I know what that sounds like, but I'm not trying to be evasive this time. Fact is, there's still a lot to this investigation that I just don't understand."

Pacilio ate the last bite of his sandwich. "You wanted to know if Carol Sefchek is delusional," he said. "I can't tell you for certain, since I wasn't in the hotel room with her. But, from everything I know about this case, I'd be inclined to give her the benefit of the doubt. I really would."

Muriel Rojas' eyes narrowed. "Even that business with the mirror? You believe that really happened?"

Pacilio twitched his mouth to one side. "I wasn't there, like I said. But, yeah, I think something occurred along the lines of what she told us."

"So, what kind of theory are you following here? That Barbour pulled off some sort of magician's trick in his motel room, just to fool that poor, dumb hooker? For what purpose?"

"No purpose that I can think of. No, Muriel, I don't think it was a stunt rigged up to impress Carol Sefchek."

She spread her hands a couple of feet apart. "Then what? You're running out of possibilities pretty fast." She began ticking them off on her fingers. "Carol's not delusional, you say, which means what she told us really happened, allowing for inaccuracies of memory, perception, and so on. And she's not the victim of a hoax, you say, which means there is no rational explanation for what she described. Which leaves us with what?"

Pacilio was slowly shredding his empty potato chip bag. Without looking up, he asked, "You ever read any of the Sherlock Holmes stories when you were a kid?"

"No, they weren't too popular in *el barrio*. I read a few of them in college, for some English class or other. There's a point to this, right?"

Pacilio nodded. "There's a story where Holmes explains one of his deductions by saying, 'When you have eliminated the impossible, then whatever's left, no matter how improbable it might sound, is the truth.' The man knew what he was talking about, I think."

For almost half a minute, she just sat there and stared at him. "Let me be sure I understand this," she said finally. "You and Sherlock Holmes are asking me to accept Ms. Sefchek's account as an accurate representation of something that actually took place."

"What I'm saying is that you might want to avoid making a knee-jerk diagnosis that the kid upstairs is wacked, based only on her story. Some of it's hard to accept, I grant you, but that doesn't necessarily mean that either the story is a lie or that the girl is crazy."

Muriel swirled the remains of her coffee around in the cup. "We'd better stop dancing around this," she said, frowning. "You're positing that Carol Sefchek witnessed something . . . supernatural, paranormal, whatever the current buzzword is?"

"I could qualify it about nine different ways," Pacilio said, "but the short answer is *yes*."

He expected disbelief, or anger, or a diagnosis that he himself was delusional. Instead, she said, calmly, "Tell me why a man like you would believe a thing like that."

"All right, but before I do, I'm going to ask for something you offered me earlier: your word. What I'm going to tell you mention to nobody, and I mean nobody at all – not at work, not at home, not anywhere in between."

She shrugged. "All I have at home is a hamster named Theodore, and I suspect he wouldn't find the subject very interesting. As for work" – she smiled grimly – "I have no intention of undermining my credibility as a physician by sounding like the front page of *The Weekly World News*. You need have no fears on that score, Mike."

"Maybe not, but I still want your word," he said.

So she gave him her word. And then he told her.

It took quite a while.

After Pacilio had finished, Dr. Muriel Rojas sat silently, as she had throughout his entire account. Finally, she blinked several times, then rubbed her eyelids with the tips of her fingers. After a moment she asked, with a slight smile, "Are you sure you don't normally work with a female partner? Redheaded Irish girl with a medical degree, maybe, who's always trying to disprove your theories about alien abductions?"

Pacilio's answering smile was restrained, as well. "Yeah, I used to watch that show, too," he said. "It was kind of fun, but it's just TV. It's not real."

"And this is? *Demonic possession?* I mean, are you fucking *serious?*"

Before Pacilio could reply, she cut him off. "Yes, of course you are, you've made that quite clear," she said apologetically. "I just needed to vent a little, I guess. I must be upset, to use that particular obscenity."

Pacilio's smile had more wattage this time. "I believe I've heard the word a few times before, Muriel."

She shook her head. "No, that's not what I mean. I'm neither a prude nor a prig, nor did I think that you were, but I do tend to be very proper in my speech. My mother raised me from the cradle with the idea that only low-class people use vulgar language – and Mama was very big on upward mobility. If I even said so much as "damn" in the house, she'd practically blow a blood vessel. So it's pretty much second nature with me now -- unless something, or someone, gets to me in a big way. And not much does that, anymore."

Pacilio might have been interested in exploring the implications of her last statement, but before he could, Dr. Rojas looked at her watch and made a sound of dismay.

"I have patients to check on," she said, "and I'm already late." She pushed her chair back, but did not stand immediately. "Listen," she said,"are you leaving town today?"

"No, the last flight to D.C. took off over an hour ago. I'll stay in Albany tonight and get an early plane in the morning." He was careful to keep his gaze focused on her face, not her body, as he said that, and to keep his tone businesslike.

"Why don't you come over to my place for dinner tonight? We need to talk about this at greater length, and I don't imagine it's the kind of subject you want to share with people at nearby tables in a restaurant."

The phrase "greater length" seemed to hang in the air between them, Pacilio thought. He inclined his head slightly and said, "It would be my pleasure to dine with you. Where do you live?"

From a pocket in her gray plaid skirt she brought out a small gold case and extracted a business card. After scribbling something on the blank side she handed it to Pacilio. "I put my home address on the back," she said, "and the phone number, in case something comes up." Those last two words also seemed to acquire a special quality which caused a momentary awkwardness, until Pacilio asked, "What time is best?"

"Say around 7:30?" At his nod, she went on, "Listen, I had enough tortillas and enchiladas in my first eighteen years to last me a lifetime, so I hope you like basic American cuisine – steak, potatoes, salad?"

"Sounds fine to me. How about I bring a bottle of wine?"

"Fine, do that. But now," she said, rising "I really have to get back to my patients."

"Okay, then. I'll see you tonight."

And with that she was gone. Pacilio sat alone at the table for another ten minutes, and it is a credit to his professional dedication that he spent almost half that time thinking about Peter Barbour.

———◆———

Pacilio needed a room for the night and thought the Holiday Inn on Wolf Road would do as well as anywhere. He could talk to any hotel employees who had encountered Peter Barbour, and he wanted a look inside the room Barbour had occupied the night before.

Pacilio had stayed in a number of Holiday Inns over the years, but he had never seen one that was laid out like this. It was as if the architect couldn't decide whether to put in a hotel or a motel, and so had ultimately gone with both. There was the central building that rose up five stories and was a clone of any modern urban chain hotel. But spreading out from the central structure was a series of single-story wings that would allow you to park your car right in front of your room, just like a conventional motel.

The motel-style rooms were cheaper, and Pacilio was mindful of the anal-retentive accountants back in D.C. who would be scrutinizing his travel voucher. With a discrete flash of his federal credentials, he was able to get a room only three doors down from the one where Carol Sefchek had been tortured and terrorized.

Getting into Peter Barbour's former room was easy. Responding to the entreaties of the Holiday Inn's manager (who was worried about scaring off paying customers), the Albany Police Department had refrained from plastering the outside of Room 128 with yellow crime scene tape. There was a policeman at the door, but he was in plain clothes. Detective Second Grade Karl Melling was clearly bored out of his mind and only too willing to open up the sealed room after a look at Pacilio's credentials. He explained that he had let some FBI people in earlier in the day, but that no one had been by for the last four hours.

As he closed the door behind him, Pacilio saw that the room was typical of what the motel chain offered worldwide. One of the double beds was still made. The other, clearly the one Barbour had employed for his amusements, was a mess. The bedspread had been removed, and the thin, camel-colored blanket and top sheet had been pulled down and folded a couple of times to give full access to the bed.

The fitted sheet bore stains in several places. Some of them appeared to be dried perspiration, whether brought on by passion or agony Pacilio didn't know. Then there were the bloodstains, already dried brown, from where Barbour had amputated Carol Sefchek's nipples. A large discolored area in the center of the sheet puzzled Pacilio for a moment, until he bent over and sniffed. Urine. It looked as if Carol had lost control of her bladder at some point, whether out of pain or fear or both.

Strips of fabric, the same color as the sheets, dangled from the four bedposts; each showed a clean cut at the end, probably from scissors employed by the EMT crew that had been summoned to the scene. Ugly images of the lab in Fairfax came back to Pacilio for a moment, and he wondered if Carol Sefchek would ever learn enough about Peter Barbour to look back on what had happened to her in this place and consider herself lucky.

Pacilio took a quick turn around the room, glanced in the bathroom and the closet, opened a couple of drawers. He didn't really expect to find anything that the Albany P.D. and the FBI might have missed. As he went through this desultory examination, his eyes were time and again drawn to the mirror.

It was a perfectly ordinary hotel room mirror, about five feet by three, fastened to the wall above the dresser by brackets that clamped it tightly in twelve places. Feeling slightly ridiculous, Pacilio checked the mirror and its clamps for signs of tampering. He found none.

He then took a close look at the wall opposite, to see if there might be some way that an image could have been projected onto the mirror from across the room. There was nothing. He had not expected that there would be. Whatever had happened in here, he was fairly sure that cheap conjurer's tricks had played no part in it.

As he stood there in the utterly mundane motel room, hands in his pockets, gazing absently at a mirror that was surely identical to thousands of other mirrors in thousands of similar rooms, he could hear Carol Sefchek again, her voice shaky with fear as she talked about the mirror.

Hades Project

"I must have passed out after he did my other nipple, it hurt so bad, I never knew anything could hurt so much. I don't know how long I was out, but when I come around the first thing I see is him standing over me, and as soon as he notices I'm awake, he moves around to the front of the bed and kneels on the mattress. He's got me tied to the bedposts hand and foot, so I'm spread wide open. So there he is, kneeling between my legs. With one hand he starts rubbing my pussy, just stroking it with his fingers, you know? In the other hand he's got this thing, I think they call it a box-cutting knife – it's got a big handle like a pocketknife, but it has this little blade that's real sharp, like a razor. And he's holding this knife, making sure that I can see it, and he's still gently stroking my pussy with his other hand, and he's telling me about clitorectomy, about how it's this real old tradition, been around for hundreds of years, they still do it in some parts of the world, and he's going on and on, a real fucking professor, and even though I didn't go to some fancy college, it don't take me too long to catch on to the fact that as soon as the lecture is over, Professor fucking Barbour is going to take that thing and he's going to cut off my clit with it, and I start to wonder if it's possible to get so scared that you start to lose your mind, 'cause I think I'm beginning to lose mine, on account of it looks like something is going on in the mirror that's on the wall across from the bed. There's all these colors and patterns, and they're like swirling around in there. It's a little bit like the time I tried some acid that a friend of mine gave me, except now I can see that the colors in the mirror have started to like come together in the shape of a face, but it's not a human face, really, except that it is. I mean, it was kind of like that movie, I saw it on HBO once, about some doctor who had this island, and he took these people and combined their genes with animal genes and ended up with people who looked like animals, and that's what this face in the mirror was like, except it was huge, it *practically filled up the whole fucking mirror, and I'm starting to wonder if I really am nuts except I don't get to think about it very long because that fuckface Barbour has decided to stop talkin' and start chalkin'. He's got the razor knife in one hand and he's trying to get hold of my clit with the other one, and I'm squirming around as much as I can but I can't move very much and I know he's gonna do it in the next two or three seconds and I'm wishing he would just kill me and get it over with and then there's this SOUND. I mean, it was like the roar of a fucking lion or something, except it said a word, some word in a language I never heard before. And it seemed so loud, I swear people across the street must've heard it. I guess Barbour didn't have no idea what was going on in the mirror, 'cause his back was to it and me being gagged like I was, I couldn't exactly tell him. But as soon as he hears this — sound, word, whatever it was — he just freezes. And the look on his face is probably the way I was looking about two seconds earlier, I mean the bastard looks terrified. Then, after a couple or three seconds, he jumps off the bed and turns around so that he's looking right at the mirror. And as soon as he sees that face, bam! — he falls to his knees faster than a nun in front of the Pope. He's like kneeling at attention, you know? And his head is kind of bowed, he never looks right at the face in the mirror again. Hell, I can't look at it very long, either. I mean, it's like a man with the face of an animal — the kind of animal that eats people. So I just lie there kind of staring at the ceiling and wondering what's going to happen to me when Barbour gets done with whatever the fuck it is he's doing. And this thing in the mirror like talks to him, and it's not sounding too happy about things, either. I couldn't understand the words, but the tone of voice wasn't hard to follow. I mean, this dude is PISSED. And Barbour mostly just listens, except once in a while he says something back in the same language, and the way he says it sounds like it must've been 'Yes, sir,' or 'You bet,* boss,' something like that, you know? And this goes on for I don't know how long, but finally it seems to be winding down. The face in the mirror barks out some sorta order or something, and Barbour falls on his face with his arms stretched out like he's worshipping in front of a fucking idol or something. And then, for the first time since the mirror started getting weird, I can feel this thing looking at me. I close my eyes tight – last thing I want is to get this guy's attention – but I can still feel it somehow, and I can tell he's looking at me the way a big fat guy at a buffet looks at a piece of cheesecake, kind of like, 'Should I eat this now, or save it for later?' and I'm just starting to think that I might have been better off when it was just me and Barbour, when, all of a sudden it's like somebody turned a light off, or something, so I open my eyes and look and the mirror is just a mirror again. Then Barbour gets up off the floor and I think, 'Oh, fuck, he's gonna pick up where he left off,' but what he does instead is get dressed and then he starts packing, and he's not wasting any time about it, either. And he doesn't even act like I'm in the room, but I know he's gonna kill me before he leaves. He might not take the time to have any more fun, but he can't let me live: I mean, I've seen his face, I've looked at his driver's license so I know his name, my testimony can put him in jail if they catch him, I know about that weird shit with the mirror, whatever that was, so he has to kill me. And, you know, I didn't mind too much, really. I was hurting pretty bad, my hand and my tits, especially, and I had been so scared for so long that I just wanted it to be over. No more pain and no more fear, that was looking pretty good to me about then, and if I had to die to get it, well, okay, it seemed like a fair price to pay. So I closed my eyes and waited. I figured he'd do me last thing before he left. It didn't matter to me how he did it, as long as it was quick. I was lying there waiting to die, and I felt more peace than I could ever remember feeling, because I knew it was almost over. Then I *hear the door to the room open and, a second later, it closes. I open my eyes, and he's gone. But he can't fool me, the prick. He's just having a little bit more fun, trying to fake me out. Any second now, he's going to open that door and come back in, maybe make some smartass remark like 'Oops, almost forgot something,' and then slit my throat. That's all right, let him have his fun. But the door doesn't open. Then I hear a car start up outside. And eventually it dawns on me that he's not going to come back and kill me, after all. And I start to cry, worse than before. Worse than I ever have in my life, because I'm still tied to the bed. I'm helpless, get it? I can't move, which means I can't kill myself. I have to live. That motherfucking, cocksucking bastard, WHY WOULDN'T HE KILL ME?"*

Pacilio stared at the mirror for a while longer, then he looked at the bed some more. Finally, he shook his head a couple of times and left the room.

He talked to the desk clerk who had done the check-in on Peter Barbour the prior evening, but learned little. Then it took him the better part of an hour to determine that no other Holiday Inn employee on duty the night before could remember having any contact whatever with Barbour.

Pacilio went back to his own room to make phone calls. The first was to the toll-free number for USAirways. He learned that the first flight to Washington D.C. the next day left at 9:20 a.m. Seats were available, so he reserved one.

His next call was to McGraw.

"What have you got, Mike? Peter Barbour's head on a plate, I hope." McGraw sounded tired.

"No," Pacilio said. "Bastard was long gone by the time I got here. Christ knows where he is now."

"Were you able to get anything out of the victim?"

"Some. But I'm not sure at this point how useful it is. For what it's worth, she's pretty well confirmed that it was Barbour."

"Hell, we were sure about that already," McGraw said. "The hotel registration, remember?"

"That's not necessarily definitive. We knew that somebody calling himself Peter Barbour got a room and gave them a credit card imprint. They don't always ask for a picture ID at hotels, Mac, especially if the credit card goes through the computer all right. So, conceivably, somebody could have buried Peter Barbour face down in a shallow grave somewhere in Virginia, after first taking Barbour's wallet."

"Yeah, I guess that's true. But you say the girl confirmed it's him?"

"Yes, she did. You were right – she's a hooker. Part of her routine involves checking the ID of the John, to determine if he's a vice cop."

"Makes sense, I guess. So she saw his license?"

"Yeah. She remembers the name, and she also checked the picture on the license against the guy's face. It's him."

"All right, good. Did he leave anything behind that might connect him with the murders in Fairfax or Wilkes-Barre?"

"One thing in particular: lots and lots of jism."

"That's right, I was forgetting the sexual capabilities that he showed in Fairfax."

"Well, seems like he's still got them. According to our working girl Carol, they made it something like ten times in the space of two hours, each ejaculation duly contained in a condom."

"So where are all these used rubbers now?"

"Albany P.D. must have them," Pacilio said. "Although, with ten to play with, they're probably sharing with the FBI. The Feebies have better lab facilities, anyway."

"Okay, good. Listen, about the victim, any idea why he didn't do her like he did the others? We know what his idea of fun is, so why the change in pattern? Why is this hooker still alive?"

Pacilio didn't want to try explaining the phenomenon of the mirror to McGraw, not over the phone. "I don't know for sure," he said. "It seems he changed his mind fairly early in the proceedings and just left." Pacilio thought the mild lie was in order, under the circumstances. "The girl was in and out of consciousness by that time, so she's not sure what happened. She thinks she remembers Barbour talking to someone. Maybe he made or received a phone call," Pacilio said, then added blandly, "Or he could have had a visitor."

McGraw grunted. "Well, maybe we'll find out someday, if they manage to take the bastard alive. In the meantime, you might as well head on home."

"I was planning to, at least for a day or two. There are some aspects to this case that we need to talk about, face to face. My plane gets in before lunchtime tomorrow."

"There's no 'day or two' about it, Mike. Our part of the job's over."

The knuckles of Pacilio's left hand, the one holding the phone, were suddenly pale. "What are you talking about?"

"It's a straight manhunt now," McGraw said. "New York has issued a warrant on Barbour, charging him with abduction, aggravated assault, and so on, all stemming from what he did to the hooker. That doesn't exactly make him Public Enemy Number One, but every cop in the state will have his photo from the driver's license and the car's description and license number. Also, based on what you've told me, I'm pretty sure the U.S. Attorney for Northern Virginia is going to file federal charges tomorrow, charging Barbour with interstate flight to avoid prosecution for multiple murder."

"None of that puts our Mr. Barbour behind bars," Pacilio said.

"No, it doesn't, but it sets a system in motion, and the system will take him down sooner or later. Even if he gets out of New York State, it won't help him much. Copies of the circular on him will be in every State Police cruiser east of the Rockies. Remember, Mike, this guy isn't a career criminal. Prior to Fairfax, his lawbreaking experience consisted of two speeding tickets. He doesn't know what a dragnet is, probably, let alone how to avoid one."

"Maybe," Pacilio said doubtfully. "But it looks like he's learned a lot in the past few days."

"Besides, the FBI wants us out of this. Pennypacker was very clear with me about that. It's their case now. Anyway, what are you going to do – cruise the interstates hoping for a sight of the guy's car?"

"No," Pacilio said, "that's not exactly what I had in mind."

"Come on back, podner. Stop by the office after lunch tomorrow for some debriefing so we can close our file on this thing. Shouldn't take more than an hour. Then take a couple of days off and get some rest. See if you can ease this whole mess out of your head."

"Yeah, okay, Mac." Pacilio's voice was calm now. "I'll see you tomorrow afternoon."

After hanging up the phone, Pacilio remained seated on the bed for several minutes. Mostly he looked at nothing in particular, although, from time to time, his gaze drifted over to the mirror above the bureau, a mirror identical in all respects to the one in Room 128. Finally, he picked up the telephone and tapped in a number he had written down earlier. His call was answered on the fourth ring.

"Hello," he said. "I have a reservation on one of your flights for tomorrow . . . Flight 297, Albany, New York to Washington, D.C. . . . yes, departs at 9:20. The name is Pacilio. P-a-c-i-l-i-o. Yes, in coach."

There was a pause while the voice on the other end asked a question. Then Pacilio said, in the same quiet voice with which he had lied to McGraw, "I need to cancel that reservation."

Chapter 11

"Mirrors?" Dirty Eugene's voice sounded both puzzled and irritated. "What the fuck am I supposed to know about mirrors?"

"You told me last night that there was such a thing as demonic visitation," Pacilio said into the phone. "Kind of the flip side of visits by angels, like the one that appeared to Mary, right?"

"That particular occasion is known as The Annunciation, you heathen. Yeah, there are some reports of demonic visitation, apart from conjuring. So?"

"So, have you ever heard of it happening through a mirror?"

There was silence on the line for ten or twelve seconds. "Eugene? You still there?"

The old priest's voice came back at once. "Just thinking," he said. "It takes longer these days than it used to. The memory isn't as good as it used to be either, unfortunately. But there was something . . . oh, right, got it now. There are several accounts dating back to the Twelfth and Thirteenth Centuries, or thereabouts. These are testimonies of demonic visitation that somebody, probably the local Bishop, decided were believable enough to enter into an official record someplace."

"And these stories talk about demons using mirrors to communicate with humans?"

"No, not mirrors," Dirty Eugene said. "I'm not even sure they *had* mirrors, as we know them today, back in those days."

"Then *what*?" Pacilio said impatiently. "Come on, Eugene, this is important. Don't jerk me around."

"Well, in a couple of cases, the demon was described as appearing to the subject in a pool of still water. Not a mirror as such, but the basic principle is the same, I would think."

"Yes, so would I," Pacilio said. "All right, anything else?"

"Well, I also vaguely recall reading something about a visitation that supposedly occurred in the face of a highly polished metal shield. Some Spanish Conquistador claimed the Devil had tempted him by appearing in the reflective surface."

"Did anybody believe this guy, do you know?"

"I presume so. They burned the poor bastard at the stake for consorting with Satan. The Inquisition used to take that sort of thing very seriously, you know." Dirty Eugene snorted in scorn. "That probably put a bit of damper on any future reports of a similar nature by other soldiers."

"Okay, well, it seems to me that there's –"

"Wait a minute," Dirty Eugene said. "Something else just broke through the fog. A couple of months before they shipped me off to Bolivia, I had dinner with another Jeb – a guy I had first met in Rome, at the Gregorian, years earlier. He told me a weird story about an exorcism he'd performed in France, in or around Rhiems, I think. The expulsion of the demon was successful, and the victim, a fella in his late thirties, was actually in pretty good physical and mental shape afterwards. That's not always the case, by the way. So, my friend tells me that the two of them talked a little, a couple of days after it was over. The French guy described the experience as like being a passenger in a car that somebody else was driving. He knew everything that was going on, but he couldn't do anything about any of it. Pretty good analogy, don't you think?"

"Sure, great," Pacilio said bleakly. "Go on."

"Well, this guy tells my friend that at one point while he was possessed – I gather the whole thing lasted a couple of months before the exorcist was finally called in –something appeared in a bathroom mirror, an image that had nothing to do with a reflection of the man standing in front of it. The victim, to the extent his consciousness was present, found the image terrifying. However, his unwelcome tenant, the demon, seemed to recognize the entity in the mirror, and appeared to converse with it. I gather that the visitor in the mirror represented a demon further up in the hierarchy than the one that was possessing the Frenchman, since the possessor demon was very respectful to the thing in the mirror, paid obeisance to it, and so on. What the point of it all was, I don't know. Maybe the demon in our world was being given some kind of instructions, but got exorcised back to Hell before it could carry them out, and good riddance, too."

After several seconds of pensive silence, Pacilio said, "What could those instructions, if that's what they were, have been about? I mean, what's important enough to Satan, or whoever, that he sends out Hell's equivalent of Western Union to a demon that's possessing somebody?"

"Christ, who knows?" Dirty Eugene said. "I'm not about to try and second-guess the schemes of the Evil One. Tell you this much, though: if those were instructions that were issued, they weren't intended for the benefit of you or me or anybody else in this world."

"No . . . no, I don't suppose they were," Pacilio said quietly. "Okay, Eugene, thanks for the info. It was a help. But there's something else I need, and fast."

He spoke for several minutes, and in the end the old Jesuit agreed to do his best to comply with Pacilio's request. Then they were done – or very nearly.

"Mikey, listen to me," the priest said, and for the first time in the phone call there was real urgency in his voice. "If you're messing around with what I think you're messing around with, you need to be very careful. There could be a lot at stake, here."

"Oh, yeah?" Pacilio tried for blasé, but didn't quite make it.

"Yeah. Your immortal soul, for one thing. And maybe a hell of a lot more."

"Pun intended?"

"You bet your fucking ass," Dirty Eugene said.

———◆———

Pacilio glanced at his watch and calculated he had time for one more call. He picked up the receiver again and punched in a number from memory.

The phone at the other end rang five times, followed by a click. A moment later, a female voice said, "Hi, this is Shari Sexpert. If you're a hot woman who knows when to nibble and when to lick, wait for the beep and leave a filthy, perverted message. Be assured that I *will* get back to you. On the other hand, if you're

a man, may I suggest that you wait for the beep, too –
and then commence to eat your heart out."

When the "beep" tone sounded, Pacilio said into the
phone, "It's Mike, Sharon. Pick up if you're there."

A couple of seconds later, there was another click as
the line opened. A voice, female, contralto, and
recognizable as the same one on the answering machine
tape, said, "Michael! How the hell are you?"

"I'm not too bad," Pacilio said, "but I was wondering
– does your publisher find that answering machine
message amusing?"

"Oh, I have a separate line, with its own answering
machine, for business stuff. This line is just for personal
calls, and very few people have the number. Just
important folks – like you."

"Well, flatterer, can you spare a few minutes, or did
I call at a bad time?"

"I always have time to talk to you, you know that.
Just a second."

It sounded like she had put her hand over the
receiver, but not very tightly. He heard her say, "It's my
brother. Do you mind if I spend a few minutes?" There
was a pause, then Pacilio heard his sister say, "No, please,
don't stop now. It's all right."

Then she was back on the line with him. "So, what's
up?"

Pacilio said, "Is somebody there? Am I interrupting
something?"

"Well, yes and no, actually."

"Don't be coy, Shar. If you want me to call back, just
say so."

She chuckled softly. "Coy, Michael? Are you

referring to *moi?* No, what I meant by 'yes and no' was that yes, someone is here, and no, you're not interrupting anything. Whatever was transpiring when the phone rang a minute ago is continuing to transpire even as we speak."

"I see."

"Do you, really? It's my newest friend, Crystal. She's a lawyer with one of the biggest firms in town. I'd ask her to say hello, but one of the things she learned at Swarthmore is that a lady *never* talks with her mouth full."

Pacilio sighed into the phone. "Come on, Shar, save the smut for your next book, okay? Where you're concerned, I'm shockproof."

"Well, you can't blame a girl for trying. All right, we'll declare a smut moratorium, for the time being. So, what's doin'? Are you coming out to the Coast?"

"Not anytime soon, I'm afraid," Pacilio said. "The main reason I called is because I need help with something."

"Sure, sweetie. Anything I can do I will, you know that."

"Well, the thing is, I need to get in touch with one of your old girlfriends."

"Really!" Sharon Pacilio chuckled. "Well, *there's* a first. I assume your interest isn't social, since you never approved of any of my girlfriends."

"Not true. I just didn't like the ones who were real hard-core dykes."

"Michael, *I'm* a dyke!"

"Yeah, I know," Pacilio said. "But you're a *nice* dyke."

His sister erupted into laughter. As it subsided, she said, "Well, I can't argue with that. When you're right, you're right!" After a moment or two she was serious again. "So, who among my former paramours are you interested in?

"I don't remember her name, but she was the one who claimed to be a witch."

"A *witch*? Are you sure you don't mean *bitch*? That won't narrow the field much, I'm afraid. Oh, wait – are you thinking of Sarah McPherson?"

"I think Sarah was her first name, yeah. Black hair, pale, you said the two of you met at some kind of strip club?"

"Right, that's Sarah. I was in the audience and she was performing on stage. What on earth do you want to find *her* for?"

"It's business, and I can't tell you more than that, right now. Not over the phone. Look, when it's over, I promise I'll come out and buy you dinner at Ernie's and tell you all about it. But I warn you, after I do, you may start sleeping with a night light."

"I *already* sleep with a night light, dummy. But if that's the way it's got to be, far be it from me to compromise the national security."

"I appreciate your understanding," Pacilio told her. "So, can you put me in touch with Sarah?"

"Not immediately. She and I broke up in, let's see ... the winter of '99. I haven't seen or heard from her since. I haven't even heard anything *about* her, and that tells me she's left town. Gossip is the local gay community's life blood, and I haven't come across even a morsel about Sarah in quite some time."

"Shit," Pacilio said, with feeling.

"I expect that I can get a line on her, though," his sister said. "I still know some people who knew her, Biblically and otherwise, and they should be able to refer me to still other people, and one of them will probably know where she is. I'll make some calls."

"Hate to rush you, but can you do it tonight? There's a time factor."

"Sure, that's no problem. I was planning to stay in tonight, anyway. Where can I reach you later – at home?"

"No, I'm in Albany, New York. Here's the hotel's number." He read off the area code, the phone number, and his room number. "I'll be out for a while, but if you leave a message, I'll get it and call you right back."

"Okay, Michael, you may, as they say, rely upon me."

"I knew I could," Pacilio told her. "But why are you breathing like that all of a sudden?"

"Well, if you *must* know, Crystal's been devouring me all the time we've been talking, and now she's got a couple of fingers going in and out, as well, and this girl *really* knows her way around a G-spot. I've been trying to ... to concentrate on what we were saying, but I think I'm about to lose the battle, Michael. Would you like to listen?"

"No, thanks," Pacilio said hastily. "That's a little more Freudian than I can handle. Enjoy, and call me later, all right?"

Sharon Pacilio sounded as if she were speaking through clenched teeth. "Sure, honey, no problem. I'll find her, I'll . . . yes, baby, like that . . . oh, yes, *yes* . . . ."

Pacilio hung up without waiting for his sister to break the connection. There were a few beads of sweat on his forehead, but it was, after all, a warm evening.

In San Francisco, Sharon Pacilio listened to the dial tone in her ear and hung up, a wide grin on her face. She leaned back in her desk chair, tapped a Virginia Slims out of the pack next to her computer, and lit up.

"Shockproof," she said to the empty room, and erupted into laughter again "Not just yet, big brother."

She used the computer's mouse to save what she'd been writing, picked up the phone again, and began to tap in numbers.

———◆———

Muriel Rojas lived in a condo complex a little way north of the city of Albany. The modernistic architecture and natural wood construction suggested the place was pricey, and since the cars in the parking areas tended to favor Mercedes, Lexus, and BMW, Pacilio figured that the tenants probably weren't having trouble with the mortgage payments.

Pacilio pushed the downstairs buzzer and announced himself. Muriel Rojas' voice, slightly distorted by the intercom speaker, invited him to enter and come upstairs. Then the outer door clicked open.

Dr. Muriel Rojas answered the door of her condo wearing snug, faded blue jeans and a gray sweatshirt that said "Notre Dame Fighting Irish" on it. Her small feet were clad in gray and white running shoes. Taking in Pacilio's suit, she said, "I meant to tell you to dress informally, but I forgot, in my rush to get back to work. Sorry about that."

Pacilio shook his head with a smile. "Wouldn't have mattered," he said. "I don't have a lot of clothes with me, and what I did bring is suits, so I'd be dressed like this, anyway."

He handed her the paper bag he was carrying. "You said we were having steak, so I asked the guy at the liquor store for advice. Once he saw I wasn't going to spring for the $120 bottle of Dom Perignon he was pushing, we settled on this. I hope it will do."

Muriel pulled the bottle out and looked at the label. "Pinot Noir? It should be fine," she said. "I'll open it up and let it breathe a little. In the meantime, get comfortable. Doctor's orders: off with the suit coat, off with the tie. Roll up your sleeves, too, if you like. I will not be made to feel underdressed in my own home."

"Sounds good to me." Pacilio removed his coat and tie as she went off in search of a corkscrew. It occurred to him for a moment that "underdressed" was just one syllable away from "undressed."

The living room's furniture was mostly Scandinavian modern, made with a lot of teak and shiny metal. The couch, which looked like it might conceal a sofa bed, was done in a nubby beige fabric, as were two matching armchairs. In the middle stood a large coffee table with a glass center framed by some kind of blond wood. Against one wall was a Mitsubishi television set with what looked like a 35-inch screen and a free-standing speaker on either side.

There were a few pictures on the walls, mostly abstracts in bright colors, but most of the wall space was taken up by built-in bookshelves. He walked over to take a closer look, expecting medical books and journals. Instead, Muriel Rojas' bookshelves were crammed with novels in both hardcover and paperback. Her tastes seemed to lean toward mystery, suspense, science fiction and fantasy. Pacilio was looking over the titles when Muriel returned to the room.

"Sighted wine, opened same," she said. "It'll be ready for us when we're ready for it."

"You've got some interesting books here. I guess I was expecting to find four editions of *Gray's Anatomy* and maybe the last ten years of *Journal of the American Medical Association*."

"All that's in my office," she said. "I don't leave for the day until I've read everything I need to know for work. Then, when I finally get home, I can read whatever I want for relaxation and not think about medicine at all." She gave a wry smile. "That's the theory, anyway."

Pacilio made a gesture that took in the whole of Muriel Rojas' library. "Looks like you do a lot of that relaxation reading."

"True," she said. "It's my principal way of unwinding – and in the ER, the spring gets wound pretty tight, as you might imagine. Reading novels also helps me get to sleep at night."

"Wouldn't a glass of wine or a shot or two of Chivas Regal do as well?"

She shook her head. "When you're my size, it doesn't take much alcohol to induce a pretty good buzz. And if I go in to work with a hangover, I could make a mistake – and you know what they say about doctors and mistakes, don't you?"

Pacilio shook his head.

"Cooks cover their mistakes with mayonnaise," she recited, "and architects use ivy – but doctors cover theirs with earth." She smiled at him and shrugged. "I find light fiction better for both the head and the liver. Not to mention the patients."

"Then why did you say 'okay' to my bringing over a bottle of wine to go with dinner?"

"Why not?" she said. "I don't want to deprive you of the chance to have some wine with the meal, if that's what you like. Besides, I plan to join you – for half a glass, anyway. Taken with food, it shouldn't affect me very much."

Pacilio feigned disappointment. "So that pretty

much puts the kabosh on any fiendish plan to get you drunk and take advantage of you, I guess."

"Looks that way, I'm afraid," she said with mock sympathy. "Guess you'll have to try it while I'm in full possession of my faculties."

She took a step back toward the kitchen. "I was going to put the steaks under the broiler, but I came out to ask how you like yours."

Pacilio shrugged. "Medium rare is fine, but don't fuss over it too much. I can enjoy anything that's between the two extremes."

"Extremes?"

"You know – between 'charcoal briquette' and 'still breathing.'"

She laughed lightly. "Well, that sounds like a window big enough to fit even my cooking through. Let me see what I can do."

She turned, took a step away, then turned back. "Look, why don't you come into the kitchen with me? I want to keep an eye on the steaks and get a couple of other things ready. It hardly seems polite to leave you out here by yourself."

He followed her through a small dining room into the kitchen, which was done in the same modern style as the rest of the condominium. The oven was set against one of the walls, with a Formica counter running above it. Atop the counter, a microwave oven was working on some potatoes that were visible through the glass. Muriel Rojas busied herself putting a couple of rib-eye steaks under the broiler.

The kitchen was spotlessly clean, and seemed to be equipped with every cooking gadget known to humankind. There was a new-looking food processor, a juicer, a toaster-oven, and several devices that Pacilio didn't recognize. "I've seen mess halls that weren't set up as well as this place," he said. "Do you entertain a lot?"

"Actually, no. I had some ambitions along that line when I first moved in here. For a while, I suspect, I was the Williams-Sonoma catalog's best customer. But I don't seem to have the time or energy for dinner parties. In fact, I don't even cook for myself all that much, so it's nice to have the chance to fuss a little bit. Usually when I get home, I'm too whipped to contemplate something fancy, so I just munch some raw vegetables and follow that with a couple of reheated slices of pizza."

"Pizza!" Pacilio pretended shock. "After the way you sneered at my little bag of potato chips this afternoon, I'd never have figured you for a junk food junkie."

She shook her head. "Pizza's not junk food, really. It's pretty well balanced, nutritionally, and fairly low in fat – unless you cover it with stuff like pepperoni or sausage, or insist on eating six or seven slices."

"Cuts."

She raised her eyebrows. "Sorry?"

"Where I grew up, we used to call them 'cuts' of pizza, not slices."

"Really? I hadn't heard that one before. Where's your home town?"

"Little hole in the wall in Northeast Pennsylvania, called Pittston. It's between Wilkes-Barre and Scranton."

"Those two I've heard of, but not Pittston."

He shrugged. "No reason why you should have. It's not famous for much of anything. A lot of coal mining went on there once, but it petered out in the early 1950s. A couple of guys from Pittston are sort of semi-

167

famous, although I've never met either one of them. Jimmy Cefalo used to play for the Dolphins, and there's a guy named Jay Parini, who's an English professor at some college in New England, I think. He's written several novels and I see reviews by him in the *New York Times Book Review* sometimes, too, so I assume he's a pretty heavy hitter in literary circles."

She was looking at him a little strangely. "Do you, uh, read the *Book Review* often?"

"Every Sunday, if I'm not working. Besides, I find the paper stock that the *Times* uses is very absorbent, which comes in handy when I oil my Tommy gun on those long, rainy Sunday afternoons." Pacilio didn't put much sarcasm into his voice, but he didn't need to.

Muriel studied the linoleum of her kitchen floor for a few moments. Then she looked at Pacilio squarely. "I was patronizing you, wasn't I?"

Pacilio nodded once, his face impassive. "Yes, Doctor, I'd say you were."

"Think I could save the evening with a sincere apology and a promise not to do it again?"

He nodded again, but his expression was softer this time. "There's a pretty good chance of that."

"All right, then. I'm sorry I patronized you, Mike. I won't do it again."

"Okay, fine," he said pleasantly. "Just remember, will you, that just because I'm a government thug don't mean dat I ain't got no cooth."

"To be sure," she murmured. Stepping over to the oven, she checked the progress of the broiling steaks. "Just a few more minutes."

"Sure there's nothing I can do to help?" Pacilio asked. "I'm pretty handy in a kitchen, if I say so myself."

"Really? Well, let's try you out in another room, instead." She hastily added, "The dining room, I mean. Why don't you take the salad out there, along with the salad bowls. Oh, and would you pour some of the Pinot Noir? Wine glasses are on the table. Just half a glass for me, remember."

Ten minutes later they sat down to eat. They tried at first to keep their talk politely superficial, but it was no use. Inevitably, they were drawn to the subject that had brought them together in the first place. Despite what their mothers had once told them, their digestion did not suffer from their choice of dinner table conversation. They were not delicate flowers, either of them.

After a while, Muriel swallowed a mouthful of steak and salad, then said, "Your boss might actually have a point, you know."

Pacilio put down his wineglass. "And that point would be what?"

"Assuming, for the sake of argument, that this Peter Barbour is actually a victim of demonic possession, how are you going to find him? If there are warrants out for him now, why not leave it to the police? A state trooper somewhere will spot his license plate, pull him over, and that's that. Case closed, right?"

"Maybe," he said. "It could work out that way, and nobody would be happier about it than me. But Dirty Eugene –"

"That's the Jesuit? Father Brady?"

"Grady. Yeah, that's him. He warned me to keep in mind what I might be dealing with here."

"You mean the alleged demon? I wouldn't think you'd be likely to forget a thing like that."

"No, what he meant was for me not to forget what a demon is: a fallen angel."

"So?"

"So that means it was pretty damn smart to begin with. God wasn't making dummies in those days. And it's had a very, very long time to learn since then. I'm not at all sure that whoever is pushing Peter Barbour's buttons is dumb enough to go driving along the New York Thruway in broad daylight. And there's something else that's bothering me, too."

Muriel's mouth was full, so she made a "Go on" gesture with her fork.

"From what Carol Sefchek told us about what went down at the Holiday Inn, it seems pretty likely that the demon got some kind of marching orders from whoever appeared in that mirror."

Muriel nodded. "He certainly seemed purposeful all of a sudden, if Carol's account is to be believed."

"I'm inclined to believe it. What I keep thinking about is that this creature was told to go *somewhere* and do *something*. And whatever his purpose is, it's a pretty safe bet that it wasn't intended to help heal the sick, comfort the afflicted, or insure that Tom Green never makes another movie."

Muriel considered for a moment. "It makes sense, I guess. Always assuming you grant the basic premise of demonic possession."

Pacilio nodded. "Yes, assuming that."

"But that still doesn't explain how you can catch him if the State Police of three states can't. I mean, he could be anywhere. How do you know where to begin looking?"

"At the moment, I don't," he said grimly. "But I've kind of got an idea where I might find out."

She frowned. "Where on earth do you expect to get that sort of information?"

"Actually, I don't expect to. Get it on earth, I mean."

She looked at him in mock exasperation. "You know, if you were to explain that, I probably wouldn't have to tie you to the table and remove your pancreas with my steak knife," she said. "I mean, it could still go either way, but the odds would be in your favor if you stopped being cryptic and actually told me what the heck you were talking about."

"Well, I always try to go with the odds, when I can," he said with a smile. Then the smile vanished as he went on, "I'm trying to find someone who can conjure me up a demon."

———◆———

"I don't usually do this kind of thing," the woman said, carefully guiding the Mercedes through the dark residential streets. She was a little bit drunk.

"Of course not, I never thought you did." The lie came easily, as always.

"I mean, it's not like I don't try to be a good wife to him. For seventeen years I've been a good wife to him. But he leaves me alone so much. Him and his sales conferences."

"He neglects you terribly, doesn't he?" If she had not been drinking, she might have noticed the boredom in his voice. But perhaps it would have made no difference.

"The bastard. He's been neglecting me for too damn long. Even when he's home . . . he hasn't touched me in over a year. He's got something going on the side. A wife knows these things. I asked him once, 'Do they have secretaries at these sales conferences of yours?' And he gives me this look, you know? Like I'm a four-year-old and he's trying to explain why the sky is blue. 'Of *course* there are secretaries,' he says to me. 'After all, we have to have someone to take notes, and type up the minutes, and handle all the paperwork.' I bet he's got someone handling *his* paperwork, that's for sure. Some bottle-blonde with a silicone chest who wants to get out of the typing pool, the little whore."

"If that's true, then you're entitled to your revenge, aren't you?"

"That's right. That's exactly right. My revenge. And that would be you, wouldn't it, honey?"

"If you want me to be. I'm certainly willing to play the part, if it's required."

"Oh, you've got something I require, don't you worry about that, uh, I'm sorry, Paul, is it?"

He smiled indulgently at her. "Peter, actually."

"Sure, I remember now, Peter. Do you go by Pete?"

"Actually, my very oldest friends call me Asmo."

"Asmo? What the hell kind of a name is that?"

He laughed at the question, for some reason. "It's sort of a nickname, actually. Short for Asmodeus."

"Asmodeus? You mean like that guy, they did the movie about him, he was a musical genius back in the old days? Mozart?"

"You're thinking of *Amadeus* I believe. Sounds similar, I agree, but entirely different. You're right about Mozart, though. He *was* a genius. A very interesting fellow, too. Lots of soul, you might say."

"Well, you're an interesting fellow, too, Peter."

"I'm glad you find me so. I do try not to be dull."

"We're going to have fun, aren't we? While the cat's

away the mice will fuck their brains out, isn't that how it goes?" Raucous laughter followed.

"Yes, that's right," he told her after they had regained their composure. "We'll have fun that hasn't even been invented yet."

———◆———

Muriel Rojas put down her knife and fork and gave Pacilio her full attention. "In light of all that's happened, I won't ask you if you're kidding me. I am curious, though, about how you expect to find someone to conjure a demon. Is it fair to say that the Yellow Pages isn't too helpful for that kind of service?"

"I haven't actually checked, but it doesn't seem like the kind of thing the phone company would want to get involved in."

"So where do you look?" she said, returning to her meal.

"I'm going at it two ways. One is through Dirty Eugene."

"Does he do that? I thought you said he was an exorcist, which sounds like just the opposite of what you're looking for."

"No, Eugene doesn't conjure demons, but he knows it's possible. In fact, he tells me that he's seen it done – by another Jesuit, believe it or not."

"At this stage, I don't know what I believe anymore," she said. "So this priest, Dirty Eugene, is going to put you in touch with this other priest who knows how to conjure a demon?"

Pacilio shook his head. "No, that guy's dead. Apparently he was doing a conjuring once and fucked it up, somehow. Excuse my language."

"No, please, it's all right," she said. "Just because Mama conditioned me to talk like a nun doesn't mean I'm easily offended. Besides, in the ER you hear a constant stream of profanity. Some of it even comes from the patients."

Muriel ate the last bite of her steak, then said, "So if your Jesuit friend doesn't know anyone who conjures demons, how is he going to help you?"

"He's making phone calls, trying to find someone who *does* know. If there's somebody in the Jesuit order doing that stuff today, Eugene will find out. I just hope it doesn't take too long."

"You said you had two lines of inquiry. What's the other one?"

"My sister."

She stared at him for a moment. Then she said, with the air of someone who suspects her leg is being pulled, "You've got a sister who conjures demons."

Pacilio allowed himself a slight smile. "No, not as far as I know," he said. "That's probably one of the few things she *hasn't* tried. But I happened to remember this afternoon that she used to have a girlfriend who was some kind of a witch, and a witch may be just what I need."

"When you say 'girlfriend,'" Muriel began carefully, "do you mean someone she would go shopping with, or do you –"

"My sister's a lesbian," Pacilio said. "No need to tiptoe around it, although I appreciate your tact. I've had a lot of time to get used to the idea. She came out, to me, anyway, when she was sixteen, and that was –" He calculated briefly. "– twenty-two years ago." He shrugged. "She's my kid sister, I love her, and she happens to like girls. I'm used to it. She says she loves me too, despite what she calls my 'blatant heterosexual tendencies.'"

Muriel nodded. "Sounds like you two have a pretty good relationship."

"I think we do. I don't get to see her as often as I'd like to. She lives in San Francisco, and I don't get out to the West Coast very much. But she sends me copies of each of her books as they come out. She's kind of a cultural critic – especially those parts of the culture that deal with sex, and not just gay sex, either. She edits anthologies of erotica and writes some herself, as well. Real hot books, as we used to say when I was a teenager."

Muriel was looking at him with narrowed eyes. "What's your sister's name?"

"Sharon. To save embarrassing our parents, who were tight-ass Catholics from the word go, God rest them, she adopted a pen name: Sharon Purcell."

"Sharon Purcell? You're telling me that *Shari Sexpert is your sister?*"

Pacilio smiled at the expression on Muriel's face. "Yeah, I guess I am. Sounds like you're familiar with the name."

"Yeah, I guess I am," she gave back to him. "Excuse me just a minute, will you?"

She tossed her napkin onto the table and went into the living room. Pacilio thought he could hear her rummaging among the bookshelves.

Within a minute she was back, holding two trade-size paperback books. Pacilio recognized them at once. One was entitled *Smut: Erotic Tales for the New Millennium*. The other was *Pornography and the Sex-Positive Woman*. Each cover bore the name of Sharon Purcell.

Muriel sat down again and spent several seconds studying the author photo on the back of one of the books. "Yes, I can see the resemblance," she said, "especially in the eyes and nose. Your sister is a very attractive woman."

"Should I take that as an implied compliment, or are you saying I look like a girl, and a lesbian at that?"

She gave him a shrug combined with an enigmatic smile. "Make of it what you will." More seriously, she said, "But this is one heck of a surprise. I mean, I've read her books, and you're right, they're pretty hot stuff. And I've seen Shari Purcell on TV a couple of times, too. She was on one of those HBO "Real Sex" programs last year. That was the first time I'd ever seen her, apart from the jacket photo. And didn't she show up on Letterman during this past winter, sometime?"

"Yeah, she did. Called me up a week before and told me she was going to be on. She had a lot of fun doing that. So much, she told me, that they'll probably never invite her back again."

"I know what you mean. She was pretty wild." Shaking her head, Muriel said, "God, I still can't get over you being her brother."

"Why?" he asked. "All sorts of people have siblings. Even literary celebrities like Shari Sexpert."

"I know. It's just that she seems so uninhibited, so outrageous, and you . . . ." She let the thought trail off unfinished.

"And me, I'm so repressed, proper, and boring?" He didn't say it as if he were taking offense.

"Well, I wouldn't have put it exactly that way."

"Remember, Muriel, I work for the federal government. Civil service doesn't exactly encourage the fostering of free spirits, you know? Flamboyance is not regarded as a career-enhancing trait, except maybe at the National Endowment for the Arts."

"I know that, Michael. I didn't mean that you were boring. It's just that your sister is so . . . spectacular."

"That she is," he agreed. "But, you know, I've been known to be kind of spectacular myself, under the right circumstances." He was looking at Muriel very intently now.

She accepted his gaze, and sent something similar right back to him. "Spectacular, you say." There was a husky quality in her voice that he had not heard there before. Listening to it, he found himself getting an erection.

"Sometimes." He nodded without breaking eye contact. "Really, it all depends on the circumstances . . . and the company."

Muriel looked at him for a moment longer, then pushed her plate away and stood up. "Well, listen," she said, "since we're all finished here and everything, what do you say we adjourn to another room, the one with a bed in it, and we'll see if you can be spectacular all over me."

Without taking his eyes off her, Pacilio got to his feet as well. "Best idea I've heard this lifetime," he said.

———◆———

The Rev. Eugene Grady opened the French doors and walked haltingly out onto the second-floor terrace of the University of Scranton's Jesuit residence. His room upstairs, where he had been making telephone calls for the last two hours, was stuffy and warm, even with the window open. Dirty Eugene had a headache that he thought some fresh air would improve, and the terrace often picked up a nice breeze in the evening.

The old priest was frustrated. He had made more than a dozen phone calls in an effort to find out whether any Jesuit was still authorized by the Society to conjure a demon. More than half of the people he had spoken with had claimed not to know what he was talking about. That was unsurprising, in a way; it was the kind of thing that was kept under wraps and restricted to those few with a genuine "need to know." Neither Mother Church nor the Jesuit order was interested in having the world at large become aware that they sometimes did business with the Infernal.

But some of the priests he had called were, he knew, privy to the policy that allowed conjuring when dire necessity arose. To a man, they had denied knowledge of anyone who had the training and experience necessary to undertake this dangerous task.

Dirty Eugene suspected that at least two of them had been lying, but there was nothing he could do about it. He had been away too long, up on his godforsaken Bolivian mountain. Most of the Jebs he had known who had access to information about conjuring were either dead or caught in the unrelenting grip of senility. Grady was, in the words of a former President, out of the loop.

So he walked, and thought, and cursed under his breath, and thought some more. He was just reaching into his pocket for a cigarette when the evening breeze freshened, bringing with it a new, but strangely familiar, odor. It took Dirty Eugene several moments to realize that he was not smelling it with his nose. Then he knew.

In the Middle Ages, those entrusted to seek out the servants of Satan were often called "witch smellers." It was believed that such people had a special talent for sniffing out the Evil One and those who were in league with him.

A great deal of that business was nonsense. Most of the witch smellers were actually smelling nothing, because usually there was nothing to smell. The witch hysteria that gripped parts of Europe, as well as a certain village in colonial Massachusetts, was largely based on religious mania combined with a mundane desire to settle old scores. Most of those executed for witchcraft were almost certainly innocent of any crime, unless stupidity is a capital offense.

Dirty Eugene was aware of all of this. But he also knew that the real servants of Satan sometimes gave off a distinctive psychic manifestation that was perceived by some sensitive humans as an odor. The average person might smell nothing at all, while someone standing three feet away, if he was both attuned and experienced, might perceive a foul stench that said, as clearly as Shakespeare or Ray Bradbury ever did, "something wicked this way comes."

Father Eugene Grady stood on the terrace in the night and sniffed the breeze with more than just his nostrils, and what he smelled would have made the crematoriums of Bergen-Belsen seem fragrant by comparison. He sensed in the air the presence of something savage, and he was afraid.

"What the fuck is this? Is this the demon that Mikey is after? What is it doing here, for God's sake?

The night brought him no answers, and so he headed back to his room, which was warm and stuffy and, mercifully, received little of the outside breeze. He did not walk slowly, nor did he look over his shoulder, in the very real fear of seeing what might be coming up behind him.

Justin Gustainis

Chapter 12

Michael Pacilio awoke from a light doze. He considered closing his eyes again and letting himself fall into the deep sleep that his body and mind craved, but then he remembered the phone calls he had made to his sister and to Dirty Eugene Grady. Slowly and carefully, so as not to disturb his companion, he eased himself into a sitting position on the edge of the bed.

His feet had just touched the floor when Muriel Rojas' voice said softly from behind him, "It's all right, I'm awake."

Pacilio looked over his shoulder at her. She lay on her stomach, her long hair in a tangle. Her nude body seemed to glow in the light from the bedside lamp, although some of that may have been due to the sheen of perspiration that was still drying on her. Her face was turned toward him, and the gray eyes seemed even larger than usual. "Sorry if I woke you," Pacilio said.

"You didn't," she said. "I was just lying here, treating myself to a mental replay of the last couple of hours. Not as much fun as the real thing, of course, but still quite pleasant." She smiled at him, and there was affection there that he had not seen before. "And was it good for you, too?"

"Isn't that supposed to be my line?"

"I suppose so, if you're a traditionalist. Are you?"

He shook his head. "No. Once, maybe, but not any more. Well, just in case it wasn't obvious: yes, Muriel, it was *very* good for me."

"I'm glad. I wanted it to be, but with first times . . . well, you know."

"Yeah, I do. But not this time."

"No, not this time." She turned over on her side so that she was facing him. Squinting suddenly, she said, "What's that in your armpit? A birthmark?"

"No, it's a tattoo showing my blood type, A-positive. I had it done when I was in the service. A lot of guys in my unit did."

"But why go to the trouble? Didn't you all wear – what do they call them – dog tags containing that kind of information?"

Pacilio shrugged. "Dog tags get lost sometimes. And they can be noisy, too, so we didn't always wear 'em."

"Silence is that important?"

"It was, back then. I let myself get a little noisy sometimes, these days. You might have noticed that earlier."

That brought out a smile. "Yes, you're very –" She searched for the word. "– intense. I like that."

"Thank you," he said. "And you're very verbal."

"Sure you don't mean 'oral'?"

"I had noticed that, too. No, I mean you like to talk."

She lowered her eyes and then, to Pacilio's amazement she actually blushed – and it did not stop at her face. His mind flashed to the memory of the nude Muriel, on her hands and knees on the bed with Pacilio standing behind her, the two of them coupling in a posture beloved by canines everywhere. He heard again in his mind Murial Rojas' voice, coming to him through her clenched teeth but loud and clear nonetheless in an unending X-rated litany that had gone on for most of their lovemaking.

Muriel returned her gaze to Pacilio's face and said softly, "I'm kind of embarrassed about that."

Pacilio's neck was getting stiff from looking over his shoulder, so he turned around and knelt on the bed, facing her. "Why embarrassed?" he asked. "If you can't talk dirty in bed, where *can* you talk dirty? Anyway, I found it quite a turn-on."

"Well, I'm glad of that. But it makes me sound so... I don't know... slutty, I guess."

"I hate to keep repeating myself, but if you can't be slutty in bed ...."

She smiled into his eyes. "You're very sweet. And a very good, uh, screw, too."

"My God," Pacilio said in wonderment. "You really can't do it, can you? You can't talk dirty, except in the throes."

She nodded. "That's pretty much true. When I'm aroused, I seem to want to talk that way, and doing so serves to heighten my excitement, as well. After all, a great deal of excitement, sexual and otherwise, comes from the transgression of boundaries."

"Anybody ever tell you that you talk like a doctor?"

"As a matter of fact, yes." She grinned at him. "But not in bed." After their shared laughter subsided, she went on, "Anyway, the thing with boundaries is –"

"I think I get it," Pacilio said. "It's exciting for people to do stuff they know they shouldn't. Your mother taught you that you shouldn't say dirty words, so it's exciting when you do. And if you only allow yourself to use them when you're having sex, then that probably adds to the excitement, too."

She looked at him, her head tilted a little to one side. "You're not just a pretty face, are you?"

"Some say I'm not even that. I met a woman recently who told me that I look like a lesbian."

"I didn't mean it that way, and you know it. Anyway," she said, reaching over with one hand and gently touching him with a fingertip, "I never met a lesbian with one of these."

"Really? And have you met a lot of lesbians?"

"No, not a lot. A few. I understand that some people at the hospital think I *am* one."

"I think I've had ample proof of your heterosexuality, lady." Pacilio swallowed hard. "In fact, most people would probably consider what you're doing right now as blatantly heterosexual behavior."

"Do you want me to stop?" Her index finger was moving, back and forth, back and forth.

"I didn't say that. But, the thing is, I do need to check with my motel, to see if Sharon or Dirty Eugene have called back. It's kind of important. Mind?"

"Of course not," Muriel said, removing her hand. "I must say, though, I admire your dedication to duty, considering the way that thing is throbbing."

"I was just planning to make a phone call or two," Pacilio said, "not join a monastery."

"Imagine my relief. Okay, listen, you can use this phone," she said, indicating one on the nightstand next to her, "or, if you want privacy, there's one in the living room."

"Privacy seems a pretty dead issue as far as you and me are concerned," he said. "You already know more about what's going on than my boss does, so you might as well stick around for the next episode. Scoot over a little, will you?"

Sitting on the other side of the bed, Pacilio called the Holiday Inn and learned that he had received calls from both a Ms. Purcell and a Father Grady. Pacilio thanked the desk clerk and hung up. Then he began tapping in Sharon's number.

Muriel was kneeling behind him on the bed, her breasts pressed up against his back. She murmured in his ear, "Was your sister actually receiving oral sex from another woman while you were talking to her on the phone earlier?"

"She said she was," he replied absently, "and, knowing Shari, I believe it."

The phone began ringing at the other end. Pacilio was only dimly aware that Muriel had disengaged herself and was leaving the bed. He waited through five rings, listened to the answering machine come on.

"Hi, this is Shari Sexpert," the recording began, followed by the rest of the message. As soon as he heard the "beep," Pacilio said, "It's Mike, Shari. Pick up, will you?"

A moment later, his sister's voice came on the line, saying, "Hi, Michael, I wondered if I'd hear back from you tonight."

"Well, like I told you earlier, it's kind of urgent. Were you able to locate Sarah?"

The nude form of Dr. Muriel Rojas appeared in Pacilio's field of vision. She had come around the bed and was standing directly in front of him. Then, in one fluid motion, she dropped to her knees.

"Yes, I think so," Sharon said. "I found somebody

who told me that she was in Denver as of two months ago, working with some kind of Wicca Center."

"Denver? Shit. I was hoping for someplace I could get to faster."

Kneeling between his legs, Muriel Rojas was suddenly competing for his attention in a very effective way.

Pacilio said "Hold on," then put his hand over the phone and asked, softly, "What the hell do you think you're doing?"

"The technical term is 'fellatio,'" Muriel said, "although, if you like, you can call it 'sibling rivalry.'"

Then she began to devour him in earnest.

Having no choice, Pacilio went back to his phone call. "Do you get an address in Denver?" he asked.

"No, the friend who told me about Sarah didn't know where she's living, apart from the city. Michael, is someone there with you?"

"That was the room service waiter. I got hungry and ordered a sandwich. It came quicker than I thought. The food, I mean."

"Well, anyway, I wasn't able to get an address for dear Sarah, but I'm pretty sure she's still in Denver. I called Directory Assistance to see if she has a phone under her name. They told me the number is unlisted – which is way different from saying there's no such person in the system."

"Yeah, I know."

"I assume you have the federal clout to shake Sarah's Denver address out of the telephone company."

"Probably. There's lots of ways to do it, once you know what city you're . . . dealing with."

"Michael, are you all right?"

"Yeah, sure, just tired, I guess."

"You sound like you're in pain. Did you get yourself hurt in the service of Uncle Sam again?"

"It's just my head . . . headache. Bad one."

"Poor baby. I get those sometimes. Are you taking anything for it?"

"I've got a doctor helping me with it. I think it'll be okay soon . . . pretty soon."

"All right, then I'd better let you go. Good luck in finding Sarah. And if you succeed, don't bother giving her my love – the bitch and I did *not* part friends."

"Okay, sure. Thanks, Shar. I'll get in touch when this job is over and tell you what I can."

"Terrific. Oh, and Michael?"

"What?"

"Be sure to have your lady friend wipe up the jism when you're finished. It makes such a mess for the hotel maid, once it's dried – or so I've been told."

Shari Sexpert's laughter pealed from the telephone receiver as Pacilio hung up, three seconds before exploding into Muriel Rojas' warm and hungry mouth.

———◆———

"What time is it?" he asked lazily.

"Huh? I dunno. Late." She had been dozing.

"Could you be a little more specific? The clock is on your side, remember?"

"All right, all right." She rolled over and looked. "Twenty after two – although this thing runs a little fast, so it's probably more like a quarter after."

"As you say, it's late." He stretched luxuriously on the silk sheets. "So tell me, what would that husband of yours say if he walked in here right now?"

"Don't worry yourself, honey. He won't be back until day after tomorrow. And he never comes home early from one of his 'sales conferences.' Not as long as there's bosses to suck up to and bimbos to bang."

"But what if he did come back early, just this once?"

She chuckled deep in her throat. "Richard? He'd probably have a coronary if he walked in and found us lying here – buck naked, the bed a fucking mess, and me with come leaking out of every orifice ... well, you did leave my belly button alone, I'll give you credit for that much."

"Well, if you'd like, I could probably manage –"

She slapped him gently on the thigh. "Don't even think about it, you maniac. My God, I don't think I've had a working over like that since eleven years ago."

"Oh? And what was that happy occasion?"

"Back in the days when Richard was still interested in trying to spice up our marriage, we went to a group scene at the house of these people we'd met at the country club."

"You mean an orgy? How charming!"

"That's not quite the word I'd use for it, but it was interesting, all right. I would have thought that kind of party would be for couples only, you know? But, along with the seven or eight couples, there were two women, I think, and four or five men who'd come stag. Do people still say that – 'going stag' for arriving without a date?"

"Not where I come from."

"Well, anyway, there was a surplus of guys at this little soiree. I didn't think too much of it at the time, but a couple of hours later I found myself pulling a train for six of them. Mind you, I had been drinking quite a bit."

"I'm not familiar with that expression – 'pulling a train.'"

She chuckled again. "Spend most of your time in a refined atmosphere, do you?"

"I wouldn't say that exactly, no. But I don't think I've come across that particular term before."

"I first heard it in college, back in the Sixties. Some of those fraternity parties . . . well, anyway, 'pulling a train' in my case meant that these six guys wanted to fuck me, and I let them, one after another, with everybody else watching."

"And did you enjoy yourself?"

"As a matter of fact, I did. And do you know what part of it I liked the most?"

"Yes," he said.

"Richard had to watch," she went on, heedless of his comment. "I mean, I was pretty sure he was going to poop out early, and he did. He threw a fuck into this chubby little redhead – he didn't think I was watching, but I was – and that was it, as usual, for one-shot Richard. He sat around watching the others, but he didn't take part in the rest of the festivities. I, however, took part quite a lot. And when I put on my little exhibition with those six guys, well, I thought Richard was going to *die*."

"But surely, as your husband, he could assert certain rights . . . ."

"And make a scene? No, not Richard the Chicken-Hearted. He takes more shit from people, me included, just to avoid a fuss that somebody might notice. He has his mother to thank for that, take my word for it – you won't find a bigger tight-ass than Mama this side of the Vatican. But, you know what? If he had stood up right then and said to me, 'Jessica, enough of this bullshit! Get your tawdry ass up from there and get dressed right now. We don't belong here, and we're leaving!' If he had just said that to me, if he had just told me to stop acting like a fucking whore and come home with my husband, well I'd have done it in a heartbeat."

"But he didn't."

"No," she said, and that one word held more pain and loss than it should be possible to contain in a single syllable.

"And that was all of eleven years ago, you say."

"Eleven years, four months, give or take a week."

"And yet you describe it as if it were yesterday."

"I guess there isn't a day that goes by that I don't think about some part of it or other."

"Your own private Hell, you might say."

"Oh, fuck that shit. Self-pity's for losers. And how about you, studly? Don't you have any private vices or torments?"

"Torments? I suppose I've known a few over the years, although on that score I've found that it's far better to give than to receive. And as for vices, well I should think I've tried them all, with one or two exceptions."

"Anybody who can fuck like you shouldn't have much trouble finding company for any kind of vice at all. Which ones?"

"Which what?"

"Which vices haven't you tried?"

He thought, or pretended to. "Well, there's necrophilia, of course."

"I don't think I know that one, but it sounds dirty."

"Dirty enough, I would think. It refers to sexual relations with the dead."

She laughed incredulously. "You're kidding me, aren't you? People *do* that?"

"Some people do. An acquaintance of mine told me once how interesting it was to do a before-and-after comparison with a sexual partner. To see if she were improved by death, as it were."

"You actually met somebody who was *into* that? How utterly *creepy*."

"Oh, he had been 'into' many things in his time. His name was Caligula."

"Sounds Italian."

"Yes, he was – Roman, to be precise. Listen, what's the time now?

"Almost ten of three."

"Are there any service stations still operating at this hour, do you think?"

"In town, probably not. Off the highway there are some that are open twenty-four hours, and the turnpike rest areas never close. But what do you care about gas stations? Back at the bar, you said you don't even have a car."

"So I did. But I think I know where I can get a good deal on one." He cracked his knuckles, then flexed the long, powerful fingers. "Well, time grows short, which is a pity, in some ways. We could have shared some really stimulating experiences . . . but I have a rather important matter to attend to, and if I don't take care of it soon, well, there'll just be Hell to pay. Still, I *would* like to find out if he was right, before I go."

"You lost me on that last curve, Peter. Find out if *who* was right?"

"My old Roman friend, Caligula."

There was fear in her voice now. "Right about . . . what?"

"Comparisons."

And then he was on her, like Judgement Day.

———◆———

Muriel Rojas sat back on her haunches and looked up at Pacilio. He thought she appeared smug, like the cat that had been at the cream – an image that was encouraged by what was running down from one corner of her mouth.

"I'm tempted to say, 'You shouldn't have done that,'" Pacilio murmured, "but most of the evidence of how I really felt is probably just now making its way down past your tonsils."

"Well, it's nice to know that hypocrisy is not one of your vices," she said with a grin.

"Still, I wish you had picked another time to be impulsive. Sharon is never, *ever*, going to let me live that down."

Muriel shrugged, which caused her naked breasts to jiggle very attractively. "Why should she get to have all the fun with you stuck in the role of straight man?"

"Well, I am, after all, a straight man."

"A fact for which my gratitude knows no bounds," she said. "Listen, will you be offended if I excuse myself to go brush my teeth? The aftertaste of that stuff is much less pleasant than the process of acquiring it."

"Sure, go ahead. I'll give Dirty Eugene a call, and see if he's found me somebody closer than Denver who might know how to conjure a demon."

"Good luck," she said, and padded off toward the bathroom.

Pacilio started tapping out numbers. It was late, but he knew that Dirty Eugene Grady was an erratic sleeper and as likely to be awake as not.

The phone at the other end was picked up midway through the first ring. That fact was enough all by itself to send alarm bells jangling in the back of Pacilio's mind, even before he heard the fear in the old priest's voice.

"*Mikey?*"

"Eugene, what's wrong? What happened?"

"*He's here. The motherfucker is here.*"

With an effort, Pacilio made his voice remain calm and reasonable. He knew one thing already – the Rev. Eugene Grady was stone cold sober, and that frightened Pacilio as much as anything the priest had just said.

"Eugene, listen, I want you to bear with me. I'm going to ask what are probably some very stupid questions, but I want you to put up with it and just answer me, okay?"

Without waiting for a response, Pacilio went on, calmly, patiently, the way you talk to a retarded child, or a drunk, or someone teetering at the edge of panic. "When you say 'he,' I assume you mean Peter Barbour."

"That's not its name. This Barbour is only its vessel."

"Okay, I understand. But that's who you mean, right?"

"Yes, of course, who'd you think I was talking about, the Mormon fucking Tabernacle Choir?"

"Okay, fine, I said these were dumb questions, I know they are. Just indulge me a little more, all right? Now, when you say, 'He's here,' . . . ." A sudden thought caused

Pacilio's pulse rate, already elevated, to start racing. "Eugene, tell me you're not looking at him right now."

It only took the priest a second to reply, but to Pacilio the wait seemed like an hour on the rack. "Bite your fucking tongue, Mikey," Dirty Eugene snapped. "Did you actually think I'd be calmly having a telephone conversation with you if that fucking thing was in the room with me?"

Hasn't been all that calm so far, Pacilio thought, but the rush of adrenaline was starting to ease off. "So, where is he?"

"Somewhere close, I can't say exactly. Probably in the city somewhere."

"How do you know? Something on the news about more killings?"

"No, I haven't seen the news. I don't need to, not for this."

"Then, what? Come on, Eugene, talk to me, will you?"

Dirty Eugene sighed into the phone. "Look, sometimes when you've spent time dealing with demons, you develop a kind of sixth sense about them, something that grows out of one of your other senses. With me, it's an odor, very distinctive. Well, I smelled it tonight, Mikey, and, believe me, it ain't Chanel Number Five. There's no mistaking it for anything else."

"All right, assume that whatever you smelled tonight is a reliable indicator of the presence of a demon. How do you know it's the same one we're interested in?"

"Because visitations by the Infernal Ones are pretty rare, thanks be to God. For reasons known only to the Most High, demons don't get to cross over to our side very often, at all – just as well, considering how much havoc they usually cause. Let us both sincerely hope that there isn't more than one of those things running around the Eastern United States these days."

"Okay," Pacilio said. "Say that it is Barbour, or whatever is possessing him. How do you know he's in Scranton? If you're sensing him at a distance, how do you know the distance isn't a hundred miles?"

"Because I *do*," Dirty Eugene said impatiently. "Look, it's hard to explain, but the sense doesn't work at long range. All right, I may have overstated things a bit when I said he was in town. I suppose he could be a little farther away, Carbondale, maybe, or Wilkes-Barre, someplace like that. But I tell you this: the son of a bitch is close, no error."

"All right, I believe you. I guess I have to. The next question is, what do we do with the information?"

"What do we do? We find the bastard, that's what we fucking do! We find the human host and hog-tie him, so I can perform the ritual and send this thing back where it came from."

"Fine, great, but just how are we supposed to do that? Scranton's got, what, about 100,000 population?"

"Yeah, more or less."

"And you're telling me that he might be as far away as Wilkes-Barre, which means, even if he stays put, he could be anywhere in the Wyoming Valley, right? Old Forge, Pittston, Wyoming, Nanticoke – Christ, I forget half of those little burgs after all this time. But it's a lot of territory, and a hell of a lot of people, Eugene."

"Well, Jesus Christ, Mikey, you're supposed to be the hotshot federal agent, aren't you? Put out an alert on this Barbour, turn out the boys in blue from here to Hazelton – can't you do that?"

Pacilio sighed. "No, Eugene, I can't."

"Well, why *not*, for God's sake? Hasn't this creature killed enough people yet to be worth some serious attention from the law? How much higher does the pile of corpses have to get?"

"It's not a question of body count, Eugene. Believe me, I want this bastard as much as you do, but there are two problems. One is, just what am I going to tell the Scranton P.D., the Wilkes Barre P.D., and the Chiefs of Police of all those little towns in between, not to mention the State Police and the FBI field office? 'Calling all cars, calling all cars. Be on the lookout for Peter Barbour, serial killer and possible demonic possession victim. He is believed to be in your area, because the Reverend Eugene Grady, S.J. *smelled* him.' How well do you think *that* would go over?"

"Well, Jesus, can't you just –"

"Wait," Pacilio said. "I haven't told you the other problem yet, and it's a dandy: I've been taken off the investigation."

There was silence on the line for several seconds. When Dirty Eugene finally spoke, his voice sounded tired and old. "When did this happen?"

"This afternoon, when I talked to McGraw on the phone. It's not me, personally, who's being told to take a hike. The FBI is asserting its right to the turf, and McGraw had no choice but to agree. I'm supposed to go home tomorrow."

"So that's it, then?" Dirty Eugene asked dully. "You go back to Washington, I go back to teaching, and we can just read about the possessed Mr. Barbour's future exploits in the paper?"

"Fuck, no. It means I'm going on leave, beginning tomorrow. I've got plenty accumulated, about five weeks' worth. But I'll be strictly on my own, with no official status and no way to call on other agencies for assistance. And that's the main reason your 'Calling all cars' scenario just ain't gonna happen."

"All right, we can't approach it that way," Dirty Eugene said, with more life in his voice now. "So what the fuck *can* we do? I can't believe the Lord sent me this sign of the demon's presence and there's no way we can use it."

After a few seconds, Pacilio said, "There's got to be some importance attached to the fact that Barbour is back in the Wyoming Valley. He was there two nights ago, then went on to Albany. Now he's doubled back, or so it seems. I wonder if this ties in with the message he received through that motel mirror?"

"Message? What message? Is that why you were asking me about mirrors earlier today?"

"Yeah, it was," Pacilio said, and told him about Carol Sefchek's account of the apparition in the mirror at the Holiday Inn.

When Pacilio finished, Dirty Eugene said pensively, "So it's been given instructions of some kind."

"Sounds that way. I wonder if those orders involve something in the Valley, or if he's just passing through on his way somewhere else. Listen, Eugene, would your sixth sense or whatever it is pick him up if he were just going by – maybe driving south on Route 81?"

"I don't know, Mikey. This knack of mine didn't come with a book of instructions. I've never picked up something in transit before, to the best of my knowledge, but that doesn't mean it can't happen." Dirty Eugene snorted in disgust. "Maybe I should have been on top of the University library with a pair of binoculars – I might have sensed the son of a bitch's car as he went by on the highway and waved to him, maybe made the Sign of the Cross in his direction as a farewell gesture."

"I was just – wait, what did you say?" Pacilio's voice was suddenly tense.

"Don't pay that crap any mind, Mikey. Old farts like me have to get cranky sometimes. It's in our contract."

"No, you were saying something about spotting him on the highway . . . . Holy Shit, Eugene, I think I know what he's doing in Scranton."

"And what's that, Sherlock Holmes?"

"*The bastard needs a car.*"

———◆———

The thing that was controlling Peter Barbour almost got away cleanly. It knew that Jessica Ackerman's husband would not return for two days to find the little surprise that had been left for him, and that would be far too late to cause interference with The Task. By her own account, the late Jessica Ackerman had no children who might pay a surprise visit, and no close friends among the neighbors.

Her violated corpse should remain undiscovered for more than forty-eight hours, and, more important, her car would not be missed for at least that long – which was more than long enough.

As it backed the maroon Mercedes out of the Ackermans' garage, the demon Asmodeus was well pleased. Everything about its sojourn in this dimension had been so much *fun*.

And the real amusement had not even started yet.

———————◆———————

Jessica Ackerman had told the truth to the demon Asmodeus, but not the whole truth. She had, as she'd said, no children, and it was true that among her neighbors she could claim no close friends.

But she did have an enemy.

Her adversary's name was Monica Ackerman, and she was Jessica's mother-in-law. Monica had considered Jessica a stuck-up bitch from their first meeting, and the passage of seventeen years had not mellowed her views.

Whenever Richard Ackerman went out of town on business, (*working himself into an early grave, and for what – to keep a respectable roof over that ungrateful sow's head*) his mother took it upon herself to keep her eye on Richard's house, which was directly across the street from her own. She especially tried to keep an eye on Richard's worthless slut of a wife.

The surveillance had always been futile. Whatever wild oats Jessica Ackerman sowed in her husband's absence (and Monica was convinced that those oats were plentiful), she had been too clever to sow them in her own home.

Until now.

Despite her 68 years, Monica Ackerman's eyesight remained excellent. She had seen the Mercedes return last night about 10:30, and she had noted with great interest the presence of a passenger in the front seat. Whenever the garage door went up, a bright interior light came on automatically. Thus, Monica Ackerman had no trouble determining that the passenger was a slim man with dark hair, a man who was definitely *not* blond, portly Richard Ackerman.

Monica had been equal parts outraged and intrigued by this turn of events – so much so that she had stayed up all night watching from her darkened living room. At her age, she didn't sleep very much, anyway.

She had grimly observed the lights burning upstairs in her son's home until well into the wee hours, and she had also been watching at 3:20 a.m. when the man had come out to the garage alone, raised the door, and driven away in Jessica's Mercedes.

At first, Monica Ackerman thought the man would be returning soon. *He probably went off looking for one of those all-night drugstores. Maybe his girlfriend Jessica wants some ice cream. Or maybe she sent him to buy some more of those rubbers, so they can have another nice, safe screw in my son's bed.* But the man did not return, and the house across the way remained as silent as a tomb.

At about 5:15, the blackness outside began to give way to the gray of incipient dawn, and Monica Ackerman decided that enough was definitely enough. She stormed upstairs, flung her nightgown onto her still-made bed, and began to get dressed. Less then ten minutes later, the light of the new morning found her crossing the street in a beeline to her son's house. Monica would confront Richard's whore of a wife. She would lay out the evidence of betrayal as dispassionately as one of those lawyers on television. She would listen to the denials, followed by the tearful pleas not to tell Richard of the whore's transgressions. She would promise to consider keeping silent, if the whore would take a vow of faithfulness and, incidentally, apologize to her mother-in-law for all the slights and insults the whore had inflicted on her over the past seventeen years. Monica would then promise to keep mum about the whole sorry episode. Then, as soon as Richard returned home, Monica would blow the whistle on his wife's slutty ways and wait for him to make the only honorable choice open to him: departure, divorce, and return to the bosom of his mother, the only woman who had never betrayed his love.

Monica Ackerman rang the bell of her son's home, waited two seconds, then rang again. The whore must be sleeping soundly after her night's exertions. Monica gouged the button with her thumb, as if digging into Jessica's eyeball, and kept it there for well over a minute, but there was still no response from within. She tried the door: locked, and she had no key. But there was a pantry door around back, and Richard had complained more than once that the whore kept forgetting to snap the lock on it.

Monica walked with a determined stride to the back of the house. To her great relief, the whore had been careless yet again – the pantry door was unlocked.

She was familiar with the inside of her son's house, despite the whore's reluctance to invite her over more than once or twice a month. The pantry led into the kitchen, which was dim and still, as was the adjoining dining room. There were no lights on anywhere on the ground floor, but enough daylight was seeping in past partly drawn curtains to allow Monica to see where she was going, which was to the stairway. At its base, she found the light switch and flipped it on, illuminating the stairs as well as the upper and lower landings.

Monica Ackerman ascended those stairs like Patton crossing the Rhine. Once she reached the second floor landing, four rapid steps brought her to the bedroom that her son and the whore slept in. The door was slightly ajar. Monica, ever mindful of propriety, knocked first – but she was careful to strike hard enough for the bedroom door to swing open under the impetus of her fist. The first of a planned series of angry denunciations on her lips, Monica Ackerman took a deep breath to guarantee a good, loud volume for her overture, and strode into the room.

The tall, skinny police officer with the prominent Adam's apple came out of the front door of Richard Ackerman's home and went over to the patrol car that was parked at the curb just behind the ambulance. The red lights atop both vehicles were flashing. Up and down the street, neighbors, mostly women, stood on their porches or doorsteps and watched.

The policeman opened the passenger side door of the cruiser and got in. He took the microphone of the police radio off its hook and brought it to his mouth. "Dispatch, this is thirty-four."

A moment later, a tinny-sounding female voice replied, "Go ahead, three-four."

"This is Patterson. Let me talk to Sergeant Builder."

"Wait one, three-four."

Half a minute or so later, a male voice came through the radio's speaker. "This is Builder."

"It's Patterson, Sarge. Me and Ruane are on that 911 call from 834 Linden."

"Yeah, Patterson, what've you got?"

"We have two female DOAs in an upstairs bedroom. One's a female Caucasian, age early to mid- forties, nude, lying in bed. Extensive bruising on throat and neck, the EMTs say probable death by strangulation, but that's preliminary. There's evidence of recent sexual activity. In plain English, there's half-dried come all over the place."

"Hope that's not 'cause you got all excited and did something you shouldn't, Patterson." The voice was dry.

"Not me, Sarge, I like my broads still breathing. But I'm keeping an eye on Ruane, just in case he's got any necro tendencies. Okay, the other DOA is also female Caucasian, late sixties or early seventies. This one's fully clothed, sitting on the floor with her back against a wall. No obvious cause of death, but it looks like heart failure. She had a phone in her lap, so there's a good chance she's the one made the 911 call, before she checked out. Oh, and there's some weird shit written on the walls in what looks like lipstick."

"What do you mean by 'weird shit?'" the Duty Sergeant asked.

"Well, like, over the bed it reads, 'Welcome home, honey!' or something like that."

"Okay, Patterson, I'll get on the horn to Homicide and get some detectives out there. Keep civilians out of the crime scene in the meantime, copy?"

"Got it, Sarge: will follow SOP for crime scenes."

"Yeah, and, listen: is there a car parked there, in front of the house or in the garage?"

"Negative, Sarge. Nothing's parked near the house, and I can see into the garage from here. *Nada.*"

"The woman who made the 911 call said something like, 'He took the Mercedes.' Could be a reference to the perp. While you're waiting for Homicide, check with the neighbors and see if you can put a name on one or both of your DOAs. When you get the IDs, contact Motor Vehicles to see if there's a Mercedes registered to either one of them. If there is, get the model, color, and the tag number. Maybe we can nail this guy before he gets too far."

"Will do, Sarge."

"Builder out."

Officer Kevin Patterson replaced the microphone in its clip and carefully levered his lean 6'3" frame out of its cramped position in the patrol car. As he bent backward to stretch his spine a little, he looked up at the sky through the overhanging elm trees. The sun was well up now, and not a cloud could be seen.

It was shaping up to be a beautiful day.

Chapter 13

McGraw took a swallow of pineapple juice and placed the glass on Kimura's desk, taking care to use the coaster provided. Kimura had taken the trouble to learn the preferred beverage of each of his department heads, and to keep a supply of each in his office refrigerator. McGraw figured the least he could do was avoid leaving rings on the furniture.

Kimura sat behind his desk, a half-empty glass of tonic water in front of him. He looked at McGraw expectantly, as if to say, "You requested this meeting, and at very short notice, so let's get on with it." He was, of course, far too polite ever to say such a thing out loud.

"There have been developments," McGraw said, "involving that awful business in Fairfax."

Kimura's eyebrows went up in surprise, then quickly came back down as his eyes narrowed. "It was my impression, Mac, from what you told me yesterday, that the Fairfax investigation was out of our hands, at the very explicit invitation of the FBI."

McGraw nodded. "It was a little more than an invitation, unless I misunderstood Special Agent Pennypacker's use of the phrase 'obstruction of justice.' But you're right, Kim. That's what I told you, because that's what I believed at the time. But, as I said, there have been ... developments."

Kimura sighed. "This is all very Pavlovian, Mac. In the space of a few moments, you have conditioned me to regard the word 'developments' with the same emotions that General Tojo probably experienced whenever he heard the name 'MacArthur.'"

Both men laughed, then Kimura said, "I believe you've done enough foreshadowing, Mac. I am adequately prepared to receive bad, if not disastrous, news. Out with it."

"I'm not sure if it's disastrous, but it sure is strange," McGraw told him. "For starters, I got a phone call at home this morning, just after 7:00, from a guy who identified himself as Father Eugene Grady, S.J., calling from Scranton, Pennsylvania. Said he's a friend of Mike Pacilio's."

Kimura produced a small smile. "Somehow, I've never pictured Mr. Pacilio in the company of members of the clergy."

"I think Father Grady may have been one of Pacilio's professors in college," McGraw replied. "Grady didn't say so, but it ties in with something Pacilio said to me on the phone a couple of days ago."

"And what did Father Grady want with you?"

"He said that Pacilio wanted me to know that Peter Barbour was loose in Scranton."

Kimura just stared at him. "My God," he said, finally. "And how did Mr. Pacilio come by this information?"

"The priest didn't say. He did tell me that Pacilio would be in touch with me soon to explain everything."

"An explanation that you await as eagerly as I do, I'm sure," Kimura said. "Did Father Grady give you an address where Barbour could be found?"

"No, he didn't. In fact, he said that Barbour had

probably already left the area, for parts unknown."

Kimura frowned. "So the information, if that's what it was, had no real value?"

"I'm not sure. He also told me that Barbour had apparently killed a woman in Scranton, and probably stolen her car, as well."

"And did he come by this intelligence using the same undisclosed method?" Kimura was beginning to suspect that his time was being wasted, and impatience was starting to erode his usually courtesy. "A Ouija board, perhaps? Or maybe he called one of those '900' numbers and spoke with a 'certified professional psychic.' Either way, I assume he was unable to provide you with the name of the alleged victim, or any specific information about her supposedly missing automobile."

"Well, actually, he did a little better than that," McGraw said, and dipped two fingers into his shirt pocket to produce a slip of paper. Glancing at it, he said, "The murdered woman, according to Father Grady, is one Jessica Ackerman, age 43. The car's a maroon 2001 Mercedes SEL, Pennsylvania license number ANR 773."

Kimura dropped his eyes to the blotter on his desk. After several seconds, he said, "Please accept my apologies, Mac. Such rudeness on my part is quite inexcusable."

"Think nothing of it," McGraw said. "This whole business is pretty bizarre – it's got us all acting hinky."

"Without a doubt," Kimura said. "But how did the priest come by this information concerning Peter Barbour? Was it on the radio in Scranton, or in the morning paper, or what?"

"He got it from a radio, but not in the sense you mean. At Pacilio's suggestion, Grady says, he stayed up all night monitoring the police radio band with a scanner – you know, one of those things that automatically goes up and down all of the wavelengths used by police, fire fighters, ambulance crews, and so on, and lets you listen in?"

"Yes, I know," Kimura said. "A neighbor of mine has one. He listens to it at night when he can't get to sleep."

"Well, Grady told me that another priest, who has a room down the hall from him, had one of those scanners. So Grady borrowed it and started listening. Said he hit pay dirt around 6:30 this morning."

"When the police discovered the murder of this woman, I assume."

"Right. As Grady began to pick up the details, he says, it looked more and more like our boy."

"What sort of details, dare I ask?"

"Nothing too grotesque this time," McGraw said, "assuming you use Fairfax as your standard for measurement. But it was still pretty distinctive. The woman, prior to being strangled, was sexually assaulted – 'copiously,' in Father Grady's words, by which I gather there was semen all over the place. Also, there was writing on the wall, in lipstick again. Something like 'Welcome back, honey,' which was presumably intended for the woman's husband, or boyfriend, or whatever. That would seem to clinch it."

"Yes, so it would," Kimura said softly.

"And then there's that business with the stolen car."

"Why is that important?"

"Because Pacilio apparently told Grady, before this murder was discovered, that Barbour was probably looking to pick up a new set of wheels. After the attack on the hooker in Albany, Barbour's car was hotter than El

Paso chili. Pacilio figured that Barbour was planning to dump that Toyota of his in favor of something that wasn't on the hot sheet of every cop in a three-state area."

"But the police now know about the stolen Mercedes, so Barbour has gained nothing," Kimura said.

"True," McGraw said. "I assume he thought the murder, and the theft of the car, wouldn't be reported for a while, which would give him the chance to put some miles on that Mercedes without anybody official looking for it. But something went wrong, apparently, and the Scranton cops got on to the murder soon after it happened. I don't have all the details on that, but I can probably get them later, if you want."

"We'll see." Kimura thought for a moment. "So the Scranton police know that this stolen car is being driven by a man suspected of murder," he said. "Do they know that the person they seek is Peter Barbour?"

"They probably do by now. I called Pennypacker more than an hour ago, and he should have passed on the information to the Scranton police, as well as the Pennsylvania State Police, by now."

"Now *there's* a conversation I'm glad to have missed," Kimura said with a thin smile. "Did Agent Pennypacker threaten to clap you in irons for interfering in his investigation?"

"Not in so many words, no. He was kind of curious as to how I came by the connection between the Scranton murder and the earlier ones. But when I declined to tell him, he accepted it with fairly good grace. Even thanked me for the information, although it didn't sound like his heart was in it."

"He was probably in a hurry to start making calls to Pennsylvania," Kimura said. "But I wouldn't be surprised if you hear from him again."

"No, me neither. But I *was* surprised by something that was waiting for me on my office voice mail when I got in this morning."

"Another 'development?'" Kimura put ironic quotation marks around the word with his voice.

"Yeah, kind of," McGraw said. "It was a message from Pacilio. He's taking some annual leave, effective today. He doesn't know how much of it he'll need, yet, he says. I checked with Human Resources, and he's got more than a month accumulated."

Kimura shrugged. "If he wants some time off, that's understandable. He's had a very stressful time of it these last few days. I'm curious to know how he determined that Barbour had found his way to Scranton, but I can wait to find that out until Mr. Pacilio returns from his vacation."

McGraw shook his head dubiously. "I don't think he's going on vacation, exactly. Not if I heard the last part of his message correctly."

"What do you mean, Mac? Do we need to get you fitted for a hearing aid in your old age?"

"No, not yet. But there was a lot of background noise where Pacilio was calling from. Sounded like an airport, presumably the one in Albany. A really loud PA system started announcing the arrival of some flight or other just as Pacilio said the last part, so I may have misunderstood him." McGraw paused. "But it sounded like he said he was flying to Denver to find a witch."

———◆———

Pacilio looked upon flying the way that Victorian ladies of a certain class used to regard sexual intercourse: as an unpleasant duty to be performed only when absolutely necessary, and with no prospect of enjoyment whatever. Pacilio had been required to fly plenty of times as a SEAL, sometimes parachuting out of the damn plane, as well. But he had never completely mastered his fear, even if he had learned not to show it.

Sometimes, as a way of alleviating his anxiety in the air, Pacilio would recite under his breath the SEAL's Prayer. Its origin was uncertain, but every SEAL who served in Vietnam seemed to know by heart this blasphemous version of Psalm 23:

> *Yea, though I walk through the valley of the*
> *shadow of death, I shall fear no evil.*
> *For I am the meanest, the baddest,*
> *the deadliest motherfucker in the valley.*

Finally abandoning his fantasy that sheer will power was going to keep the plane in the air, Pacilio let his thoughts drift to other subjects, like Muriel Rojas, M.D.

Since she wasn't on duty at Albany Medical Center until noon, Muriel had accompanied Pacilio to the Albany airport. While waiting in the departure area for his flight to be called, they had talked desultorily about unimportant things. It was only when the airline clerk announced over the P.A. system that boarding was about to begin that Muriel Rojas had grabbed Pacilio's lapel and spoken with urgency in her voice.

"Listen, Michael, I'm still not sure what's going on here, except that I seem to be getting myself involved with a guy who thinks he's one of the crew from *Ghostbusters*."

Pacilio shook his head and smiled weakly. "Wrong movie," he said. "I'm afraid this one's closer to *The Exorcist*."

"Whatever. The point is, sooner or later, you're going to need some help with this supernatural snipe hunt that you're on. If you're merely delusional, and I almost hope you are, then somebody's going to have to get you out of whatever looney bin they throw you into. As a physician, I can probably find a way to spring you. On the other hand, if all of this spooky stuff you've been telling me is real, you'll need somebody, sooner or later, to give you a hand in catching this guy Barbour."

"It's impossible to say right now how this investigation is going to shake out. For all I know, some State Trooper is arresting the son of a bitch right this minute. I hope so – but somehow, I don't think it's going to be that easy."

"I want *in*," she said. The voice was quiet, but her eyes were fierce, as was her grip on his lapel. "I can get time off from the hospital whenever I need it. Several of my colleagues owe me big favors and will take over for me in the ER if I ask. So I want you to promise that you'll call me when you get a lead on Barbour, or Beelzebub, or whatever his name really is."

Pacilio looked at her for a long moment. "*Why*, Muriel?" His voice mingled affection with exasperation. "Tell me that, will you? You don't impress me as the clingy type, despite what you're currently doing to my suit jacket."

Slightly embarrassed, she relaxed her grip. "Don't misunderstand me, Michael. I'm not going all moony over you, and this isn't some kind of "Stand by Your Man" nonsense. I'm not at all sure that last night means you *are* my man. And you're not sure, either, are you?"

Pacilio started to speak, but she stopped him with a finger to his lips. "Spare me your reassurances. You're right: I'm not clingy, and I'm not desperate. Maybe we'll decide that we want something long-term out of this, or maybe last night was just the best one-night stand I've ever had. But in the meantime, *I want in on this.*"

Pacilio shook his head in puzzlement. "Look, I'm not turning you down, all right? I can't afford to. Without my agency to fall back on, I may need all the friends I can get. But if you're not doing some kind of 'I wanna be your girlfriend' number – and I believe you when you say you're not – then what's in it for you?"

Muriel Rojas glanced toward the departure gate and saw that only a few passengers remained to be boarded. "You're going to miss your flight if you don't get moving pretty soon," she said.

"There's time yet," he said. "Time enough for you to answer me. Why do you want to get any deeper in this swamp than you already are?"

She looked up at him with a wry smile. "Why do you think I specialized in emergency medicine, you jerk?"

"How the hell do I know? To heal the sick, comfort the dying, make a pile of money – all of the above?"

She shook her head. "No. I wanted to do all of that, but it comes with virtually any kind of medical practice. But from my first day on the EM rotation when I was an intern, I knew it was going to be emergency medicine for me, and you, of all people, ought to understand why."

Pacilio just looked at her, his face showing nothing.

"*Adrenaline*, dummy! The pure rush that comes from using everything you've got for as long as it takes to win. The thrill of knowing that you've looked the Grim Reaper right in the face and then spit in his eye. *That's* why I work in the ER, and that's why I'm going to be part of this hunt for the elusive Peter Barbour."

Pacilio was still looking at her, but in a different way now. His expression was that of a man recognizing an old friend, someone he hasn't seen in many years but knows very well.

"You and me, Michael," she said to him, and now the excitement was clear in her voice, as pure and sweet as the sound of Roland's horn. "You and me, and maybe that old priest in Scranton, if he's willing. We are going to find Peter Barbour, man or demon or whatever the hell he is. We are going to pursue him and we are going to catch him."

She abruptly put an arm around Pacilio's neck, pulling his head down until it was close to her face. For a moment she stuck her tongue in his ear, an act so unexpectedly sensual that he found himself instantly becoming erect. Then she removed her tongue, and, her mouth still right up against Pacilio's ear, whispered, "And then we are going to kick his diabolical ass!"

———◆———

Pascoe was sitting at his desk reading the most recent Arbitron ratings for his cable-TV channel when the telephone buzzed softly. He pushed a button with one manicured finger and picked up the receiver. "Mr. Waxmonsky is here," his secretary's voice said. "He says he has an appointment, but I have no record of it, Reverend."

"That's all right, Francine, it's probably just some kind of mix-up," Pascoe said. "As long as he's here, I guess I can spare a few minutes. Send him on in, will you?"

Jerry Waxmonski did, in fact, have an appointment, but Pascoe was careful that no record of it would appear on any document that might one day be the subject of a subpoena. For the same reason, he always paid Waxmonski out of his own personal funds, and in cash. No church money was involved, so there was no danger that someday Waxmonski might be the subject of an audit that would spread from his books to Pascoe's.

It wasn't that Waxmonski was either disreputable or careless, but Pascoe only employed the private investigator for confidential matters, and he believed in caution. He had so many enemies – the government (when the Democrats were in power, anyway), rival religious leaders, and, of course, the press – that one misstep could bring his whole empire down around his ears.

There was a discrete knock at the door. Pascoe called, with practiced cheerfulness, "Come on in," and another secretary opened the door and ushered Jerry Waxmonski into Pascoe's office. Pascoe waved Waxmonski into one of the chairs arranged in front of his desk.

Pascoe had long thought that Gerald Stanislaus Waxmonski was the total antithesis of every Polish joke that Pascoe had ever heard as a boy growing up in Cleveland. According to Pascoe's adolescent peer group, Polish guys were big and beefy, but Waxmonski was of average height or a little less, slim, and wiry. The stereotypical Polack was unkempt and dirty, his clothing often stained by beer and the juice of hastily-consumed kielbasa; Jerry Waxmonski, on the other hand, always wore three-piece suits in quiet patterns of blue or gray, and the white shirts and dark silk ties that accompanied the suits were never sullied by the slightest hint of either stain or wrinkle. Finally, of course, Polacks were dumb, poorly-educated, little more than brutes. Everybody among the young Tommy Pascoe's circle of friends knew that, and the adult Pascoe sometimes wondered what he and his snot-nosed little playmates would have made of Jerry Waxmonski, honors graduate of the

University of Wisconsin, fluent speaker of three languages, former star Special Agent of the FBI and, most amazing from Pascoe's point of view, author of two published volumes of poetry.

With the dazzling smile that accompanied most of his utterances, Pascoe said, "Good to see you again, Jerry."

Waxmonski let his blond head dip forward about an inch. "Reverend," he murmured. "Always a pleasure."

"You said yesterday that you had been successful in your inquiries."

Waxmonski began to unfasten the straps and buckles on the slim, archaic-looking briefcase that rested on his lap. It was the sort of valise that a senior partner in a white-shoe Philadelphia law firm might have brought to mortgage foreclosures around 1930. "I said I had been 'reasonably successful,'" he told Pascoe. "By that, I mean that I've been able to find out most of what you wanted to know, while following your instructions to be discrete. As things stand now, it's highly unlikely that anyone is aware that I've been digging around in this matter for you. But if I go any deeper, it will be very difficult, I would think, to prevent my efforts from coming to the attention of the authorities."

Pascoe frowned. "When you say 'authorities,' who do you mean, exactly?"

"Someone in the federal government, most likely," Waxmonsky said, removing some papers from his case. "The FBI is in charge of the investigation, and their people certainly might catch on if I push my inquiries further. There's also another agency, called" — Waxmonsky consulted his notes — "the Office of

Scientific Accountability. They normally investigate fraudulent use of federal grant money, but they have a rather wide brief, I understand. They've been involved in the case as well, although it would not surprise me if the FBI moves them to the sidelines very soon. The Bureau doesn't like outsiders getting involved in its investigations."

"But so far, you're confident that none of these agencies is aware of your own activities?"

"Completely confident," Waxmonsky said.

"Well, then," Pascoe said, "Maybe you'd better tell me what all this discrete investigating has turned up."

"Very well." Waxmonsky shuffled papers for a moment. "The information from your caller, the old woman, proved to be substantially correct, although incomplete as to details, of course."

Pascoe nodded. He had learned from experience to pay attention to his hunches, and there had been something about the old lady's story that made it sound like more than the recycled trash from supermarket tabloids that people sometimes called up with.

"Four nights ago," Waxmonsky continued, "there was apparently a mass murder in a building in Fairfax, Virginia. Ten people were killed, and each corpse showed evidence of torture, or mutilation, or rape, or some combination. I have the full particulars, based on the autopsy results, should you desire to hear them."

Pascoe suppressed a shudder. "No, that won't be necessary. But I *am* interested in the motivation for this brutality. Were these people tortured to make them divulge some secret, do you think?"

Waxmonsky pursed his lips for a moment. "Hard to say for certain, of course, but my opinion is no. It doesn't have the earmarks of implemented interrogation. There are too many . . . refinements."

"What, then?" Pascoe asked. "Savagery for its own sake?"

"Possibly," Waxmonsky said after a moment. "It's conceivable that it was done to send a message to someone, as a kind of demonstration of ruthlessness, or perhaps as an act of revenge. But that would be rather more likely if we were dealing with criminals here. This sort of violence happens in the drug trade from time to time, although the Fairfax murders are still rather more sadistically elaborate than you usually find among that crowd. Whoever did this, even if they were operating under orders, enjoyed their work. That's quite clear."

"A psychopath, you mean."

Waxmonsky shrugged his well-tailored shoulders. "Abnormal psychology isn't my field, but if you want a layman's opinion – yes, a psychopath. Or perhaps a gang led by a psychopath."

"The FBI doesn't know how many people were involved?"

"No," Waxmonsky said. "There are several theories being discussed at the Bureau, each of which is supported to some degree by the evidence. But they're a long way from being certain. They do know that all of the sexual assaults were carried out by the same person – the DNA evidence shows that conclusively."

"You mentioned a moment ago that the victims were not involved in drug dealing," Pascoe said. "So, who were they?"

"They were scientists. Mostly theoretical physicists, whatever that means, although one of them was an electrical engineer. Ten utterly respectable scientists, in a perfectly legitimate laboratory, with a nice fat government grant, doing something that nobody will talk about."

Pascoe frowned. "The project was classified?"

Waxmonsky shook his head. "That's the strange part," he said. "As best I can determine, the project had no security classification at all. But, despite that, the clamps are on tight now. That extends to the nature of the crime, and even the question of whether a crime took place at all."

"So there *is* a cover-up," Pascoe said.

"For lack of a better term, yes there is. Ten scientists, ten funerals, ten closed coffins. Oh, and ten death certificates, all containing variations on the theme of 'industrial accident'."

"But what on earth is the point? I know that there are any number of people in the federal government for whom secrecy is a reflex, but why would anybody want to cover up a mass murder?"

For the first time since the conversation began, Waxmonsky broke eye contact. "I don't know," he muttered, suddenly busy with the straps and buckles of his old-fashioned briefcase. "I don't know," he repeated, more loudly. "And I may not be able to find out, unless you're willing to risk my activities coming to the attention of the Bureau. That's your decision, of course. But I do know this much: something truly, profoundly evil took place in that laboratory, and the government is trying very hard to make sure that no one else finds out about it."

"Something evil," Pascoe repeated softly, and his gaze was distant for a few moments. Then he stood and said, "Thanks for coming in, Jerry. Do you have your bill with you?"

"Of course." The other man produced a folded sheet

of paper. Pascoe glanced at it and said, "Fine, quite reasonable. Payment in a few days, by the usual method. All right?"

Waxmonsky nodded, knowing that he would soon receive at his P.O. box a small package containing his fee in cash – a sum that would not be mentioned on his tax return.

Waxmonsky asked, "Do you wish me to continue inquiries in this matter, given the risks of discovery?"

Pascoe shook his head. "Let's not attract the notice of the FBI. Once they start poking around in your affairs, it can be enormously difficult to get them to stop. But there may be another way to approach this. See what you can find out about the research they were doing in that laboratory. If they were on a government grant, there should be information about it somewhere. Perhaps if you can find out what they were working on, that will give us a clue as to why they died. At any rate, proceed cautiously, and don't attract undue attention. All right?"

"Of course, Reverend." The voice was slightly huffy. "I *always* proceed cautiously."

"To be sure," Pascoe said with a reassuring smile. "Do you have a copy of your report for me?"

"Yes, certainly. Here you are." The investigator handed over a manila envelope, received Pascoe's thanks and professionally hearty handshake in return, and was shown the door.

Pascoe returned to his desk, the faraway look back in his eyes. He picked up the phone and pressed a button. "Francine? Cancel my eleven o'clock, will you? And don't put any calls through until I tell you otherwise."

A few moments later, Pascoe was absorbed in

Waxmonsky's report on the murders in Fairfax. After reading it twice, he spent several minutes looking at nothing at all. Finally, he opened a desk drawer and took out a fresh yellow legal pad. Removing his Mont Blanc pen from his pocket, he began to draft a memo to himself. Pascoe often used this method to organize his thoughts and test ideas.

He wrote for almost an hour before his hand became tired and his stomach began to suggest that some lunch would be appreciated. Before locking the pad in his desk, Pascoe glanced at the first page again, where he had begun the memo with the words, "Something utterly evil has taken place in Fairfax."

The phrasing was Jerry Waxmonsky's, which showed that, in one sense at least, Pascoe possessed true humility: he was never too proud to steal a good idea from anybody.

———◆———

Pacilio was usually not able to sleep on airplanes, but the prior two nights had not afforded him very much rest. Besides, there was nothing of importance he could do before the plane brought him to Denver. His plans, such as they were, were made. So he let his eyes close somewhere over Ohio. Pacilio slept; in time, he dreamed.

At first, it seemed like the same dream that had haunted his sleep ever since Vietnam. He was alone, searching the jungle for his missing partner, Carl Chopko. But this time, Pacilio did not hear the gradually growing sounds of insects feeding. Instead, as he made his cautious, apprehensive way through the undergrowth, there came a familiar voice from off to his left.

"I was wonderin' when you'd get here, man. Took you fuckin' long enough." *The voice was Carl Chopko's.*

Pacilio turned his head slowly, his stomach in a knot, not knowing what vision of horror was going to greet him. But Chops seemed okay, not the way he usually appeared in the dream. Sitting atop a large rock, wearing sweat-stained jungle fatigues, Carl Chopko looked the way he always had – except that his tropical tan was replaced by a pallor that Pacilio had never seen on his partner's lean face before.

Pacilio took a rag from the pocket of his own jungle fatigues and wiped his sweaty brow and scalp as he studied his friend. After a few moments, he said, "You're pale as a fuckin' ghost, man."

"That's 'cause I *am* a fuckin' ghost, man."

After a long pause, Pacilio said, "Yeah, I guess you must be, come to think of it. Couple of months after I rotated home, I heard that Charlie caught up with you. Took you alive, too, you dumb bastard. The letter I got from our C.O. didn't go into much detail, but it didn't have to. I knew what had happened to other guys from Phoenix who'd gotten captured."

Chopko nodded. "Yeah, it was pretty fuckin' bad. An intense experience, you might say. Tell you this, though: I didn't give them anything. Not a fuckin' word, unless you count the things I said they did with their mothers. They wanted to know all kinds of shit. Some of it I knew, some I didn't. Tried to tell me that if I only gave them the information, they'd stop what they were doing to me." He snorted derisively. "Yeah, right, and I'm Ho Chi Minh's kid brother. So, I didn't talk, and they kept on with it. I got a little hazy towards the end there, but I think it lasted two days, off and on, before I went into shock and finally croaked."

"I was back stateside when it happened, but I keep

dreaming about it. I dream that I'm the one who finds you."

Chops nodded again. "Yeah, I know, Mike. You got to give that shit up, man. Just let it go. It was a long time ago, and I'm okay, now. No more fear, and no more pain. What else can a guy ask for? Besides, you got other stuff to worry about."

"What do you mean?"

"That motherfucker you're trackin', what's his name, Barbour."

"So you know about that."

"Yeah, sure, and I also know that's not his real name."

"That's the name on all the ID that he's been using," Pacilio said.

"No, man, Barbour's just the host. You've been right all along. You just don't know how right you've been. It's a fuckin' demon, Mike, just like before. Just like Do Lac. Only this bastard is ten times worse."

"We didn't know what we were dealing with in Do Lac. Not until the end – and even then I didn't let myself believe it."

"Better believe it this time, man. You can't afford to screw up now – the stakes're too high."

"What the fuck are you talking about?"

Chops shook his head. "Never mind, man, you don't need to know that now. But here's one thing you *do* need to know: the motherfucker's name is Asmodeus. Remember that: Asmodeus. It'll most likely come in handy somewhere along the way."

"Since you know so much, why don't you tell me what the hell I'm supposed to do with Barbour or Asmodeus or whoever the fuck he is? Assuming I can find him in the first place."

"Can't tell you that, man, 'cause I don't really know. You'll have to play it by ear. You were pretty good at that back in the old days, if I remember right. But, in general, I'd take the broad's advice."

"What broad?"

"That doctor broad, man. Rojas. Hang on to that one if you can, buddy. She's about as tough as you seem to think you are."

"We'll have to see about that. But what advice are you talking about?"

"What she said this morning, man, just before you got on the plane: find him and kick his fucking ass!"

"Listen, Chops, what're you —"

"Can't talk much longer, Mike. One thing, though: you're not gonna have that dream any more. The one where you find me lookin' all gross with the bugs and shit. You deserve some rest from that crap. So, it's over for you."

Chops got up from the rock he'd been sitting on. "Take care of yourself, buddy, and watch your back. Especially now."

Carl Chopko stepped forward and clasped Pacilio's hand in the Special Forces handshake, an overhand grip that looked something like arm wrestling without the table. "Airborne!" Chops said through his grin.

"All the way!" Pacilio replied, completing the ritual. "But, Chops, why can't we —"

"'Cause you're about to wake up, man."

Pacilio's eyes snapped open and he was once again in seat 23E of a USAirways Boeing 727. A few seconds later, one of the flight attendants, a tall redhead with green eyes, bent over his seat.

"I didn't want to wake you when we had the

beverage service earlier, but we have plenty left," she said, smiling. "Would you like something to drink?"

Her newly-awake passenger, a compact, fit-looking man with dark hair and eyes, looked at her as if she were the last person he expected to see. Jen Wilson was used to that; people waking from slumber in an airplane sometimes needed a moment to get their bearings. She tried again. "Sir? Can I bring you something to drink?"

The man blinked two or three times, then smiled at her. "Do you have any ginger ale?"

"Sure, we have plenty of Schweppes. Would you like a can, with some ice?"

"That would be great, thank you."

When Jen brought him his ginger ale he thanked her again, but she noticed that the faraway look had not yet left his eyes. Well, she thought, some people just take longer than others to come back to the real world. He seemed like a nice guy; she hoped his dreams had been pleasant.

Chapter 14

Pacilio's flight touched down at Denver International Airport only two minutes behind schedule, and did so smoothly enough to avoid causing undue anxiety in even the most skittish of passengers.

His suitcase, an enormous old leather thing he had bought in London years ago, was too big for carry-on, so he'd been forced to check it through to his destination. He hoped that he wouldn't have to spend the next day without a change of clothes because some dimwit airline employee had sent his bag to Seattle. Besides, his gun was in there.

Despite the fact that the SEALs had trained him in the use of every kind of firearm, Pacilio was not a gun freak. He carried a pistol because he had to. Sometimes he was required to arrest people, and occasionally those people objected – violently. He had personal discretion as to the type of weapon he carried, so he had sought advice from a couple of friends who *were* bona fide gun freaks. One of them worked for the Executive Protection Division of the Secret Service; the other was a member of the FBI's Hostage Rescue Team, the best SWAT unit in the country.

Both of Pacilio's friends had recommended several models of the 9mm Glock automatic. Pacilio had borrowed a Glock Model 19 from his buddy in the

Secret Service, taken it out to a range for a couple of hours, and liked it. He now had one of his own.

Fortunately, Pacilio's bag showed up where and when it was supposed to. Ten minutes later, he was in a cab on his way to the Brown Palace, a pleasant old hotel that Pacilio found a refreshing change from the national franchise lodgings where he usually stayed. The rooms were attractive and comfortable, but Pacilio especially enjoyed the lobby, which featured a lot of red leather on the furniture and oriental rugs on the floor. The lobby's stained-glass ceiling was something to see when the sun was shining – and in Denver, it usually is. So Pacilio always stayed at the Brown Palace when in the Mile-High City, even though the room prices usually led to squabbles with the curmudgeons in Accounting. Well, this time he was paying for it himself, so the bean counters back in D.C. would have to seek other sources of aggravation.

A clerk at the registration desk found Pacilio's reservation in the computer, and was happy to check him into a $200 single. The assigned bellhop was a blond and deeply tanned young man who looked to Pacilio as if he belonged on the beach in Malibu, shooting the curl and saying "Dude" a lot. But like all the hotel staff, the young man knew his business. He got Pacilio and his outsize suitcase into the proper room, demonstrated the light switches and TV remote, collected his tip, and departed, all within five minutes.

After unpacking, Pacilio went looking for the phone book, finally finding it in one of the nightstands. He took the thick volume over to the writing table and sat down.

There was no point in looking up Sarah McPherson in the White Pages, since Sharon had said the number was unlisted. But there are all kinds of methods to get fur off a feline. He might be able to induce the local telephone company to divulge his quarry's address and phone number, but then word might get back to McGraw that Pacilio, on leave, was claiming to be acting in an official capacity. It wasn't that Pacilio thought McGraw would be unreasonable or unsympathetic; given an explanation, he might prove to be neither. But Pacilio liked the older man too much to put him in a difficult position with Kimura. For now, the less McGraw knew about this, the better. Pacilio already regretted the last part of his voice-mail message to McGraw, mentioning his search for a witch in Denver.

Opening up the Yellow Pages, he searched under the "W"s to see if there was a listing for "Wicca." Nothing. He thought for a moment, then turned to the "C"s. Sure enough, there it was, right below "Churches -- Wesleyan." Under "Churches -- Wiccan," there was one entry: "Algard Wiccan Church and Healing Center" with an address on Arapahoe Road. Pacilio picked up the phone. If nobody at the Wicca Center knew Sarah McPherson, he was going to have to fall back on Plan B. Trouble was, he didn't have a Plan B.

After two rings, the phone at the other end was answered by a cheery female voice that said, "Church of Wicca."

"Hello," Pacilio said. "I'm trying to reach Sarah McPherson." He hoped he didn't sound like a bill collector.

"Sarah's not here right now," the bubbly voice informed him. "Hold on a minute."

In the silence, Pacilio could hear his pulse in his ears as his heartbeat accelerated -- clearly, they knew Sarah at this place. That was a start.

The young woman's voice came back on the line. "It says here that Sarah will be on the desk tonight from seven 'til ten. Can I take a message?"

"No, that's all right. I'll give her a call this evening."

"Okay, then. Bye!"

Pacilio hung up, wondering if all witches were usually that perky. Times had certainly changed, he thought. If Shakespeare's three weird sisters were around today, instead of bedeviling Macbeth on the Scottish moors, they'd probably form a rock band and end up opening for Melissa Etheridge at Madison Square Garden.

Pacilio looked at his watch: coming up on 4:50 local time. A shower and change of clothes, followed by something to eat, should take him close to the time he ought to be leaving.

He decided to order room service for dinner. That way, he could eat while catching some network news, and maybe a half-hour of CNN, too. Then it would be time to see if he could find the witch who had been his sister's lesbian lover, and ask her to conjure up a demon for him.

Pacilio shook his head at the sheer weirdness of it all. Then he stood up and began to unbutton his shirt.

The building housing the Algard Wiccan Church and Healing Center looked to have once been the property of the F.W. Woolworth Company. The architecture had the distinctively tawdry Woolworth style to it, and the company name was still faintly visible in the stone over the big ground floor windows.

The former dime store now appeared to house some kind of social service agency on its ground floor, but there was another doorway off to the left with steps leading upward. Pacilio opened the door and saw a hand-printed sign informing him that the Wicca Center could be found on the next level.

The second floor contained only two offices. One, a resumé service, had a sign on its door proclaiming that "Better resumes lead to better-paying jobs!" Across the landing, another sign read "Algard Church of Wicca and Healing Center. Walk In." Pacilio did.

He found himself in what appeared to be a reception area, from which two doorways apparently led deeper into the Church's facility. From somewhere in the back he could faintly hear voices; they sounded female and seemed to be chanting, but he couldn't make out the words.

The anteroom contained a number of cheap-looking chairs in orange plastic, and several mismatched tables stacked with pamphlets of different kinds. There were some sepia-toned framed photos on the wall, featuring people Pacilio didn't recognize. The largest item of furniture was a beat-up wooden desk, with a new-looking Dell PC off to one side.

Behind the desk, just looking up from a clipboard on which she had been writing, sat an intense-looking woman in her late thirties. It was Sarah McPherson.

It had been more than five years since Pacilio had seen her, but he was sure. Sarah hadn't changed much: still slim, still pretty in a brittle sort of way, the raven-black hair worn differently than he remembered, in a French twist now. Her skin was as pale as ever, the coloring of someone who stays indoors a lot.

Or who only comes out at night, he thought.

The glasses Sarah wore were new, although Pacilio wondered what good they were doing with the lenses pushed up to rest on top of her head. Maybe she just liked the look.

"Good evening," she said, with a measured smile that contained no hint of recognition. "Welcome to the Church of Wicca."

Pacilio smiled back. "Tell me, who or what is 'Algard?'"

"It's a particular rite within Wicca," she said. "The name itself is a combination of two men's names: Alexander Saunders and Gerald Gardner. Both of them were influential in the revival of the Wiccan religion in this century, although our church was actually founded by a woman, Mary Nesnick."

Before Pacilio could say anything, she went on, in a pedantic tone, "The best analogy I can give to help you understand this would be Catholicism: you have the Roman Rite, with the Pope as head, then you have the Eastern Rite, also known as Greek Orthodox, with the Patriarch of Athens as its head. They share many beliefs in common, but their rituals are rather different. It's the same with our religion. I have a pamphlet describing the Wiccan Church's history, if you'd like one."

Pacilio shook his head. "No, that's all right, but thanks for the quick lesson, Sarah."

She stared at him for a moment, then reached up and brought the glasses down onto her nose. After a moment she said, "I know you from somewhere."

He nodded. "Mike Pacilio, Sarah. Been a long time."

"The name doesn't ring a bell, but your face is familiar. Did you go to –"

"Sharon Purcell is my sister," he said. "We met in San Francisco, about five years ago, when I was out visiting."

In the silence that followed, Pacilio could again hear the chanting from the other room, although the actual words remained elusive. Sarah McPherson was staring at his face as if she were planning to sketch it later from memory.

Finally, she said softly, "*That's* why I thought I recognized you. I wasn't remembering you, but her. There's . . . so much of her in your face."

He nodded. "When we were growing up, people always said we looked alike."

"But you're not twins, are you? You look older than – than her."

"I am," Pacilio told her. "By six years."

Sarah McPherson took a deep breath, let it out, and put a smile on her face that was as bright as it was synthetic. "I think this is where I'm supposed to say something about a small world, Mike. So what brings you to the Church of Wicca? Do you live in Denver now? I seem to recall that you worked in Washington before."

"I still live near there. I'm just in Denver for a day or two."

"And this is how you spend your free time on business trips? Learning about arcane religions?"

"Not exactly, Sarah. I came to Denver to see you."

The smile was suddenly gone. "Did you, now? And how did you know where to find me?"

Pacilio considered whether mentioning his sister's involvement would help matters. He decided it wouldn't. "I work for the federal government, Sarah. I have access to a lot of databases – IRS, Social Security, agencies like that. It took me about half an hour at a computer terminal to locate you."

She made a face. "That sounds almost sinister. Very *1984*."

"It's the electronic age. Everybody's in some computer somewhere."

"Well, big brother, here you are," she said, with a tinge of sarcasm. "So what the fuck do you want?"

Pacilio studied his hands for a moment, then looked up. "I needed to find a witch," he said simply.

"Well, you've found one," she said, and her voice was flat. "Now what?"

The emptiness of Pacilio's voice matched her own. "I want to talk to you about conjuring a demon."

Sarah McPherson stared at Pacilio from across the Wicca Center's reception desk. "This is not, I take it, your idea of humor," she said.

Pacilio shook his head. "Doesn't seem funny to me."

She tapped the desk in front of her several times with her right index finger. Her unpainted nails were long enough for each tap to make an audible click. Finally, she said, "This room is a little too public for us to talk about that subject. Come with me."

She led Pacilio through the open doorway to his right. He followed her down a dimly lit hallway with an old wooden floor that creaked and groaned as they walked along.

Sarah stopped at the third door. Like all those along this hallway, it was painted a dark shade of red that bordered on maroon. She opened the door, reached in, and flicked on a light switch. "Come on in."

As he entered, Pacilio noticed that a white index card was taped to the door, with *Sarah McPherson* written on it in elegant-looking calligraphy. Underneath the name was a hand-drawn symbol that looked like an Amish hex sign.

Sarah closed the door. "Have a seat," she said, gesturing toward a worn couch done in nubby brown fabric. She sat down in an armchair that looked as if it had once been part of someone's living room set.

The room was small, about fifteen feet by twenty. Its only other furniture consisted of a small metal desk pushed against one wall, a couple of bookcases filled with books and knick-knacks, and an end table on either side of the couch where he was sitting.

Pacilio noticed the poster on the far wall, just above the desk. Against a white background was a silhouette of the traditional witch figure, conical hat and all, astride a broom. From the end of the broom a line looped and swirled down below the figure until it formed the letters of the words, "SURRENDER DOROTHY!"

Sarah McPherson was very serious now. "So, tell me – how did you find out about us?"

Pacilio shrugged. "You're in the Yellow Pages."

"No, I mean about our practice of the Black Arts. Conjuring demons, and so forth."

"I don't have any specialized intelligence about this place. I remembered you from five years ago. You told me back then that you were a witch, but you didn't seem inclined to discuss the subject further. So we left it at that."

"Are you telling me that you flew all the way out to Denver just because I once told you that I was a witch?"

He nodded. "That's about it. I figured you would remember me, and therefore might be more inclined to trust me than you would some stranger who just waltzed in here."

"I see." Sarah McPherson's gaze rested briefly on the witch poster. "And you assumed, based on our prior acquaintance, that I would just summon a demon for you, the way I might call out for a pizza, or something?"

"I don't know what's involved, whether it's complicated or easy, or what. Until very recently, I didn't even know that it was really possible."

"But now you do? Or think you do?"

Pacilio nodded again. "Someone I trust told me it could be done, said that he had actually *seen* it done. And I'm pretty sure that's what I need. Why I need it is kind of a long story."

Sarah McPherson raised an eyebrow. "And you believe that I would do this – summon one of the eternally damned so you can have it perform some . . . *service* for you?"

"You're a witch, you told me so yourself," Pacilio said. "I assume that's what witches do. I'm prepared to pay you for your services."

"Yes, of course," she said softly, almost to herself, "How foolish of me to think that we could keep our little secret indefinitely."

She rose and walked over to one of the bookcases and picked up a small object from one of the shelves. Returning to her seat, she asked Pacilio, "Do you know what this is?"

She was holding a miniature teddy bear, brown, about four inches tall. Its nose was a sewn-on triangle, its eyes the same kind of triangles but upside down. The fur was worn thin in several places.

Pacilio decided to play straight man until he found out what the joke was. "Looks like a little teddy bear," he said.

"This is Terry Bear," she said, her face and voice serious. "He is my Familiar." Her voice gave the word a capital letter.

"I thought black cats, and live ones at that, were preferred for that kind of thing."

"You don't think he's alive? Well, I grant you he's not very outgoing right now. If I ever do conjure a demon for you, perhaps you'll see another side to little Terry

Bear, here. He can be very useful. But be careful of him: he bites."

Pacilio nodded. Keeping his face impassive, he said, "If you say so."

Sarah McPherson stared at him for several seconds, her expression unreadable. Gradually, though, her face began to reveal something very like contempt. "Do you know what a witch is, Mr. Pacilio? Do you really?"

"Beyond what I've already said, no, I don't." *But I bet you're going to tell me.*

"A witch today does what witches have always done: healing and divination. The curing of disease, and the foretelling of the future. The healing is often done with herbs and other earth-medicines. The divination is mostly through the Tarot. No cauldrons. No crystal balls. No black cats. And no brooms. But do you know why so many women were burned at the stake in the Middle Ages, after first being tortured into false confessions? Do you know why?"

"For consorting with the devil, wasn't it? And using magic to hurt people, through curses and so forth. Right?"

"Those were the charges, yes." The last word came out with a hiss. Sarah McPherson was working herself up into a fine fury. "Those were the pretexts under which hundreds, perhaps thousands of women died in unimaginable agony all over Europe, not to mention Salem, Massachusetts. But those were not the real reasons, Mr. Pacilio."

Pacilio hadn't come for a lecture, but he seemed to have no choice but to listen to this one, so he fed her the line she wanted: "Then what *were* the reasons?"

"Because they were considered competition by the doctors and the priests. The women's herbal healing often worked much better than the quackery that passed itself off as medicine in those days. And their worship of the Goddess, the Mother of All, who they saw as the source of their power, well, that veneration was seen as paganism by the Church. Those women challenged the prevailing power structure of their age by their very existence, and for that they had to die."

She stood up and began to pace the small room. "And because the Church controlled the society, its view of witchcraft is the one that prevailed. 'Consorting with Satan,' oh, sure, there's a fucking joke for you. Any woman who didn't kneel down and kiss the local Bishop's ass was said to be consorting with Satan. Over all the centuries, that vicious caricature prevailed. And it became part of our popular culture – legends, and books, and later, movies and TV and the Goddess knows what all."

She was looking right at Pacilio now, and there was fire in her eyes – perhaps the fire of a woman being burned at the stake. "And so today we have millions of ignorant fools, steeped in their stupid cultural superstitions, who know nothing of witchcraft beyond what they see in their idiotic television shows, who assume that any woman who worships the Goddess, who offers to heal using herbs, who tries to read the future using the Tarot cards, that any woman who does those things, even today, is guilty of consorting with the Evil One."

Sarah stopped pacing, and stood behind her desk now. "And some of these people are so steeped in their own ignorance," – she picked up the little bear and held it toward Pacilio – "that they are even willing to believe that a teddy bear, a toy for children, a small stuffed toy bear who's been with me since I won him at St. Mary's

Church carnival in seventh grade, is actually some sort of magical creature used in the summoning of demons!"

Sarah McPherson laughed derisively. "Take your superstitions back to Washington and write up a report on me, why don't you? And be sure to put *this* in your fucking report: there's no Black Magic in the Church of Wicca, you stupid cocksucker, and there never has been. The only demons you're ever likely to meet are the ones living inside your own empty, worthless head. Now, GET THE FUCK OUT OF HERE!"

———◆———

Pacilio raised himself up from the bed far enough so that he could take a swig from the can of ginger ale without spilling it all over himself. The clock radio said it was 1:12 a.m.

Wish I still smoked. Nothing like a cigarette, or a whole pack of them, when you're by yourself in a hotel room, feeling like the asshole of the Western world. Despite this gloomy meditation, he was not tempted in the slightest to go down to the lobby in search of a cigarette machine.

He kept the TV's volume low for the sake of his neighbors, in case any of *them* could sleep. One of the Denver stations was showing *The Magnificent Seven*, the greatest Western ever made and a movie that, by Pacilio's estimation, he had seen twenty-eight times. Its being on tonight was, as far as he was concerned, the high point of his trip.

He didn't know what to do next. The Church of Wicca was clearly a dead end. *If I ever go back there, they'll probably burn ME at the stake.* He wondered if Dirty Eugene Grady remembered many details from the conjuring he had once witnessed – enough to make the attempt himself. Even if the old priest were willing, did

Pacilio have the right to ask him? He had the impression, from what Dirty Eugene had said, that if you were conjuring a demon, and you fucked it up somehow, the consequences were a little rougher than if you were making a soufflé and burned it. In fact, "burned" was probably an appropriate word for what might result.

The telephone rang as he was watching Charles Bronson trying to teach some Mexican farmers how to shoot a Winchester. Pacilio tried to think of who might know where he was staying, and realized that the easiest way to find out was to answer the damn thing.

"Hello?"

"The one you want is Victoria Steele." Sarah McPherson's voice contained none of the rage Pacilio had listened to earlier in the evening.

"Give me that name again, will you?" Pacilio said, reaching for a pen.

"Victoria Steele, with an 'e' at the end." Sarah sounded as if she might be drunk.

"Why do I want to talk to her?"

"Because she's what you're looking for."

"You mean she's –"

"She performs the Dark Magic. For money. She was in the Church for a while, until we found out. Then we expelled her."

The way she pronounced 'expelled' told him that Sarah McPherson was *seriously* drunk.

"Okay, thank you. Thank you very much. Where can I find this Victoria Steele?"

"Maybe she's in the book, I dunno. If not, what you do is, get a copy of *The Denver Reader*."

"What's that?"

"Local 'alternative' paper. Get it free at any liquor store, newsstand, like that."

"Okay, I know what you mean. Lots of big cities have rags like that. Is this Steele woman the publisher, a writer, what?"

"No, uh-uh. She advertises in there. Find the part with all the sex ads. Biggest section of the damn paper. Look for 'Mistress Victoria.' That's her."

"*Mistress Victoria*? You're not kidding me about this, are you, Sarah?"

"No, not kidding. It's what she does, besides the black magic stuff. Whips and chains and all that. Makes lotsa money, too. That's what I hear."

"Okay, I'll check it out, Sarah. Thank you again."

"All right. Welcome."

"Tell me one more thing, will you?"

"What?"

"How'd you know I was at the Brown Palace?"

"Didn't. I been calling them all, asking for you. Good thing you're under the 'B's."

"Yeah, I guess so," he said gently. "Well, thanks again, Sarah. Maybe you ought to get some sleep, huh?"

"So much like her."

"Excuse me?"

"You look so much like her. So much. S'enough to break your fucking heart."

"Sarah, listen —"

"I still love her, you know."

"I know," he said softly. "I know."

———◆———

A mile or so across town, Victoria Steele was in what she called her "studio," hard at work at one of her two professions.

The floor of the large room was highly polished hardwood, with no rugs to soften it. There was no softness anywhere in that room.

The heels of Victoria Steele's boots rapped sharply on the floor as she strolled away from the naked man and toward a table where she kept her implements. The man was blindfolded, but he was able to keep track of her movements by the sounds her heels made as she walked. He knew she was going over to one of the tables and would return to him shortly. He awaited her, and whatever she might bring with her, with a mixture of eager anticipation and sheer terror.

Although unable to see the woman now, he had gotten a good look at her before she had tied the black leather blindfold around his head and yanked it tight. He held her image firmly in his mind as he waited for her to return.

Victoria Steele stood 5'8" in her bare feet, and she gained an additional three inches from the boots, which were made of black patent leather and came three-quarters of the way up her formidable thighs. The rest of her outfit consisted of a bustier in black PVC that had the look of wet leather. The garment extended down to snap closed at the crotch but left the firm breasts bare. Her ensemble was completed by long gloves, also in black PVC, that stopped just below the elbow.

Victoria Steele's shoulder- length hair was blonde, in odd contrast to her black eyebrows. People assumed the eyebrows were natural and the hair dyed, but, in fact, the reverse was true. Her lips were full, her nose small, and her slate-gray eyes gazed upon the world with all the warmth and generosity of a tax assessor. She worked out with weights four times a week, and looked it.

Victoria Steele stood in front of one of the wooden tables for a moment, considering. Then she picked something up and sauntered back to the man suspended from the ceiling, her heels tapping out her progress like the ticking of some terrible clock of doom.

As she approached the naked man she said, "I do hope you're comfortable like that, Ronald. Because if you're not, I'm afraid I'm not going to do a blessed thing about it." She spoke teasingly, with a hint of laughter in her voice.

Whether anyone could have been comfortable in the man's position is doubtful. His hands were shackled, the padded shackles attached to chains which had been raised by a pulley set firmly in the ceiling. A few minutes earlier, Victoria Steele had worked the crank that operated the pulley, hoisting the man by his hands until he was on tiptoe. Then she had locked the mechanism in place, leaving the man with about half his weight on his toes and the rest suspended from the shackles. The amount of weight involved was not considerable, in any case, for the man was slim verging on skinny. His black hair was thinning, although the moustache below the long, narrow nose was full. He was in his mid-forties, which made him appear about ten years older than the beautiful but stern-looking woman who was standing behind him. He wore only the blindfold and a throbbing hard-on.

He had paid Victoria Steele five hundred dollars for what she was going to do to him.

"Now this," she said conversationally, "is just a small whip. Almost a toy, really. One can't possibly hurt anyone with it, so I don't want to hear any yelping out of you, or I'll give you something to yelp about, do you understand me?"

"Yes, I understand," the man said in a trembling voice.

Victoria Steele immediately swiped the whip across his buttocks, putting a lot of shoulder muscle into it. "Yes, *what*, you worthless scumbag?"

"Yes, mistress," he replied immediately.

"Oh, Ronald," she said in mock despair, "I do hope you're not going to be insolent with me tonight. Because if you are, I will have no choice but to punish you very severely. And it would hurt me to have to do that, Ronald, really it would, after all that we've meant to each other. But, do you know what?"

"What, mistress?"

"It will hurt *you* a great deal more. Not just a little tickle like *this*." And with that, she raised the whip and went to work on him in earnest.

Chapter 15

Sunlight bright in the window behind her, Victoria Steele looked across her austere teak desk and asked, "So, Michael, how did you come to hear about the services I offer?"

It was a little past 1:00 in the afternoon. Pacilio sat in Victoria Steele's office, which served as an anteroom to her studio – the place where a man named Ronald had suffered so much the night before, loving every minute of it.

Pacilio had expected Victoria Steele's domain to be decorated in Early Dungeon, and was surprised to find the small office businesslike and modern-looking, featuring a lot of blonde wood and several pastel colors. Pacilio thought the place was about as sexy as a podiatrist's office, except for the woman herself, who sat across from him behind an expensive-looking Scandinavian Modern desk.

Victoria Steele was not tricked out in the black leather and PVC ensemble that had been her working outfit the night before, but no one would have mistaken her for Rebecca of Sunnybrook Farm. She wore a sleeveless black turtleneck top that displayed her well-toned arms to good advantage. Below that were black denim jeans, starched and pressed to give the legs a sharp crease. Her feet were clad in casual lace-up shoes of soft black leather. A long, slim gold chain surrounded the ivory column of her neck. From it, at a level just above the full and clearly bra-less breasts, dangled a gold pendant that looked like a figure "8" on its side. Pacilio recognized it as the ancient symbol for Infinity.

In answer to Victoria Steele's question, Pacilio said, "Well, uh, I saw your ad in the *Reader*. It sounded like something that I would find . . . fulfilling." On the phone, he had passed himself off as a submissive who was interested in the pleasures of female domination. He decided to continue that pose, until he got a better sense of the woman sitting across from him. He'd learned from Sarah McPherson that asking someone to conjure a demon was not necessarily the best way to begin a conversation. Besides, if she were to offer him sex for money, he might be able to use that as leverage.

Victoria Steele looked at him dispassionately, clinically. "Have you had any experience with a dominant woman?"

Pacilio nodded. "I used to have a girlfriend who liked to take the dominant role," he lied. "We had different games that we'd play, stuff like that. I found that I enjoyed submitting to her, enjoyed it very much. But we broke up about a year ago."

"What caused you to break up?'

Pacilio made a face and tried to sound resentful. "She decided she liked her dyke girlfriend better than she liked me."

She nodded, as if this answer made perfect sense. "Have you had any other experience as a submissive since then?"

"Well, yeah. Since my girlfriend left, I've been to see a professional dominatrix a couple of times. I found that I liked what she could do for me."

Victoria Steele raised her eyebrows briefly at that, but sat in silence. She and Pacilio had been regarding each other for ten or twelve seconds when she suddenly snapped,

"Stop looking at me!"

Pacilio's brow furrowed, but his gaze did not shift. "Why?" he asked in puzzlement. "What's wrong?" An instant after the words left his mouth, he realized he'd made a mistake – a conclusion that was reinforced by the soft but contemptuous laughter coming from Victoria Steele.

"'What's wrong?'" she quoted, mockingly. "Why, there's nothing wrong, officer. Not a blessed thing."

"Officer? What the hell are you talking about?" Pacilio was trying for an indignant tone, but he knew it was no use.

She shrugged her muscular shoulders. "Play dumb, if you want to," she said. "I expect it comes easy for you."

"Ah, fuck it," Pacilio said, with feeling.

"So, who are you with?" Her voice was matter-of-fact now. "Denver Vice? The County Sheriff's Office? Or that new State Attorney General's Task Force that's been in the papers lately?"

Pacilio shook his head in disgust. "None of the above, lady, for what it's worth."

She went on as if he hadn't spoken. "I don't know why you people bother any more, I really don't. I'm thoroughly familiar with state, county, and local statutes as they relate to this area of activity, and I've taken professional legal advice, as well. My work does not constitute prostitution in any sense of the term, the law included. I am not a whore, Michael – or whatever your name really is. You couldn't have sex with me for the amount of money you make in a year. What I do is beyond sex, and it is certainly *not* prostitution."

"How did you make me?"

Victoria Steele thought for a moment. "You referred to your seeing a 'dominatrix', but a true submissive would call her a 'mistress.' And you said you had enjoyed what she did for you, but you should have said that you found pleasure in the chance to serve her." She made an impatient gesture. "You see? The difference is one of attitude. So I tested yours by ordering you to stop looking at me. You reacted like a normal man, with puzzlement and confusion. But a real, trained submissive would have dropped his eyes instantly, without question."

"I think I follow you," Pacilio said. "This whole thing is a lot more subtle than I realized."

"Yes it is," she said. "Now, if you're through wasting your time, not to mention my own, that object in the wall to your left is called a door. You probably know how it is employed. Try not to let it hit you in the ass on your way out." She smiled thinly. "If it does, I might have to charge you for the pain."

Pacilio stayed where he was. "You're very sharp," he said, "but you're only half right. You're correct about my pretending to be something I'm not, and I apologize for coming to you under false pretenses. I came up with that submissive routine because it seemed the quickest way to get my foot in the door, not because I was looking to bust you for hooking."

Victoria Steele arched her eyebrows. "Well, what, then?"

"I contacted you because I'm interested in what I understand is another aspect of your work." He paused. "I want you to conjure me a demon."

She looked at him for a long moment, absently fingering the "Infinity" symbol that hung from the chain around her neck. Then she began to laugh. There was no scorn in it now – her amusement seemed quite genuine. Eventually, the laughter subsided. For the first time, there was real interest in the cold gray eyes.

"Well, goodness gracious," she said pleasantly, "why didn't you say so in the first place?"

———◆———

Pacilio held the phone to his left ear and listened to faint clicks as the long distance connection was made. A moment later came the sound that meant the phone at the other end was ringing. It was picked up midway through the third ring.

"Dr. Rojas."

"Hi, Muriel. It's Mike."

"Michael! Are you still in Denver?"

"Yeah, I'm afraid so. Until tomorrow, at least."

"How's the, um, witch hunt going?"

"Well, the answer to that is one of those 'good news, bad news' kind of deals."

"Uh-oh. Well, you'd better start with the good news, I guess."

"The good news," Pacilio said, "is that I've found someone who says she can call up a demon for me."

"You mean this Sarah what's-her-name that your sister located for you?"

"No, it's not Sarah McPherson. I did find her, but, it turns out, I was operating under a false assumption. She doesn't do that kind of thing – she makes that *very* clear.

But she did pass me on to another woman, and this one claims to be the real deal."

"Well, that sounds promising."

"Yes, it is, I think. But it also leads me into the bad news."

Muriel Rojas sighed. "You don't really need to milk this for drama, Michael," she said. "I mean, the subject is dramatic enough all by itself, don't you think?"

"I guess you have a point, although I wasn't consciously trying for a theatrical touch. Anyway –" Pacilio hesitated briefly, then plunged ahead. "The bad news is that the genuine article, whose name is Victoria Steele, wants ten thousand dollars up front to do the conjuring."

There was silence on the line. Finally, Muriel Rojas said, rather absently, "I don't suppose that's something you can put on your American Express card, is it?"

"No, it's strictly on a cash basis, or so she tells me. I can maybe squeeze two grand in cash advances out of the credit cards I have on me. I've been trying to call Sharon – there's good money in genteel porn, and I know she'd help me out with a loan. But all I keep getting is the damn answering machine. She could be just out shopping, or she might be off at a book signing in Cleveland, or someplace."

"And you can't wait indefinitely, can you?"

"I sure as shit don't want to," he said. "This Steele lady is willing to do the conjuring tonight, but she's got to have the cash in hand before she'll even pick up her magic wand, or whatever it is she uses. And I don't much like to think about what our buddy Peter Barbour might be doing right this minute, or who he might be doing it to."

"Yes, I know."

"But I'll tell you this much: I'm sick and fucking tired of reading his witty little messages, written on a wall in blood someplace, with mutilated corpses used as visual aids. I *want* this bastard."

"Of course you do," she said. "Me, too."

There was another pause, but when Muriel Rojas spoke again, her voice had lost its preoccupied quality. "I'm trying to figure if somehow this whole scenario of yours could possibly be the world's most elaborate con game. But, try as I might, I just can't see it that way. Or maybe I don't want to."

Pacilio sighed into the phone. "Can't say I blame you for entertaining the thought, Muriel. In your place, the idea would sure as hell occur to me. And I guess that anything I say right now to reassure you would only make it look worse, wouldn't it?"

"Yes, it probably would," she said. "Of course, your pointing that fact out might mean that you're about the best con man in the world."

"And is that what you think I am?" he asked softly.

"No, Michael, I don't. If the whole story had come from your lips alone, I might, just might, start to wonder. But the presence of Carol Sefchek negates that hypothesis. Her injuries are undeniable, and far from minor. And if her story about how she got those injuries is really an act, then Meryl Streep had better start thinking about retirement, because that Sefchek kid is the best ever. And one other thing occurs to me, as well."

"What's that?"

"I don't know much about con artists, but it seems to me that this would be an incredibly complex and expensive scam to put on, just for the sake of tricking one lady doctor out of ten thousand dollars."

"Eight thousand, actually," Pacilio said. "I can come up with the other two grand on my own, as I told you."

"Only eight thousand?" She laughed briefly. "Well, that proves it, then: you *must* be on the level." Then her voice became serious again. "Actually, Michael, I never really doubted that you were. On the level, I mean."

"That's good to hear, Muriel."

"However, I probably should mention that, if I'm wrong, and you really *are* just a crook who wants to steal my money, I'll track you down."

"I know, Muriel."

"I'll find you, somehow."

"I know, Muriel."

"I'll cut your heart out, without benefit of anesthesia."

"I know, Muriel."

"I'll use a dull scalpel."

"I would expect nothing less, Muriel."

She laughed again. "All right, I've got that out of my system. Now, then: how are we going to get the money to you? You need it today, is that right?"

"Yes, I do. I want to get the conjuring done tonight, if at all possible. The sooner I get a line on Barbour, or whatever he is, the better. For the money transfer, how about Western Union?"

"No, not for a sum this large. I don't think most Western Union offices keep that much cash on hand." She thought for a moment. "Where are you now?"

"In my room at the Brown Palace Hotel in Denver."

"Is there a bank close by?"

"There must be. I went out this morning on foot, but I wasn't paying attention to banks. Hold on a second, will you?"

He was back on the line within thirty seconds.

"Muriel? There's a branch of Wells Fargo just up the street. Will that do?"

"It should. Okay, here's what you do. Go over to the bank, and tell them you want to open an account for the express purpose of receiving a wire transfer."

"Okay, I can do that."

"When you leave the bank, be sure you have your account number, the bank branch's name and address, and the telephone number they use for wire transfers. Then you call me back. I'll phone the information in to my bank, and they'll take care of the transfer. Barring a glitch of some kind, you should have the money within an hour, I would think."

"That sounds fine. But how come you know about stuff like wire transfers? I thought doctors were supposed to be inept with money."

"Oh, we are," she replied. "In fact, some of us are so dumb about our finances that we have been reputed to loan thousands of dollars to a government thug we hardly know, based on nothing more than a spooky story and one night of incredible sex."

"And the thug hasn't even properly thanked you yet."

"*De nada*, as we say back home. Just try to live long enough to pay it back. And be sure to let me know how this conjuring thing works out."

"I will. But there's one more thing, Muriel."

"What?"

"Do you really think it was incredible sex?"

"Go to the bank, Michael."

It took, in fact, an hour and ten minutes before a Wells Fargo assistant manager named Ramon Martinez started counting out hundred dollar bills in front of Pacilio. When the man had finished, Pacilio looked at the neat pile of cash in puzzlement. "I'm not usually one to turn away money," he said, "but the amount of the transfer was supposed to be eight thousand, and you just counted ten."

Martinez, a neatly-groomed man in his mid-thirties, nodded. "Yes, sir, I remember that eight thousand's what you told me when we made the arrangements. But the actual amount of the wire transfer was ten thousand dollars. When I saw the discrepancy, I checked back with Marine Midland in Albany. There was no error, Mr. Pacilio. The amount authorized for transfer to your new account here was ten thousand dollars."

"I see. Sorry about the confusion."

"Not at all. If there's a problem, perhaps you might wish to consult with the account owner in Albany. You can use my phone, if you like."

"No, that won't be necessary," Pacilio said. "I think I've got it figured out."

"Demonic possession?"

Kimura had been sitting with his forearms resting on his desk, but now he leaned back, letting the back of his neck press against the cool leather of the headrest. After several moments he contnued, "I won't insult you by asking if you're joking, Mac."

"I know how it sounds, believe me. I keep asking myself whether it makes any sense on its own merits, or am I just clutching at straws for the sake of making some sense out of this awful Fairfax business."

Kimura nodded. "And so your presence here means, *ipso facto*, that you've decided there's merit in the theory."

"I guess I must have." He leaned forward in his chair. "I've spent most of today and all day yesterday going through the literature on serial murder – the psychology stuff, of course, and psychiatry, along with criminology and sociology and God knows what all."

"There must be a lot of it," Kimura said. "It seems to have become quite a popular topic for research, these last few years."

"It is," McGraw said. "Thing is, quite a few of those studies raise questions about the motivations of particular serial killers – questions that can't be answered."

"Unless one posits demonic possession as a causative agent?"

"Yeah, that bridges the gap. It explains why certain men, with no history at all of mental illness, no record of antisocial behavior and no physical abnormality – like a brain tumor or something – will suddenly go out and start carving up other people for fun." McGraw sat back, and drank some more juice. "I reached this nutty conclusion more or less the same the way scientists discovered quarks."

Kimura's brow furrowed. "Come again?"

"I'm no physicist, but I gather that quarks're some kind of subatomic particles. I read an article someplace that said the people who discovered quarks weren't on the prowl looking for them. They couldn't have been, since nobody knew the things existed. But apparently there's something weird about the way atomic particles behave under certain conditions, a pattern that said to these scientists, 'There's *something* there.' And, eventually, they found it."

"Just as you found your, uh, demons."

"Yeah, just like that." McGraw smiled crookedly and said, "If you decide to have me committed, you ought to know that Nancy will be plenty mad. She's got tickets for us to go hear Soovin Kim play at Kennedy Center this weekend."

"That *is* a problem," Kimura said with mock seriousness. "Louise and I are quite fond of Nancy, and it would be a shame to distress her by having you institutionalized." Then the seriousness in Kimura's voice became real. "Assuming, just for the sake of argument, that you're not a deserving candidate for a strait jacket, and assuming further that I decide to go along with this macabre fantasy – just what on earth are we going to *do* about it?"

McGraw shook his head. "I don't know, really, but I bet Pacilio does. I'd better get in touch with him, if I can."

"You believe that Mr. Pacilio is pursuing this matter privately, while supposedly on leave?"

"You know I do," McGraw said. "If he's in Denver looking for a witch, then it can only be because of this case. Dealing with demons is what witches do, or so people used to believe."

"Yes, I know. I can only hope that our pursuit of this line of inquiry does not get us all burned at the stake, professionally speaking."

"Me, too, Kim. And that raises an important question: how much backing can Pacilio and I expect if we pursue this?"

Kimura took off his glasses and rubbed the bridge of his nose, a sure sign that he was distressed. Then he replaced the spectacles and said, "Very little, I'm afraid. If I commit any significant resources to this, after our being explicitly warned off by the FBI, it could all blow up in our faces. You and I, along with Mr. Pacilio, could all find ourselves very suddenly unemployed, not to mention facing criminal charges of obstruction."

McGraw nodded, as if he had expected little else. "So does this mean that you think that Pacilio and I are both acting like little kids – scaring each other with ghost stories around the campfire?"

"No, it doesn't," Kimura said. "In fact, I'll grant the possibility that you may be on to something. But can you see me trying to convince Mr. Loomis of that?"

McGraw gave a disgusted snort. Hal Loomis was Kimura's boss, a political appointee, the number three man in the whole department, and a shining testament to the validity of the Peter Principle. He was not famous for being either open-minded or tolerant of those whom he regarded as fools.

"Yeah, all right, you've got me there," McGraw said. "He *would* have me committed, and probably you, as well."

"Very likely. I'm sorry, Mac. There's just not a lot I can do, apart from helping a little here and there."

"Helping how?"

"If you want to put your other cases on hold for a few days, I won't object. If you need to do some traveling, to Denver or wherever, I can authorize both the time off and reasonable expenses. I can dissemble to Agent Pennypacker about your whereabouts if he calls here looking for you. Beyond that. . . ." Kimura shrugged apologetically.

"I know, Kim, and I understand completely. Your moral support means a lot to me, though. I want you to know that." McGraw stood up. "Well, if you'll excuse me, I'd better get on the phone to Denver and see if I can find out where Pacilio's staying."

"And if you succeed, what then?"

"I'll ask him if he's found his witch yet."

———◆———

It was a few minutes shy of 10:00 p.m. when Pacilio walked out the front entrance of the Brown Palace, got in a cab, and gave the address of Victoria Steele's studio on Colfax Avenue.

The driver, a Latino in his late twenties with weightlifter's forearms and a shaved head, nodded and said, "Sure, no problem." He had a tattoo, in the shape of a single teardrop, adorning the right side of his thick neck. As he pulled into traffic and accelerated, a cool breeze began to blow through the cab from the windows, which were open a few inches.

The driver glanced over his muscular right shoulder and said, "The breeze bothers you, you let me know, okay?"

"It's fine," Pacilio said. The day had been warm, but Denver was cooling off rapidly with the coming of darkness. Pacilio thought about the darkness, and the midnight hour that the night would soon usher in. Victoria Steele had been very definite about the time that the "summoning," as she called it, should take place.

"Midnight is the traditional time," she'd told Pacilio that afternoon, shortly after she'd finished counting her ten thousand dollar fee. "I could make up some mystical-sounding mumbo-jumbo to explain why, but the truth is, I don't know. I can tell you that midnight affords the best chance of success, in my experience – and, in these matters, my experience is considerable."

Pacilio's eyes had narrowed. "'Best chance of success?' You mean, it might not work?"

"There's always that possibility." A shrug of the elegant shoulders. "Sometimes the demon I'm summoning won't come, or can't, for some reason. And there's a limit to how hard I can push things."

"This may be a dumb analogy, but, if you call one number and get a busy signal, can't you call another one?"

Victoria Steele had shaken her head. "I know what you're getting at, but it doesn't work that way. I can only summon a demon that I have signed a pact with. I have pacts with several, but demons are not all the same, they have different attributes and skills. Some are good at treasure-finding, others can predict the future, within limits, and still others are useful if you want someone killed. You said you were interested in learning about another demon, one you believe is loose in our world. Well, I have a pact with a demon named Machiste who might be helpful. He's rather a gossip, and he can even be made to tell the truth, under certain conditions. But if he doesn't appear when summoned, I don't have pacts with any other demons who are likely to be very useful for what you want."

"So what if you try for this demon Machiste, and he doesn't show?" Pacilio had asked. "What am I paying you ten grand for?"

"You're paying ten grand for me to try again tomorrow night, and each night thereafter if need be, until I succeed. Of course, you can call the whole thing off at any time, and your money will be refunded – less one thousand dollars for each summoning I attempt. That's for my time and trouble, which will be substantial."

Pacilio had frowned. "So, I'm paying you ten thousand all at once if you succeed, or one thousand a night, every night, even if you fail? This is starting to sound like a gypsy scam I heard about once."

Victoria Steele's gray eyes had flashed, and her voice, normally cool, had gone positively Arctic. "I am not a gypsy, and this is not a scam. If you have any doubts about that, then take your fucking money and get out, right now."

Seeing that Pacilio was making no move to depart, she'd continued, "But if you decide to go forward with this, may I strongly suggest that you not speak to me like that again. Otherwise, some dark night when I'm in an especially bitchy mood, I might do a summoning on my own account, perhaps of the demon Asmodeus, whose particular joys are murder and rape. And then, who knows, I might induce him to pay a little call on *you* – or on someone you love."

Pacilio had let nothing show on his face at her mention of the name "Asmodeus," although he had felt a ghostly finger trace its icy path down his spine. "Asmodeus" was the name given to him by Carl Chopko in his dream. It was supposed to be the name of the demon that Pacilio was hunting. Was Victoria Steele's use of that name just coincidence, or did she know more about this business than she was letting on? Pacilio decided to wait and see.

In the meantime, he needed Victoria Steele, who was now royally pissed off at him. But apologies are cheap, and they don't make people any more bulletproof later, if it comes to that. "I'm sorry for my flippancy," he'd told her, solemnly. "I intended no disrespect. It was a careless remark and I regret making it."

After a moment or two, she had nodded. "All right, forget it. Be here tonight around ten. There are some preparations to be made, and I also want to brief you about the procedure."

Pacilio had stood up and looked across the desk at Victoria Steele. "Do you think the chances are good for success tonight?"

She had shrugged again. "They're not bad. I'd say there's about an 80 percent chance of success. Don't worry, Mr. Pacilio. It will either work or it won't. If it doesn't, we'll keep trying until it does." She'd given a bark of laughter then, and Pacilio had been surprised that a human voice could make a sound that bitter. "Unless something goes wrong," she'd said, "in which case we'll both have more important things to concern us."

The taxi slowed as the driver searched for the street number that Pacilio had given him. "Next block," Pacilio said. "Third building in from the corner, on the right."

"Okay, got it," the driver replied. His name was Rogelio Quesada, and he was a reformed gangbanger who'd found Jesus and given up his life of crime and violence four years earlier. As he pulled the cab into a parking spot, Quesada was gratified that his fare appeared to be a godly man, too. The passenger in the back seat was muttering to himself very softly, but Quesada was sure he'd caught enough of the words to recognize the Twenty-Third Psalm.

———◆———

The demon Asmodeus opened Peter Barbour's eyes and saw by the motel clock that it was after 11:00 p.m. Barbour had been asleep more than twelve hours. That would have to do.

Asmodeus did not need to sleep – indeed, had never slept once in its long, long life. But Peter Barbour, creature of flesh and blood, did require slumber. Asmodeus had been able to get more out of Peter Barbour than the Creator had ever put in – including increased physical strength and speed, as well as greatly augmented sexual capacity – but there were limits to what even Asmodeus could do with such poor material. Peter Barbour's body had been driving south through Delaware when Barbour suddenly began to suffer heart palpitations. Asmodeus had made a quick assessment and realized that Barbour had not had any of what humans call sleep for over seventy-two hours. The human's body was close to complete biochemical failure at a time when Asmodeus, along with the Master he served, could afford no failure.

So Peter Barbour had checked into this little Mom and Pop motel just off Route 95, and, under the command of Asmodeus, he had slept. Even after twelve hours of rest, Peter Barbour was a long way from best of health, but Asmodeus calculated that the human would last long enough for the demon to reach its destination. Then Asmodeus might let him die – painfully, of course.

Twenty minutes later, they were checked out and on the road again. Asmodeus had been tempted to amuse itself with the elderly couple who owned and ran the motel, but it did not want to run the risk of attracting official attention at this point. There would be time for fun after it reached its destination and completed its assigned task. Then there would be amusement in abundance – such slaughter and burning and sexual violation as this world had never seen.

Asmodeus had made sure that Peter Barbour was driving the speed limit exactly, and was not concerned when they passed the Delaware State Police car parked in the median strip. The patrol vehicle was only visible for a few moments in the headlights of Barbour's car. But ten or twelve seconds later – the length of time it might take an alert State Trooper to double-check a license number on his hot sheet – the rearview mirror showed Asmodeus that the police car was pulling onto the highway, red lights flashing.

The trooper's intentions were clear, since no other vehicles were traveling that stretch of Route 95 at the moment. Barbour had not been speeding, so the red lights could only mean one thing: the police knew who was driving the Mercedes. Somehow, they *knew*! From Peter Barbour's lips spewed a curse in a language no human would recognize. A moment later, Barbour's right foot pressed down on the accelerator as far as it would go. The State Police car, its siren sounding like the scream of a damned soul, followed in pursuit.

Justin Gustainis

Chapter 16

Victoria Steele let Pacilio into her office and locked the door behind him. She was wearing a loose-fitting garment that resembled the robe of a Buddhist monk, but done in maroon with black accents instead of the saffron associated with Buddhism.

She was also bald as a doorknob.

Pacilio wondered if she had been wearing a wig earlier in the day to conceal her hairless skull, but then he noticed a small razor nick behind her left ear; it had oozed one drop of fresh-looking blood.

"Why did you shave your head?" he asked.

Victoria Steele shrugged. "Sometimes departing demons, on their way back to Hell, have been known to grab a careless summoner by the hair and bring him along. This is not, as you may imagine, a desirable outcome from the summoner's point of view. I always take steps to prevent anything like that from occurring, but, with demons, it's best to plan for the worst. So I shave, just as a precaution."

Victoria Steele went to the door leading to her studio "Come on," she said. "There are some things I need to explain to you."

The first thing that Pacilio noticed was what appeared to be an altar, set up in the middle of the room. It was small, compared to those he remembered from the Catholic churches of his youth – about the size of a coffee table, but taller, about four feet high. The altar was covered with a black cloth through which was woven, in maroon thread, dozens of horizontal figure-eights – the same "infinity" symbol that Victoria Steele had worn on a chain around her neck earlier in the day. The colors were the same as those of Victoria Steele's robe, although in reverse proportion.

Atop the altar were a number of objects, including a miniature charcoal brazier, a large leather-covered book that looked very old, two ceramic bowls, a small hand bell, and a long, black staff that resembled a shepherd's crook.

On the floor directly behind the altar was a circle, about four feet in diameter. It had been drawn on the floor in some kind of ink or paint that had dried brown. To the left of the circle and about ten feet behind it was another circle, about half the size of the first.

On the other side of the altar, perhaps fifteen feet beyond it, was the pentagram.

The encircled five-pointed star had been made using strips of black masking tape on the surface of the expensive-looking hardwood floor. Pacilio thought that a lot of tape must have been called for, since the pentagram measureed at least ten feet across. At the tip of each point was a squat black candle contained by a small ceramic bowl painted maroon.

Victoria Steele led Pacilio over to the smaller circle. "Stand in here," she said, then walked over to the larger circle that was behind the altar. "This is just a quick dry run," she told him, "but I wanted to be sure you had a sense of where everything is going to be and what you have to do, along with what *not* to do."

The cold gray eyes bore into Pacilio's. "Now, I want your full attention, so stop gawking around," she said. "What I'm about to tell you now can save your life – and your soul, for that matter."

"Go on, I'm listening."

She turned to face the altar and rested her hands on the black and maroon cloth that covered it. "I will conduct the ritual of summoning from here, using these instruments and reading aloud from this book." She turned back to Pacilio. "While all that is going on, there is nothing for you to do, and that is what you will do – nothing. Don't speak, don't ask questions, and keep your smart-ass observations to yourself. Above all, *do not leave the circle.*"

"Why not? I'm not arguing, just curious."

"Because that circle is your protection. Before we start, I'm going to reinforce it with some material that demons are averse to, and I'll use the same stuff around the Great Circle, where I'm standing. No demon that I would summon will have the power to break that circle, so as long as you stay inside it, you're safe. But if you leave the circle, or somehow break it from inside . . . ." Victoria Steele shook her head, as if contemplating a fate beyond imagining.

She walked over to where Pacilio was standing, and her face and voice lost a little of their hardness. "Look, Pacilio, you'll probably go to Hell when you die, because most people do. But I think you'll agree that if one is facing damnation sooner or later, then later is far better. And above all, you do *not* want to be transported to Hell in the body. That is the absolute worst fate that can befall a human being, and I have that on *expert* authority, all right?"

Pacilio nodded. "You're in charge," he said. "I realize this is a serious business, and one which I don't know anything about."

"Well, you'll find out something about it tonight," she told him. "And, with any luck, you'll also learn what you came here to find out. But don't say anything during the summoning, until I tell you. Once the demon appears, keep your eyes on him, and him alone – it's safer that way. And don't be surprised at anything you see. Demons, even fairly minor ones like Machiste, are very skillful at creating illusions. Just don't ever let yourself forget what you're dealing with."

"And what's that?"

"Something that could spend a hundred years making you scream, and regard it as time well spent."

Pacilio noticed the sheen of perspiration on her forehead, although the room was pleasantly cool.

"You really don't like doing this stuff, do you?" he asked gently.

He saw her start to bluster, then change her mind. "No, I don't," she said. "It frightens me every time. Dealing with demons is stressful enough, in itself. And there's always the risk, however slight, that something might go wrong."

"So why do you keep doing it?"

She shrugged. "The money's good, for one thing. And the knowledge to be gained – that's another reason. Demons have been around since before the world was created. They know a lot of secrets, and sometimes they can be induced to share." Her mouth twitched in something like a smile. "There are some other benefits, as well."

"Like what?"

"Well . . . how old would you say that I am?"

Pacilio studied her face for a moment. "I'm not good at this," he said, "but I'd say thirty, thirty-two."

She nodded. "That's what my mirror tells me, too. Except it's a lie. I'm actually fifty-eight years old."

"Jesus Christ," he said softly.

"No, I can assure you that He wasn't involved in the arrangement."

"So, you're telling me that you don't age?"

"Well, I do," she said, "but much slower than normal. I was a bona fide twenty-eight when I discovered that a bargain made with a certain demon would allow me to slow my biological clock dramatically. I estimate that, in physical terms, I've grown four or five years older since then. I expect to live a long, long life."

"With certain damnation waiting at the end?"

Victoria Steele shrugged. "Who knows what bargains might be made in the meantime? Or, maybe I'll join a convent of Carmelite nuns and spend forty or fifty years on bleeding knees, in fasting and prayer." She paused. "Well, perhaps not, since I'd probably have problems with the celibacy requirement. Speaking of which –" she looked at her watch " – time's growing short, and we have something else to do by way of preparation. Come on."

She led Pacilio back into the anteroom and over to an expensive-looking couch done in white leather.

"You *are* straight, aren't you?" she asked.

He stared at her. "Say what?"

"Heterosexual," she said, drawling the word with a touch of mockery. "A scientific term meaning, in this case, that you like to fuck women – as opposed to men, or sheep, or Shetland ponies. Actually, I don't care about the men, sheep or ponies, as long as you like women, as well. You *do* fuck women, don't you?"

"Yeah, sure, but what's *that* got to do with anything?"

"It'll make this easier, that's all. I figured you liked girls, the way you were so carefully not staring at my breasts this afternoon."

She reached back, grasped the collar of her robe, and pulled it up and over her head in one smooth motion. She wore nothing underneath, apart from her sandals, and she kicked those off a moment later. Pacilio noticed that the blonde pubic hair was silky and extremely long, and that she had the kind of body a top-dollar stripper might have envied.

Victoria Steele cupped her breasts and held them up like offerings. "You can look at them now, if you want to," she said. Her voice was a caress. "I won't mind. In fact, I think you should do more than look."

Trying to ignore his growing erection, Pacilio said, "What are you after, lady? A quick lay to settle your nerves before the main event? You ever hear of Valium?"

She shook her head. "I wouldn't take Valium before a summoning, I need to be able to concentrate fully, and drugs can hinder that." Her voice became harder. "Besides, this isn't for my nerves, you impertinent bastard. It's part of the ritual."

"Having sex is part of the ritual," he said dubiously.

"In a way, it is, yes," she told him. "Look, in most religious traditions, the priest, minister, shaman, whatever, engages in a ritual of purification before conducting an important rite. Sometimes this involves only a prayer, or maybe a symbolic washing of hands, or, in some religions, a period of fasting and meditation."

Pacilio shrugged. "So?"

"So when you're dealing with the Nether World, everything is reversed: white is black, virtue is vice, and purity becomes defilement. The deliberate commission of a sin is necessary, as an offering to the Lords of Darkness. It's the opposite of the purification ritual. And it's necessary."

Victoria Steele walked over to Pacilio and stood right in front of him, her hard nipples not quite touching his chest. "Just take my word for it, will you? As the summoner, I have to do this in preparation, and what does it matter to you, anyway? Just think of it as the opportunity to get your rocks off." She began to rub his chest with the palms of her hands. "Come on, this is what every man wants, and we both know it – a quick, hard fuck with an attractive woman, if I may flatter myself. No promises beforehand and no commitments afterward. It won't even cost you any money, and I'm a better lay than any whore you've ever had. Come on, baby, I want to feel your cock deep inside me, what do you say, hmmm?"

She moved her hands down to his waist, where her left hand came into contact with the edge of the holster on Pacilio's right hip. She pushed the edge of his suitcoat back and looked at Glock 19. "And what did you think you were going to do with this?"

"Nothing in particular. I've been wearing it ever since I started on the trail of this guy I'm after. It's habit now."

"I just hope you didn't think this will do you any good with the demon I'm going to summon," she said, "because it won't."

"I never thought it would," he told her. "I probably wear it as a security blanket, as much as anything."

"Just as long as your need for security doesn't make you do something stupid . . . all right, never mind." Her hands started moving again. "Now, then, where were we?"

"Listen, Victoria, I don't think this is going to work," Pacilio said. "Casual, meaningless sex doesn't have the attraction for me that it did when I was twenty. I don't mean to mess up your pre-game ritual, but if you'd told me earlier, I could have let you know then. Sorry."

Victoria Steele checked her watch again. "We haven't got time for this prissy nonsense," she muttered irritably. To Pacilio's relief, she turned away and went over to her desk. Pulling open a drawer, she removed a small glass bottle with a plastic spray nozzle. It looked like a perfume atomizer, Pacilio thought. *If she thinks some Chanel No. 5, or maybe Red Door, is going to make me change my mind, she's going to be one disappointed witch.*

As she walked back toward Pacilio, Victoria Steele sprayed some of the bottle's contents on her neck, between her breasts, and lower, below her navel. Then, standing in front of him again, she said, "I dabble in perfumery now and then, and this is one of my more successful efforts. Do you like it?"

She applied a good amount of perfume to the palm of her right hand while muttering something in a language Pacilio had never heard before. Then she cupped the hand and held it up to his face. He sniffed, and found that the perfume had a pleasant sandalwood scent to it.

Pacilio was about to complement Victoria Steele on her creation when strange things began happening inside his head.

His pulse began to hammer in his ears, and he could feel beads of perspiration break out on his face, a sensation that was soon duplicated all over his body.

The room suddenly began to feel very warm, and after a few moments he realized that he was looking at the woman through what seemed to be a red haze, as if he were a photographer using a filter to take her picture, and a damned pornographic image it would be, too. He found himself becoming hard again, and this time the erection was so demanding that he thought it might burst right through his zipper. Dimly, as from a great distance, he felt Victoria Steele's urgent hands on his tie, his jacket, his shirt – tugging, unbuttoning, removing. Then she was unbuckling his pants, pulling down his shorts, and he thought he heard a voice that might have been hers say, *"Oh yes, that's better, that's exactly what we needed, and so big, too! Yes, I think this will do just fine."*

Then his mind seemed to go away for a while.

Thinking about the experience later, he decided that the photography comparison was especially apt, since what he remembered about that incredibly carnal half-hour with Victoria Steele kept coming back to him as a series of images frozen in time, like snapshots in some X-rated photo album.

Click: Victoria Steele kneeling in front of him, her mouth engulfing him. Her shaved head, earlier a turn-off to Pacilio, now incredibly erotic as he looked down at what she was doing while she looked back up at him, holding his eyes with her own. . . .

Click: Victoria Steele's formidable body supine on the white leather couch, Pacilio lying atop her but facing the other way in the sixty-nine position, their faces moistly buried in each other's groins. . . .

Click: Victoria Steele bent over one arm of the couch, Pacilio behind her, squeezing the mounds of her incredible ass as he drove into her with a vigor and urgency he had not known since his teenage years. . . .

Click Pacilio bent over the couch's arm now, hands holding his ass cheeks apart, Victoria Steele rubbing lubricant over her eight-inch strap-on dildo while cooing something about "Fair's fair, after all. . . ."

Click: Both of them on the white couch, Pacilio atop Victoria Steele, thrusting as if to pound her clear through the cushions, and damn near succeeding. . . .

Click: Pacilio crying out like a lost soul as he emptied himself into Victoria Steele, in a series of spasms that seemed to last an eternity of pain and pleasure. . . .

Later, he returned to himself to find Victoria Steele wiping his face with a damp cloth that smelled like Witch Hazel. He was sitting, nude, on the floor with his back resting against the couch. "Well, back among the living, I see," she said pleasantly.

Pacilio could speak only with difficulty, since his vocal cords had just been through an unaccustomed workout. "What the hell was *that*?" he croaked.

She stood up and walked over to her desk, where her ceremonial robe lay in a wrinkled heap. "I'm not sure, but I think they call it *fucking*," she said. "That, plus a few other things, as I seem to recall." She slipped the robe over her head, then slid her feet into the sandals she had discarded earlier.

"You'd better get dressed," she said to Pacilio. "We'll need to start the ritual in a few minutes, so that I'm ready to do the Invocation at midnight."

Pacilio stood up, discovering in the process that his knees were wobbly. "I want to know what you *did*." His voice was working a little better now.

"What I *did* was treat you to the best sex you've had in your life," she snapped, "so spare me the outraged innocence." After a moment she said, in a more reasonable tone, "The perfume has an enchantment on it. All it did was heighten your libido for a while."

"And turn off the rest of my mind," he said.

Victoria Steele shrugged. "I've found that usually happens when the libido is in control, haven't you? What's that saying – there isn't room for many brains in the head of a hard cock?" She looked at her watch again. "Look, if we don't start the ritual within the next five minutes, there's no point in trying at all tonight. Of course, if you want to repeat this all over again tomorrow. . . ."

Pacilio began to pull his clothes on. "Okay, we'll go through the ritual and see what happens. And when it's over, win or lose, you and I are going to have some conversation about what just happened here."

"Fine, let's do that," she said irritably. "Few things amuse me more than watching a supposedly adult man carry on like a gang-banged virgin." She walked over to the studio door. "I'm going to get ready," she told him. "Join me when you're dressed – and don't forget to re-lock your chastity belt."

The hardworking Germans at Mercedes Inc. put together some well-engineered automobiles. Unlike a lot of cars that have speedometer numbers reaching up to 120, the Mercedes 550 SEL will actually give you an honest 120 miles an hour – just in case you ever find yourself on the Autobahn, where speed limits are as irrelevant as a politician's promise and receive about as much respect.

U.S. Route 95 is not the Autobahn, but the Mercedes being driven by the thing that inhabited Peter Barbour was nonetheless roaring along with the speedometer needle as far to the right as it would go. This kind of speed is highly illegal, but that was the least of the driver's concerns. It was also of limited interest to the man behind the wheel of the Delaware Highway Patrol car that was currently in hot pursuit. Corporal Frank Trowbridge had other things on his mind – such as how to stay on the Mercedes' tail, keep control of his own vehicle, and talk on his police radio all at the same time.

"Dispatch, this is Patrol 47," Trowbridge said into the microphone. He was almost shouting, in order to be heard over the noise that his siren was making. "I'm Southbound on Route 95, just south of mile marker 71. Am in pursuit of a maroon Mercedes, Pennsylvania tag number PRC 977, listed as stolen by a subject wanted for questioning in connection with a homicide in Pennsylvania. Subject vehicle is traveling at a high rate of speed, in excess of 100 m.p.h., and has resisted all efforts on my part to pull him over. Next exit ramp is approximately nine miles south. Request roadblock at the end of the exit ramp and another roadblock across Route 95 just beyond the ramp. If we can fake him into taking the exit and nail him at the end of the ramp, all the better. Over."

"Roger that, Patrol 47," the female dispatcher's voice came back calmly. "I will relay this information to Captain Bateman. Continue pursuit and await instructions. Over."

"Acknowledged."

The dispatcher was back on the air within a minute. "Patrol 47, be advised that your request for a roadblock is confirmed. The barracks is scrambling at this moment, and blocking units should be in place before the suspect vehicle reaches the exit in question. Please advise when subject vehicle is one mile away from roadblock point. Do you copy?"

"That's affirm, Dispatch. Will continue pursuit and advise you when we're one mile out. Over."

"Dispatch out."

Frank Trowbridge could feel the sweat under his armpits and the collar of his uniform shirt. Things were going to get interesting when the driver of the Mercedes realized that the road ahead of him was blocked off by a wall of State Patrol cars. The driver would have very few options then, none of them very promising. The smart thing would be for him to pull over and surrender, but the suspect was apparently wanted for murder already, and thus could not be counted on to do the smart thing. But it didn't matter, really. One way or another, this guy was toast. It was only a matter of time.

———◆———

Pacilio stood in what Victoria Steele called the Lesser Circle and tried to keep his attention on what the woman was doing. But it was difficult to stay focused; his body kept finding ways to remind him of what it had been up to while his mind had been suspended in the red velvet fog of Victoria Steele's enchantment.

He decided that he didn't really like Victoria Steele very much.

She was kneeling within the Great Circle, putting down on the floor a ring of putty-like substance that followed the circumference of the Circle exactly. A few minutes earlier, she had done the same thing to the Lesser Circle. "This material is your protection," she'd explained. "No demon called up under the constraints that I will impose will be able to penetrate it."

"What is this stuff, anyway?"

"The paste itself isn't all that special – some hand-ground flour, water, sea salt, a few more esoteric ingredients. But the main thing is that it holds some other ingredients in suspension and evenly distributed throughout the circle."

"What kind of ingredients?"

"What do you care? Are you planning on taking up the Art, yourself, perhaps?"

"No, but when somebody tells me that my life depends on something she's made, I get kind of curious about what it is, that's all."

"It would take more time than we have right now to explain it, but one of the principal ingredients is the Eucharist."

Pacilio stared at her. "A consecrated Host? Are you kidding me? Where the hell did you get that?"

"It doesn't matter," she said. "Come on, face front. It's time we got started."

"I want to know where you got the Host."

"From a priest who's in love with me," she snapped. "Or thinks he is. Now shut up and let me get to work."

Turning to the altar, Victoria Steele opened the ancient-looking book to a page marked with a red ribbon. With her left hand, she made a motion in the air that looked to Pacilio like the sign of the cross, but upside down – a gesture that she repeated four more times. Then she began to read aloud, in a firm, clear voice.

"By all the powers of light and darkness, by all the Lords of Blood and Pain, by the four dark winds that blow across the earth, whose names are War, Pestilence, Famine and Death, I urge and entreat the attention of the One who guards the gateway to the place of sorrows, which is known as Gehenna. I invoke Him to allow brief passage to the one that I summon, to vouchsafe him to come hither and do my bidding, as he has agreed to do in accordance with a bargain between us freely made and duly signed in mutual obligation."

She picked up the bell from the altar and rang it five times. Then, replacing the bell, she reached into one of the bowls and came out with a fistful of blue powder, which she sprinkled into the brazier with five sweeps of her right hand. She then reached into the other bowl, came out with a handful of rust-colored powder, and repeated the procedure. Once both substances were in the brazier, she passed her left hand over it five times, making a different gesture with each pass. A few moments later, a thin stream of smoke began to issue from the brazier and drift in the direction of the pentagram, even though there was no hint of breeze within the room.

Pretty good trick, Pacilio thought, *to get smoke to go where you want it to. Almost as good as starting a fire without matches or a lighter.*

Turning the page of her grimoire, Victoria Steele continued the invocation. "Powers of Darkness, hear my prayer. Oh Fallen Ones, grant my entreaty. Rebels against Heaven, look favorably upon my petition. Dwellers in torment, hearken unto me. Send into my presence the one who is called Machiste, a loyal and trusted servant of the Father of Lies. Let him come unto the five-pointed star, the pentangle, the Star of Solomon, whose power over the netherworld is known to all. Let him be adjured to harm none present. Let him be compelled to observe the boundaries between the world of darkness and the world of light. Let him be bound so as to do my bidding, to obey my will, to speak as I may command, and then to return to his place of damnation. Let this be done in the fearful name of Leviathan, in the dread name of Beelzebub, in the awful name of Mephistopheles, in the black name of Astaroth, and in the terrible name of Baal."

Victoria Steele reached into one of the bowls again, and added more of the blue powder to the smoldering brazier. She did the same with the dark-red powder, the color that looked to Pacilio so much like dried blood. Then she picked up the bell and again rang it five times. Then she began to speak again, but this time did not refer to the book before her. Instead, she picked up from the altar the long staff made of black metal. Holding the curved end in her left hand, she pointed the staff at the pentagram.

Pacilio had noticed earlier that there was an unlit black candle in a maroon bowl at each of the pentagram's five points. As Victoria Steele declared, "I conjure you, Machiste, in the name of Leviathan!" one of the candles flared and began to burn steadily.

Victoria Steele shifted the staff's point of aim slightly. "I invoke you, Machiste," she chanted, "in the name of Beelzebub!" A second candle was suddenly alight.

Again the staff moved a few inches. "I command you, Machiste, in the name of Mephistopheles!" Three of them were burning now.

"I call you forth, Machiste, in the name of Astaroth!" A fourth candle ignited.

"I manifest you, Machiste, in the name of Baal!" All the candles had now been ignited.

Victoria Steele took in a deep breath, and her next words were almost a scream: "I summon you, Machiste, in the unholy name of Lucifer!"

For a long, aching moment, time seemed to stand still – there was no sound except for Victoria Steele's stentorian breathing, no movement other than the flickering of the five candles and the swirling smoke from the brazier.

Then Pacilio noticed that the smoke from the brazier was starting to collect over the pentagram. The miniature cloud rapidly grew thicker, although the rate of burning in the brazier did not appear to have increased. Within a minute, the smoke in that small area had concentrated into a fog that would, on a larger scale, have done justice to London at midnight – although Pacilio did not remember the London variety giving off the strong odor of sulfur that now permeated the room.

The pungent smell was making Pacilio's eyes water, but he kept his gaze focused on the pentagram. Even so, he was unable to say precisely when the smoke thinned sufficiently to reveal the secret it had held.

There was Something standing in the middle of the pentagram.

———◆———

When Peter Barbour's eyes picked out the State Police roadblock just beyond the upcoming exit ramp, the demon Asmodeus immediately discerned the humans' feeble stratagem: he was supposed to take the exit to avoid the roadblock, and only when he was halfway through the long curve of the exit ramp would the second roadblock, the one at the end of the ramp, be revealed. The pursuing police car would be behind him, and the Mercedes would be trapped, with no room to manuever.

Peter Barbour's lips sneered with Asmodeus' scorn. They would play their intellects against his, would they? Well, perhaps they had enough mental capacity to learn something about strategy from him, who had been a General in the greatest war that either Heaven or Earth had ever seen.

Asmodeus was not familiar with the expression "bootlegger's turn," nor was the phrase part of Peter Barbour's vocabulary. But the demon understood physics better than Einstein ever had, and it calculated in a millisecond what combination of speed, motion and inertia would produce the result it desired. The roadway was wet from a recent rainstorm, which would help. Using Peter Barbour's foot on the brake, Asmodeus began carefully to slow the Mercedes. It was all a matter of timing, and Asmodeus knew all there was to know about time.

Following about a hundred yards behind, Corporal Frank Trowbridge saw the Mercedes' brake lights come on and immediately began to slow his patrol car, to avoid rear-ending the other vehicle. Was the guy in the Merc slowing down to take the exit, or was he going to pull over and give it up in the face of such overwhelming police opposition? Or was he going to do what more and more of them seemed to do these days – come up with a gun and start blasting away in suicidal defiance? Frank Trowbridge was prepared to cope with any of these choices that the suspect might make.

He was *not* prepared to see the Mercedes slow to about thirty-five and then brake hard while the driver twisted the steering wheel a quarter-turn to the left. He was not prepared for the Mercedes' rear end to whip around in a controlled skid that ended up, 180 degrees or so later, with the Mercedes facing back the way it had come. He was not prepared to have the rapidly accelerating Mercedes charging right at him, its high beams on, its horn blaring. He was not, in short, prepared to die.

Frank Trowbridge frantically twisted his steering wheel to the right in a desperate effort to avoid the head-on collision that seemed only seconds away. The manuever worked, although the Mercedes' bumper gave Frank's the slightest possible nick as the two vehicles passed each other. The patrol car was suddenly careening off the road into some high weeds, while the Mercedes fled north on Route 95 south at an ever-increasing rate of speed.

The demon Asmodeus was not versed in the expression "playing chicken," either, but did understand what it meant to break an enemy's nerve. It was well pleased with the way its plan to escape the clumsy police trap had worked.

This enjoyment lasted at least six seconds, until the Mercedes' right rear tire, which had just been subjected to a degree of torque the manufacturer had never anticipated, exploded like the clap of doom.

———◆———

The smoke that had collected in the middle of the pentagram gradually cleared, revealing more of the figure that stood there. Whatever Pacilio was expecting, it was not the blond, aristocratic-looking young man with the shy smile who was before him now. The visitor, who looked to be in his mid-twenties, was dressed in a blue blazer, a white shirt open at the collar with a yellow ascot underneath, gray flannel slacks, and black, tassled loafers. The blonde hair was worn over the ears, and the handsome face bore an expression of well-bred attentiveness.

"Hail, Machiste!" Victoria Steele declared formally. "You have kept our bargain by appearing when called. I, too, shall honor the bargain when giving you leave to depart." Then, in a more conversational tone she added, "Your corporal manifestation is a surprise to me."

"Why?" the young man inquired mildly. "Do you find my appearance distasteful? I did *so* want to cut a dashing figure." The voice was slightly campy in tone, with a British accent so refined as to make Prince Charles sound Cockney by comparison.

Victoria Steele shook her head. "No, not distasteful at all. But I do recall that you appeared in a rather different form the last time I summoned you."

The demon smiled ruefully. "Yes, I'm afraid I was trying to disconcert you on that occasion. How naughty of me. And how very foolish, to think that I could frighten a practitioner of the Art as experienced and courageous as yourself, my dear." A slight bow in Victoria Steele's direction. "Still, I am rather surprised that you invited me to return quite so soon."

"The last time was more than six years ago, Machiste."

"Yes, my point exactly," he said in that well-bred drawl. "But, upon reflection, I'm not surprised that you find me irresistible. So many women do, you know."

"I summoned you for a reason, Machiste," Victoria Steele said sternly. "I require information concerning the whereabouts and intentions of another of the Fallen."

Machiste raised two perfectly-groomed eyebrows. "*You* require? Then what explains the presence of this rather swarthy gentleman to your left?" He made a slight gesture in Pacilio's direction. "What does *he* require? Someone to restore his power of speech, perhaps?"

"He will speak when it is time for him to speak," she snapped. "But first, you will give *me* your pledge to answer truthfully!"

"Truthfully?" The blond aristocrat seemed to find the word amusing. "Well that's rather difficult to promise, old girl. It's such a slippery thing, this *truth* that you're going on about. Why, I can still remember my old chum Pontius Pilate asking that Galilean fellow, 'What *is* truth?' And I rather think he had –"

"Silence, obstinate one! You will swear to speak the truth, and you will swear *NOW!*" With the last word, Victoria Steele slammed the point of the staff into the floor at her feet. Instantly, the demon Machiste gave a howl of pain – a sound that, to Pacilio's ears, was more animal than human.

After a few seconds, Machiste seemed to recover from his anguish. Still affecting his House of Lords accent, he said mildly, "That wasn't really very sporting, old girl."

"Swear!" Victoria Steele cried, followed by another thump of the staff. "Now!" The staff came down yet again.

The sounds of agony were even louder and more unpleasant than before. After the pain appeared to pass, Machiste looked at Victoria Steele, and his blue eyes appeared to burn with a fire all their own. The equanimity of the upper-class Brit twit was gone now, replaced with a chilling malice. "On the day that you pass over from this plane to my own," he said hoarsely, "we must have a discussion about pain, you and I. A long, long talk, punctuated frequently by your screams and fruitless pleas for mercy."

Victoria Steele raised the staff again. "Swear!"

The demon held a hand up, palm outward. "Very well, I swear, I swear. By the name of my father, who is Lucifer, by the name of my home, which is Hell, by all that is unholy, I swear to speak the truth and to utter no falsehoods."

Without taking her eyes off Machiste, Victoria Steele said to Pacilio, "All right, ask your questions. He won't lie, probably, but remember that everything you hear is given under duress, so assess it accordingly. And don't waste time – we only have until those candles at the points of the pentagram burn down. Then he'll be compelled to go back where he came from – it's part of the spell. I estimate about twenty minutes."

"Pity you didn't use bigger candles," Pacilio said.

By way of reply, Victoria Steele said, "Nineteen minutes."

"All right, all right," he muttered, then raised his voice to call, "Machiste!"

The demon, back in full possession of his genteel persona, sketched another bow. "Your servant, sir."

"Do you know the demon called Asmodeus?" Pacilio's excellent peripheral vision picked up the movement of Victoria Steele's head as she heard that name. She started to turn and look at him, but caught herself and kept her eyes on Machiste. Pacilio knew she must have been thrown by the name of the very demon with which she had threatened him earlier in the day.

"Of course," Machiste said urbanely. "All of the Fallen know each other. We've had a good deal of time in which to become acquainted, you know."

"And where is he now?" Pacilio asked.

"Where?" Machiste affected puzzlement. "What did you have in mind, old chap? Do you want his address, complete with postal code? Planning to send him an asbestos birthday card, are you?"

Pacilio controlled his impatience with an effort. "What I have in mind, for a start, is whether Asmodeus is in your world, or mine. You swore an oath to speak the truth, so speak it!"

Machiste smiled sheepishly, like an Oxford don caught watching *Absolutely Fabulous* on his telly. "Well, when you put it like that, I suppose I can tell you that he's in your world at present. Much nicer climate here, really."

Pacilio nodded. "And has Asmodeus taken possession of a man named Peter Barbour?"

"Didn't catch the fellow's name, actually," Machiste said. "But I do believe Asmodeus is using one of your chaps to stroll about in, yes. Saves a lot of wear and tear on the wings, you know, if you can find someone to give you a lift."

"Where – no, *precisely* where in this world is Asmodeus now?"

"That's a bit of a tough one, I'm afraid." Machiste smiled apologetically. "He's in transit, you see. If I were to tell you, um, *precisely* where he is – well, by the time I finished telling you, he'd be somewhere else, wouldn't he?" The smile became wider. "You see my dilemma, I'm sure."

"Of course I do," Pacilio said. Without taking his eyes from the demon, he said, "Victoria, could I impose on you to bang that staff down four or five times? And could you do it extra hard, please?"

"Certainly," Victoria Steele replied, and raised the staff with both hands.

"Hang on, now, there's no need to be hasty," Machiste said. "I did tell you the truth, you know. Asmodeus *is* in transit even as we speak."

"All right," Pacilio said. "So, suppose you tell me, as *precisely* as you can under the circumstances, where the son of a bitch is right now."

"Oh, dear, vulgar insults," Machiste said with a show of dismay. "Asmodeus will be so upset when he hears. He's really quite sensitive, you know."

Through clenched teeth, Pacilio said "Victoria. . . ."

Victoria Steele, who had lowered the staff to the floor after Machiste's apparent acquiescence, raised it again.

"Oh, very well," Machiste said sullenly. "If you must know, he is now in the district you call Delaware, on the roadway known as Route 95 South, just north of mile marker 73, traveling at what is, for you creatures, a high rate of speed – around 120 miles per hour. Is that *precise* enough for you, old boy?"

"It'll do," Pacilio said. "Is Asmodeus, or Barbour, still driving the Mercedes he picked up in Scranton?"

"Yes, I believe he is. He sent us the car's owner, you know – a woman, Jessica something-or-other. I made her acquaintance quite recently. She apparently thought she knew something about what you creatures so quaintly call 'gang bangs.'" Machiste's grin was quite horrible. "She has a somewhat better idea now, I believe."

"Never mind," Pacilio said. He glanced at the black candles, saw that they were significantly lower. "Does Asmodeus have a specific destination in mind?"

"Well, he does *now*. I mean, when he first arrived on this side, all he thought of was his own pleasure, or so it seems. The naughty boy simply went cavorting about, enjoying himself with no thought to the *marvelous* opportunity that had been presented to him."

"What opportunity was that?" Pacilio asked.

"Why *sharing*, of course. I mean, selfishness is not exactly unheard of amongst us, but there comes a time when one simply *must* give some thought to others. So the Master sent Lucifuge Rofocale to remind Asmodeus of that little fact. To put the fear of the Devil into him, you might say."

Pacilio's eyes narrowed. "Sent *who*?"

Victoria Steele answered him, her voice thoughtful. "Lucifuge Rofocale is a demon very important in the hierarchy of the Fallen. Believed to be third after Satan Himself, who is, of course, the Master that Machiste is referring to."

Pacilio nodded. "So that's who appeared in the mirror at the Albany Holiday Inn?"

"Your mirrors have sometimes been useful to us," Machiste admitted.

Pacilio took a deep breath, then asked the $64,000 dollar question: "So where is Asmodeus going, in the body of Peter Barbour, and what is he supposed to do when he gets there?"

Machiste frowned, like a Bishop hearing his first dirty joke. "Surely, you don't expect me to answer that."

"Surely, I do," Pacilio said.

"Do you have any conception of what would be done to me, upon my return, if I were to reveal that to you? No, of course you don't, you couldn't possibly."

Victoria Steele had been content to let her client take the lead up to this point; after all, he was paying. But now she was intrigued. Pacilio had apparently stumbled onto something of immense importance, although he was, of course, in no position to comprehend the possible ramifications. But it now seemed vital that Machiste answer Pacilio's question. Depending on what the response was, Victoria Steele might find herself in a position to gain more knowledge than she'd ever dared hope for – and in the Great Game she played, knowledge was power.

Pacilio might try to interfere with any plans she would make to use that information, but he could be dealt with easily enough. She could do another summoning tomorrow night and send Something to take care – permanently – of any danger that Pacilio might pose.

But first, Machiste had to answer that question. Victoria Steele raised the staff and prepared to slam it down, knowing that a minor demon like Machiste would be unable to resist for long the pain that she could inflict upon him.

The reason for what happened next is unclear. Victoria Steele may have been overtired, or possibly her mind was so full of the possibilities stemming from what she had just heard that she lost her concentration. All of that is speculation. But the undeniable fact is that, in thrusting the ensorcelled staff into the floor, Victoria Steele unconsciously took half a step forward. As a result, her point of aim was off by almost a foot. Instead of striking the hardwood floor cleanly, the staff was driven into the Host-impregnated putty she had laid down *and broke the circle.*

———————

When the Mercedes' right rear tire blew out under the kind of abuse it was never intended to handle, Asmodeus calculated the proper response in about one-tenth the time that an intelligent human could have done it: steer with the skid, foot off the brake, let inertia slow the car down. The demon was already calculating what to do after the car was back under control, and so it failed to realize, for a crucial three seconds, that Peter Barbour's body was not responding with the speed required by the situation. The recent rest notwithstanding, Barbour was still at the edge of exhaustion, and his reflexes were much slower than normal – certainly slower than Asmodeus had been counting on. Consequently, the decision to steer with the skid, which was a sound idea, was implemented just a little too late.

The uncontrolled skid carried the Mercedes across the highway and off the left shoulder, where soil erosion caused by bad drainage had allowed a shallow ditch to form.

Asmodeus was just beginning to regain control of the steering when the left front wheel slid into the ditch. At the speed the Mercedes was moving, that was enough.

The Mercedes rolled twice before smashing into a wall of boulders that was used to reinforce the highway median strip. At the moment of impact, the car was traveling, sideways, at 58 miles per hour. With that kind of momentum involved, it is not surprising that the Mercedes' gas tank split open, gushing Hi-Test Unleaded all over everything. The motor was still racing, producing sparks in abundance, and so less than ten seconds after impact, the Mercedes went up like the world's biggest Molotov cocktail.

The first of the state troopers on the scene was tempted to call for an ambulance immediately, but then changed his mind. The trooper had seen a lot of wrecks, and more than a few car fires. His experience told him that nothing human could survive this one.

———◆———

Until that night in Victoria Steele's studio, the fastest living thing that Michael Pacilio had ever seen had been a King Cobra he'd once observed in Vietnam. While lying in ambush one rainy afternoon in the Mekong Delta, Pacilio had watched the deadly snake from thirty feet away as it took down a rat, and the speed of its strike had been awesome.

The demon Machiste made that cobra look like a garden slug. The instant Victoria Steele broke the continuity of the Great Circle with her staff, before she was even aware of what she had done, Machiste was on her.

His body never left the center of the pentagram. But his right arm suddenly stretched out, impossibly long, looking to Pacilio like something out of an animated cartoon. But there was nothing funny about what Machiste was doing. The hand at the end of the absurdly elongated arm flashed under the hem of Victoria Steele's robe and went straight for her groin. There, it somehow got a grip – and began to pull.

For a moment, Pacilio was baffled. Then he remembered her pubic hair – blonde, silky, and extremely long. *She said that a demon may try to grab you by the hair and take you back with him. That's why she shaved her head, but she forgot how long her pussy hair is and now that bastard has got a handhold!*

Machiste yanked hard, and Victoria Steele's feet shot out from under her. Now she was on her back, with her legs already outside the useless circle, and the demon was dragging her toward the pentagram, all the while giggling in a manner that would have been unnerving if it were not mostly drowned out by Victoria Steele's screaming: *"PACILIO! DO SOMETHING! STOP HIM! HELP ME! HURRY, DO SOMETHING!!"*

Pacilio stood absolutely still, but his mind was in overdrive.

He would not have thought it possible that a normal-sized adult could be dragged by the pubic hair, but maybe it was some kind of symbolic sorcery thing -- otherwise, the demon could just as easily grab you by the arm.

So, what could he *do*? To leave his circle would probably mean joining Victoria Steele in her predicament. Machiste had two arms and would no doubt be overjoyed to have a second plaything. How could Pacilio help her without leaving the circle? His eyes flickered over to the metal staff, which Victoria Steele had dropped when Machiste had yanked her off her feet – no, too far away. He couldn't reach it from within his protective circle, and had no way to know if it would work for him even if he could get his hands on it.

Victoria Steele was fighting hard. She had somehow found a purchase on the hardwood floor with her bare heels and had slowed the rate at which Machiste was able to drag her. Now she used her strong abdominal muscles to raise the upper half of her body from the floor. Pointing her right index finger like a gun at Machiste, she cried, "Machiste, spawn of Satan, know the wrath of your Creator, Jehovah, and his Son, Jesus!" With the last word, her index finger traced the sign of the cross, upright this time, in the air.

The curse had an effect – Machiste howled in an agony greater than any he had shown earlier when being chastised with Victoria Steele's staff. *But he did not let go.*

Victoria Steele drew breath to try the curse again, or perhaps she had something else in mind. But Machiste recovered quickly from his anguish and gave a sharp tug that pulled her forward again and banged her head on the floor at the same time. Victoria Steele frantically tried to gain another purchase with her feet, but the hardwood floor was slick. Plus, her frantic struggles were tearing the skin off her heels, and the resultant bleeding was making traction even more elusive. She was being dragged slowly but steadily now, and was more than halfway to the pentagram and whatever awaited her there.

"PACILIO!" Her voice was a screech.

Never, under any circumstances, leave the circle.

"STOP HIM! PLEASE!"

Pacilio thought about Victoria Steele's description of a demon: *Something that could spend a hundred years making you scream and regard it as time well spent.*

"PACILIO, YOU FUCKING BASTARD! DO SOMETHING!!"

He could feel the holstered Glock 19 against his forearm through the suitcoat. *I hope you didn't think this was going to do any good with the demon I'm going to summon, because it won't.*

"PACILIO, GOD DAMN YOU!!"

She was almost there. Inside the pentagram, Machiste's aristocratic face split in a grin of triumph. Pacilio could hear Victoria Steele's voice describing what it meant to be transported to Hell "in the body": *It's the absolutely worst fate that can befall a human being.*

"PLEASE, GOD, DON'T LET HIM TAKE ME!!!"

The demon Machiste had supernatural speed, but, for a mere human being, Michael Pacilio did pretty well.

It took him three-quarters of a second to draw the Glock and bring it to aim two-handed, and only a little more time than that to fire two 9-millimeter rounds into the top of Victoria Steele's smooth, shaven skull.

———◆———

Frank Trowbridge, who had finally worked his State Police cruiser out of the mud and undergrowth, was the next to arrive at the blazing wreck that had once been a Mercedes sedan. Leaving his vehicle's flashing red light going, he walked over to the other trooper, whose name was Steve Wozniak. The two men knew each other slightly.

"Looks like the crazy son of a bitch lost it, big time," Trowbridge said by way of greeting.

"That's for sure," Wozniak said. "I think one of the tires blew on him, threw him into a skid. That was kind of a slick move he put on you, though, wasn't it?"

Trowbridge shook his head in wonderment. "The old rum runner's turn. Christ, I haven't seen that since I was a kid, fooling around with my Mustang on those dirt roads back home. Did you call the meat wagon?"

Wozniak shook his head. "Not yet. Figured there was no special hurry, you know? No way that asshole is getting out of there, except in a body bag."

"Yeah?" Trowbridge was looking over Wozniak's shoulder now, in the direction of the still-burning wreck, and there was a stricken expression on his face. *"Then what the fuck do you call THAT?"*

Wozniak turned to see the front passenger-side door of the Mercedes swing open and disgorge a human figure that crawled out of the car, staggered three or four paces, and collapsed on the ground. The man, like the car itself, was burning like a torch.

"Holy fucking Jesus!" Wozniak yelled, then ran to his cruiser for a fire extinguisher. Trowbridge sprinted the other way, toward the still-burning shape lying on the ground. He tore off his uniform shirt as he ran, losing most of the buttons in the process. When he reached the man, he began to beat at the flames with his shirt, all the while yelling, "If you can hear me, roll! Roll to your left, it'll put the fire out! Roll left, c'mon, man! Roll, goddammit!" All the while, even as he was shouting and trying to extinguish the flames, Trowbridge was thinking, *"I hope the son of a bitch dies right now. Nobody deserves this, nobody should have to go through this, I don't care what he's done, let him die, please, God, just let him die."*

Wozniak ran up with a fire extinguisher and sprayed the recumbent form, although Trowbridge had already put out most of the fire that had engulfed the man. Whether either trooper had done any good was a moot point. The still figure on the ground reminded Wozniak of photos he had seen of napalm victims in Vietnam, except the pictures had failed to convey the distinctive odor produced by burning flesh. Steve Wozniak privately decided that he was never going to eat roast pork again.

Trowbridge, who was kneeling on the ground by this time, looked up at Wozniak and said, "Better call for that ambulance now, I guess, for all the fuckin' good it'll do. We're gonna need a fire engine, too."

Wozniak could not take his eyes off the still, silent thing on the ground. "Christ, I would've tried to get him out, if I'd known . . . I mean, did you ever see anybody survive a crash and burn like this one? And no screamin' – you notice that? The son of a bitch is in there on fire but there's no screamin'! You ever see that? How was I supposed to *know?*"

"Not your fault, man," Trowbridge told him. "I would've thought the same thing, in your place. Anyway, the poor fuck's dead now –"

That was when Peter Barbour's right hand, what was left of it, snapped out to grab Trowbridge's wrist. "Jesus!" The trooper yelled in both surprise and revulsion.

The husk that had once been a human being named Peter Barbour held on to Frank Trowbridge with a grip that was amazingly strong. Then the charred lips moved. A sound came from the seared throat, then another, followed by several more. Then the grip relaxed, the hand let go, and Peter Barbour, who had suffered greatly for his sins, finally found the peace of death.

Wozniak had a stunned look on his face. "Did he say something? Did you catch it, Frank? What did he say?"

"I think he said, 'Thanks for the lift,' Frank Trowbridge replied, and there was no fear at all in his voice now – no fear, and no compassion. There may even have been a touch of amusement.

Justin Gustainis

Chapter 17

It was just past 1:30 in the morning when the taxi brought Pacilio back to the Brown Palace. There was no doorman on duty, and for this Pacilio was grateful. He wanted to get inside unnoticed and unremembered – just in case Denver Homicide came around asking questions later.

He had walked three blocks from Victoria Steele's studio before finding a bar that was open, and had used the pay phone there to summon his cab. The driver, a middle-aged black man with the thickened nose and ears of a former boxer, had politely asked to see some money before pulling away from the curb. Pacilio understood that guys leaving bars late at night don't always have the cab fare they claim, so he'd flashed some green without complaint.

There were a few people scattered around the lobby even at that hour. Pacilio paid no attention to them and was careful not to make eye contact. He crossed the lobby swiftly, and if any of his fellow guests made note of his passage, it is unlikely that they were close enough to see the haunted expression in his eyes. Pacilio was heading directly and discreetly to his room, where he was going to lock the door behind him, and bolt it, and then put the chain on. He would try to resist the impulse to push the room's furniture up against the door as a barricade.

His brisk stride brought him to the main bank of elevators. None of the doors was standing open, so Pacilio pushed the call button. He had been waiting only a few seconds when a voice behind him said, pleasantly, "I was wondering when you were going to show up."

Three reactions passed through Pacilio's brain and central nervous system in very rapid succession.

The first was a startle impulse, and it was strong enough so that Pacilio almost, but not quite, jumped a foot in the air. The second was a defense reflex that had him pivoting rapidly on his left foot to face the speaker, his right foot sliding back to maintain perfect balance even as his arms began to move, very fast, into a combat stance, that would allow him to block a blow or deliver one, as needed. The third reaction was recognition, prompting Pacilio to abandon his fighting posture before it was fully developed and to sigh with exasperation before saying, in surprise and annoyance but most of all in relief, "Jesus Christ, Mac, what the fuck are you doing here?"

Pacilio closed the door of his hotel room and chained it. "Sit down, Mac, anywhere you like." He went around the room, turning lights on. "What were you doing down in the lobby at this hour, anyway?"

McGraw shrugged. "I don't sleep well in any bed but my own, which just shows you what an old fart I'm turning into. I tried watching TV, but after a while the walls started to feel like they were closing in. So I thought the lobby might offer a change of scene and some open space, if nothing else."

Pacilio started to take off his suitcoat, then stopped and seemed to notice for the first time that the side pockets were bulging slightly. He reached in and began to toss packets of twenty dollar bills onto the bed nearest to him. After the side pockets were empty, he reached into the jacket's inner pockets and added several more stacks to the collection on the bedspread. Each packet of bills was held together by a new-looking "Wells Fargo" wrapper.

McGraw stared at the pile of cash, but his voice contained nothing more than mild curiosity when he asked, "Have you taken up bank robbery as a second career? I mean, what you've got there doesn't look like much of a haul by Willie Sutton's standards, but I suppose it's not bad if you're just starting out."

Pacilio was looking at the money, too. "No, it came from a bank all right, but my method of withdrawal was entirely legal. I used it to pay for services rendered, and 'rendered' is a good word for what happened. But I'm pretty sure the woman I paid won't be complaining about the refund."

Pacilio took off his suit jacket and laid it on the bed next to the small pile of bills, but not before McGraw noticed the faint but rather large stain around the breast pocket.

"You're usually pretty careful about your clothes," McGraw said. "Did you have an accident at dinner tonight?"

Pacilio shook his head, and his expression was bleak. "No, that was later," he said. "And it was no accident; it was on purpose." He picked up the suit jacket and looked at the stain critically. "I washed off as much as I could with some cold water before I left, but it's going to need dry cleaning. That'll have to wait until I get home, though. The Denver P.D. might be checking around, tomorrow or maybe the day after, to see if any of the local cleaning places have been asked to deal with bloodstained clothing. Besides, I'll be flying out tomorrow, since I got what I came for, more or less."

McGraw was not short on either intelligence or empathy. He already knew what Pacilio looked like when shaken to the core; he had seen that only a few days earlier, after Pacilio had returned from the lab in Fairfax. But this was worse, McGraw thought, because Pacilio was more than shaken. This time he looked scared. McGraw was not used to seeing fear on that face.

"It was pretty bad tonight, wasn't it?"

"Bad?" Pacilio just shook his head. "Fucking awful is what it was. I haven't run into anything that nasty since the war, and even then . . . ." Pacilio might have been talking to himself. "This time, I really had no idea what I was getting myself into. Hell, I was half-prepared to believe that it was all going to turn out to be nothing more than an elaborate con game. But I had to find out for sure."

"And you found out that it wasn't a con." McGraw said quietly.

"No, it wasn't a con. It was real – if you can describe something so fucking incredible with words like 'real.'"

McGraw nodded, as if everything Pacilio had just said made perfect sense to him. "I'd like to hear about it, if you feel you can tell me," he said. "But first things first. I flew out here to see if you needed a hand, and I'm still ready to lend one. I gather there's some possibility that you may be attracting the attention of the local *gendarmes*. Do we need to move you to another hotel, under a different name? Or do you want to get out of town fast, to avoid being picked up for questioning? If it's one of those deals, the cops will probably be watching the airports, but I can rent a car for you in my name, if that's what you need."

Pacilio thought for a moment. "None of that should be necessary," he said, "but thanks, Mac. The police aren't involved yet, and they probably won't even know they have something to investigate for another day or so. It ought to take them even longer to get around to me, if they ever do, and by then I'll be back East. By the time they could get an extradition warrant signed and served, assuming they feel it's worth the trouble, this Peter Barbour business ought to be over with."

"Is that all that matters to you – getting this case closed?"

"For now, yeah, that's all that matters," Pacilio said, and McGraw was glad to see some of the old determination returning to Pacilio's voice. "There are bigger stakes involved here than we thought, Mac. A lot bigger."

"Is that what the witch said when you found her?"

"That, and more. A hell of a lot more."

"Maybe you'd better tell me about it."

Pacilio began to loosen the knot in his tie. After a moment, he said, "Yeah, maybe I'd better."

Pacilio sat down on one of the beds. "Do you believe in demonic possession, Mac?"

He seemed surprised when McGraw pursed his lips, nodded a couple of times, and said, "As a matter of fact, I think I do."

Pacilio blinked. "That's not what I expected you to say, to be honest."

"Three or four days ago, that's not what I *would* have said. But I've learned a lot in the past few days, and none of it has gone very far toward improving my peace of mind. Anyway, go on."

"Well, I got the idea into my head that our elusive psychopath Peter Barbour might possibly be a victim of possession. So I went to see a Jesuit I know at the University of Scranton . . . ."

———◆———

". . . so I pulled my weapon and shot her in the head. Twice."

There was silence in the room then, and it seemed to go on for quite some time. Finally, McGraw said, "I can see now why you're concerned about the Denver police. It might be difficult to convince them that your shooting this Steele woman actually constituted an act of mercy killing."

"Yeah, I figured that I might have a few problems with that."

"And if you told them what you've just told me, they'd probably think you were just angling for an insanity defense."

"Which means I'd be headed for a long spell in a state loony bin instead of one of Colorado's maximum security prisons."

"Not much of a choice there," McGraw said.

"No, not much at all. So I did what I could to cover my tracks. That's the reason I took back the money – well, one of the reasons, anyway. It might have been possible to trace the bills back to Wells Fargo, and I had to use my real name to arrange for the wire transfer. So I cleaned up at Victoria Steele's as best I could, including wiping everything down for fingerprints. Then I turned the air conditioning up to the max, locked the place up tight, and dropped Ms. Steele's keys down a sewer grate a couple of blocks away. She'll be found eventually, of course, but there's no way to predict when. Somebody else with a set of keys could go waltzing in there today, who knows? But even if nobody else has access to the place, sooner or later she's going to get ripe enough for it to become noticeable elsewhere in the building. But the air conditioning will slow decomposition somewhat and buy me a little more time."

"Wait a minute." McGraw was frowning. "You killed Victoria Steele to prevent this demon, Machiste, from taking her back to Hell with him while she was still alive, right?"

"The phrase she had used earlier was 'in the body,'" Pacilio said, nodding

"But after you spoiled his fun by killing her, he was still there, wasn't he? You said that the Steele woman told you he'd be stuck inside that pentagram thing until those candles burned out."

Pacilio nodded again, wearily. "Yeah, you're right, Mac. The son of a bitch was still there."

"So, what happened after you shot her?" McGraw was less interested in learning the answer than he was in having Pacilio tell it. Clearly, the memory was eating at him even now. McGraw thought the only way to reduce some of the immense pressure on Pacilio's psyche was to get him to open up about it, to share the burden of whatever terrible thing had happened.

Pacilio started to speak, cleared his throat, then tried again. "Well," he said, "that's actually when it got kind of ugly."

———◆———

Two hours earlier:

Pacilio stood inside the Lesser Circle, the smoking pistol still in his hand, and watched Victoria Steele die. Death by gunshot is rarely instantaneous, even with two bullets in the brain. Victoria Steele's central nervous system protested its imminent extinction with a series of large-muscle spasms that lasted four or five seconds. Then her limbs stopped twitching and she was still.

Pacilio looked at Machiste, who was staring at Victoria Steele's corpse with a mixture of rage and disbelief on his aristocrat's face. Then the demon turned his gaze on Pacilio, and for just an instant the human mask fell away and Pacilio saw Machiste as he really was. There are no words in any human language to describe the monstrousness of that vision, but it is fair to say that many people who were less resilient than Michael Pacilio would have suffered an immediate and complete mental breakdown at the sight.

Pacilio did not go mad, but he did start to become faint, a gray mist clouding his eyesight and becoming thicker by the second. However, as his knees started to buckle, Pacilio suddenly heard a voice shouting in his ear, as clear and loud and urgent as if its owner were standing right beside him: "Hey, Mike! Get your shit together, man! Pass out now and you'll fall outside the fuckin' circle. Then your ass is grass and that blond motherfucker's the lawnmower! STAND TO, YOU ASSHOLE!!" The voice, Pacilio realized, was Carl Chopko's.

A surge of adrenaline sped through Pacilio like an electric charge. His vision cleared almost immediately and his knees straightened. A few seconds later, he risked another look at Machiste, but the demon was now fully back in its human guise. The rage seemed to be under control, but Machiste was looking faintly disappointed, as if Pacilio's recovery had spoiled another of his plans.

"Well, old boy," Machiste said suavely, "your answer to the lady's plight, what one of your race's greatest statesmen would call 'the final solution,' was rather ingenious, I must say. I have no doubt the soul of the recently deceased Miss Steele will be waiting for me when I return to my abode, and will provide me and my brethren with many centuries of amusement. Still, I was rather looking forward to bringing the whole package back with me. One so rarely gets the chance to enjoy that sort of treat, you know. There was that Faustus fellow, of course, but his corporal form didn't really last us very long. . . ."

Pacilio glanced at one of the fat candles, still burning in its bowl at one tip of the pentagram. A well-placed bullet from his pistol would probably blow the candle to pieces, extinguishing it in the process. There were eight rounds left in the Glock, more than enough to destroy all five candles. But would doing that have the same effect as letting the candles burn out on their own? Would it send Machiste back to Hell immediately – or free him from the pentagram and turn him loose upon the world? Pacilio had no way of knowing, and the risks of guessing wrong were immense. No, he would have to let the candles burn down naturally.

Machiste noticed the shift in Pacilio's gaze, and understood its object immediately. "Oh yes, the candles," he said. "They have some little way to go yet, don't they, before inducing my regretful departure."

Machiste put an index finger to his lips in an affected way. "However shall we spend what time remains to us, hmmm? Shall I describe, in exquisite detail, what Hellish delights await you when you cross over from your plane of existence to mine own? Oh, dear, I detect a certain lack of enthusiasm. Well, then, what about poetry? I do so love a good bit of verse, don't you? So uplifting for the spirit! Here's one of my favorites."

Machiste put a mock-serious expression on his face, stuck out his chest, and, in an absolutely dead-on imitation of the late Richard Burton doing Shakespeare, recited:

> *There once was a fellow named Dave*
> *who found a dead whore in a cave.*
> *Though she'd been there a spell,*
> *and had started to smell,*
> *he just thought of the money he'd save!*

Machiste pretended bemusement. "Now why does that remind me of the late Miss Steele?" he wondered aloud. "Well, she was a whore of sorts, wasn't she? All those naughty whips and things." Machiste looked right at Pacilio, and his grin was evil incarnate. "Well," he said, "I suppose you could say she's damaged merchandise now. You know what that means, don't you?" Machiste mimed delight. "She's on *sale*."

Machiste's arm again defied nature as it stretched out beyond the pentagram and grasped the ankle of Victoria Steele's corpse. It took only a few seconds for him to drag the unresisting form into the pentagram with him.

The ceremonial robe had ridden up around Victoria Steele's waist as a result of her final exertions, but Machiste apparently still thought it would cramp his style. It took him only a moment to tear the garment from hem to neckline and discard it. The demon gazed at the nude body and said to Pacilio, "She kept herself rather nicely in trim, didn't she? But of course, I was forgetting: you had the opportunity to enjoy her charms while she was breathing, didn't you? I'm quite envious, old man. Well, I expect she's still warm, at least. . . ."

Machiste unbuckled his belt, undid a fastener, then pulled down his zipper. He let the gray worsted slacks fall, and then followed them with the pale blue boxer shorts that he wore underneath.

Pacilio tried not to stare, but failed utterly. Machiste had the largest penis that Pacilio had ever seen on a human being, and it might have stacked up well against many a stallion, too. The immense organ was already semi-erect, and Machiste lovingly improved its condition with both hands. Then he smiled coquettishly at Pacilio and asked, "See anything you'd like to nibble on, old boy? Homosexuality runs in families, you know. There's just *tons* of scientific evidence to that effect, and since your sister is such a total *dyke*, haven't you ever wondered about your own latent faggotry, Michael? No comment? Not interested? Pity, that. Well, I suppose I'll just have to make due with the material at hand."

Then the horror show really began.

To say that Machiste raped and sodomized Victoria Steele's corpse is accurate, but incomplete. To say that he did things to her body sexually that were never intended by nature to be done to a human form is also true, but fails to capture the full rapacious cruelty of what took place. To say that the demon Machiste then mutilated the woman's body savagely is factual as far as it goes, but mercifully, still leaves a great deal to the imagination.

Pacilio knew no such mercy. He was afraid to take his eyes away from the *Grand Guignol* performance going on in front of him, much though he desperately wanted to – Victoria Steele had been very clear on that point: for your own protection, keep your eyes on the demon at all times. So he watched, as Machiste knew he must. What Pacilio was forced to look at went from disgusting to horrifying to unspeakable – all within the space of a few minutes.

Then it went beyond unspeakable, and still Pacilio watched, for the sake of his own self-preservation.

It seemed the length of an Ice Age before the candles finally burned out and the blood-splashed form of Machiste was forced to return to Hell, calling cheerfully to Pacilio as he faded away, "We'll see each other again soon, old boy – sooner than you think! Oh, and sorry about all the mess! Cheerio!"

———◆———

After Pacilio finished his account, McGraw said, "So, is that when you got the stain on your coat, during that ghastly 'performance' he put on for you?"

Pacilio nodded. "It looked a lot worse before I was able to run some cold water over it."

"I'm reluctant to ask," McGraw said, "but what's it from?"

Pacilio was quiet for several moments, then asked, "You ever play dodge ball when you were a kid, Mac?"

"You mean like when one kid has a ball, a soccer ball or volleyball or something, and throws it at another kid, who tries to jump out of the way and avoid getting hit?"

"Uh-huh, that's the one."

"Sure, we played it. I think every kid does."

"We played it back in Pittston, too," Pacilio said. "I was fast on my feet, even then – hardly ever got hit, no matter who was throwing the ball."

McGraw, who was unsure where this was headed, contented himself with "Uh-huh."

"But inside that Lesser Circle," Pacilio continued, "there wasn't a hell of a lot of room to move around, you know? Fucking thing couldn't have been more than three feet in diameter. Made it kind of hard to dodge anything."

"So you got the stain on your jacket. . ."

Pacilio's voice held no expression at all as he said, "It's from when he threw Victoria Steele's heart at me."

Pacilio lay on the hotel bed, watching as Robert Shaw led a team of World War Two commandos through Yugoslavia. Pacilio was glad the good guys had the scriptwriter on their side; in a real war, all of them would be either dead or captured before the third commercial break.

Once McGraw had gone off to his own room, Pacilio had taken a long shower, put on clean undershorts and a t-shirt, and flopped on the bed with the remote control to see what was on the tube at that hour – which was how he'd ended up with *Force Ten from Navarone*. It wasn't that sleeping didn't occur to him – his mind was crying out for the chance to turn off. But Pacilio was fairly sure what was waiting for him the other side of consciousness, and he was in no hurry to renew his acquaintance with either Victoria Steele or the demon Machiste, even in his dreams. He knew he would have to sleep sooner or later, but waiting a while seemed like a good idea.

The window was starting to brighten with morning as Pacilio watched Robert Shaw and his companions blow an immense dam to smithereens, thus drowning what looked like half the *Wehrmacht*. A little later, as the closing credits rolled, Pacilio's eyelids started to droop. He was at the point of dropping off to sleep when the phone rang.

"Sorry if I woke you, yet again," McGraw's voice said.

"You didn't," Pacilio told him. "What's up?"

"I just got a call from Kimura. He said that he had just heard from our old friend, Special Agent Pennypacker."

"Heard what, exactly?"

"That Peter Barbour was killed last night in Delaware. The car he was driving, the same Mercedes he stole in Scranton, crashed while he was trying to avoid a State Police roadblock."

Pacilio was silent for a long moment. "Are they sure he's dead?" he asked finally.

"As the proverbial doornail. Upon impact, the Mercedes went up like an incendiary bomb, I understand. Our Mr. Barbour went up with it."

"So they *do* have a corpse," Pacilio said.

"They do, for sure. Burned to cinders, I guess, but a corpse, nonetheless."

"So, if he's burned beyond recognition, how do they know it's him?"

It was McGraw's turn to be silent. After several seconds he said, "You know, that's actually a pretty good question – one that never occurred to me. Most likely, any paper ID he might have been carrying would've burned up in the fire, wouldn't it? They must have made their identification based on the car he was driving."

"So, because Peter Barbour is believed to have ripped off this Mercedes in Scranton, and since there is a male corpse in the same burned-out Mercedes, therefore the corpse is Peter Barbour? It's been a long time since I took Logic 101, Mac, but I know there's something wrong with *that* reasoning."

"I didn't ask Kim how the Delaware cops identified the body," McGraw said thoughtfully. "He probably doesn't know, anyway. Most likely, Pennypacker just gave him the broad outline, as a courtesy. Damn, I never thought to question the identification – I was so busy being happy that it's finally over."

"I'll be happy, too, Mac. I'll be fucking ecstatic. As soon as I *know* it's over."

"So, how are we going to determine that? How do you identify a charred lump of meat – which is, I guess, all that's left of Barbour."

"Or whoever," Pacilio said.

"Or whoever. Can they get fingerprints?"

"My guess would be, no. A fire, if it's hot enough, destroys flesh, including the flesh that contains the fingerprints."

"Dental records, then?"

"I don't know for sure," Pacilio told him, "but I have an idea where I can find out."

———◆———

"Good morning, Muriel," Pacilio said into the phone. "I hope I'm not taking you away from important doctor stuff."

"Hi, Michael. No, it's all right. I worked the night shift, and I was just finishing my notes for the day staff who'll be treating my patients. You're up pretty early – or have you not been to bed yet?"

"No, I haven't, I'm afraid."

"What have you been doing – conjuring demons all night?" Her tone of voice was light.

"No, not the whole night," Pacilio said grimly. "And not 'demons,' plural. Just one." He made a sound that might have been a sigh. "One was enough."

"My God, you mean it *worked*? That woman was able to call up an actual *demon*?"

"Yeah, it worked," Pacilio said. "Maybe a little too well. And I promise I'll tell the whole story, face-to-face, the next time I see you. I owe you that much, considering you paid for the whole thing. But not now, okay? I've got a problem, and I need your medical expertise."

"All right," she said briskly. "Ask away."

"Let's say you've got a dead body, badly burned in a car fire. No chance of fingerprints. How do you identify who it is?"

"Well, the usual method is through dental records. You make a standard dental chart, maybe take X-rays, too. Then you circulate that stuff to the local dentists to see if any of them has something on file that matches."

"And that's it?"

"Well, it's not foolproof, of course. A dental chart isn't unique, the way fingerprints are. But the likelihood that two people in a given area would have the exact same configuration of fillings, caps, extractions and so on is pretty remote."

"How long does the ID process usually take – a couple of days?"

"I don't know for sure, but I imagine it depends on how hard the police push it, and how cooperative the dentists are. Plus, there's no guarantee it will succeed. Some people just never go to the dentist."

"I see," Pacilio said glumly.

"I would have thought that you'd know all about this kind of stuff, Michael," Muriel Rojas said. "I mean, it's pretty basic police procedure."

"I'm not a cop, Muriel. At least, not in the generally accepted sense of the term. Mostly, I investigate scientific fraud, which rarely involves charred human remains."

"My guess is it rarely involves demons, either."

"Hardly ever," he said. "So, listen, what do you do if the dental records don't lead to a positive ID?"

"Well, there's DNA, of course. The advantage is that, unlike dental charts, a DNA profile *is* unique. The downside is, you have to have something to match it to."

"What kind of something?"

"Anything that carries DNA in it. Blood, of course. Semen. Tissue samples, although not burned tissue – that won't work. Hair is okay, I think."

"But if burned tissue won't give you a DNA match, what's the point –"

"The point," she said, "is that an incinerated body is usually not 100% burned tissue. It depends on how hot the fire was and how long the body was in it, but, except for extreme cases, you can usually get some usable tissue from some of the internal organs. And you don't need a lot of it to do a DNA profile."

"Okay, Muriel, that's very helpful. Thank you."

"Listen, Michael, this is a long way from my specialty, you know? If you want more detailed information, I can talk to one of the pathologists on staff here, or maybe spend some time searching the MEDLINE data base."

"No, that's all right. Don't put yourself to a lot of trouble. If I need more info, I'll call you back later."

"It's not much trouble," she said, "but I'll leave it up to you. Can you at least tell me why you need to ID a severely burned body?"

"Well, the Delaware State Police claim they've got a badly burned guy named Peter Barbour down there. On a slab in the morgue."

The silence on the other end of the line lasted so long that Pacilio finally asked, "You still there, Muriel?"

"I was initially going to say 'Wow, that's fantastic,' because it means he can't hurt any more people. My second impulse was to commiserate with you, because I know you wanted to be the one to catch him. But then I realized the implications of what you've been asking – badly burned corpses and all. They're not certain it's him, are they?"

"Oh, I think *they* are," Pacilio said. "He was driving the Mercedes that was stolen from that woman murdered in Scranton a couple of days ago, so it's not a hard connection to make. They're sure it's him. *I'm* the one who's not sure. Not yet, anyway."

"So, what are you going to do?"

"Go and find out for myself."

The Reverend Tom Pascoe was at his desk early. He had to be in Washington, D.C. by evening, to give a speech at a political fundraiser, and wanted to clear his desk of accumulated paperwork before leaving.

Pascoe was making some minor changes in the speech when his telephone began to buzz softly. He glanced up and saw that the call was coming in through his private line. Very few people had that number.

"Hello?"

"Good morning Reverend, this is Gerald Waxmonsky."

"Good morning, Jerry. To what do I owe the pleasure?"

"I've been discreetly poking around in that Fairfax business you asked me to look into, and I've turned up a couple of things that I thought might interest you. Can you spare a few minutes now, or would you rather I come by in person?"

"I'm leaving town this afternoon, Jerry, and the morning is really jammed," Pascoe told him. "So why don't you run it down for me now?"

"All right, then. I thought you might like to know what those scientists, the ones who got themselves killed in such memorable ways, were actually up to. As far as I have been able to determine, their research was aimed at determining the possible existence of a parallel dimension."

"A parallel *what?*"

"Basically, it's the idea that our plane of existence is not the only one, that one or more alternative planes may be out there, parallel to ours but in a different part of the time-space continuum. What Clayborn's team was trying to do was prove this mathematically, and, if they were successful, attempt one thing more."

"And what was that?"

"To make contact."

Pascoe was silent for several moments. Then he said, "There's got to be more to it than that, or you wouldn't be calling. What's the other piece of the puzzle?"

"Well, Reverend, that has to do with the rather unusual theory that underlay Clayborn's work. Much of this is not well known, not even within the scientific community, but Clayborn presented a paper two years ago at the annual convention of the American Society for Theoretical Physics. His presentation, I gather, was not well-attended. Afterward, he submitted the paper for possible publication in *Scientific American*."

"That's considered a pretty heavyweight place to publish, isn't it?" Pascoe asked.

"Indeed it is," Waxmonski said. "Of the five scientists who reviewed Clayborn's paper – one of whom is a Nobel Prize winner, by the way – two recommended immediate publication with no substantial revisions."

"That's two reviewers," Pascoe said. "What about the other three?" He found that he was getting caught up in Waxmonski's tale despite himself.

"The other three recommended that the manuscript should be rejected as completely unacceptable. One of them suggested, tongue-in-cheek I assume, that the author consider submitting it to *The Magazine of Fantasy and Science Fiction*. Anyway, the senior editor sided with the majority, which included the Nobel winner, and that was that. Clayborn's paper was ashcanned. He never submitted it elsewhere, as far as I can tell."

"And the subject of all this academic dithering was what?"

"A little essay entitled *'All We Know of Heaven and All We Need of Hell': The Physics of the Supernatural.*'"

"Is that right?" Pascoe sounded intrigued.

"He basically argues that the Heaven and Hell described in the Bible may well be real places, but places that exist in dimensions parallel to ours."

"Well," Pascoe said, "I can't remember ever hearing it put that way in the seminary, but I suppose such a viewpoint isn't inconsistent with Christian teaching – as long as we recognize that access to one or the other of those 'dimensions' is restricted to pure spirits: angels, demons, the souls of departed human beings, as well as the Good Lord Himself, of course."

"That's just it," Waxmonski said. "Clayborn didn't recognize that at all."

"Come again?"

"Clayborn claimed that it should be possible to access those parallel dimensions from the one in which we live, using supercharged electromagnetic fields. I confess the physics of the thing is far beyond me, but here's one idea that I think I grasped pretty well: he believed that it had already been done."

"Really!" Pascoe exclaimed. "Then it's been one hell of a well-kept secret!"

"Funny you should use that term, Reverend, since that's more or less what Clayborn had in mind: witchcraft."

Pascoe saw the point quickly. "Clayborn is saying that witches really *did* consort with the Devil."

"He puts it differently, but, basically, yes. He says that there were those who somehow discovered how to manipulate electromagnetic fields to the point where they could achieve access to one of those parallel dimensions. The hot, nasty one, in this case."

"That's not exactly the point of view popular with the PC brigade these days, is it?" Pascoe said. "I thought the feminazi party line was that the witches of the Middle Ages were poor, persecuted healers and midwives whose practices challenged male hegemony and thus resulted in the ruthless sexist persecutions of the witch trials, and blah, blah, blah."

"I wouldn't know about that, Reverend. But Clayborn had the notion that what we refer to as 'magic' is just science that hasn't been discovered yet. I was able to obtain a copy of the paper that he presented at the

Theoretical Physics conference. Let me read you one paragraph that I've highlighted."

Pascoe listened to the shuffling of papers in the background, then the private investigator was back on the line. "Still there, Reverend?"

"Still here, Jerry. It's just starting to get good."

"I hoped you'd find it so. Okay, here we are." Waxmonsky began to read aloud:

"One need not indulge in ignorant superstitions to recognize that certain rituals and rites practiced by those once referred to as 'witches' may well have been grounded in sound principles of physics – principles unrecognized as scientific simply because science has yet to discover them. If you give a man a sugar pill and tell him that it's a magic cure for his headaches, in some cases the headaches will subside. Our ancestors would have deemed such a cure sorcery; today, we call it the placebo effect. The witches of old, who were able – some say – to summon so-called demons at will, may well have thought of themselves as wielders of supernatural power. But, in time, we may come to view them as the first physicists."

"Well, there it is, Reverend," Waxmonski said. "Make of it what you will."

"So, this is the kind of thing that was going on in that Virginia laboratory – an attempt to test these ideas of Clayborn's experimentally," Pascoe said pensively.

"That I cannot say for sure. The government is keeping a tight lid on everything to do with the actual project – which in itself would seem indicative of *something*, wouldn't you agree?"

"I would, indeed. Listen, can you fax me a copy of that scientific paper you just read from?"

"Of course. I can do that right now. I assume you want this sent to the private fax number?"

"You assume right, Jerry. And, while you're faxing things, send along your bill, will you? I want to take care of that right away."

"My pleasure, as always, Reverend. Do you want me to continue inquiries in this matter?"

"No, nothing further," Pascoe said absently. "I think I have everything I need."

Corporal Frank Trowbridge of the Delaware State Police usually had dinner with his wife before starting his shift. Jolene worked as a secretary at Dupont Chemical, but she was usually home from work early enough to cook and share the evening meal.

Tonight, dinner was her special meat loaf, with gravy, mashed potatoes, and peas and carrots. It was one of Frank's favorite meals, but he was not tucking into it with his customary enthusiasm.

After watching her husband push the food around on his plate for ten minutes, Jolene Trowbridge finally asked, "Frank, what is it? What's wrong?"

"I don't know, exactly, and that's the truth," he said with a sigh. "I've just felt *weird* ever since last night."

"You mean, since that guy got burned up in his car," his wife said softly.

Frank nodded. "It's hard to describe, but I can't seem to get him out of my head."

"Well, gosh, I can understand that," Jolene said. "A horrible sight like that, I guess it would be pretty hard to stop thinking about it. But that'll pass, sweetie. It just needs a little time."

Trowbridge shook his head. "That's not what I mean, though, Jo. It's not just that I keep seeing him all burned up but still alive, grabbing my wrist like that. . . ." He shuddered, but went on. "It's like he got inside my head, somehow, you know? I can almost *feel* him in there sometimes. It's like a big ol' bear breaking into a hunter's cabin, or something. He's in there, looking around, checking under the bed, knocking stuff off the shelves. And he's hungry. Oh, God, is he hungry. . . ."

Jolene Trowbrodge was trying hard to keep the alarm she was feeling from showing on her face. She knew Frank had seen some ugly things in the course of his job, but nothing had ever got to him like this before. Finally, she said, "It's just the stress, Frank. It's natural, I guess, for a guy who does the kind of work you do. You just need some rest, is all. You're off tomorrow and the next day, right?"

He nodded, and suddenly there was a light in his eyes that had not been there before. "Yes, that's right," he said, as if to himself. "They won't expect me at work for three days. That will be very good."

"Sure, it will," his wife said reassuringly. "You just need to catch up on your sleep and chill out a little." After thinking a moment, she said, "If you like, I can get in some of that nice wine we like, that Black Tower stuff. And, you know, the Video Palace is just a couple of doors down from the liquor store. I could maybe stop in and pick up a couple of movies for us. You know, from their back room."

He looked at her blankly. "The back room. Yes, good idea."

She went on, oblivious to his puzzlement. "I used to feel embarrassed going back there, the only woman in the room every time, and you can feel the eyes of all those guys on you, it's like they're trying to look at you without being caught looking. Well, the hell with them."

"Yes, I expect so," her husband said, very seriously. "All of them, eventually." Again, Jolene Trowbridge paid no attention. She was warming to her subject.

"And if that teenage kid behind the counter, the one with the freckles, gets a hard-on from knowing that I rent a dirty movie once in a while, well, let him, I don't care."

Frank nodded absently. "Sure, whatever."

"Would you like that, Frank?" Jolene had convinced herself that she knew how to cure her man's blues, and it wasn't going to take any fancy psychiatrist to do it, either. "A nice dinner, a little wine, a sexy video on the VCR . . . maybe I could put on that outfit you got me last anniversary, the one with the garter belt and the high heels and all . . . hell, who knows what might happen then?"

He was grinning at her now, and if that grin was more vulpine than anything that had ever appeared on her husband's face, Jolene Trowbridge didn't appear to notice.

"You're right," he said, his voice heavy with excitement. "Who knows what might happen then?"

Justin Gustainis

Chapter 18

Trooper Steve Wozniak parked the red Trans Am in his usual space behind the Troop B barracks. He killed the engine, which also cut off the car stereo that had announced his arrival from a full block away. Walking toward the back door of the building, he vaguely noticed the sound of a car door closing off to his left but paid no attention until a voice said, "Officer Wozniak?"

Wozniak turned to see a man standing about twenty feet to his left, a medium-sized man with dark hair and eyes, wearing a well-cut blue suit. The man carefully kept both his hands in plain sight, then raised one to display a credential folder containing what looked like a badge and an identification card.

The well-dressed stranger lowered his hand and walked a few steps closer. "My name is Pacilio," he said. "I'm a federal investigator, and I wonder if you can spare me a few minutes."

Wozniak's eyes narrowed. "Federal?" he said suspiciously. "Those weren't FBI creds you just flashed, buddy. I've seen 'em before and I know what they look like."

"No, I'm not FBI," the man said. "I never said I was."

"Maybe you'd better let me get a closer look at that ID of yours."

"All right. Here you are."

Wozniak examined the badge, then the laminated ID card. "Office of Scientific Accountability?" he read aloud. "What the hell's that?"

"It's an agency that investigates fraud in government-funded scientific research."

"I think you got the wrong guy, mister," Wozniak said with a snort, and handed back the credentials. "I'm not involved in any kind of scientific research, and the only money that Uncle Sam ever give me was in my income tax refund, and damn little of that, too."

Pacilio nodded. "I understand, but the man who burned to death in his car last night was a suspect in the murder of several people who *were* doing research under a government grant. That's what I want to talk to you about."

Wozniak shook his head and stepped back, the way you do when the Jehovah's Witnesses show up on your doorstep during the Super Bowl. "Nope, can't help you. I've got start-of-shift roll call in about five minutes, and I haven't got time for this crap. Sorry."

"I've already spoken with your duty sergeant," Pacilio said, and this time there was some snap in his voice. "He's the one who described your car for me, and advised me that I'd hear you coming from a long way off. Sergeant Strubeck said he wouldn't mind if you were a few minutes late for your shift. He understands that this case I'm working is important to a lot of people back in Washington, not to mention several in the state government here."

Wozniak stared at Pacilio. "Look, mister, I don't know what the feds have to do with this, but I'll tell you what I told the duty Sergeant, and what I told the Captain, and what I'm gonna tell the fuckin' review board at the hearing three days from now: *I didn't do nothing wrong.* I saw the crash and the fire, okay? I've been on the job long enough to know that nobody is gonna live through something like that. Trowbridge said so, too, you can ask him."

"Trowbridge is the other officer who was on the scene," Pacilio said.

"That's right, and he's a damn Corporal, and *he* didn't think there was any big fuckin' hurry to call in the rescue squad. He was as surprised as I was when the guy came crawling out of that car, burnin' like a moron's barbecue. Nobody should have been able to do that, and Trowbridge agrees with me."

"So, you're saying the suspect was completely engulfed in flames when he left the car."

"Yeah, engulfed," Wozniak said sarcastically. "He was 'engulfed' like you wouldn't believe. And it wouldn't have mattered if I'd called it in the second I got there, anyway. The bastard only lived for another couple of minutes after he got clear of that wrecked Mercedes. No way the paramedics could've shown up in time to do anything but pronounce him, and you can take that to the fuckin' bank."

"How did you know he was still alive after he collapsed outside of the car? Did you check for vital signs, or what?"

"No, but he sure as hell *looked* dead, once I ran my fire extinguisher over him and put the fire out. I mean, we are talkin' third degree burns over 100% of his body, far as I could tell. A real crispy critter, as they used to say in the 'Nam."

"Is that what they used to say?" Pacilio's voice contained nothing but polite inquiry.

"Yeah, you know, napalm victims and like that. Anyway, we both figured that was all she wrote for this dude — then he reaches out and grabs ahold of Trowbridge's wrist, grabs it real hard, looked like. Scared the shit out of both of us."

Trooper Wozniak did not notice that the federal man's face suddenly went very still. "Some kind of post-mortem reflex, do you think?" Pacilio's voice was casual.

Wozniak shook his head. "Not hardly, because then his mouth starts moving, like he's trying to say something, except his lips and tongue weren't in such great shape right about then, you know? Hell, Trowbridge told me the guy actually *did* manage to get something out, but I figure he was just busting my balls."

"What did the man say, according to Trowbridge?"

"Ah, he said the burned guy croaked something like 'Thanks for the ride,' but I think it was just bullshit. Anyway, he died for sure a couple of seconds later, long before the meat wagon could've got there, even if I had called right after the crash, you understand?"

"No, not entirely," Pacilio said softly. "Not yet, anyway."

———◆———

Hiroshi Kimura nodded at McGraw and said, "So it's all over but the shouting – or, shall I say, the identifying."

"Yeah, I suppose so."

"You sound dubious, Mac, but I don't understand why. Barbour was driving the car, Barbour was killed in the crash, and the authorities will almost certainly establish Barbour's identity to the satisfaction of all concerned, probably within a few days. So, why the doubts?"

"I don't know, exactly," McGraw said. "But this whole thing has me spooked, Kim. Maybe Pacilio's paranoia is contagious. Of course, if he's right about where Barbour was headed, and why, then I'd say paranoia would be a pretty mild reaction."

"He believes that the demon-controlled Mr. Barbour was headed back to the laboratory in Fairfax, the place where all of this awful business started."

"That's right. And Barbour's travel pattern since Albany is consistent with that premise, for what it's worth."

"And if he had succeeded in reaching Fairfax, Mr. Pacilio believes, the demon was going to use Mr. Barbour to repeat the experiment that supposedly led to Mr. Barbour's possession in the first place," Kimura said. "To open the 'door' that poor woman was referring to on the answering machine tape."

"To open, in effect, the Gates of Hell," McGraw said, "and, believe me, I know how late-night-TV-movie that sounds. But that's what Pacilio thinks Barbour had in mind."

"And Mr. Pacilio garnered this information from yet another demon, who was called up –"

"The correct term is 'conjured,' I believe."

"Of course," Kimura said with a tight smile. "A demon who was conjured by a witch whom Mr. Pacilio found in Denver, Colorado."

"That's my understanding," McGraw said.

"Then what are you worried about? Even if we take this fantastic hypothesis on faith , it doesn't matter anymore. Clearly, Mr. Barbour's not going to be opening anything now."

"I'm sure you're right, Kim," McGraw said. "I just wish we could be sure that it's Barbour who's down there in Delaware, in the morgue."

Kimura spread his hands. "Who else could it be? Who else is going to be driving that car? Who else would take such drastic measures to escape the police?"

McGraw's face was showing the weariness that he felt, only some of which was physical. "Those are all good questions, Kim, and I haven't got answers to any of them. But here's a question for *you*: If you've got somebody who's possessed by a demon, and the person dies while in this possessed state, *what happens to the demon?*

———◆———

Pascoe sat at his desk, shuffling papers around idly. This was not usual behavior for him; he did not get to be who he was, or to own what he owned, by sitting around playing with paper clips. But this morning his concentration was disrupted the lingering effects of the dream.

After giving his well-received speech at the fundraiser the evening before, Pascoe and his small entourage had stayed overnight in Washington, at the Hay-Adams Hotel. Perhaps sleeping in a strange bed had contributed to the bizarre drama that had been staged by Pascoe's subconscious.

Pascoe was a believer in the power of dreams, but not in any bullshit mystical sense. Rather, he regarded a dream, especially a vivid one, as his subconscious mind's way of directing his attention to something important.

His dream in the hotel bed had been nothing if not vivid.

Pascoe was alone in the middle of an immense field. There was lush grass in abundance, along with wildflowers and rolling hills as far as the eye could see. Pascoe was sensitive to natural beauty, and he took in the vista with pleasure. But then clouds began rapidly to roll in, blotting out the sun and threatening a violent storm. Pascoe was afraid, for he was completely exposed to the threat of lightning, and even if he ran from the spot, there was nowhere to run to, only the gently sloping but completely open ground. He remembered that, in case of lightning, you should get as low to the ground as you can. Pascoe threw himself flat, but feared that the lightning might still find him. He began to dig with his hands, reasoning that even a shallow trench might afford the protection he needed.

Fortunately, the ground beneath him was soft. The top level of grass peeled away easily, as if it were sod recently laid down. The dirt underneath came up as if his hands had the touch of magic. In fact, it must have been something like magic, because, before Pascoe realized it, he had dug a hole at least ten feet deep and about half as wide. "I can stop now," he thought. "The lightning will never reach me if I stay down here." But something urged him to go just a little deeper, so he kept on. Sure enough, he had dug down only a few inches further when his hands encountered something hard. "What's this?" he wondered. "Did I finally hit rock?" Pascoe tried to excavate around the hard, flat object, but it seemed to occupy most of the floor of his hole. So he began to brush the dirt away to get a better look at it, and was greeted by the gleam of metal. He thought it was brass at first, but as he uncovered more and more of the clearly man-made artifact, he became sure of two things: that it was made of gold, and that it was a door. The floor of the hole he had dug was almost completely occupied by a golden door.

There were three words carved or engraved into the middle of the door: FACILIS DESCENSUS AVERNO. Pascoe recognized the phrase from Virgil's "Aeneid": EASY IS THE DESCENT INTO HELL.

Pascoe realized that he was kneeling on top of the gate of Hell.

There was no knob in the door, no latch or handle or any other way to open it.

But there was a keyhole.

And it was then that Pascoe realized there was something dangling from around his neck by a thin gold chain. A key.

As keys go, it wasn't fancy. It didn't gleam with precious stones, nor did it appear to be made of anything but the basest metal. But it felt so good in his hand, so right somehow, that before he even thought about what he was doing, Pascoe found himself lifting the gold chain over his head, fitting the key into the keyhole before him, and, without hesitation, turning it.

Immediately, the door began to grow warm, then hot, then unbearable. Pascoe scrambled to get off the metallic surface before he was fried, and he somehow managed to squeeze himself into the few inches of space between the door and the edge of the hole. He got clear barely in time. The great golden door exploded open as if from a mighty pressure that had built up behind it. The source of that pressure was soon clear, as a great stream of winged creatures flew screeching and screaming, yowling and howling, through the newly-opened doorway, out of the hole, up and away. None of these Hellspawn gave Pascoe so much as a glance, and for this he was grateful, for what he could see of them as they rushed past him was horrible to behold.

Eventually, the flood of denizens from the netherworld slowed to a trickle, then stopped altogether. Above the surface of the hole he had dug, Pascoe could hear the fury of the storm continuing unabated. Lightning flashed, thunder boomed, and there were occasional bursts of hail. Mixed in with the sounds of the storm's fury, Pascoe thought, he could also hear other sounds, as if from a great distance: screams and shouts, bugles blowing, and the harsh clash of swords. It seemed to go on for hours and hours, but, finally, the storm subsided. As the noise of nature's fury faded, so did the sounds of battle. Now there was quiet – complete, total, and, somehow, awful. No birds sang, no tall grasses rustled in the gentle breeze, no insects buzzed and fretted. Nothing.

Then, from the middle of that aching silence, Pascoe heard a Voice, stronger and louder and richer than any he had ever heard in his life. And that Voice said, with a force that shook the ground, "WHERE IS MY BELOVED SON, IN WHOM I AM WELL PLEASED? FOR HE HATH BROUGHT ABOUT THE FINAL BATTLE, THE LAST STRUGGLE BETWEEN LIGHT AND DARKNESS, THE ARMAGEDDON PROMISED SO LONG AGO. AND NOW JUDGMENT SHALL BE RENDERED UPON ALL THE EARTH, FOR MY KINGDOM IS COME AT LAST. WHERE IS THOMAS, MY OWN TRUE SON, THAT I MAY SEAT HIM AT MY RIGHT HAND AND MAKE HIM ONE WITH ME FOREVER MORE?"

His heart pounding in his chest, Pascoe frantically began to climb out of the hole he had dug. He tried to shout, "I'm here, down here!" but his voice, so dependable in a hundred pulpits over the years, refused to work. He was fiercely clawing his way up and out of that hole, desperately, insanely, but with joy ready to burst inside him, he was ripping and tearing his way to the surface where his Father awaited him, where his eternal reward was waiting for him, and he was almost there now, his head was just about to reach the surface of a world reborn in the Second Coming of the Lord Jesus –

Pascoe awoke in his bed at the Hay-Adams, sweating and gasping like a marathon runner.

He lay there for a few minutes, waiting for the dream to let go of his consciousness, taking with it the taste of disappointment that was like bitter gall and wormwood in his mouth.

Pascoe's wakeup call was not due for over two hours, but he knew that more sleep was simply not a possibility. His brain was burning like a church fire as he struggled to understand what his subconscious was trying to tell him with that bizarre but strangely appealing vision – appealing, that is, apart from its abortive ending.

Consequently, the Reverend Pascoe, now back at his desk at the church's Atlanta headquarters, was having trouble focusing on his paperwork. His mind kept drifting to other matters – to the extraordinarily compelling dream, to Waxmonsky's report on the Fairfax massacre, to the scientific paper that had been written by the doomed research team's leader, and to the near-total news blackout the government had draped over the whole matter like a convenient shroud.

Finally, Pascoe decided to stop dithering. He gathered all the file folders, memos, requisitions and correspondence together into a pile and shoved the whole mess over to the far corner of his immense desk. Reaching into a drawer, he pulled out a fresh legal pad and gave his considerable powers of concentration to the subject that had been obsessing him.

For more than an hour he thought, and doodled, and wrote, and thought some more. Finally he put down his pen and sat back, absently massaging the writer's cramp out of his right hand. He read what he had written, then went back and read it again. He could find no flaw in either his analysis of the situation or in his planned course of action. There were risks involved, but if Pascoe had been afraid to take calculated risks he would still be an obscure assistant pastor stuck in that run-down little Baptist church in Radford, Virginia.

There can be no great victory without a correspondingly great risk, Pascoe reminded himself. Then he picked up the telephone receiver and began to make the calls that would put his vision into action.

———◆———

The phone at McGraw's bedside rang as he was buttoning his pajama top.

"Hope I didn't wake you," Pacilio's voice said, "although I think that's supposed to be your line."

"No, it's all right," McGraw told him. "I haven't been to bed yet, although I will be as soon as Nancy gets done brushing her teeth."

"Sorry I didn't have the chance to call earlier. I wouldn't disturb you now, but you did say that you wanted a progress report."

"Yes, I did. And I do."

"Well, my report is that I haven't got a hell of a lot of progress *to* report."

"Where are you now?"

"I'm at the Ramada in Dover, Delaware, room 242. Let me give you the phone number, in case you need to reach me before morning."

McGraw wrote the number on a notepad, then asked, "So, what's been impeding your progress?"

"Mostly a couple of clowns in the Delaware State Police."

"How so?"

"Well, it started out pretty well," Pacilio said. "I was able to talk to, what's-his-name, Wozniak, one of the two troopers who was there at the crash site when Barbour, or whoever it was, died."

"So, what did you get out of him?"

"I learned two things. One is that Wozniak is kind of a jerk, and two is that the guy I *really* need to talk to is the other trooper who was there that night, a Corporal named Trowbridge."

"Why him?" McGraw asked. "What did Trowbridge see that the first guy didn't?"

"It's not what he saw, but what he might've heard. Wozniak says that the driver of the Mercedes spoke to Trowbridge before dying."

"Might be interesting to know what he said. Unless, of course, he was just calling for his mother. Lot of guys in Korea used to do that, when they were hurt bad."

"We won't know which it was until I see Trowbridge. Thing is, he works out of a different barracks from Wozniak. Apparently Trowbridge spotted the Mercedes, recognized the license plate from his hot sheet, and gave chase. He requested a road block and got one, but it was set up in the territory covered by another command, which is how Wozniak got pulled into it."

"Why is that a problem for you?"

"The problem is that by the time I figured out that I had to talk to Trowbridge, and found out that he was assigned to another barracks, and drove over there, Trowbridge was already out on patrol," Pacilio said, and now the frustration was clear in his voice.

"And the duty Sergeant at the barracks, it turns out, is never going to have hemorrhoids because he is already a perfect asshole. He won't call Trowbridge on the radio and ask him to come in – not for somebody as unimportant as me. And he won't tell me what area Trowbridge is patrolling – doesn't want me bothering the officer while he's out there saving the state from speeders and drunk drivers."

"So what are you going to do," McGraw asked, "catch up with Trowbridge when his shift is done?"

"Can't do that, either. Sergeant Bilko, or whatever his name is, says Trowbridge will probably have paperwork to do once he gets back to the barracks, and the Sarge doesn't want him disturbed. He won't even tell me what the number of Trowbridge's cruiser is, so I can't intercept the guy in the parking lot."

"Pretty tough luck, your running into a prick like this Sergeant," McGraw said. "Listen, I can probably get some juice sent down the line to make him more cooperative, but not before morning. We're not even supposed to be involved in this investigation, so I can't get away with waking people up tonight."

"There's no need, Mac, but thanks. I'll stop at Trowbridge's house around mid-morning tomorrow, after he's had a chance to get some shut-eye. He'll likely be more amenable to some conversation at that hour than if I show up at one o'clock in the morning, which is probably the time he gets home."

"His Sergeant gave you Trowbridge's home address?" McGraw sounded surprised.

Pacilio snorted. "The Sarge didn't give me anything but a pain in the balls. But he did happen to mention that Trowbridge's wife's name is Jolene. Can't be too many Frank and Jolene Trowbridge around these parts. In fact, there's just one, according to the nice lady at the phone company. Trowbridge lives in one of the southern suburbs of Dover. I already got directions from the clerk at the desk downstairs when I checked in. It doesn't sound too hard to find."

"So you're going to ask this Statie what Barbour said to him there at the end."

"Barbour, or whoever. Yeah, that's the plan."

"Then what are you going to do?" McGraw asked.

"That kind of depends on what he tells me."

———————◆———————

Frank Trowbridge finished his shift at midnight and arrived home half an hour or so later. It had been an uneventful evening, for which he was glad – he'd had enough excitement two nights earlier to last him for a while. Trowbridge's peace of mind was enhanced by the fact that he had completely lost the feeling that something strange was going on inside his mind – almost as if another intelligence had invited itself in and was looking around before deciding whether to buy the place. The creepy sensation of playing host to another mind had not recurred once today, and Trowbridge was confident that he had turned the corner on it. *Guess Jolene was right,* he thought, pulling into his driveway. *I just needed to get some distance on the memory of that guy in the car. I let it get to me for a little while, that's all.*

As he approached his front door, Trowbridge noticed that the lights in the house were out, but he could see the flickering of the TV screen through a gap in the living room curtains. Jolene was still up, then, unless she had fallen asleep on the couch waiting for him.

Frank Trowbridge let himself in without making unnecessary noise, and he refrained from calling, "Hey, it's me!" as he sometimes did. If Jolene had dozed off, he didn't want to startle her; he knew she hated that. He decided to wait a minute for his eyes to adjust to the dark, so that he could avoid bumping into furniture when he went over to gently shake her awake.

Then he noticed what was playing on the TV.

It was sure as hell wasn't *The Tonight Show* – not unless Jay Leno had made some pretty drastic changes in the program's format. As Trowbridge watched, a naked blonde lying on a large bed writhed in apparent ecstasy as a kneeling man performed oral sex on her. The woman, who appeared to be in her mid-twenties, had large breasts that were too firm and evenly matched to be anything but silicone, but Trowbridge liked them, anyway. As the blonde continued to wriggle and moan, another man, naked like the first, approached the bed. He stood so that his erect penis was close to the woman's face, and his initiative was soon rewarded, as she began to gobble his formidable organ with both skill and enthusiasm.

There was a giggle from off to Trowbridge's left. He tore his gaze away from the TV and looked toward the unmistakably female sound. His eyes had adjusted enough for him to make out the figure reclining on the couch.

Jolene Trowbridge was wearing around her slender waist an old-fashioned black garter belt which was attached to the tops of the smokey-shaded nylons that graced her long and well-formed legs. A pair of shiny black shoes with four-inch heels completed the ensemble. She wore nothing else but skin. Even in the dim light from the TV, Trowbridge could see that her nipples were erect. His uniform trousers suddenly began to feel too tight in the crotch.

Jolene Trowbridge looked at the movie for a moment. "Hmmm, looks like those fellas are giving her an awful fine goin'-over," she said teasingly. "Think you could do as good all by yourself?"

Trowbridge glanced back at the screen, where the blonde now had one of the men on his back and was straddling him, while leaning forward far enough for the other one, who was kneeling behind her, to slowly enter her anus. The position looked both unlikely and uncomfortable, but managed to be highly erotic nevertheless.

Frank Trowbridge grinned and was about to say something lascivious when he suddenly jerked like a man who has received a mild electric shock. He stood perfectly still for several seconds, as the grin slowly faded from his face, leaving it cold and empty. Then, after five or six more seconds, Frank Trowbridge grinned again.

It was the same face, but it was not the same grin.

Whatever had just happened, the darkness of the room and the distraction offered by the porno movie had kept it from Jolene Trowbridge's notice. Another few moments passed before she turned her attention back to her husband and said, "Well, what do you say, stud? Think you could make me moan like that?"

Something that had recently been her husband nodded and said, "I do believe I can," then started unbuttoning the State Police uniform shirt.

"You sure?" Jolene Trowbridge replied in mock challenge. "Looks like she's gettin' quite a work-out."

"No problem at all," Asmodeus replied. "I believe I can promise you the work-out of your life."

It was coming up on ten o'clock the next morning when Pacilio parked his rental car in front of the Trowbridge house. He hoped Trowbridge was up and about – people get grumpy when you wake them up on their day off. If the trooper was willing to cooperate and answer questions, Pacilio would probably be in and out of there in fifteen minutes. Maybe then he could go back to Washington and try to forget this whole mess. Or maybe this case was going to require even more from him than it already had – a prospect that filled Pacilio with something like dread.

The house was a small white colonial with green accents at the eaves and on the decorative shutters. The paint job looked relatively fresh, and carefully applied. Pacilio wondered if Trowbridge had done the work himself. The yard, although not huge by the standards of the neighborhood, was neat and well-kept. The Trowbridges probably weren't affluent, but it looked as if they took good care of what they had.

Pacilio ascended the three concrete steps leading to the small porch. He rang the front doorbell, waited, then rang again. Nothing.

Well, shit. Is he still asleep, or in the shower, or already gone off somewhere?

The driveway that ran alongside the house curved around toward the back yard, which probably meant a garage or carport. Pacilio decided to see if there was a car parked back there.

He was halfway to the garage when he noticed the flies.

The Trowbridges had installed a window air conditioner in one of their first-floor rooms. Pacilio knew this model; years ago, his parents had bought something similar for the family home in Pittston. The idea was that you raised your window and screen far enough so that the rear of the air conditioner protruded outside to take in fresh air, cool it, and then blow it into the house. To keep bugs from flying into your house through any open space at the sides, this kind of air conditioner came with an expandable plastic screen on either side. You could pull out the little screens as far as you needed, fasten them to the window frame on both sides, and block any gap between the air conditioner and your house.

But one of the plastic screens had come loose, pulling back toward the main unit and creating a gap three or four inches wide. It was through this that all the flies were finding their way in and out of the house. Watching the busy insect traffic moving through that opening, Pacilio felt his stomach do a slow somersault.

The window was too high for him to look through the opening into the house, so he stood underneath it, raised up on his tiptoes, and inhaled a deep breath through his nose. The odor that greeted him, reminiscent of freshly-sheared copper, was all too familiar.

Pacilio turned and walked briskly toward the back of the house. The longer he lingered around this window the more likely it was that some neighbor was going to get nervous and call 911.

The locks on back doors are usually cheaper and easier to circumvent than those in front, and the one on the Trowbridge house was no exception – you'd think a cop would know better. No alarm system, either. Maybe they'd told themselves that nobody would dare try a home invasion at a State Trooper's house. *Well, there's all kinds of invasions, some of them in ways you'd never expect.*

He had the back door open within seconds and let himself into the kitchen. He closed the door quietly and stood still, listening. There was no sound except for the humming of the refrigerator and the erratic buzzing of flies from the next room. The copper-like odor was strong in here.

Pacilio followed the insect noise, and it led him into the living room and what remained of the woman who was now the focus of the flies' interest. In life, Pacilio judged, she had been an attractive woman in her mid-thirties – a woman with a healthy sense of sexual fun, judging by the garter belt, hose and high heels that formed her only clothing.

Because he had been prepared for what he would find, the things that had been done to the woman did not overwhelm Pacilio with the same disgust and horror that he had experienced a few days earlier in the Fairfax laboratory. He felt some of that, but it was outweighed by the sense of sadness and pity that flooded him as he looked at Jolene Trowbridge's ravaged body.

There was a stairway leading to the second floor. Pacilio headed for it, careful not to step in the blood or to tread on any of the intestines that were strewn about the floor.

He ascended the stairs quietly, the Glock ready, just in case the one he sought was still in the house. But the second story was deserted. In one room, Pacilio found a Delaware State Trooper's uniform left in a careless heap on the queen-size bed. He noticed that the holster belt that went with the uniform had been left behind, too – but the holster itself was empty, as were the pouches that should have contained extra ammunition. Whoever had been wearing that uniform, wherever he might be now, he was clearly prepared for trouble.

Back in the slaughterhouse of a living room, Pacilio considered calling the police, and decided against it. Even with his federal ID, he'd be hours answering questions, and he did not have hours to spare. He silently asked the spirit of the dead woman to forgive him for leaving her that way. He tried to console her with the thought that he might yet be able to offer her vengeance.

Judging by the coagulation of the blood on the floor, Jolene Trowbridge had been dead several hours. Pacilio thought he knew where the creature that had killed her was headed, and he knew also that the bastard had a long head start on him.

———◆———

As Pacilio was letting himself out through the back door of the Trowbridge home in Delaware, something that had once been Frank Trowbridge was driving, at the legal 65 miles per hour, along Route 95 in northern Virginia. There was a green highway sign in the distance, and in another fifteen or twenty seconds its message became legible: "ALEXANDRIA, FAIRFAX, NEXT 3 EXITS."

The driver of Frank Trowbridge's Subaru Outback smiled with delight and anticipation. It was a smile that the late Jolene Trowbridge would have recognized all too well.

Chapter 19

Pacilio drove back to the Ramada Inn as rapidly as the traffic would allow. The room was his until 1:00 p.m. checkout, and he wanted a secure place to make telephone calls. The things he needed to talk about ought not to be discussed from a pay phone. They might attract the wrong kind of attention.

His first call was to Washington.

"Mac, we've got a problem."

"I hate it when you say that, especially lately," McGraw said with a sigh. "All right, how bad is it?"

"As bad as it gets. I just came from Trowbridge's house."

"Who's Trowbridge? Oh, right, he's the state trooper you mentioned last night. What did he have to tell you?"

"He didn't tell me anything," Pacilio said. "He wasn't there. But he did leave something behind."

"What? A message?"

"No, a body, who I assume is Mrs. Trowbridge. She was butchered, just like the victims in Fairfax. I'm no medical examiner, but based on the condition of the body I'd say she's been dead something like six hours."

"Was there anything written on a wall or mirror this time?"

"No, nothing," Pacilio said. "I don't think he intended this one to be found. But it's our boy, Mac. This poor woman, the way he . . . well, it's something I've been seeing a lot of lately. It's his signature. I know it's him."

"Dear sweet sufferin' Jesus," McGraw said softly. He was silent for a few seconds, then said in a normal tone, "So you were right, after all? It wasn't Peter Barbour who was incinerated in that car?"

"Actually, I think it probably *was* Barbour. I figure our demon has found a new host, and its name is Trowbridge."

"Shit," McGraw said, with feeling. "So if the demon is in control of this trooper, then most likely he's headed –"

"For Fairfax," Pacilio said. "For the lab. To do what he's been sent to do. And the son of a bitch must have left hours ago."

"Left how, do you think? Driving, flying, what?"

"I'd say driving. There's no car parked in front of the house or in their garage. Besides, it's tricky getting a gun on a plane these days, even in checked luggage, and it looks like Trowbridge took his duty weapon with him."

"What's his route, do you think? Delaware into Maryland, across Chesapeake Bay on that toll bridge near Annapolis, what's it called?"

"The Severn River Bridge," Pacilio said. "Yeah, that's the most direct way, by car."

"Then he gets on the Beltway, which will take him damn close to Fairfax, won't it?"

"Yes it will, and that's probably how he'll go – if he hasn't done it already."

"All right," McGraw said, "so we put out an alert to the Maryland and Virginia police, and some state cop will spot Trowbridge's car and pick him up, same thing as happened with Barbour. End of story."

"Who's going to put out the alert, and on what basis?"

"Well the FBI can get in touch with –" There was a long pause, then McGraw said, "Oh, goddammit."

"My thoughts exactly," Pacilio said. "The Feebies might be kind of reluctant to send out an alert based on your claim that the subject of said alert is armed, dangerous, and possessed by a demon, and is believed to be on his way to open the gates of Hell."

"Okay, so we forget that part of it. We treat it like a straight murder investigation, and if Trowbridge crosses a state line to avoid prosecution, that puts it right in the FBI's lap, anyway."

"Prosecution for the murder of Mrs. Trowbridge, you mean."

"Right, exactly," McGraw said.

"I'm afraid there's a problem there, too – the cops don't know about Mrs. Trowbridge yet, because I didn't tell them."

"You didn't *what?* Jesus Christ, why the fuck not?"

"Because I didn't want to spend the rest of the day and half the night answering questions," Pacilio said patiently. "Look, Mac, if this thing is going down the way we figure, we haven't got all day to fuck around. Trowbridge, or whoever he is now, has got a job to do, and he's gone off to do it. And he's going to do it soon, unless somebody gets in his way."

There was a long pause from the other end before McGraw said, wearily, "Yeah, okay, I guess you're right. But I hope to Christ you have some notion about how to stop the sumbitch, then, because I'm fresh out."

"I've got the beginning of an idea," Pacilio told him, "but I'm going to need some help."

"What kind of help?"

"For starters, I need surveillance of that lab in

Fairfax. Listen, there's an empty storefront across the street from the place – I noticed it when I was down there last time. Used to be a printer's, I think. It's a couple of doors up the street from the lab building, and it ought to have a good view of the front door and the windows on one side. Put somebody in there as soon as you can, and I'll check in with him when I arrive."

"What do you want him to do, exactly?" McGraw asked.

"Just keep track of any activity. If anyone goes in or out, I want the time and a description of the subject or subjects. If there's any sign of life within the building, lights going on, somebody passing in front of a window, anything like that, I want it noted, along with the time."

"All right, those are the instructions I'll issue."

"One thing more," Pacilio said. "Be very clear that this is a watching brief only. Whoever you send down there is to take no other action, no matter what he sees, okay? He just keeps his eyes open, makes note of anything interesting, and reports to me when I get there."

"I'll pass that on," McGraw said, "but why the insistence on surveillance only?"

"Because this infernal motherfucker has killed enough people already. I'm not interested in feeding him any more victims. Let the bastard pick on somebody his own disposition – once I catch up with him."

"Don't talk like that, Mike," McGraw said. "*His own disposition*? That's not you."

"It is now."

Pacilio's next call went to the Jesuit residence at the University of Scranton.

"Eugene, what happens when someone who's

possessed dies before an exorcism can be carried out? What happens to the demon?"

"Good question, Mikey," Father Eugene Grady said pensively. "Mother Church doesn't have a definitive answer to that, which is unusual, since Mother Church likes to have a definitive answer for everything. I've read learned monographs on the demonic, but all it amounts to is polysyllabic guesswork."

"Well, shit, that's helpful."

"There was one thing that I heard when I was undergoing my training to be an exorcist. This isn't written down anywhere as far as I know, but the fella who told me, an old Jeb named Darst, said it was something that everybody with exorcism experience agreed on: *don't make physical contact with the possessed*, especially if there's a chance he or she is about to die. It's believed in some circles that the demon can pass from its host to another human at the moment of the host's death, if there's physical contact between the two. Me, I always avoided physical contact with the possessed, in any case. Fucking demon'll tear your eyes right out of your head, given half a chance, then laugh about it. Anyway, that's one theory, for what it's worth."

"Your theory may be due for an upgrade to a law, or whatever the next step is," Pacilio said. "Because I'm pretty sure it's happened again."

"Oh, fuck, don't tell me."

"Afraid I've got to," Pacilio said, then explained about Peter Barbour's fiery death and its apparent effect upon Frank Trowbridge of the Delaware State Police.

When Pacilio was done, Dirty Eugene said, "So you figure the demon is using its new host to get to this lab, fire up whatever equipment they used the last time, and invite all his buddies to come over to our side."

"That's what I think, all right. He got his marching orders in that hotel room in Albany, and has been trying to get back to Fairfax ever since."

"Then why the fuck are you wasting time with phone calls?" the priest shouted. "Get your ass over there to that laboratory and stop him! Do you know what's going to happen if that creature gets the passageway open again?"

"I kind of have an idea, yeah."

"Take the carnage that this one demon has caused thus far and multiply it by a thousand – shit, maybe ten thousand or even a hundred thousand. I don't know how many of the Fallen there are, nobody does. But tell me this: are you familiar with the expression 'Hell on Earth,' Mikey?"

"I've heard it, Eugene."

"Well, that phrase is going to take on a *whole new meaning* if that bastard isn't stopped somehow. So why are we still talking?"

"Because I need your help," Pacilio told him.

"Aw, Christ," Dirty Eugene said. "I was afraid you were gonna say that."

———◆———

Pacilio's third call was to Albany, New York.

"Muriel, we have a problem."

"I saw that movie," Dr. Muriel Rojas said. "Tom Hanks, right? It made me glad that I passed up the chance to study flight medicine and work for NASA. But what's the problem?"

"I think the demon has jumped to another host. Peter Barbour probably *is* dead, but I think there's a

Delaware State Trooper named Trowbridge who's been acting real funny lately."

"How funny?"

"Last night he tortured, mutilated and murdered his wife, in a style that's been getting pretty damn familiar lately."

"Oh, my God, the poor woman. They can do that? Demons, I mean. They can just pass from one person to another like some kind of infectious disease?"

"Dirty Eugene says it happens sometimes, especially if there's physical contact at the moment of death. Apparently that's what happened with Barbour. Another cop who was on the scene told me that Barbour managed to grab the wrist of this trooper named Frank Trowbridge. It was the last thing Barbour did, and it looks now like he did it for a reason."

"So where is this Trowbridge now?" she asked. "Do you know?"

"Not for certain, but I'm pretty sure he's on his way to Fairfax – if he's not there already."

"Fairfax?" Muriel Rojas sounded puzzled. "Isn't that where all those people were killed, in that laboratory?"

"Right. That laboratory is probably where he's headed."

"But why? What's the point?"

"The point, I believe, is to duplicate whatever experiment those people were doing the other night, the one that opened a door long enough for our demon to jump into the body of that poor bastard, Peter Barbour."

"The demon wants to go back? He's homesick for Hell, of all places?"

"No, I'm pretty sure that he wants to open the door so that he can let all the other demons cross over to our side. I'm betting those are the instructions he was given by whoever contacted him through the mirror in that motel room in Albany."

"Is that purely conjecture, Mike? Or do you know something that you haven't told me?"

"It's not conjecture. I couldn't have come up with that idea in a zillion years. No, I got it from something said by the demon that I had conjured up in Denver."

"That's right, you said you had succeeded in contacting a demon, but you still owe me the details."

"I know, Muriel, but there isn't time now. If I'm right about what's happening, the shit's going to hit the fan, in a big way and real soon. I need you to help me, although I hate to ask."

"Why the reluctance? Are you going to ask me for more money?"

"No, I don't need your money – I need *you*. And the reason I'm kind of reluctant is because I don't know how dangerous it might turn out to be."

"Hey, you're talking to the original adrenaline junkie, remember? What do you want me to do?"

"I need Dirty Eugene in Fairfax as soon as possible, but he can't get there without help."

"Why not? I'm not refusing, just curious."

"His legs don't work too well anymore, and he has trouble with stairs. Also, he tells me he's had some health problems, although he won't go into detail on what those are. He's willing to make the trip, but he needs help getting around, and you're in the best position to give it. You're pretty close to Scranton, you know what we're dealing with here, and you're a doctor, besides." Pacilio took a breath. "Muriel, I hate to ask –"

"Where do you want Father Grady, and when?" Her voice was crisp now, the same tone she used in the ER when casualties were coming in there was no time to waste on social niceties.

Pacilio, who had learned a similar mindset in the SEALs, responded to it, telling her, succinctly and precisely, what he wanted. The logistics were worked out quickly.

"Last question, before I hang up," Muriel said. "What exactly are we accomplishing with all this hurly-burly? Why do you need the old priest with you in Virginia?"

"I would have figured that was obvious," Pacilio told her. "I want him to perform an exorcism."

———————◆———————

Pacilio's last phone call resulted in a message that was left on an answering machine in San Francisco.

"Sharon, it's Mike. Sorry I missed you again. I just wanted to say thanks again for the information you dug up for me, and also to tell you I love you. I don't say that very much, do I? Not often enough, I guess. But I love you, little sister. Always have." There was several seconds of hissing silence on the tape, then: *"Good Bye."*

———————◆———————

McGraw left Kimura's office with his mouth set in a thin, hard line. He did not slam the door on his way out. Returning to his office, he walked down three flights of stairs, spurning the elevator. In the elevator, someone might have tried to talk to him, and McGraw knew how unwise conversation would be right now.

Reaching the outer office of his section, McGraw noted that his secretary was away from her desk. Just as well. Dorene was a good secretary, and did not deserve to have McGraw blast her head off just because she was handy.

McGraw went into his private office. He did not slam that door either. Inside, he kicked no furniture, did not fill the room with snarled obscenities, and refrained from throwing small, breakable objects at the walls just for the sheer joy of watching them smash into pieces.

He was too old for such adolescent displays of temper, although he briefly considered each and every one of them.

Kimura had not been unpleasant – he was never that – but he had been adamant. "I cannot authorize an investigator from this department to rush down to Fairfax on some kind of watching brief that has nothing to do with our work here," he'd said. "Especially if there is a risk that the whole business might blow up in our faces. And, since Mr. Pacilio is involved, I think such an outcome is not entirely impossible."

"Doesn't it concern you that Pacilio himself is already involved in this?" McGraw had hoped to catch Kimura in an inconsistency. Fat chance.

"Mr. Pacilio is still officially on leave," Kimura had replied blandly. "How, and where, he spends his time off is his own concern and none of mine. Or this department's."

"Damn it, Kim, don't you understand what's at stake here, if Pacilio's right?"

Kimura had taken off his glasses and began to polish them with his tie – a tactic that he sometimes used to avoid making eye contact while saying something that made him uncomfortable. That was when McGraw knew that he had lost.

"What I understand is that Mr. Pacilio has built a structure of supposition and fantasy that may yet prove to be no more than a house of cards. I gather he has made a convert of you, and you may dwell in that structure with him if you wish. But beware of the first stiff breeze, Mac."

"I thought you believed it, too, Kim. At least, that was the impression you gave."

"I'm sorry if I inadvertently misled you." There was silence for a while as Kimura's tie continued to rub lenses that no longer needed cleaning. Finally, he said, "Who knows, perhaps I did convince myself for a short while that there was some validity to Mr. Pacilio's theories. But that was foolish of me, I think."

"And when did you change your mind?" McGraw's quiet voice showed nothing of what he felt.

Kimura sighed. "At about the time I envisioned myself trying to explain to Mr. Loomis how I had expended significant resources of this department in an effort to forestall a demon from bringing about the end of the world."

Back at his desk, McGraw did some deliberate deep breathing in an effort to calm down so that he could think clearly. The thinking, once begun, didn't take long; there was only one option left. He picked up the telephone and made two brief calls. The first was to the department's Human Resources Office. The second was to his wife.

———◆———

The demon Asmodeus and its human host made a right turn onto Sager Avenue in Fairfax, which put them only three blocks away from the former high school gymnasium that had been converted into a government-funded laboratory. Asmodeus was almost ecstatic with joy; if all went well, in a few hours it would be reunited with its brethren in an orgy of terror and destruction beyond anything to be found in the feeble human imagination. Compared to the coming invasion, the Nazi blitzkrieg through Europe would look like a schoolyard fistfight.

And Asmodeus would be the one to make it possible, would be the catalyst for a New World Order unlike any that the banal human politicians had ever conceived of. Truly, for this, Asmodeus would find favor with his Master, would be elevated to sit at His left hand, and would be rewarded with the choicest opportunities for slaughter, rape and plunder.

So involved was Asmodeus in its bloody fantasies that it failed to notice the people in front of the laboratory building until Frank Trowbridge's vehicle was almost abreast of them. There were dozens of the humans, and they paraded in a double line around the whole perimeter of the converted Catholic school gymnasium. Many carried signs over their heads. Asmodeus did not want to attract attention by stopping, but slowed the Subaru a little to get a better look at the procession. Many of the marchers appeared to be women of middle age, but there was also a good number of young people of both genders who looked to be in their early twenties.

Asmodeus was also able to read several of the signs that were being held aloft by the marchers. One said "CLOSE DOWN THE DEVIL'S DEN," another proclaimed "STOP SATANIC RESEARCH!!" while a third urged "TELL THE TRUTH ABOUT THE MURDERS." The last impression the demon Asmodeus received of the protesters before they began to recede in the Subaru's mirror was of an elderly woman in a cheap blue-and-white patterned housedress with a slip that protruded a full three inches beneath her hem. She proudly held up a sign that read "SATAN SUCKS!"

Even as Asmodeus drove on, fury rose within it like lava in a volcano. "No!" it snarled. "No! They will *not* interfere with the Task! No!" Louder, now. "NO!" It began to pound the steering wheel with Frank Trowbridge's right hand in rhythm with the words. "NO! NO!!" Pounding harder, now. "NO!! NO!!!" The voice became a scream from the bottom of The Pit. "**NO! NO! NO!**"

Pacilio parked his rental car one street over from Sager Avenue so that he could approach the defunct print shop from the rear. He didn't want to show himself anywhere that might be visible from the laboratory building. Given the nature of the enemy, Pacilio wanted every advantage that he could get, including surprise. The long package that he was carrying under his arm represented his effort to gain another kind of advantage.

In Vietnam, there had never been more than three hundred SEALs deployed in-country at any one time. Demand for these highly-skilled warriors was understandably high, so the SEALs were spread thinly in each of their areas of operation. This meant that they were seriously outnumbered every time they went into the field. The SEALs learned that survival depended on their ability to turn every possible factor in a mission to their advantage. They found ways to make use of terrain, weather, darkness, firepower, speed, endurance and stealth – and each of them discovered for himself that the deadliest weapon of all is the one that's located between your ears.

As Pacilio approached the rear door of the former home of "Printers, Inc.," he noticed that the lock appeared to have been forced, probably with something like a tire iron. He was almost certain that the lock had been jimmied by the agent McGraw had sent to keep the lab under surveillance, someone who was probably waiting inside for him even now. But "almost certain" and "probably" were not enough to make Pacilio careless.

He quietly placed the long, paper-wrapped package on the ground, then drew the Glock 19 from its holster. He reached across his body with his left hand, grasped the doorknob, and threw the door open. He stepped inside in one fluid motion, then quickly shuffled to his left so as not to be silhouetted in the doorway.

The windows of the place, including the big display window facing front, had been waxed over for whatever reason people do that with empty buildings. Consequently, the interior of the old print shop was gloomy. But there was enough light for Pacilio to make out the single figure sitting in a chair near the front window, next to which a small rectangle of wax had been scraped off to allow a view of the outside. The man near the window had started in surprise when the back door had been flung open. Now he got out of the rickety wooden chair, placing on its seat the notebook and pen that had been resting in his lap.

Pacilio thought there was something familiar about that shape, and then the man began to walk toward him.

A moment later, Pacilio found himself saying, for the second time in less than forty-eight hours, "Jesus Christ, Mac, what the fuck are you doing here?"

———◆———

Following instructions, Muriel Rojas and Dirty Eugene Grady checked into adjoining rooms at the Fairfax Hampton Inn. Then they settled in to wait for Pacilio's call. On TV, Dirty Eugene found some professional wrestling – a form of entertainment which, like papal encyclicals, he enjoyed greatly and believed not for an instant. He flopped on his bed, lit up a Winston and prepared to watch The Rock do simulated battle with an opponent who looked for all the world like a muscular Saddam Hussein. In the next room, Muriel Rojas tried, to concentrate on an article in The Lancet about a new drug that held promise for increasing survival rates among heart attack victims.

Muriel had taken emergency leave from her duties at Albany Medical Center, calling in favors from other doctors to be sure that her shift at the ER would be covered. Then she had made airline reservations: Albany to Scranton for one passenger, Scranton to Washington for two. Her travel agent had asked "Round trip or one-way?" and, after a moment's hesitation Muriel had replied "One-way." As she spoke, she tried to ignore the uneasy feeling that the phrase had turned loose in her gut.

At the Jesuit Residence in Scranton, Muriel was fairly certain that the balding little priest with emerald-green eyes who answered the door was the man she had come to meet.

"Father Grady, I presume," she said.

"Dr. Rojas, I presume," he replied, gravely, and with a slight bow.

She grinned, then, and stuck out her hand. "Muriel."

He took it. "Eugene," he replied, with a grin of his own. "Well, we'd better get this show on the road. Mikey will be pissed off if he has to take on the Forces of Darkness all by himself." He'd spoken with a light tone, but there was an underlying seriousness to his words. And there was something else, as well.

"Just a second," Muriel Rojas said as the priest bent to pick up his bags. He stopped, then turned back to face her.

"What's the matter?"

"That's my line, I think." She leaned forward, murmured "Pardon me," then gently placed the first two fingers of her right hand underneath Dirty Eugene's eyes and carefully pulled down, exposing more of the eyeballs to her view. Her left hand went to his wrist, and the priest realized she was taking his pulse.

After ten or twelve seconds, Muriel released Dirty Eugene's arm and straightened up. She looked at him for several moments longer, then asked, quietly, "How long?"

Dirty Eugene Grady shrugged in annoyance and said, "How long have I got? Six months to a year, they tell me, but fucking doctors don't know shit from shinola." He forced a smile, then said, "No offense."

"That's not what I was asking," Muriel said. "What I meant was, how long have you known?"

"About the incipient fallibility of my ticker?" Another shrug. "Couple of months, more or less. That's why the Order sent me home from Bolivia, to let one of their tame cardiologists subject my aging carcass to every medical test known to science. Yeah, it was about two months ago that he sat me down, put on that funeral director's face that I swear they must practice in the mirror, and gave me the awful news that I seem to be mortal, after all."

Muriel saw through the bluster as if it were a clean picture window, the curtains wide open to reveal the fear dwelling behind it. "Does Michael know?"

Dirty Eugene shook his head. "Naw, I haven't told too many people. I've seen how most folks act around somebody who they know is going to check out pretty soon, and it makes me want to puke. I prefer not to have my funeral start while I'm still breathin', thank you very much."

"He should be told, Eugene."

The old Jesuit snorted with disgust. "Like hell, he should, especially now. What's he supposed to do, worry about my health? Tell me to sit up here and wait for the Reaper to tap me on the shoulder while Mike's down there in Virginia taking on a power that was old before this world of ours even existed? He should be concerned about the strain on my poor old ticker while this creature is trying to open wide the very gates of Hell? *Have you lost your fucking mind, lady?*" The last sentence was delivered in a bellow, the words hanging in the air, echoing around the cavernous anteroom before fading into nothing.

Muriel Rojas blinked, then blinked again. After another few seconds, she said pleasantly, "That taxi's got his meter running. Would you like to go now, or would you prefer to stand here and show me more about how big your balls really are?"

Dirty Eugene smiled as he bent to pick up his two

small cases. "Tell you what, Muriel," he said as he shuffled out onto the porch. "I won't show you mine if you don't show me yours."

Now, in her room at the Fairfax Hampton Inn, Muriel looked up from her medical journal to see Dirty Eugene standing at the connecting door. There was no twinkle in the green eyes this time. "Muriel, darlin'," he said, "there's something we need to talk about."

———◆———

McGraw walked toward Pacilio, his feet kicking up dust bunnies that chased each other haphazardly across the floor. "You know," he said with a weak smile, "if you keep saying that every time you see me, sooner or later it's going to start hurting my feelings."

"No offense intended, Mac," Pacilio told him. "But you do surprise me. I asked you to send somebody down here – I wasn't expecting you to come yourself."

"Kimura wouldn't go for it," McGraw said. "He refused to let me assign someone. So, since the job seems to be one that badly needs doing, I assigned myself. Actually, I'm officially on leave, as of –" McGraw checked his watch – "about three hours ago."

"I was under the impression that Kimura was with us on this. At least, that's what I thought you told me in Denver."

McGraw made a face. "I told you the truth, as I understood it." He turned away from Pacilio and paced a slow figure-eight in the dusty floor. "Kim's in a difficult position. He's accountable to that asshole Loomis, you know. So far, there isn't anything much to account for. But if he starts assigning personnel to this thing now, sooner or later he's going to have to explain why. And that could be a problem, especially since Peter Barbour, who was supposed to be the object of this exercise, is currently occupying a small, cool cubicle in a Delaware morgue. Kim doesn't want to have to explain your theory of demonic possession to Loomis, who isn't likely to be an open-minded audience."

"I've met Loomis a couple of times," Pacilio said. "He's about as open-minded as Jerry Falwell."

McGraw nodded. "Kim could lose a lot of face if he gets called on the carpet over this, and Loomis would never let him forget it, either."

"So, instead of running the risk of a loss of face, he's convinced himself that what's going on down here is no more than a figment of my imagination?"

"Yours, with mine aiding and abetting," McGraw said. "Actually, I think that's what he *needs* to believe, Mike. Otherwise, he'd be forced to do something, with all the professional risks that would involve."

Pacilio nodded gloomily. "So here we are," he said. "Just you and me. Well, not quite – I've got Muriel Rojas and Dirty Eugene waiting at the Hampton Inn."

"I've talked to your friend Father Grady on the phone. Seems like an interesting man. Are he and the doctor going to be joining our little stakeout, too?"

"Not until I get a better idea of what's going on," Pacilio said. "I want to keep them out of the line of fire for as long as possible."

"Will there be one, do you think? A line of fire, I mean."

"Hard to tell," Pacilio said. "But I do know that Corporal Trowbridge took his service pistol with him when he left home, along with all the ammo that was in his belt pouch. And let's keep in mind that the dude who seems to be in control of Trowbridge these days hasn't exactly been showing a deep and abiding respect for human life."

"Just wondering," McGraw said, a little too casually. "Hell, I haven't been shot at since Korea."

"The enjoyment of the experience doesn't improve with time," Pacilio said. "That reminds me – excuse me a second."

He walked back to the rear door and stepped outside. When he returned, he was carrying something long and narrow wrapped in brown paper. He brought it over to the print shop's counter and began to tear the paper away.

"What've you got there?" McGraw asked. He received no answer, but a few seconds later, said, "I see."

Pacilio picked up the object reverently, like an offering to a bloodthirsty god. "You ever use a shotgun before, Mac?"

McGraw nodded slowly. "For hunting, when I was growing up in Texas. Ducks, mostly. Geese and doves sometimes." He looked from the shotgun to Pacilio's face. "It's been quite a few years, Mike."

"Well, let's hope it's like what they say about riding a bicycle." Pacilio worked the slide underneath the shotgun's barrel, producing a crisp *clackety-clack* sound. He pointed the barrel toward the ceiling and pulled the trigger with a dry click. "Remington pump, 12-gauge. Holds five shells in the magazine. We won't worry about maximum effective range and all that crap – if you have to use it, it'll be from up close."

"I would have thought you'd go for one of those automatic shotguns that I keep reading about," McGraw said.

"They're illegal in the state of Virginia, except for police use. There's no way the gun shop across town where I bought this would have sold me an automatic shotgun, even if they had one in stock. I could probably requisition it through government channels, but you know how long that would take. Anyway, a good pump gun, like this one, will give you a rate of fire that's almost as fast as an automatic, and it's a lot less likely to jam."

Pacilio worked the slide again, followed by another dry pull of the trigger. "Smooth, clean action, which Remington is known for," he told McGraw. "Fucking thing'll kick like a mule, though, so be sure that you're well-braced if you have to fire it. You want to be able to deliver quick and accurate follow-up shot. In a firefight, that can make all the difference."

"I'll take your word for it," McGraw said. "I assume the SEALs taught you all about that stuff."

"That they did. Now here," Pacilio said, picking up a smaller box that had been wrapped up with the shotgun, "we have double-ought buckshot, twenty rounds."

McGraw's eyes narrowed. The pellets in double-ought buckshot are the largest made, each about the size of a dried pea, fifteen to the shell. It's the load hunters use when they intend to kill something big. "I once knew a fella who brought down a full-grown grizzly with double-ought buck," he said quietly. "You're not fucking around, are you?"

"No, I am most definitely not fucking around." Pacilio handed the shotgun to McGraw, then opened the box of shells and held it out. "Here," he said. "Let's see if you still remember how to load one of these things."

All pump shotguns load the same way, through a port just forward of the trigger guard. McGraw was pleased that his fingers seemed to remember what to do without fumbling. He took a shell from the box and loaded it, followed by four more. As he did so, Pacilio kept talking, in a detached, lecturer's voice. "This is a useful weapon for our purposes," he said. "It's loud as a bastard, which will scare people, and that's good. Sometimes it even causes them to freeze for a second or two, and that's even better. Also, with this load, if you hit somebody anywhere in the trunk with the full shot pattern, you've got an instant kill. Even if you get them with only part of the pattern, it's a serious injury."

McGraw pumped the slide, bringing a round into the chamber. "I just hope I can avoid scaring myself," he said.

"An old Gyrene like you?" There was affection in Pacilio's voice. "You'll do fine." After a brief, awkward silence, Pacilio returned to his businesslike tone. "Try to remember to open your mouth wide when you fire, which will reduce the impact on your eardrums. You'll feel ridiculous, but do it anyway. Indoors, that thing is going to sound like the end of the world."

McGraw made sure the safety was on, then placed the shotgun gently on the counter. "I don't know what the end of the world sounds like," he said. "Do you?"

"No I don't," Pacilio said. "And I'm not looking to find out anytime soon, either. That's why I'm interested in that building across the street. Has there been any activity since you've been watching?"

"Oh, Christ, that's right, you don't know. There's been activity, all right, but I don't think it's what you had in mind." McGraw returned to his vantage point at the front window and motioned Pacilio over. "Take a gander at *this*."

The demon Asmodeus got control of its anger quickly, realizing that rage was unproductive and that continuing to slam the steering wheel was going to break bones in Frank Trowbridge's hand – a hand that would be needed a while longer. It pulled the Subaru Outback into a supermarket parking lot, turned off the engine, and sat quietly, pondering the problem posed by the human fools who were marching around the building that housed The Door.

Asmodeus did not need much time to arrive at a satisfactory solution. Clearly, some shopping was in order. Asmodeus remembered passing a billboard that advertised something called the Fair Oaks Mall, which boasted over 200 stores. A marketplace that size would surely have what the humans called a hardware store. With any luck, the mall would also offer an establishment where Asmodeus could buy an ice cream bar. There would surely be a service station nearby, as well.

The humans marching with their signs and their hymns might well grow weary and leave sometime in the next few hours. If they did, so much the better. But if they were trudging around that building by around 9:00 p.m., then Asmodeus would deal with them – in a way that would not only solve the problem they posed but would offer considerable amusement, as well.

Asmodeus and its human host started the Subaru and drove off in the direction of the Fair Oaks Mall. Meanwhile, three blocks away, the praying, chanting and hymn-singing of the protesters continued, with no sign of abating.

———◆———

Pacilio gaped at the demonstrators through the little rectangle that McGraw had cleared in the print shop's wax-covered window. "God almighty," he muttered. Then, to McGraw: "Who are those assholes?"

McGraw shook his head in bewilderment. "It appears, judging by those picket signs and the chanting that I've been able to hear, they're protesting the research that was done in that lab. Protesting on moral grounds."

"Religious nuts, do you think?"

"That's a strange question, coming from a guy who says he's here to prevent Armageddon."

"You know what I mean, Mac," Pacilio said impatiently. "The self-appointed guardians of public morality. The last time I saw a bunch like this, they were marching and praying in front of a theatre that was showing *The Last Temptation of Christ*."

"Yeah, there is that aura about them, isn't there? But if they're fundamentalists run amok, they're pretty well organized."

"How do you mean?"

"I was already set up here when they arrived. First, three vans pull up, all the same make, model and color – dark blue, if it matters. People start getting out, and it looks like each van holds seven or eight passengers. This bunch is mostly middle aged and older, the majority of them women. But a guy is in charge of things – tall skinny fella with real thick eyeglasses. He supervises the unloading, helps distribute the picket signs, gets them started on the marching. Then he climbs back into one of the vans and all three vehicles take off."

"*Well organized* is right," Pacilio said.

"It gets better." McGraw consulted the notebook he had left on the wooden chair. "Another ten or twelve minutes goes by, and this full-size bus pulls up, and out comes a bunch of college-age kids — the kind of young folks the phrase 'clean-cut' was invented for. No long hair on the guys, no miniskirts or short shorts on the girls, and the only earrings are being worn by females. I'm looking at these kids, and it's like 1957 all over again."

"So, how many of these throwbacks got off the bus?"

"I'd say about thirty," McGraw replied. "And here's something interesting — it was a school bus."

"You mean one of those yellow–"

"No, not that kind of school bus. It was a bus that belongs to a school — a college, to be exact. The name of the place was painted on the side."

"Don't keep me in suspense, Mac. What school was it?"

"Paraclete University."

"That name's familiar from someplace. Wait — isn't that one of those Bible-thumper schools? No drinking, smoking, dancing or jerking off?"

McGraw nodded. "That's the one. It's down in the southern part of the state."

"Paraclete University," Pacilio said musingly. "It's part of this whole fucking religious conglomerate started by that TV preacher, right? There's the school, and the television network, and a political organization — right-wing, naturally."

"Naturally," McGraw said. "Yeah, it's all part of the same little empire. I read an article about it in *Newsweek*. It's all controlled by the same guy."

Pacilio's thumb and index finger were lightly pinching the bridge of his nose. "You know, it's probably a mental block brought on by my deep sense of revulsion, but I can't remember that creep's name."

"It's Pascoe," McGraw said. "The Reverend Tom Pascoe."

———————◆———————

Jeff Truax was feeling pretty good. He had been allowed a one-hour dinner break from the picket line outside the Devil's Den (as he thought of the deserted laboratory), and Cindy had traded times with another girl so that the two of them could go together. Dinner had consisted of Big Macs and fries at McDonalds, but Jeff didn't care what he ate as long as he could be around Cindy Greene while he did it. They had been dating since November, and he had been in love with her since Valentine's Day. Better yet, Cindy had told him over dinner tonight that she thought she was starting to feel the same way about him. That news was enough to set him walking on air, even if the walking currently involved a slow, monotonous circuit around this red brick building that looked like the site of high school basketball games, not a place of evil.

But Reverend Donnelly, Paraclete University's Chaplain, had said the place was diabolical. He had explained everything to them before asking for volunteers to picket. There had been no shortage of eager participants. After all, a willingness to do the Lord's work was what had drawn these young men and women to Paraclete University in the first place, rather than to some heathen state institution of allegedly higher learning.

Jeff had been back on the march for about forty minutes when the maroon and gray SUV slowly rolled up in front of the building. The driver cut his engine, then put his flashers on before exiting the vehicle.

The task of dealing with the press had been given to

Mr. Fothergill, one of the adults from the church group that was sharing the picketing duties. However, he was in another part of the line and nowhere in sight. Besides, Jeff didn't think the man with the Subaru was a reporter. They usually wore coats and ties, and this man was dressed casually, in jeans and a sweatshirt. Also, he didn't have the look of curiosity that Jeff had seen in the journalists who had come around earlier. This man looked worried, and Jeff felt it was his Christian duty to see if he could help.

"Can I do something for you, mister?" Jeff asked, leaving the line and walking over.

"I don't know," the man said, frowning. "It's my car – I lost power about fifty feet back, had just enough momentum left to coast over here. I wanted to get out of the way of traffic, you know?"

Jeff nodded sympathetically. "It kind of sounds like the electrical system, but I'm bound to tell you, I'm no mechanic. But if there's anything. . . ."

"Thanks, I appreciate that, I really do. You know, you're probably right about the electrical, but there's one other thing I want to check first. There's a special modification to the fuel tank in these models that might be causing the trouble."

Jeff put down his picket sign (it read "NO DEALS WITH THE DEVIL!") and looked at the vehicle more closely. "This is one of those Outbacks, isn't it?"

The man nodded again, and smiled "Sure is. You're pretty sharp." He was over at the Subaru's gas port now, on the opposite side from the sidewalk where Jeff was standing.

"These things have a new kind of fuel line, and I wonder if mine has gotten knotted up, somehow. If it has, that would prevent gas from reaching the engine. Listen, you could really help me out, if you can spare a minute."

"Sure, that's okay," Jeff said. "Give my feet a rest from all that walking. What do you need me to do?"

"Can you crouch down next to the car on your side, and put your ear against the gas tank? I'm going to stretch this fuel line out of the tank to see if it's tangled up. What I'd like you to do is to let me know if you hear a pinging sound from inside the tank. Can you do that? Just take a minute."

Jeff's brow furrowed. He didn't know much about cars, it was true, but. . . . "You want me to listen for a *pinging noise?* From the *gas tank?*"

The man nodded reassuringly. "Yeah, I know it sounds kinda weird, but the guy at the dealership said that might happen with these newer models. If it does, I'll have to call for a tow truck. Otherwise, I should be able to drive it as far as my hotel and deal with it in the morning. Come on, what do you say? It won't take us long."

Jeff shrugged. "Okay, I'll give it a try, but I hope I recognize your pingin' sound if I hear it."

"You'll do fine," the man said with a wide smile. "Okay, why don't you crouch down next to the gas tank on that side and let me stretch this fuel line out where I can get a look at it."

Jeff squatted next to the car, feeling a little silly. Behind him, his fellow demonstrators continued their slow circuit around the building, some of them glancing at Jeff curiously. Then he heard a familiar female voice behind him. "Whatcha doing, Truax? Goofing off again, or have you moved up to stealing hubcaps?"

A moment later, Cindy Greene was crouching on the sidewalk next to him. "Hey, what's goin' on?" she asked with a smile.

Jeff shrugged. "Aw, this guy's got car trouble, and he's trying to figure if his fuel line is messed up, or if something else is wrong."

"So you're helping out by stealing his hubcaps?" she asked teasingly. "Lighten the load a little, maybe?"

"No, bimbo-brain, he wants me to listen for a pinging sound in the gas tank while he does something with the fuel line."

"A pinging sound," Cindy said dubiously. She brushed her raven-black hair out of her eyes with a gesture that Jeff had grown quite fond of in recent months, then asked, "Do I sense somebody's chain maybe being yanked?"

As Jeff Truax tried to explain just what it was he thought he was doing, the driver of the Subaru Outback was busy on the opposite side of the vehicle. Opening the hinged gas port revealed that the plastic gas cap was missing. Instead, lying across the fuel tank aperture was a flat wooden stick about six inches long. The words "Dove Bar" were stamped into the wood. The stick was held in place by a loop of thin rope that was knotted around its center. The rest of the cord disappeared into the fuel tank.

The driver grasped the stick and pulled it toward him. It came easily, and brought gasoline-soaked cord with it. After a glance to check for traffic, the Subaru's driver walked rapidly straight back, holding on to the stick and trailing the increasing length of the cord with him – across Sager Avenue and into a nearby service alley that ran between a boutique and a stationery store. The cord that was being drawn from the Subaru was long enough so that its other end was still submerged somewhere within the depths of the Outback's gas tank.

If that helpful young man Jeff Truax had been standing up, he would have observed these things. He might have noticed that the material stretching across the street and into the alley was not fuel line, but clothesline. But it is doubtful that Jeff, a trusting soul, would even then have realized its true purpose.

It was the fuse on a bomb.

The driver of the Subaru backed down the alley a few feet, then stopped and produced a Bic disposable lighter. The driver smiled contentedly, like an epicure about to sit down to his favorite meal. Its voice said in a murmur, "When you meet my brethren, kiddies, be sure to tell them who sent you." Then the driver flicked the lighter and said, still softly, "Consider this a foretaste of Hell."

The flame raced along the length of the gasoline-soaked clothesline and into the Subaru's gas tank, which contained just under twelve gallons of high-test unleaded. In its liquid form, gasoline burns when exposed to flame. But gasoline vapor, in the presence of fire, will explode.

There was enough vapor in the Subaru's fuel tank to create a tidy little eruption – a blast powerful enough to rupture the tank in three places and spew burning gasoline over everything within a radius of some fifty feet. Jeff Truax and Cindy Greene were well inside that radius, and both were knocked sprawling by the explosion.

The electrical impulses that comprise human thought processes operate far faster than any other system in the body. It took 1.6 seconds for Jeff Truax's nerve endings to let his brain know the terrible thing that was happening to him. But in that length of time he was able to process the agonized female scream that came from a few feet to his right, understand what it meant, and formulate a silent scream of his own: "*Cindy, oh my God, Cindy, NO!*"

Then he knew nothing but the fire.

———————◆———————

McGraw was slumped in the uncomfortable wooden chair behind the print shop window, trying to stay awake, when the maroon and gray Subaru Outback coasted to a stop in front of the lab building. He watched the interchange between the driver and the young man with curiosity that turned to puzzlement as the driver began to back away from his vehicle while pulling a length of cord from the Subaru's gas tank. The driver disappeared into the mouth of an alley that was three buildings to McGraw's left, and McGraw was starting to wonder if he ought to wake Pacilio when flame sped along the length of that rope like a shooting star from Hell. McGraw had barely made it to his feet, the chair falling over behind him, when the Subaru's gas tank went up with a blazing roar.

As McGraw jumped up, Pacilio's legs were already moving, very fast, off the counter where he had been dozing. He dropped lightly to the floor, walked swiftly over to the cleared area of the window and stared out at the conflagration that was taking place. He could hear the screaming even through the thick glass of the print shop's window.

Without taking his eyes off the scene across the street, Pacilio asked, "What the fuck happened?"

Receiving no reply, he turned and looked at

McGraw, who was swearing to himself as he struggled with the locks on the front door. An instant later, Pacilio was standing next to him, one hand firmly but not painfully on McGraw's left arm, the other arm thrown around McGraw's shoulders. Since his mouth was close to McGraw's ear, Pacilio spoke softly. "Where are you going, Mac?"

"Where the fuck do you think I'm going?" McGraw's voice was loud, and there was an edge of hysteria in it. "We've got to help those people!"

Pacilio did not relinquish the grip of either hand. "Mac, stop fooling with the door," he said quietly. "I want you to think for a second."

"Think about *what*? There are people burning alive over there – can't you fucking *hear* them? We've got to help, for Christ's sake!"

"Mac, listen –"

"*Will you fucking let go of me?* Look, you stay if you want to, ice man. I'm not going to stand here and watch people burn to death."

"Yes, you are." Pacilio's hands were still in place, and McGraw suddenly felt them tighten, only a little, just enough to give a sense of the power that could be brought to bear. "You're going to do *exactly* that, and so am I."

Pacilio still had not raised his voice, but McGraw could tell that he was speaking through clenched teeth. "What are you going to do over there? What could the pair of us do? Have you got a fire extinguisher? Me, either. Got a fire hose? How about a bunch of hypos loaded with morphine? Didn't think so. So what are we gonna do? Beat at the flames with our suit coats? Yeah, we could do that, I guess, but look through the window

– there's people doing that already. How many of those fundies did we count – forty-some? Looks like eight or ten were caught by the flames. The others are doing as much as we could do, or as little."

"Well, what's wrong with *trying*, goddammit?"

Pacilio let McGraw go, but continued to stand next to him. "What's wrong with trying? Not much, except this: have you considered that Trowbridge might have done this for just one reason – *to make us break cover?*"

McGraw looked at him as if Pacilio had suddenly grown a third eye. "What the hell are you talking about?"

"Trowbridge, or Asmodeus, whatever we call him, needs to get into that building, right? And once he gets in there, he needs to work undisturbed – for how long, we don't know. Maybe he's worried about interference. Maybe he thinks the place might be under surveillance. So he pulls something that would bring any self-respecting cop running to the rescue, while Trowbridge watches from a distance. Maybe he's watching with a rifle in his hands, for all we know."

Pacilio stepped back a little. "That's what's wrong with trying to help, Mac," he said grimly. "We've come too far, and stepped over too many dead bodies on the way, to fuck it up now."

McGraw's eyes were wide. "You think he just burned up eight or ten people to see if the place is being *watched?*"

"It's possible. That might not have been his only reason – I don't see this guy as having one simple reason for doing anything – but I bet that was part of it."

"That's absolutely fucking inhuman," McGraw said hollowly.

"Of course it is. But then, so is he." Pacilio glanced out the window. "Listen, if you want to do something helpful, why don't you dig out your cell phone and call 911 anonymously. I bet none of those holy rollers across the way have thought of that yet. At least, I don't hear any sirens."

"Good idea," McGraw said, although his eyes did not meet Pacilio's. He began to dig the phone out of his briefcase.

"Mac?"

"What?"

"I'm sorry I had to put my hands on you."

McGraw looked at him for a couple of seconds. "That's okay, forget it," he said. "But if you do it again, I'm afraid I'll really have to hurt you, instead of just slapping you around a little."

Pacilio's mouth twitched in what might have been the ghost of a smile. "Thanks for the warning."

———◆———

It took the first team of paramedics only five or six minutes to arrive after McGraw's call, and they immediately called for help – a lot of it. They were followed by the police, who cordoned off the area with yellow crime scene tape and started their forensics routine.

McGraw described for Pacilio everything he had seen leading up to the explosion and fire. When he got to the part about the Subaru's driver backing into the nearby alley, Pacilio excused himself and went out the print shop's back door, drawing the Glock from his hip as he left.

He was back in about five minutes, the pistol out of sight again. "He's long gone. There's no sign of him, but I bet he didn't go very far."

"Do you think he spotted you looking around?"

Pacilio looked at him the way you look at people who ask if you've ever been abducted by space aliens.

"I withdraw the question," McGraw said.

"I certainly hope so."

They continued to observe the accident scene from their vantage point. They saw the burn victims, living and dead, carried off in a series of ambulances. The remaining demonstrators were loaded into police vans, presumably to be questioned at headquarters about what they saw. The forensics specialists finished their work, packed up their equipment, and drove off. The detectives searching for clues and witnesses completed their canvass and left. By 11:00 p.m., the area around the red brick building was deserted. The only evidence of the recent tragedy consisted of the scorch marks on the sidewalk and street, the picket signs abandoned on the ground, and the yellow crime scene tape that cordoned off the area.

Time passed, on its slow way to midnight. McGraw, for whom sleep was out of the question now, stood leaning against the print shop's counter as Pacilio sat in the chair by the window and kept watch. They had been carrying on a desultory conversation about movies they had recently seen when McGraw saw Pacilio suddenly sit up very straight.

"What is it?"

"Light just went on," Pacilio said tightly.

"A light? Where?"

"Inside the lab building. Look."

McGraw peered through the cleared space in the window. "Could it be the local cops, looking into the car bombing?"

"Cops would have come in through the front door,

and their car would be parked in front of the building. Let me have your cell phone, will you?"

Pacilio tapped in a number , then said into the phone, "Could you ring Muriel Rojas' room, please? That's R-o-j-a-s. Thanks." There was another pause, then Pacilio said, "It's me. Are you and Eugene ready to move? All right, both of you meet me in the lobby in ten minutes. Tell Eugene to bring his stuff."

Pacilio listened briefly. "No, this is not a drill. This is the real deal."

He looked through the window again at the light across the street.

"The bastard's inside the lab."

Chapter 20

The demon Asmodeus had waited for the police to depart before turning on any lights inside the laboratory building. It would have preferred to work in darkness, for security's sake, but the stupid humans were not equipped by the Creator with the ability to see in the dark.

Getting inside unnoticed had been child's play once the fiery diversion out front had been executed. The marchers who had not themselves been engulfed in burning gasoline had all gone running to the scene of the explosion and fire. Some had tried to beat out the flames with jackets and sweaters, others had dropped to their knees and begun to pray aloud, and still others had been content to dash around frantically like freshly decapitated chickens. None paid the slightest attention to the building's back door, to which Asmodeus had made its way through a series of back alleys and side streets. The lock on the back door posed no challenge to anyone with Frank Trowbridge's cop tools and Asmodeus's intelligence, and so the demon and its human host were inside the building even before the first ambulance had come screaming to a halt outside.

Turning on lights represented a risk, but only a slight one. It was unlikely that any humans could have divined its intentions. Even if some of them had, Asmodeus' transmigration from the Barbour host to

Trowbridge should have thrown even the most persistent hunter off the trail. But, just to be certain, Asmodeus had waited for a full minute in the alley where it had lit the fuse that blew up the Subaru Outback. Ignoring the fire and its attendant screams and lamentations, Asmodeus had watched the street, instead. No would-be hero had come running, from either a parked car or from one of the buildings nearby, to offer succor to those caught in the explosion and fire, and Asmodeus knew that no softhearted human police officer could have resisted the impulse to do so. The demon was confident that the building was not under surveillance by anyone.

Asmodeus ascended the back stairs to the ground floor, turned on another light, then swiftly walked down the corridor to the main laboratory, where it had recently known such delights with the members of the project research team. It turned on all the lights in the laboratory and surveyed the device that had allowed it entrance into this world. There were heavy wooden crates of electronic equipment scattered around the room – new components for the main mechanism that had not yet been installed. Well, they would never be installed now, but it did not matter: the device worked very well in its present state of development.

The apparatus didn't look like much, considering what it was capable of doing. Three big Packard-Bell turbines were linked in series off to the left. Ten feet in front of them sat the black transformer, roughly two feet square, that took the power generated by the turbines and channeled it into the rest of the machine. To the right was a bank of computers that were programmed to calculate the flow of energy passing through the system and optimize it to fit the system's needs at any given moment. A variety of programs had been developed to do this at different stages of the process. In the middle of it all was The Door.

It actually looked less like a door than a gate, consisting of two cylinders made of industrial-quality ceramic material. The cylinders were five feet high and seven inches around, and they stood upright exactly five feet apart. Each was surrounded by a thick electromagnetic coil. Various heavy-duty cables and thinner electrical wires led from the base of each of the cylinders to the turbines and computer banks.

On the floor between the posts formed by the two cylinders was another electromagnetic coil sandwiched between two thick sheets of safety glass about three feet square. The coil had been laid out in the shape of a five-pointed star surrounded by a circle.

Asmodeus had retained the contents of the deceased Peter Barbour's memory much the same way a computer user might copy the contents of a floppy disk before disposing of the original. The demon searched mentally for all information related to the operation of the infernal device that took up most of the room. The process of recall was proceeding smoothly, when the silent, empty building suddenly echoed with the unmistakable sound of a door opening and closing.

Asmodeus walked swiftly and silently over to the wall about twenty feet to the right of the room's entrance. Reaching underneath the sweatshirt that Frank Trowbridge was wearing, it produced the trooper's duty sidearm – a Sig Sauer 9mm automatic with a fourteen-round magazine capacity. The demon did not know who the intruders were, or whether they were here by chance or design. It did not matter. They would be dealt with, and then Asmodeus would return to the Task. And if the police were summoned by some busybody in response to the sound of shots, that also did not matter. By the time the meddlers in blue suits showed up, the hour of midnight would have struck and the Door would be open. When the stupid police arrived, they would find themselves with far bigger problems than determining the source of a few gunshots.

There were clearly audible footsteps now. Asmodeus thought they sounded like the treading of at least two people. Well, this room had seen a number of violent deaths in recent days; certainly it could stand a few more. These newest victims would serve as an offering to the One whom Asmodeus called Master, a fitting sacrifice to set the stage for the massive bloodletting yet to come.

Asmodeus quietly worked the slide on the automatic to bring a round into the chamber. It would wait until all of them were in the room before opening fire. Pity there was no time for fun; the intruding humans would have to be dispatched quickly. But there would be fun in abundance once the Door was opened and Asmodeus' brethren were streaming though it in a terrible tide of death and destruction.

The sound of footsteps approached the laboratory door, slowed, then stopped altogether. A confident-sounding male voice called from the hallway: "Good evening. I expect you've got something lethal prepared for us in there, but it's quite unnecessary, I assure you. We have not come to interfere with your work. On the contrary, we're here to offer our assistance. If you're as wise as I think you are, you will want to hear what I have to say before doing anything rash."

There was silence for a few seconds, as if the speaker were giving his audience time to digest this information.

Then the voice continued, "We're coming in now, and neither of us will be holding a weapon. I'd say we were putting ourselves at your mercy, except that I'm fairly certain you don't have any. But I do trust in your intelligence."

A moment later, two well-dressed men walked slowly into the room. A glance told Asmodeus that one of them was a mere minion, a servant of the tall man with silver-gray hair who spotted Asmodeus/Trowbridge almost immediately. Showing no great surprise at the gun that was pointing at him, the tall man stood still, keeping his empty hands in full view. His companion, who took up position just behind him and to his right, did the same. The minion was carrying a military-style duffel bag, which he slowly lowered to the floor. The slight impact produced muffled sounds that showed the bag contained something heavy and metallic.

"Perhaps introductions are in order," the man said cooly. "I am the Reverend Thomas Pascoe. This is my associate, Mr. Waxmonsky." The tall man gestured economically toward his companion, but his blue-gray eyes never left Asmodeus. "And I gather that you," he continued, "although, I confess, you don't look it, are what my fellow churchmen would call a spawn of Satan."

———◆———

McGraw sat alone in darkness and was afraid.

Pacilio had gone to pick up Father Grady and Dr. Rojas at their hotel, leaving McGraw behind to keep watch through the print shop's window. McGraw held the pump shotgun across his lap, and his jacket pockets were weighed down with extra rounds, but he found that all this ordnance provided him scant comfort.

He knew that a few hundred yards away was a creature that, just a few hours ago, had burned four or five people to death because their presence constituted an inconvenience. The same being had tortured, murdered, raped and mutilated ten victims inside that building less than a week ago. Scenes from Pacilio's videotape kept bobbing to the surface of McGraw's memory, despite his best efforts to think about something else, anything else.

McGraw had known fear back in Korea, especially when he'd heard the Chinese blowing their bugles prior to launching another "human wave" attack. But he had been eighteen then, and still not completely free of the teenager's delusion that he would turn out to be immortal, after all.

I'm not a kid anymore, and I know for certain now that I'm going to die someday. I'm just not ready for 'someday' to be today.

McGraw glanced at his watch, angling it so that a sliver of light from a street lamp outside could shine on its face. Pacilio had been gone for almost fifteen minutes, and would be returning soon with the lady doctor and his friend the priest.

He's going to be back any minute, and then he's going to expect me to go into that building with him. Shotgun McGraw, spurs jangling as he keeps his date at the OK Corral. Except that bastard in there, who makes Ike Clanton look like a fucking Campfire Girl, might not have heard of Wyatt Earp and Doc Holliday. He might not know that the good guys are supposed to win. He might have ideas of his own about that, and, God help me, I don't think I can do this.

McGraw looked over his shoulder at the print shop's back door. If he left now, he could be in his car heading out of town in three or four minutes. Traffic would be sparse this time of night, and he could be in his own bed, the covers pulled over his head, within an hour.

Pacilio and the others would cope well enough. Anybody trained by the SEALs ought to be more than a match for some half-ass state trooper, even if said trooper did have a demon inside him, and the priest could deal with that side of things, anyway. McGraw had volunteered to do surveillance, not take part in some half-ass commando raid. Not at his age.

I'm sixty-three fucking years old, which means I'm too young to die.

McGraw stood up quickly. He walked over to the shop's counter, gently placed the shotgun atop it, and began to empty his pockets of the extra shells. Pacilio, he was sure, would make far better use of the weapon than McGraw ever could.

They would do fine without him.

———◆———

Pacilio drove the rented Ford Taurus through the quiet streets. Fairfax, it seemed, was a town that went to bed early on weeknights. Dirty Eugene Grady, wearing a black cassock over his street clothes, a blessed purple stole around his neck and a grim expression on his leprechaun's face, occupied the Taurus' back seat and chain-smoked. If he was praying, he did so silently. Muriel Rojas sat in the front passenger's seat, her medical bag on the floor between her dainty feet as she read Pacilio her own version of the riot act.

"Muriel, listen to me," Pacilio said.

She shook her head, not for the first time in the conversation. "I'm sorry," she said uncontritely, "but I am not going to stay in the car like a good little girl while the boys go into the dragon's lair, chop his fire-breathing head off, and then send for me when it's safe. That is just *not* going to happen."

"Muriel, this is not male chauvinism," Pacilio said. "It's practicality. There's no point in putting you in the line of fire when there's nothing for you to do. Mac's going to be carrying a gun, and God knows we can use the extra firepower. You know why we need Eugene in there. But we don't need a doctor. If there's any patching up to do, you can take care of it when the job is over with."

"How do you know what's going to happen in there?" she snapped. "Did you put in a call to the Psychic Friends Network, maybe? Are you absolutely certain you won't need another pair of eyes, or hands, or simply someone at your back that you can trust? Are you?"

"Muriel, that's not the –"

"And when it comes to patching people up, as you put it, how do you know you'll have the luxury of time? A lot of trauma cases can only be saved *if* they receive proper care and *if* it's provided quickly, before shock sets in or exsanguination becomes too severe. Or did your personal psychic also assure you that only flesh wounds would be received by the home team as a result of this evening's little exercise?"

Pacilio glanced in the rear view mirror. "Eugene, can't you talk to her? Use some of that Jesuitical reasoning that you guys are so famous for."

Grady smiled slightly as he took the cigarette out of his mouth. "I'm just a simple exorcist, Mikey," he said. "I'm not trained for anything really complicated, like marriage counseling." The Winston went back between the priest's lips and its tip glowed red again.

There was silence in the car for a while. Then, as he noticed that they were coming within sight of the laboratory building, Pacilio cleared his throat. "Muriel," he said.

"*What?*"

"What does 'exsanguination' mean?"

"It means blood loss, you dolt."

"Well," Pacilio said musingly, "if exsanguination is a real possibility, maybe I'd better have someone handy who knows how to deal with it, you know?"

"Makes sense. Did you have anyone in mind?"

There was another brief silence.

"Muriel?"

"Yes, Michael?"

"Even though it's dangerous, would you be willing to accompany Eugene and Mac and me into that laboratory building tonight?"

Muriel Rojas took in a deep breath and let it out. "It would be my pleasure, Michael," she said politely.

Pacilio brought the Taurus to a stop directly across from the abandoned printer's shop. He turned out the car's headlights and sat quietly behind the wheel.

After a moment or two, Muriel Rojas asked, "Is this where your Mr. McGraw is supposed to join us?"

Pacilio nodded. "We've been using that empty storefront over there as our observation post. I asked him to stay and keep an eye out while I went to pick you two up at the hotel."

"So, where is he? Isn't he coming out?"

"Good question." Pacilio's voice showed no worry, but his hand still went quickly to the buckle of his seatbelt. "Guess I'd better go and see."

"Wait." Muriel was looking across the street. "Is this him?"

Pacilio stopped trying to unlock the seatbelt latch and looked up in time to see the gray-haired shambling figure emerge from the mouth of the alley, the shotgun carried parallel with one leg .

To Muriel and Dirty Eugene, the relief in Pacilio's voice was unmistakable as he said, "Yeah. Yeah, that's him."

———◆———

Asmodeus lowered the pistol slowly, reluctantly. Its instinct was to kill them both, but it had learned in recent days that following bloodthirsty impulses was not always the wisest course. Besides, it was intrigued by the tall man, who seemed so assured and unafraid. Let him explain his presence here and reveal the source of his knowledge of Asmodeus' true nature. Then he could die, along with his lackey.

"What's with this 'spawn of Satan' crap, man?" Asmodeus showed puzzled indignation. "My name's Frank Trowbridge, and I'm a police officer."

The tall man nodded calmly. "I'm sure you are. I expect you even have identification in your pocket to prove it." He paused. "Just as a few days ago you could probably have established your identity as Peter –" He looked over his shoulder at the man standing behind him. "What was his last name, Jerry? The first one possessed by our friend here."

"Barbour. Peter Barbour," Waxmonsky said impassively.

Pascoe faced Asmodeus again. "Yes, Peter Barbour was the last person whose body you made use of." Another pause. "But I know what you really are."

The demon permitted a smile to cross Frank

Trowbridge's face. Pretense was unnecessary, really. It did not matter what the tall man learned, since he would shortly be dead.

"Did I say something funny?" Pascoe asked sharply. The prospect of being laughed at, especially by one of the damned, was apparently not pleasing to him.

"No, you didn't," Asmodeus said, "but I find your crude theatricality entertaining." The smile was extinguished. "However, it does not explain why you are here. Please be so good as to enlighten me." The demon raised the pistol again and pointed it at Pascoe's forehead. "Now."

Pascoe did not flinch. "I'm here because I want to help you."

Asmodeus produced raised eyebrows. "Do I require help?"

"Perhaps you do," Pascoe said. "If I can figure out what you're up to, and I have, then so might others. Some of them could be inclined to . . . interfere."

"But not yourself," the demon said, giving the words a light coat of mockery. "You're not inclined to . . . interfere."

Pascoe swallowed the irritation that rose within him. "No," he told the demon calmly, "On the contrary. I want you to succeed."

Asmodeus could only stare in amazement. "And this enterprise, to which you so blithely wish success – what do you imagine it to be?"

Pascoe gestured toward the apparatus that made up The Door. "You're going to use that thing the same way it was used the last time, when you crossed over. Only this time it won't be just one of you who gets through, will it? You're going to throw open the gates of Hell."

Asmodeus regarded Pascoe silently for several moments, then said, angrily, "Who *are* you? Are you a servant of the Master? Someone whose presence on this plane I was not informed of?"

Pascoe smiled condescendingly. "I am the Reverend Thomas Pascoe, as I told you. I do not serve your Master. Rather, I serve the One who is Master to your Master – the Lord, the God of Hosts, who has dominion over all."

Asmodeus/Trowbridge's head cocked quizzically. "You serve the Creator, you say. Why do you believe that my success will be in the Creator's best interest?"

"Because your actions will surely bring about Armageddon, the final battle, in which you, all your kind, and the One you serve, will be defeated, bound, and exiled into the lowest depths of Hell forever more."

It was Asmodeus' turn for a superior smile. "And wherever did you get *that* idea?"

"It is prophesized in the Holy Bible," Pascoe said, as if addressing a simpleton.

"A wise human it is, and a rare one," Asmodeus said dryly, "who can distinguish between prophecy and propaganda."

Pascoe shrugged. "I don't expect you to agree with me. Clearly, you would not be engaged in this enterprise unless you expected a different outcome. It doesn't matter. I will trust in my Lord."

Asmodeus nodded. "And I in Mine." He lowered the pistol, but did not put it away. "But why are you here? Why not remain in your own domain and await events, such as my brethren's *supposed* defeat and exile, which you claim to believe as inevitable? What do you want?"

"As I told you, to offer assistance in the event of attempted interference. My associate, here, has been trained in the violent arts by the FBI. He only works for me on a contract basis. So I offered him a very lucrative contract indeed to accompany me here tonight. He's been watching the building from a distance since yesterday. Once he called me with news of the fire outside, I knew you were here and came right over from my hotel."

"Even assuming I might require the help of humans," Asmodeus said scornfully, "there has been no interference, unless one counts those fools who were parading around earlier. Did you send them?"

"Yes, I did. I assumed that anyone who could get past them was the man – or whatever – that I wanted to meet. And if I was wrong, and no one came, the marchers were still good publicity for my own cause."

"Several of them almost certainly burned to death, you know," Asmodeus said mildly, "not to mention those with less serious injuries."

"Regrettable," Pascoe said with a shrug. "But I learned long ago that you can't make an omelet without breaking eggs." He dismissed the subject with a wave of his hand. "But even if there is no attempt to interfere with your mission, I still desire to be part of it. I want to help you in any way I can. I seek to be God's instrument in this, the ultimate struggle. Indeed, I believe I have been chosen specifically to serve that purpose."

Asmodeus thought swiftly. Perhaps an extra pair or two of hands would be useful in making the apparatus work. The length of time that had been spent on this conversation meant the Witching Hour was fast approaching. All right, then. Let this vainglorious fool and his lackey lend their assistance. They could help

Asmodeus open The Door, then be the very first humans to taste the bitter fruits that they would help to harvest.

Asmodeus put the pistol back in Frank Trowbridge's waistband and pulled the sweatshirt down over it. "Very well, I will accept your offer of –"

Gerald Waxmonski suddenly lifted his head an inch or two, then abruptly turned to look toward the door. "*Did you hear that?*"

———◆———

Ten minutes earlier:

McGraw got into the back seat as Dirty Eugene Grady moved over to make room for him. Pacilio performed succinct introductions, and McGraw exchanged handshakes with his new acquaintances.

"I was starting to worry about you, Mac," Pacilio said. "Didn't you see us when we pulled up?"

"Sure, I did. But since I didn't have a flashlight, it took me a while to figure out that the front door of that place has a key-operated deadbolt on it. You can't open it, even from the inside, without the key. That's why I couldn't get it open . . . earlier, during the fire. It finally occurred on me to go out the back way and through the alley. Sorry for the delay."

"Well, you're here, and that's what matters," Pacilio told him.

"Wouldn't miss it for the world," McGraw said, deciding that his companions did not need to know how very close he had come to losing his nerve. "And there's something you should know," he went on. "Trowbridge, or whatever his name is, has got company."

The other three stared at him. "What kind of company?" Dirty Eugene asked.

"Two men. They drove up in that big gray Lincoln that's parked across the street. They stepped over the yellow police tape and went in the front door of the lab building, but I guess the inner door gave them trouble. That's the one with the electronic lock that you need a card-key to open, isn't it, Mike?"

"Right," Pacilio said. "So what'd they do?"

"Came out after half a minute or so. I guess they don't have an electronic skeleton key, like you do, so they went around to the rear of the building. They must have got in the back door somehow, because I saw shadows moving across the windows a little while later."

Pacilio considered the news for a moment. "Can you give us descriptions, Mac?"

"Well, both of them were wearing dark suits. One of them looked to be in his thirties. Red hair. He was carrying what looked like a military-style duffel bag, and it seemed heavy. I noticed that he seemed alert, always looking around – the roofs of buildings, store windows, parked cars, everywhere. His head was never still."

"And the other one?"

"Tall, probably over six feet," McGraw said. "Gray hair, or maybe it was white, but he moved around okay – not like somebody who's really ancient."

"Unlike myself, you mean," Dirty Eugene Grady said with a grin.

McGraw returned the grin for a moment. "Unlike either of us, Padre." Turning back to Pacilio he said, "The gray-haired guy looked kind of familiar – like someone I've seen on TV or in the papers."

Pacilio frowned. "Somebody in government, you mean?"

"Can't say for sure – but I'm pretty sure I've seen him someplace."

From the front passenger seat, Muriel Rojas asked, "What do you think, Michael? These men – are they on our side, or *his*?"

Pacilio's frown deepened. "No way to tell. Actually, neither one of those choices makes a lot of sense. I don't see who else would know what's going on in there and would be here to stop it, like we are. On the other hand, where would a demon recruit allies? And what would he need them to do?"

They were all quiet for a few seconds. Then Pacilio shook his head irritably and said, "We haven't got time to fuck around with this. We assume those two are hostile, until proven otherwise. If they turn out to be good guys, so much the better. But we don't bet our lives on it."

Pacilio reached inside his jacket pocket and pulled out a sheet of expensive, cream-colored paper that he had found in the abandoned printshop earlier in the day. It was now covered with a hand-drawn diagram of a building, and there was writing around the edges. "Now, if you will all give me your attention," he said, "I believe I have something of a plan."

The sound that had attracted Gerald Waxmonsky's attention was a loud banging from the rear of the lab building. Someone seemed to be knocking at the back door in the basement. As Waxmonsky stepped out into the hallway, he could hear the sound more clearly, and "knocking" was an understatement – something was hitting the metal door rhythmically and very hard: four blows, then a pause, then four again, then again.

In the middle of the second series of four sharp impacts on the back door, a master card-key slid into the electronic lock that controlled the lab building's front door. As the lock disengaged, it made a faint but distinct buzzing sound. Waxmonsky never heard it. His attention was focused toward the rear of the building, and the noise coming from that direction was enough to mask the sound from the front – a sound that otherwise would have been clearly audible throughout the quiet building.

Outside the back door, Muriel Rojas finished the fourth series of blows against the metal door, dropped the fist-sized rock she had been using to strike with, and ran like hell.

Pacilio's instructions had been explicit: "Four series of four, in a consistent rhythm," he'd told her. "And don't linger when you're done. You don't want to be standing there if one of those guys decides to open that door and see what's going on."

Muriel kept herself in good shape – tennis in the warm weather, raquetball in the cold – and she ran smoothly and well. Down the short flight of stairs from the back door. Around the corner of the building, then along its length to the front. Around that corner, under the yellow crime scene tape and then to the front door. The outer door's lock had been picked, and the door was braced open by a piece of charred wood that had once been the handle of a picket sign. Muriel let herself in and closed the door softly behind her.

Dirty Eugene Grady was holding the inner door open a few inches. When he saw Muriel, he gave her a wink and a quick "thumbs up" and quietly opened the door wide enough for her to pass through. Then slowly, carefully, the priest let the inner door close and lock. It did so with a barely audible click. Without speaking,

Dirty Eugene handed Muriel her medical bag, which he had been carrying.

Following their orders, Dirty Eugene and Muriel waited silently just inside the door while Pacilio and McGraw advanced slowly down the darkened hallway, their weapons ready. Although she could not see the men clearly, she knew that both would be barefoot. "We're wearing street shoes," Pacilio had said to McGraw in the car, "and they're going to make noise, no matter how softly we try to walk. We have to have the advantage of surprise, and that means absolute silence. Inside an empty building like that one, any sound is going to carry a long way."

"I can see that," McGraw had said, "but why don't we lose the shoes and keep our socks on? Be more comfortable, it seems to me, and just as quiet as going barefoot."

"Because stocking feet will slide on just about any surface except carpet – and none of those floors are carpeted," Pacilio had told him. "and if you slip once the shit starts, you stand to lose more than just your balance."

So the two of them were barefoot as they made their careful way along the corridor. The combination of bare feet with his sportcoat and tie made McGraw feel faintly ridiculous, and for that he was, perversely, glad – it helped take his mind off how scared he was.

Walking beside McGraw, Pacilio knew the sharp feeling of satisfaction that comes to the hunter after he has followed his quarry many miles over difficult terrain and finally sees the animal in his sights. But his sense of fulfillment was mitigated by memory – the memory of a village named Do Lac, and everything that had happened there. And because of this, Pacilio, too, was afraid.

———————

Inside the laboratory, Jerry Waxmonsky looked at his employer. "The banging's stopped, Reverend," he said. "Do you want me to go down to the back door and check things out?"

"No, there's no point. We weren't planning to let them in, anyway, so what does it matter who it is?" Pascoe flicked a hand dismissively. "It was probably just some kids fooling around, anyway."

Waxmonsky looked back to the doorway with narrowed eyes. "I wonder," he said softly.

"Wonder *what*?" Pascoe snapped. His nerves were growing taut in anticipation of what midnight would bring. "If it wasn't some juvenile delinquents amusing themselves, then who was it?"

Waxmonsky made a face. "There's no way to know *who* it was, but I'm getting a bad feeling about *what* it was."

"Oh, really?" Pascoe asked sarcastically. "Well, then, pray tell, *what* was it?"

"*A diversion.*"

That phrase was the very one that Jerry Waxmonsky had been planning to use, but it did not come from him.

It came from Asmodeus.

"All this time spent in human form is making me stupid," the demon snarled. "Of *course* it's a diversion! And that means they are already in the building."

Pascoe looked from Asmodeus to Waxmonsky and back again. "*Who* is in the building?" he asked in confusion.

"I expect it's your *interference*, Reverend," Asmodeus said scornfully. "It seems I may have use for you and your minion, after all."

Asmodeus looked at Frank Trowbridge's watch: 11:38. "Listen to me," it said to Pascoe. "We need twenty-two minutes until The Door can be opened. Once that is accomplished, no meddling will matter, but *we must have those twenty-two minutes.* Can your man hold the door that long?"

Pascoe looked at Waxmonsky. "Can you?" he snapped.

Jerry Waxmonsky smiled for the first time that evening. He knelt next to the olive drab duffel bag that he had left on the floor and began to work loose the clip that held its fastenings together. The smile still in place, he looked up and said "Watch me."

———◆———

In the Place of the Damned, there was a growing sense of anticipation that had not been felt there in a very long time. In another, saner, environment, it might even have been called Hope.

The multitude of the Fallen always knew what was happening on the other side of the barrier that separated their domain from that of the despised creatures called humans – the apes that the Creator had dared to endow with immortal souls, thus putting them on the same level as His beloved Angels. It was over this insult that Lucifer had rebelled, it was due to this travesty that the others had followed him in rebellion, and it was because of the misbegotten humans that all of them had been cast down, consigned to this place of darkness and pain and despair for all time.

But perhaps their torment was not to be eternal, after all. Only a short while ago, a Door had suddenly opened in this place where there were no doors. Asmodeus had been closest, and had been quick enough to slip through before the Door had disappeared again. The Fallen knew what had happened next, had watched in sick envy as Asmodeus acquired a physical body by the simple procedure of taking it away from its owner. Then Asmodeus, like a glutton turned loose in a bakery, had indulged in an orgy of rape and slaughter, with no thought given to those of his brethren left behind. But Lucifuge Rofocale, Lucifer's Prime Minister, had put a stop to that. Asmodeus had been given explicit orders, and was now on the verge of carrying them out.

The Fallen came together in the place where the Door had appeared before and would, they were confident, appear again soon. Then they could all cross the barrier, take on physical bodies and indulge in physical sensations. They would be as an army of gluttons set free in the bakery, and the bakery was likely to be the worse for their attentions.

Like vultures circling over a dying man in the desert, the Fallen gathered, and waited. They did not wait patiently.

———◆———

Waxmonsky opened his duffel bag and brought out something that looked like a cross between a Thompson submachine gun and a rifle. Then he produced a long, curved ammunition clip, clicked it into place, and worked the bolt to bring a round into the chamber. Resting the weapon on the floor, Waxmonsky began to transfer spare magazines from the duffel bag to his coat pockets.

"What on earth is that thing?" Pascoe asked. "A ray gun?" A combination of flat feet and a compliant family doctor had spared Pascoe the rigors of military service, so he knew little about firearms.

"The AK-47 is the finest assault rifle ever made," Waxmonsky said primly. "Far superior to the American M-16, or anything else that's light enough to actually carry around easily."

While the humans were wasting time with talk of their puny weapons, Asmodeus was readying the most destructive weapon that humanity had ever invented. Sitting at the main control panel, it operated a series of switches and got the turbines going, up to half speed. Looking up, Asmodeus pointed an imperious finger at Pascoe. "You! Leave your minion to his work and get over to that computer terminal. Turn it on, along with the bank of monitors, and await my instructions."

Pascoe was unused to being addressed in that tone, but time was too short to waste in argument, and when you're bringing about the reign of the Kingdom of God on Earth, you can put up with a few insults along the way. For a moment, Pascoe felt united with his Savior in shared suffering nobly borne.

Pascoe seated himself in the chair, and it did not take him long to find the switches that brought both the computer and its six monitors to life. The demon-possessed creature who had sent him there was bent over the main control panel, apparently not yet ready to issue additional instructions. Waiting, Pascoe let his gaze wander around the large room full of esoteric scientific apparatus and those mundane wooden crates, and he happened to be looking towards the doorway just as a barefoot man in a suit appeared there with a pistol in his hand.

———◆———

Pacilio's problem was that he had developed peacetime habits of thinking. In war, if you step into a room containing the enemy, you immediately start busting caps; depending on your weapon and how good you are with it, you can drop several of the opposition before they can even react to your presence. The SEALs list it under "Basic Tactics," but in the civilian world, that particular approach is called "manslaughter." Pacilio had been a civilian for, perhaps, too long.

That was why, upon stepping into the doorway of the main laboratory, he attempted to yell, "Federal Agent, everybody freeze!" – instead of following the old SEAL dictum of "Kill 'em all and let God sort it out." He actually got as far as "Federal Agent" when Gerald Waxmonsky opened up with the AK-47.

Waxmonsky was expecting trouble, but he did not anticipate that it would appear so suddenly and with no warning at all. Consequently, the first burst from his assault weapon went high, and by the time he corrected his aim the doorway was empty again.

Asmodeus responded to the sudden gunfire by glancing at Frank Trowbridge's watch, moving a switch that set the turbines to spinning faster, and calling out instructions for Pascoe to carry out at the computer.

McGraw, who was crouching in the hallway with the shotgun held ready, asked Pacilio, "Are you all right?"

Pacilio's leap from the doorway had landed him on his back, but he had rolled and regained his feet immediately. "Apart from terminal stupidity, I'm just great," he said. "I shouldn't have tried the junior G-man routine."

"You had to," McGraw said reasonably. "You know it, and so do I. But what now?"

"Cover that doorway, will you, just in case. I need to ask Eugene something. He and Muriel ought to be here any second."

As he spoke, Father Grady and Dr. Rojas rounded the corner and made their way over to where Pacilio and McGraw were now crouching, about twenty feet from the lab's doorway. Following instructions, they had remained just inside the building's front entrance, waiting to be summoned either by Pacilio's voice or the sound of gunfire. They had begun moving as soon as the first shots were fired.

The old priest was gasping for breath, but Muriel was breathing evenly and able to ask, "What happened?"

"I tried to make an arrest," Pacilio said sourly, "but the gentlemen inside declined to cooperate." He glanced back at the lab doorway. "One of those bastards has got a goddamn AK-47."

"What's that?" Muriel asked.

"Russian assault rifle. A good one, maybe the best ever made. The other two guys are at the controls of that fucking machine. I don't know if they can make it work, but they seem to be trying hard." Pacilio checked his watch. "And it is nineteen minutes to midnight, people."

Dirty Eugene Grady had enough breath back to mutter "Fuckarama."

Pacilio took him by the shoulders, but gently, as if he understood the fragility of the man underneath the priestly trappings. "Eugene, listen: for an exorcism, how close to you have to be to the possessed person?"

Dirty Eugene looked back in bewilderment. "How close? Why, you're standing right there in front of 'em."

"I understand that traditionally you do it that way. All right, the Church is big on tradition. But do you *have* to? Does the exorcism still work if you're not right in the demon's face when you perform it?"

The priest's bewilderment deepened. "Mikey, I don't know what —"

"Could you do it from here?"

———————◆———————

The demon Asmodeus used the memory of its prior human host and the body of its current one to manipulate the control panel with the kind of skill that Van Cliburn used to bring to the piano. But instead of producing a Chopin étude, this artist was using his instrument to slowly increase the power to an electromagnetic field – a field that was flowing between the two poles that constituted The Door. The amplitude and valence of the field were controlled by the main computer, which Pascoe operated according to Asmodeus' shouted instructions.

"Bring up program 'Astaroth,' the demon called. Pascoe, who had quickly gained familiarity with the computer's operation, complied.

"Program up," Pascoe called back a moment later. He had to yell to be heard over the increasing noise of the turbines.

"Execute!"

Pascoe did so, trying not to think about the possible implications of that last word. "Done!" he said.

Asmodeus reached over to turn another dial, which suddenly came loose in his hand. The demon swore vilely – although Pascoe did not understand the language, the tone of voice was unmistakable. But even while blistering the air with esoteric oaths, Asmodeus was moving. A workbench off to the side offered a variety of tools, and it took the demon only a moment to find a long Phillips screwdriver, return to the control panel and reattach the errant dial.

After confirming that the dial was now securely fastened, Asmodeus put down the screwdriver and ordered Pascoe: "Bring up program Belial."

The preacher obeyed, received the order to execute the program, and performed that task, as well. It was then that Pascoe became aware of a voice issuing from the hallway. Pascoe didn't know how long the chanting, or whatever it was, had been going on, but he found that, by focusing all his attention on the voice, he was able, just barely, to catch some of the words:

". . . and I adjure thee, thou old serpent, by the judge of the quick and the dead, by thy maker and the maker of the world, by him who has the power to send thee to Hell, that thou depart quickly from this servant of God, Frank Trowbridge, who returns to the bosom of the Church, with fear and affliction of thy terror. I adjure thee, not in my infirmity, but by the virtue of the Holy Spirit, that thou depart from this servant of God. . . ."

Pascoe was unfamiliar with the words themselves, since only the Catholic Church retains a rite of exorcism. But it was not difficult for him to discern the intent behind the prayers. He shot a glance over to Asmodeus, and saw that the demon had begun to tremble, as if from a sudden onset of chills. In a flash, Pascoe could see the whole plan going down the drain – no Apocalyptic struggle, no triumph of Righteousness, no divine reward for doing the Lord's handiwork, and, to top it off, possible indictment on a variety of felony charges. No, failure was unthinkable now, it was simply not an option, it would not be permitted!

"*Stop him!*" Pascoe screamed at Waxmonsky, who looked back uncertainly, as if asking, "*Stop who?*"

"There's someone in the hall, chanting!" Pascoe went on. "Can't you *hear* him? Stop him! Kill him, and anyone who's with him. Do it now! Now!"

Waxmonsky nodded. AK-47 at the ready, he began to shuffle, slowly and carefully, toward the laboratory's door. He paused just inside the doorway to gather himself for his assault.

Waxmonsky planned to take one quick step into the hall and empty a whole magazine into whoever was out there. The federal agent who'd appeared in the doorway was very quick. But he wouldn't be fast enough to get a shot off before Waxmonsky could blast him. Probably.

Waxmonsky took a deep breath and was all set to make his move when he realized that he was standing near the door of a brightly lit room that looked out onto a darkened hallway, which meant he was casting a clearly-formed shadow into the hall and had been doing so for several seconds which meant *they already knew he was there* . . . . Waxmonsky threw himself backwards into the lab, getting clear of the doorway just before a shotgun blast blew away a chunk of the wall as if it were cardboard. Waxmonsky, who had landed on his back, quickly flipped onto his stomach, crawled a few feet to his left to get into better position, then fired off the full thirty-round magazine at an oblique angle against the cinder block of the hallway, hoping to do some damage from ricochets. There were no cries or screams following this long burst, so Waxmonsky assumed no hits had been scored. He stood and backed up a few steps, reloading as he went. Someone out there had a shotgun and knew how to use it, which meant that Waxmonsky wasn't sticking his head out that door again. Let them come to him, if they were dumb enough, or desperate enough.

From the hall, the chanting of the exorcism ritual continued.

At the computer console, Asmodeus began to beat his right fist against the control panel, screaming, "No!

No, I do NOT depart, I will NOT surrender. You will surrender to ME, old man, to me and my brethren, and we will make of you a MEAL!"

The trembling that had racked Asmodeus' human form stopped as the demon brought to bear the full force of its will. It made a series of adjustments on the control panel, then yelled to Pascoe, "Activate Program Charon!" When Pascoe, whose attention was on the doorway, did not respond immediately, the demon screeched, "Attend to me, you moron!" When it had Pascoe's attention, Asmodeus produced Frank Trowbridge's Sig Sauer automatic and pointed it at the preacher. "Now, are you going to continue with our work, which is almost complete, or would you prefer to learn what it feels like to be gut-shot? *Well?*"

Pascoe blinked once, then again, and turned back to the computer console.

"Very Good!" Asmodeus called. "Now bring up Program Charon."

Pascoe typed, then used the mouse. "Program up!"

"Execute program."

Pascoe clicked the mouse again. "Executed!"

"Excellent. Now, stay alert, human. We are nearly there – then we shall see which is the prophecy, and which the propaganda!"

———◆———

In the hallway, Dirty Eugene Grady continued to chant the prayers of exorcism, but his breathing was becoming labored. Further, his face was taking on a slight bluish tint that worried Muriel Rojas considerably.

Pacilio looked at his watch, for the third time in two

minutes. Finally, he said, "Eugene, stop for a second. Please, just for a second."

The old priest looked up from his prayer book. "What?" he asked blearily.

"What happens when you're done with this? Does Frank Trowbridge rub his eyes and say, 'Hey, where am I?' or what?"

Dirty Eugene shook his head. "Trowbridge knows where he is. The possession victim never loses his individual consciousness, more's the pity. It's just that another, stronger consciousness has taken control – until it's driven out."

"So what happens when the ritual's done? How do we know it worked?"

Dirty Eugene shrugged wearily. "It doesn't always work the first time."

"What did you say?" Pacilio did not scream the question. Indeed, his voice became so soft that the others could barely hear him.

"The demon doesn't always depart after the first exorcism," Dirty Eugene said. Some of his pronunciation was slurred, as if he had been drinking. "Sometimes it takes, two, three, four repetitions. The record, far as I remember, is twelve times over three days."

"Twelve." Pacilio's voice was, if possible, even softer. His eyes seemed to go out of focus for a moment, then he said, in his normal voice, "Okay, thanks. You better get back to the prayers." Pacilio scrambled over to where McGraw was sitting, shotgun ready, watching the door to the lab.

———◆———

Dirty Eugene licked his lips then said quietly to Muriel Rojas, "Better give it to me now, darlin'."

"Eugene, listen, there's got to –"

He gripped her arm with a strength that surprised her. "The talkin's done," he whispered fiercely. "We talked it to death back at the fucking hotel. We agreed it was my call, and you agreed to do it if and when I said so, the American fucking Medical Association be damned. Well, I'm saying so now, *so let's see how well you keep your word.*"

He began to resume the chant of the exorcism ritual, while at the same time pulling back the right sleeve of the cassock up beyond his elbow. Muriel looked at him, helplessness and frustration chasing each other across her face. Then she reached for her medical bag and opened it. There was no fumbling around; the hypo she had prepared earlier was in one of the bag's side pockets, right where she had left it.

For the first time since her first year of medical school, Muriel Rojas prepared to give an injection without first preparing the site with an alcohol swab. Leaning over, she said softly, "Make a fist, damn you. Squeeze hard."

The priest complied without pausing in his chant. A vein obligingly popped up in the crook of his elbow, and it was into that vein that Muriel injected an 80-cc dose of adrenaline.

———◆———

Pacilio asked McGraw, "Did you hear what Eugene said?"

McGraw nodded grimly. "The exorcism might not take, first try. Problem is, we haven't got time for a second attempt, have we?"

Pacilio look at his Rolex again: 11:51. "No, we sure as shit haven't. Listen, we've got to get in there somehow. If Eugene can't exorcise the bastard back to Hell, then we've got to stop him from using that machine to invite all his buddies over here. If we do that, then Eugene can take a fucking *week* to do the exorcism, if he has to, it won't matter."

"Sure, fine, but how do we get past the guy with the machine gun?"

"We need to split his attention," Pacilio said. "And that's where you come in."

Jerry Waxmonsky didn't know what the hell was going on. Pascoe and the strange man named Trowbridge were behind him doing something with the scientific apparatus. Somebody in the hall was praying out loud, and the wording of the prayers reminded Waxmonsky vaguely of his Catholic boyhood, in the days before Mammon had become the only God he worshipped. Whoever was doing the praying had some friends with guns, too, as Waxmonsky had almost found out the hard way. Jerry Waxmonsky was a mercenary, pure and simple, and Pascoe was paying well, but all this weirdness made him uneasy.

Waxmonsky's disquiet was not improved a few seconds later when the shotgun opened up again. The shooter was firing from the hallway, but at an angle so extreme that Waxmonsky couldn't get a shot at him. Of course, that meant that the shotgunner could not get a clear shot at Waxmonsky, either. But the shotgun kept firing, the space between shots suggesting that the weapon was a pump gun. Waxmonsky was trying to remember how many rounds a pump shotgun held, thinking that maybe he might be able to catch the shooter reloading, when something hit him a glancing blow on the head. He looked up instinctively, but it was only some ceiling tile that had been broken loose by the shotgun pellets. It was just as Waxmonsky was looking back down that the flash of movement appeared. Someone had made a dive through the doorway, followed by a tuck and roll, ending up behind one of the wooden crates that lay about ten feet inside the door. Waxmonsky got off a burst at the rapidly moving figure, but he knew he was too late even as he fired. Then he realized the function of the wildly inaccurate shotgun fire – it was *meant* to bring down some of the ceiling on top of him, causing enough of a distraction to allow the quick-moving federal agent to get into the lab and behind some cover.

It had been a good plan, Waxmonsky acknowledged, and well-executed, too. There was only one thing wrong with it.

Waxmonsky quickly dropped to one knee and reached for his duffel bag again. Keeping his eyes on the crate that now concealed the federal man, he rummaged inside with one hand, relying on touch to locate what he wanted. After a few seconds, he found it.

What Waxmonsky withdrew from his duffel bag looked like nothing more than a fresh magazine for his assault rifle, but this one bore a swatch of white masking tape on which the legend "A-P" had been written in red ink. It took only a moment for him to change magazines on the AK-47.

Waxmonsky stood up then, braced the weapon's stock securely against his hip, and took aim.

Pacilio, crouching behind the wooden crate, was feeling pleased with himself. Not only had the "sky is falling" diversion worked as planned, but he'd actually been able to move fast enough to avoid getting ventilated by the guy with the assault rifle as he'd dived through the door. Now he and McGraw should be able to put this bastard in a crossfire.

Pacilio's self-congratulations were rudely interrupted when the guy with the AK-47 started putting heavy fire into the crate that was his cover. Pacilio was not greatly concerned. The wood the crate was built of was thick, and whatever the contents were, whether computer equipment or electrical apparatus or even paper, they would have enough mass to stop the assault rifle's rounds from penetrating. It was then that one of those rounds smashed clear through the crate and came out two inches from Pacilio's nose. His surprise turned to shock as another two bullets penetrated the crate, one of which missed him by a hair.

Christ almighty, what has he got in there, armor-piercing ammo? Who the hell carries THAT stuff around with him?

Pacilio knew that the crate would not protect him against teflon-coated military rounds that were designed to penetrate armored personnel carriers. He was preparing a desperation move – roll to the left, come up firing, and hope that Mac picked that precise moment to open up with the shotgun – when one of the AK-47 slugs blasted through the crate and slammed into his ribcage. Then a second round hit lower, breaking Pacilio's hip and ripping open a major artery, which began to pump blood vigorously onto the floor. Pacilio tried to reach for his handkerchief to use as a pressure bandage on the arterial bleeding, but the red haze of pain that enveloped him slowly turned to black, and then he knew no more.

Waxmonsky heard the federal man fall heavily, then saw an automatic pistol clatter to the floor just beyond the edge of the crate that still concealed the guy from view – but not from the assault rifle's deadly fire. A few moments later, a pool of blood became visible at the base of the crate and slowly spread outward. Waxmonsky fired another long burst toward the crate for good measure, and one round caught the Fed's pistol and sent it skittering away across the room. Waxmonsky changed magazines again, his movements quick and economical. The man with the shotgun would think twice before charging in now, with his buddy dead or dying. Waxmonsky smirked. He could hold this doorway all night, if necessary.

From out in the hall, the sound of chanting continued. Curiously, the voice doing it, which had sounded weak and shaky earlier, was now much stronger. Waxmonsky shrugged mentally. Whoever it was could keep *that* up all night, too, as far as Waxmonsky cared. Fuck it – a little chanting never hurt anybody.

Asmodeus knew the moment was close now. The electromagnetic field was up to 93% power, and the turbines should give the transformer the rest of the juice it needed within the next minute or so. The human at the main computer was performing satisfactorily, once Asmodeus had threatened to shoot him in the lower belly. *Mayhap I will do it, anyway, after The Door opens. It's time I did something just for myself.*

But all was not as well as it could have been. The consciousness of Frank Trowbridge was starting to assert itself for the first time since Asmodeus had seized firm control the night before, and this was occurring at a very inconvenient moment. Trowbridge's mind was full of sorrow and rage. The sorrow came from what had been done to Mrs. Trowbridge the night before; the rage stemmed from Trowbridge's being forced to be a mute witness as the demon had committed those bloody atrocities. Normally, Asmodeus cared not at all for its host's pain, except for whatever amusement value such agony might offer – but the exorcism ritual being enacted in the hall was starting to cause a potentially serious problem.

Asmodeus was losing control of Trowbridge.

But it did not matter, nothing the stupid humans did could make any difference now, because the LED readout on the control panel was showing power at 100% and the digital clock above it was reading 11:59 and Asmodeus drew in a breath and shouted over the din of the turbines: "PASCOE! BRING UP PRO–"

Asmodeus stopped, because its right hand was reaching under the sweatshirt, groping for something in the jeans' waistband.

Asmodeus had given no such order to that hand.

The hand was closing on the grip of the Sig Sauer automatic that ordinarily belonged in the belt holster issued to Corporal Frank Trowbridge of the Delaware State Police.

The hand pulled the weapon free and wrapped its index finger around the trigger.

Out in the hallway, the old priest chanted the ancient prayers of exorcism in a clear, commanding voice that might have done credit to the prophet Jeremiah himself.

The hand, which had been totally obedient since Asmodeus had taken full control, was raising the pistol toward Trowbridge/Asmodeus' head.

From the hall came: "*Therefore I adjure thee, most wicked dragon, in the name of the Immaculate Lamb, who trod upon the asp and the basilisk, who trampled the lion and the dragon, to depart from this man. . . ."*

The pistol barrel was pointing at the right temple now, the index finger tightening on the trigger.

The demon Asmodeus, calling upon his own Father, the Prince of Darkness, exercised a massive effort of will, crushed down the consciousness of Frank Trowbridge, and desperately flung the pistol across the room. It landed in a corner, bounced, and then slid a dozen feet until stopped by a bullet-riddled packing crate.

Asmodeus, spawn of Hell, screamed its triumph, then yelled to Pascoe: "BRING UP PROGRAM LUCIFER! QUICKLY!"

The words had barely left the demon's mouth when its left hand reached down, almost casually, and grasped the handle of the long screwdriver that Asmodeus had left on the control panel. At the exact instant that Asmodeus realized what was happening, a voice inside its own head seemed to scream "*THIS IS FOR JOLENE, MOTHERFUCKER!*" and in that instant, with no hesitation whatever, the left hand plunged the screwdriver deep into Frank Trowbridge's right eye socket.

The scream that followed, a mix of rage and pain and frustration, made the hair on Jerry Waxmonsky's neck stand up. It had a similar effect on Pascoe, who only dimly understood what had just happened. But he did understand that the witching hour of midnight was only half a minute away, and it did not take Einstein to figure out that the demon's command to bring up Program Lucifer would have been followed by the order to execute the program – if the one about to give the order were not currently rolling on the floor in agony, blood spurting from one of his eye sockets in a steady rhythm.

Pascoe kept his right hand near the mouse that would give the "Execute" command to Program Lucifer and watched the time display that blinked from the screen of one of the monitors. He would wait until midnight, give the command, and then everything would be changed forever.

Michael Pacilio, lying face down in an expanding pool of his own blood, had slipped into delirium. He must have, otherwise why did he think he could hear the voice of his old partner, Carl Chopko?

"You're not dead yet, man," Chops seemed to say. "You still got a chance to pull a win out of your ass, if you got the guts to go for it."

"What the fuck can I do?" Pacilio thought he asked, but his lips never moved. "That bastard put two, maybe three AK slugs into me, and I'm leaking like a fucking sieve, in case you haven't noticed."

Chops shook his head in mock sadness. "You didn't used to be such a wussy, Mike. It's this soft civilian life that does it, I guess. Suppose you stop whinin' and start thinkin'. Now, what's that about three inches away from your right hand, there?"

Pacilio made himself concentrate. "A pistol. Looks like one of those Sig Sauers that a lot of cops have gone to lately."

Chopko nodded approvingly. "Very good. The genius recognizes a handgun when he sees one. Okay, now look straight ahead. What's that over there near the wall?"

"Bunch of electronic crap. I don't know anything about that stuff."

"How about that square, black gizmo? Looks like a big metal box. Remind you of anything?"

"Looks kinda like the transformer I had on my electric train set when I was a kid – except it's maybe ten times as big."

"You win the Cupie Doll, my man. Now, how many rounds does one of those Sigs hold?"

"Law enforcement model? Probably fourteen."

"Uh-huh. So what do you suppose would happen if you used your marksmanship skills, which you always used to brag about, to put some of those fourteen rounds into that transformer thing over there? Think that might ruin anybody's day?"

"Yeah, could be. Maybe. If I can do it."

Carl Chopko snorted. "Yeah, it's a tough shot, all right. Range must be all of thirty-five fuckin' feet."

"I'm hurt bad, Chops. Don't know how much juice I have left."

Carl Chopko's smile was almost angelic. "Then you'll just have to gut it out, won't you?"

"How come you keep showing up in my head lately, Chops, after twenty-some years of nothing except in nightmares?"

Carl Chopko's smile broadened. "You needed some help, man, and there's a lot at stake this time. Besides, harps are for wimps. The Big Guy gives some of us M-16s, instead. And, hey, you know what else – *He's* Airborne, too."

Then Chops was gone. Pacilio realized his eyes were still closed, and opened them. The pain from his bullet wounds gripped him like a giant, barbed vice, but he was able to see the pistol on the floor, a few inches from his right hand. By squinting, he was able to make out the shape of the big black transformer against the far wall. That was his target. All right. All he had to do was hit it.

Pacilio tried to reach for the pistol that lay so close by. His arm refused to move. He took in a deep breath, ignoring the pain as a broken rib dug into him. The SEALs had taught him, with mud and blood and exhaustion and pain, how to keep going when he had nothing left but the will to do so. He had shown them he could do it during Hell Week. He had shown them countless times in Vietnam.

He would by God show them again.

Yea, though I walk through the valley of the shadow of death. . . .

With a tremendous effort, Michael Pacilio moved his right index finger.

I shall fear no evil. . . .

He moved a second finger, a thumb, his whole hand.

For I am the meanest. . . .

He moved the hand an inch, then two more, and grasped the Sig Sauer automatic that lay on the floor.

Thirty feet away, The Reverend Thomas Pascoe clicked the mouse, instructing the computer to execute its "Lucifer" Program.

The baddest. . . .

Pacilio thumbed back the hammer on the automatic. He prayed there was already a round in the chamber, since he lacked the strength to work the slide.

Across the room, something was happening to the electromagnetic field that oscillated between the two poles with the pentagram-shaped filaments below. It appeared to be changing, shimmering, coruscating in a way that was now visible to the naked eye. Within the field itself, it a number of humanoid shapes could dimly be perceived. They seemed to be crowding forward, jostling each other like street kids at the window of a candy store. But no urban runaway ever knew the terrible need of those who swarmed just beyond the barrier, eager for their release.

The deadliest motherfucker. . . .

Pacilio got as good a sight picture as his blurry vision would allow, took a painful deep breath, and let half of it out. That was supposed to steady your hands, although it wasn't working especially well this time.

In the valley!

Pacilio gently squeezed the trigger, and the Sig Sauer fired. The result looked like a hit dead center on the transformer, but Pacilio didn't pause to admire his marksmanship. He tried to keep his hands from shaking and fired again. And again. And again.

Waxmonsky's attention had been divided between the doorway and the bizarre activity that was taking place behind him. He had not noticed any signs of life from the government man's direction until the first pistol shot suddenly went off from behind the crate. Waxmonsky was both startled by the sound and surprised, since it was coming from what he had assumed to be a corpse.

Still alive, are we? Well, THAT problem has an easy solution. Waxmonsky raised the AK-47 to his shoulder and took careful aim.

McGraw had been crouching in the hallway, seething with frustration. He and Muriel Rojas had exchanged anxious looks, but had said nothing. Pacilio had been hit, and might be dead. McGraw could see no way to avoid a similar fate if he stuck his head through that door. He was trying to nerve himself up to give it a try, anyway, when the sound of pistol shots began coming from inside the lab. McGraw figured it must be Pacilio trying some last desperate gambit, and immediately realized that the man with the assault rifle would want to do something about that – *which meant he would not be watching the door.*

Dermot McGraw went through that doorway the way he had once hit the beach at Inchon, Korea – flat out, firing as he ran, and with all the fighting fury of a U.S. Marine in his heart.

McGraw's first shot was a clean miss – it's hard to aim straight while running, and McGraw was well out of practice. But the "boom" of the shotgun – which really *did* sound like the end of the world in that enclosed space– was enough to rattle Waxmonsky and affect his aim, so that the burst he fired at Pacilio was off by a foot, at least.

Pacilio barely noticed the near miss; every ounce of concentration he had left was being used to put accurate pistol fire into that transformer. At the sixth or seventh shot, Pacilio was blearily gratified by a thin stream of white smoke that began to issue from his target – a stream that quickly grew thicker.

Pascoe was aghast to see that something was happening to The Door. The blurred images behind it, which had started to clarify and become individually, terribly distinct, were now beginning to fade as the transformer malfunctioned. It had all been within his grasp, it had been *right there*, and now. . . .

In the hallway, Father Eugene Grady was unaware of these developments. He continued to chant the prayers of exorcism, although the pain that had been gripping his chest like a giant hand these last few minutes now felt as if it had decided to squeeze.

Jerry Waxmonsky's error was indecision. He did not know what the wounded Federal man was shooting at, but Pascoe seemed plenty pissed off about it, and that was enough for Jerry. He wanted to finish the Fed off, but there was also the elderly lunatic running at him while working the slide on a pump shotgun. If Waxmonsky continued to fire on the Fed and made a minor sight adjustment, he could kill him. But that would leave Waxmonsky vulnerable to fire from the old guy's shotgun. However, if Waxmonsky shifted his fire to the old man while he was still pumping a new round into the shotgun's chamber, Waxmonsky could kill *him*, and then deal with the Federal agent at his leisure.

Waxmonsky's reasoning was sound, but it took him far too long – at least two seconds. He held his aim on Pacilio for an instant, then decided to shift it to McGraw, instead. The barrel of the AK-47 was swinging, very fast, to its new target just as McGraw fired the shotgun again. The range was shorter this time, and McGraw was now standing still, his feet spread apart for balance. As he pulled the trigger, McGraw opened his mouth in an enraged scream, the same one his drill instructors had taught him at Parris Island all those long years ago.

Most of the fifteen pellets of double-ought buckshot took Waxmonsky full in the chest, although a few of them struck the AK-47 he was frantically trying to aim. The assault rifle tumbled to the floor, and Waxmonsky followed a moment later.

Both of them were smashed beyond any hope of repair.

McGraw quickly racked another round, scanning the room for suitable targets. The only other person still standing was the tall man with white hair, who seemed to be in the grip of hysteria. As McGraw watched, the tall man dashed over to another guy who was writhing on the floor with what looked like the handle of a screwdriver protruding from one bleeding eye socket. The tall man knelt, grabbed the wounded one by the shirt, and began to shake him frantically, screaming, "Fix it! Damn you, fix the fucking thing! You know how, you must know how! We can still do it! We *can*! The Lord commands us!"

The man on the floor was clearly dying, his passage to the Great Beyond probably being speeded up by the rough handling he was receiving. McGraw was surprised to see that the man on the floor still had some strength left, enough to grip the tall man's ankle with one hand, and McGraw thought he saw a smile cross the ravaged, bloody face just before it relaxed in death.

It was, McGraw would relate later, an eerie moment. His ears were ringing from the shotgun blasts, but they still functioned well enough. He could hear Pacilio dry-firing a now empty pistol, pulling the trigger slowly, deliberately, his aim still focused on a big, square metal box with smoke pouring out of it – a box that would later be found to have fourteen nine millimeter slugs buried within its workings.

McGraw could also hear Dirty Eugene Grady continuing to chant prayers from the hallway, although the voice sounded weak now, and very tired.

And then the tall, gray-haired man started to scream. "No, oh my God, no!" he shrieked. "Not me, I'm no one's vessel! Get out! Get the fuck out!" McGraw watched the tall man, on his feet now, backing away from the corpse on the floor in horror, backing directly toward two columns consisting of a whitish material wrapped in electrodes. There was some kind of energy being exchanged by the two poles, McGraw saw, because the air between them seemed blurred, like a heat haze rising from the desert. The tall man, who McGraw was still sure he recognized from somewhere, was screaming and backing, screaming and backing, and his path brought him right up to the weakly shimmering iridescence that flowed between the two poles. McGraw was wondering if he should yell a warning when a hand suddenly lunged out from the middle of that quivering air, a hand that looked human but which had long black claws instead of fingernails. It seized the tall man by his carefully coifed white hair, yanked violently *and the tall man wasn't there any more.* He was just – gone. And so was the terrible hand that had ensnared him.

The tall man's final scream, which contained more terror and despair than McGraw had ever heard in a human voice, seemed to echo in the air for a long time.

All of this was dumbfounding enough, but McGraw would later swear that, just before the shimmering area between the poles faded completely, another voice called from within it, a pleasant-sounding tenor with a cultured British accent that drawled, "Thanks for the offering, Michael, old chap. Be seeing you soon! Ta!"

Then there was silence. The chanting from the hall had ceased. The slow clicking of Pacilio trying to fire an empty pistol had also stopped. The electromagnetic field between the poles had dissipated. There was nothing.

McGraw ran over to where Pacilio lay in a pool of blood that seemed absurdly large. He knelt down, heedless of the mess, and felt desperately for Pacilio's pulse.

After a while, he stopped trying.

Muriel Rojas called from the hallway, "Is it all clear in there?" McGraw was still kneeling on the floor, blood all over his slacks. He couldn't have said how long he had been there before he heard Muriel's voice. He tried to speak, failed, and tried again. "Yeah, it's safe, Muriel. Come on in."

She was speaking even before she reached the doorway. "Eugene's dead," she reported solemnly. "His heart finally gave out, and I'm partly responsible. When you inject adrenaline into a –" She reached the doorway and stood rooted there, her medical bag dangling from one hand. She saw Waxmonsky's corpse. Saw Trowbridge's corpse. Saw McGraw. Saw the blood. Saw Pacilio.

"Michael?" she asked weakly.

"He's gone, Muriel. I'm sorry."

———◆———

Muriel Rojas walked over slowly. There was no hurry now. She knelt in the pool of blood next to McGraw, put her hand on Pacilio's face. "Oh, Michael," she breathed. The hand moved down to his neck, caressed him, paused, then suddenly two of the fingers pressed harder, against the carotid artery.

She looked up at McGraw then, and her eyes were wild. "Roll him over on his back," she snapped. "Gently!"

Tearing open her medical bag, Muriel found the stethoscope, put in the ear-pieces, pressed the other end to Pacilio's chest. After two or three seconds, she tore the ear-pieces out and tossed the device aside. "Gone?" she snarled at McGraw. "And where the fuck did *you* learn to check vital signs? The fucking Cub Scouts?" She unbuckled Pacilio's trousers and pulled them and the shorts down together. This exposed the hip wound, from which blood still pulsed weakly. From her bag she took a large pressure bandage, tore off the sanitary cover, and applied it, firmly.

McGraw just knelt there, stupefied. "You mean he's not –"

"*Dead?*" she said savagely. "Oh, no, he's not dead. He's *not* dead until I pronounce him, and I am not going to pronounce him, not now, not later, because this motherfucker is *not* going to die on me, do you understand?"

She tore open Pacilio's shirt and quickly inspected the other bullet wound. "Off a rib, which is probably broken, and out the back. Possible internal damage, but maybe not," she muttered, then to McGraw: "Didn't Michael say that you have a cellular phone?"

McGraw nodded. "Yeah, right here."

"Then do something useful and call 911. Tell them the paramedics will need a minimum of three units of whole blood, type A-positive. Once we stop the blood loss and get him stabilized, then we can worry about the internal damage, if any."

"Muriel," McGraw said quietly.

"*What?*"

"I'm A-positive, too."

She was silent for a moment, then said, less angrily, "Congratulations – you've just volunteered to be a blood donor. But call the EMTs first, okay?"

McGraw made the call, relaying the information Muriel Rojas had told him to pass on, and stressing that it was an emergency. Then he ran to wedge open the front door so that the paramedics could get in when they arrived.

When he returned to the lab, Muriel was wrapping gauze bandage around the bullet hole in Pacilio's side. Taking off his sport coat, McGraw asked, "Has he got a chance, Muriel? Realistically?"

The woman whose mother had raised her not to swear answered grimly, "Fuck 'realistically,' Mac. This son of a bitch is not going to die from these injuries. That is simply not an option." The expression on her face was hard to read, but McGraw thought he saw a lot of love there, and even more determination. *Could be she's right. He might not die on her, after all this. Maybe he doesn't dare.*

"What the hell are you gawking at?" Dr. Muriel Rojas said irritably. "Lie down here and roll up your fucking sleeve."

Epilogue

McLean, Virginia
October, this year

Many people who live in or around the nation's capital claim that Fall is the finest season that the area offers. Winters are sometimes harsh, and even an inch of snow on the roads throws the local drivers into a skid-crazy panic. Spring is pleasant, but lasts barely long enough for the Cherry Blossom Festival to take place – and, in some years, not even that long. And the two kindest things that anyone has ever said about the D.C. area in Summer are that the annual cholera epidemics are no more and that Congress goes home in August.

But Fall is a wonder of comfortable days and cool nights, a leaf-peeping season that seems to go on forever, and the Washington Redskins doing their damnedest in RFK Stadium.

And if the Redskins don't win too many games these days, it is still very pleasant to sit on your living room couch on a Sunday afternoon in the Fall, the game on TV serving as background to your leisurely consumption of bagels, Jamaican Blue Mountain coffee, and whatever wisdom is being offered by the thick Sunday editions of the *Washington Post* and the *New York Times*.

And if you find yourself sharing all of that with a remarkable woman – a woman who, a few months earlier, spit in the Grim Reaper's eye and yanked your mangy carcass out of his bony clutches at the last minute – well, there are many worse ways to spend a Sunday.

Pacilio put down the *Times* book review section and said, "Jay Parini's got another review in here. He dumps all over some new novel about the sex life of Lenin."

"I didn't know Lenin had a sex life," Dr. Muriel Rojas said, her nose buried in the "Arts and Leisure" section. "Not enough to fill a book, anyway."

"I think that's Parini's point."

"Parini's the fellow from your hometown?"

"Pittston, right. We've never met, but I like to see his stuff in print, anyway. 'Former local boy makes good,' and all that. He deserves his rep, too – the guy can write."

She looked up from the paper then. "Maybe so, but when's the last time he saved the world from Armageddon?"

"Who knows? Could be he's done it two or three times already, but he's just modest about it."

Muriel chewed the last bite of her bagel, washed it down with the superb coffee. "As modest as you, maybe?"

"I'm not modest. I'm just not crazy."

She nodded. "Which is exactly what people would call you if you ever told the truth about Fairfax."

"Christ, yes. Crazy – or worse."

"You're lucky you're not in jail, you know. You and Mac both. And I deserve to lose my license, for giving Eugene that adrenaline injection."

"It was what he wanted, you told me so yourself,"

Pacilio said. "And if he had to do it over again, I figure he'd still choose to go out the way he did, rather than dying a little at a time in some hospital bed. You didn't do anything wrong, Muriel, and we both know it."

"Well, the New York State Medical Board might see the matter differently, but nobody seems to have mentioned it to them. I owe your Mr. Kimura something for that – although not as much as you and Mac owe him."

"I know. For a while there I had Kimura down as the biggest prick in Washington – which is quite an achievement, when you think about it. But he really came through for us in the crunch. Called in favors from all over town, and with some Commonwealth of Virginia people, too. I never knew that he was so well-connected."

"I thought it was quite ingenious of him to claim that you and Mac were in Fairfax on official business, working undercover. And he had all those memos, suitably backdated, to 'prove' it, too."

"You know one thing I'm sorry about, though? Not being at that meeting where Kim told Hal Loomis to go fuck himself. Mac described it later in exquisite detail, but I would have loved to have been there, just to see that bastard's face when Kimura said that he was responsible for Mac and me, that we had acted properly and within our instructions, and that we had the same right of self-defense that anybody else does, and that if Loomis had a problem with that he could convene a Review Board and see where that got him."

"But he never did, did he?" Muriel said. "Call for a Review Board, I mean."

"No, he caved, and it's a good thing, too. A hearing might've led to some questions that Mac and I couldn't answer. But Loomis is basically a bully, and I think Kimura has learned a basic fact about bullies: one good kick in the balls and most of them run like hell."

Muriel frowned and said, "I don't speak from experience, of course, but isn't it difficult to run after being kicked in the balls?"

"And people accuse *me* of being literal-minded."

She laughed, then stood up. "I'm going to toast another bagel. You want anything from the kitchen?"

"No, thanks. But I do wonder where someone your size puts all the food you seem to eat."

Her answering smile was small, but wicked. "A vulgarian might say that I fuck it off."

"Who with?"

"Well, with you, jerk. On weekends, anyway."

As she walked into the kitchen, he called after her, "How about the rest of the week, when you're back in Albany?"

"Classified information!" she yelled back, and it was his turn to laugh.

When Muriel returned five minutes later, her mood was pensive. "Can you drive me to the airport in the morning? I'm on the 8:30 flight again."

"No problem," he said. "I've got physical therapy at 10:00, but I should still be able to get there on time, which is a good thing – Doris makes me do extra laps in the pool when I'm late. She's worse than any PT instructor I ever had in the SEALs."

"How much longer do you have left with that?"

He shrugged. "Doris says another six weeks. But I've been swimming at the Y on my own as well, and I bet I can cut it to four."

She nodded absently. After watching her for a few moments, Pacilio asked, "Something wrong?"

"When I made that joke about 'classified information' before, it got me thinking about something I never asked you. Whatever happened to all that stuff in the lab in Fairfax? The generators and the rest of it."

"Mac tells me that Kimura had it disassembled into its component parts and shipped off to different government departments that were willing to take slightly used equipment – and with the budget cuts, there was no shortage of takers. He had all the computer programs wiped clean, first, of course. The rest of the stuff is harmless, once you break it down. It was the computer programs and the specifications for the electromagnetic field that made it . . . what it was."

She nodded. "But the programs had to start out on paper or maybe a computer disk somewhere, right? It was all worked out by that man in charge of the project – what was his name?"

"Clayborn. He was the project director, and the whole effort to open The Door was really his baby. He was one of those who died in the lab the night the whole thing started. I wonder if he had a chance to appreciate the irony of it all as he was lying there, waiting his turn to receive the attentions of the possessed Peter Barbour."

"There's a pleasant thought," she said with a grimace. "All right, the equipment has been turned into generic components, and the man who originated the idea is dead. But what happened to his notes?"

Pacilio was silent for a long time before finally saying, "We don't know. Mac has had people trying to run them down for the last couple of months, but they haven't turned up squat, so far."

It was Muriel's turn for silence, then. She broke it by saying, "It's kind of like the Manhattan Project, isn't it?"

"Excuse me?"

"The team that developed the atomic bomb during World War Two. I read a pretty good historical novel about it last year. The technique for producing a fission reaction was closely guarded, as you might imagine. But in 1948 or so, somebody stole the secret and got it to the Soviet Union. And then the Russians had the bomb, and suddenly the world was a very different place. The knowledge was the key, of course. Once the other side had the information, they could recreate the technology. And then they could build the bomb. And so they did."

"You draw a nice analogy – unfortunately."

"The information itself – that's the crucial ingredient," she said. "The rest of it is just mechanics. And from what we know took place in that lab in Fairfax, I'd say that Clayborn's discovery might make the Manhattan Project look like pretty small potatoes. And the information is still out there, isn't it? Someplace."

"Ah, hell, the stuff is probably stashed and forgotten in a locker outside a college physics lab in East Armpit, Idaho, or someplace," Pacilio said. "Mac's people will find it, sooner or later."

The autumn sun had been obscured by high clouds a few minutes earlier, and that was probably the reason the room seemed to take on a chill as Muriel Rojas looked at Pacilio and said: *"But what if they don't?*

THE END

Printed in the United States
1376500001B/4-24

9 780971 327863